In Too Deep

Due South Book 1

Tracey Alvarez

Icon Publishing
New Zealand

Icon Publishing
Box 45, Ahipara
New Zealand
www.traceyalvarez.com

Publisher's Note: This is a work of fiction. Names, characters, places, and incidents are a product of the author's imagination. Locales and public names are sometimes used for atmospheric purposes. Any resemblance to actual people, living or dead, or to businesses, companies, events, institutions, or locales is completely coincidental.

Book Layout ©2013 BookDesignTemplates.com
Cover Art by Kellie Dennis at Book Cover by Design
www.bookcoverbydesign.co.uk

In Too Deep/Tracey Alvarez. -- 1st ed.
ISBN 978-0-473-27214-2

For my mum. You were gone by the time I started writing this book but there are traces of you in it and my grief over losing you when I was so unprepared. Love you, Mum. I hope you'd be proud.

Chapter 1.

When death revealed a pale hand to Piper Harland she didn't turn away, but kicked toward it and grabbed hold.

Sixty-five feet below Lake Tikitapu's crystal blue water, she found the seventeen-year-old water-skier who'd disappeared yesterday evening. Now that they had pinpointed his location, Piper would return the boy to his grief-stricken family, huddled above on the shore of one of New Zealand's most picturesque lakes.

Through her face mask she examined the body, while tugging on her swim-line to signal the rest of the squad that she'd found their objective. And right now she needed to be objective. Sucking air from the regulator, her gaze returned to the boy's waxen skin. Her heart clenched, stuttered, and raced faster and faster. Under her neoprene wetsuit, an icy shiver skittered down her spine.

C'mon, Pipe. Forget the past. Don't you dare lose it.

A movement to her left and her dive buddy, Senior Constable Tom Carpenter, finned to her side. His eye-brows lifted above steady brown eyes, his gloved thumb and forefinger forming a questioning "O." She nodded, mirroring the signal.

She was okay, dammit.

Piper hadn't made the elite Police National Dive Squad two years ago by allowing on-the-job stress to shake her, and she wasn't a rookie freaking out on her first body recovery dive. She'd been trained to deal with the dead.

But the teen beside her bore a resemblance to a younger Ryan Westlake, her first love. She tried to shrug it off. She hadn't thought of Ryan "West" Westlake in years. Well, maybe months. Okay, *weeks*.

Piper glanced again at the boy, his shaggy, dark hair waving in the current like fine strands of kelp. Blood thrummed thickly in her eardrums as the regulator rasped, and she inhaled a quick gulp of air. And then another.

No. She wouldn't allow her mind to go there.

But the momentary bolt of panic was enough to re-duce her smooth, coordinated kicks to fumbled thrashes of her fins as she struggled to remain neutrally buoyant. Sediment billowed behind her and swept forward over the body, momentarily obscuring its features.

Behind the face mask Tom's gaze sharpened, and he pointed at the rapid belch of bubbles escaping from her regulator, a clear indication she was breathing in and out way too fast. He made a thumbs up, a mute instruction to ascend.

Crap. She wasn't fooling anyone. Least of all herself.

The victim's lifeless eyes, focused through the deep blue to the sky above, set her heart slamming against her ribs. Tom tapped her arm and signaled again, this time with more emphasis. She released her grip on the boy's wrist, placing it in Tom's capable hands.

She had to get out of there. Right now.

Relying solely on her years of training Piper followed the line upward, keeping a check on her dive computer. She made the mandatory three-minute safety stop sixteen feet below the lake's sparkling surface. Seconds dragged as she attempted to steady her breathing. The mask dug into her face, the bottled air bitter on her tongue. For the first time she understood at a gut level the panic that drove some divers to risk the bends as they thrashed away from the claustrophobic depths.

Piper waited out her one hundred and eighty crawling seconds with her gaze fixated on the hull above, drawing on every hour of intensive training, every hard won skill, to remain static.

She was okay, dammit.

Bursting into bright sunshine she swam to the boat and didn't look back.

***

Nearly twenty-four hours after returning to the city where she lived and worked, Piper remained trapped at Wellington's Central Police Station. She collated a re-port for the coroner's inquiry and then endured a dour-faced psychologist picking through her brain—because Tom's suspicions had been aroused thanks to her near freak out. And worse? She couldn't blame him. Her re-action could've jeopardized the whole team.

Piper slammed her locker door, glaring at it while buttoning her jeans. She adjusted her tee shirt and tugged on her battered leather jacket, feeling half clothed without her pressed uniform blues and heavy stab-resistant vest.

Her pocket vibrated, and she yanked out her phone. The text from her sister said, "Call me when you get home. IMPORTANT."

Hell, what else could go wrong today?

She shoved the phone back in her pocket, snatched up her backpack and left the locker room.

"Hey, Piper?" Tom strolled along the corridor to-ward her. "You ready to tell me what *really* happened at Tikitapu?"

She froze.

"You gave me the rose-colored version at yesterday's debrief by the lake. Now I want the non-prettied up version."

"Nothing happened. I'm fine." She swung the back-pack onto her shoulder and folded her arms across her diaphragm.

"Fisher the shrink doesn't think so." He leaned against the wall opposite, a six-foot-three chunk of solid muscle with a soft side few knew about—except per-haps his wife and twin baby girls. "How long have we worked together, kid? I know when you're dodging bullets."

"I'm not a kid—ah, crap." She raked shaky fingers through her hair, pulling the short strands until her scalp stung. "Fisher stood me down from the squad today—effective for two weeks. Two weeks back to the normal daily grind of paperwork and patrol."

Tom shoved his hands into the pockets of his regulation pants. "Well, you knew we were a part time squad when you applied. You did normal duties before you became a dive cop and you continue to do it daily unless we get a call out—be thankful we're not pulling someone's seventeen-year-old kid out of a lake every day."

"Sound like a whiny cow, don't I?" Piper grimaced.

He sighed. "Look, Fisher gave me a heads-up a few minutes ago that you'd failed the assessment and I hate to say he's right—" his voice gentled "—but it's not the first trouble you've had on a body recovery, is it?"

When she glared at him, he shrugged. "Look Piper, you work like a woman possessed, so why not treat this as a holiday. Even better, go south and see your relatives. It's, what, eight years since you've been home?"

Home. Stewart Island. Bush-covered hills, cold azure ocean, and abundant birdlife.

A lump of hardened grief and loss amassed in her belly.

"Nine." She planted her feet wide apart on the pitted linoleum floor. "But it's not like I don't keep in touch. I talk to Shaye and Mum all the time." If she counted text messages and stilted phone conversations with her younger sister and mother as keeping in touch.

"Kid, you don't talk, really talk, to anyone." Her chin lifted higher and Tom tugged on his earlobe with a sigh. "It's unnatural for a woman not to yatter on about her feelings."

"Try saying that in front of your wife, boss."

"Well, my ear's here if you wanna use it. You got a little squirrelly, but we all do at one time or another. Still, you did good. We gave the boy back to his family."

"I know." She couldn't meet his gaze as the old familiar ache rose in her chest.

She did what she'd been trained to do, achieving the goals she set as an eighteen-year-old cadet entering Po-lice College. She recovered the dead this time, but nine years ago she'd been unable to return her own father to the family.

She fastened a fat, false smile on her lips. "Maybe I will take that holiday. Seats to the Gold Coast are on sale this week. See you 'round, boss."

Tom shook his head as she sauntered past. "Not if I see you first."

***

Off the southernmost tip of New Zealand, Piper clung to the ferry's handrail as it wallowed across Foveaux Strait to her hometown, Oban, on Stewart Island. Sea spray splattered onto her face, salt stinging the corners of her slitted eyes.

She was about to throw up. Repeatedly throw up. And afterward she'd have to drag her weakened carcass under a bench and curl into a fetal ball to die. The manufacturers of useless seasickness pills had better watch out, because she'd be haunting their asses.

God, she hated this stretch of water.

Unpredictable and often dangerous, the churning grey waves of the Strait reflected the gathering storm clouds above. Another howling southerly squall on the way. Perfect. She could be sunning herself without a care on the Gold Coast, but instead she'd taken a call from her panicked sister two days ago and used up all her accumulated leave to head south. Now she endured a near-death experience to try and save her older brother Ben from losing his house and business—not that he'd thank her for it.

"Just six weeks," she muttered as the ferry roiled in-to the small harbor, the anchored boats bobbing and tossing so violently she closed her eyes. "Anyone could do six weeks."

Kind of made Fisher's two weeks off squad duty al-most look appealing.

The ferry docked with a bone-rattling thump. She peered at the town's distant lights shimmering through the light rain as she stepped onto the wharf, though "town" was too big a word for the local pub/restaurant/hotel, the cluster of small stores, and the community hall.

Nothing changed. Time stood still here.

Piper tugged the baseball cap lower on her head and zipped her leather jacket shut. People swept by, surrounding her with a chatter of bright voices and the rattle of suitcase wheels along the planks. She hoisted her hiker's backpack and strode off the wharf onto Oban's main road.

Her stomach looped into a series of reef knots, each growing tighter the closer her steps carried her into the center of town. She stopped at the children's play-ground opposite the Due South Bar and Restaurant. A grassy slope led to a jumble of rocks and a beach dotted with clumps of seaweed. Overturned dinghies framed a picture-perfect island scene—ruined only by spitting skies and the choppy grey waves surging across the sand.

Raucous laughter drifted through the open doors of the bar. Someone roared, "C'mon Gav—drink, drink, drink!" The locals claimed Friday night as their own and without a doubt her brother Ben would be there. She shoved her hands into the pockets of her jacket and hunched her shoulders against the chilly air. Watching from the outside, yet again.

Light spilled from the large windows of the double-story building. The Westlake family had owned and operated Due South for the last fifty years, and the watering hole was the hub and heart of the town. Cocooned behind the glass, secure and enfolded by the warmth of familiarity, men and women she'd grown up with drank beer and gossiped.

She had to go inside and face her brother, face them all.

Face Ryan Westlake.

West.

Piper's pulse rate jetted into the stratosphere and she sucked in a gulp of sea air.

You're stronger than this, Constable Harland. You've faced gang members and addicts high on meth-amphetamines spoiling for a fight in dark alleyways. Just do it already.

Willing steel into her spine, Piper strode across the road, dumped her bag under the shelter of the railed verandah overhang, and walked inside. The scents, smells, sights and sounds of Due South were a sly jab in the solar plexus, leaving her the village idiot frozen in the doorway.

A musty wet-wool smell assaulted her nose. The same old photos of fishing boats remained mounted on olive green walls. Ford Komeke, the island's mechanic, sat on a bar stool to one side, strumming his guitar. Old Smitty was hunched at a table, emphasizing a point to his sidekick Laurie by poking Laurie's belly with an unlit cigar.

Her gaze flicked away and circled the crowded room—there he was, in her father's old spot by the corner. Slumped in a hard-backed chair, Ben stared at his empty beer glass.

One of the knots in her stomach contracted a fraction. Her gangly big brother with the easy grin and overdue-for-a-trim mop of sandy hair had changed into a broad-shouldered, short-haired, scowling stranger.

Piper adjusted her cap again, directing a quick glance at the guy working the bar. Not West, thank God. She ordered a bottle of imported lager, then impulsively held up two fingers when he returned.

Keeping her head angled down, she grabbed the beers and plunged into the crowd. The nape of her neck prickled as she weaved past table after table of familiar faces. She gave it, oh, two minutes before every Islander knew of her arrival.

Piper stood in front of her brother, since the bulk of his cast-covered ankle occupied the chair opposite. "Mum always said you'd break your neck on that mountain bike one day."

Ben didn't move but his fingers cinched almost imperceptibly around the glass. Five endless seconds stretched, his silence burned her to the bone. He rolled his shoulders under his woolen jersey and met her gaze with insolent slowness.

"Mum also said you'd always run toward trouble, not away from it." The deep timbre of his voice scraped her nerves raw. Such a long time since they'd spoken. His gaze never wavered as he drained the beer dregs from his glass. "She was wrong about that too."

Piper shrugged and put the bottles down. "Well, I'm here now."

His glass settled on the table with a hollow clink. "So you are. And I suppose I'm the trouble you're running to."

"I bought you a beer."

He turned the bottle around to read the label. "Only loopies drink this imported crap."

Loopies, the Islanders' affectionate but slightly derogative name for visitors and tourists. Piper's eyes narrowed as she took a sip from the second bottle. "Is that so? I seem to remember when you were seventeen, you and your mates pinched a couple dozen and drank until you passed out under a tree."

The corners of Ben's mouth twitched, like the muscles there battled against a smile. He slumped farther under the table lip and folded his arms. "Things have changed since those days."

"Uh-huh. You were a lot more responsible back then."

Ben winced as his foot jolted against the chair, and fired a scorching glare up at her. "Shaye told you about more than just my broken ankle, didn't she?"

Piper took another swig of beer but made no move to sit. Ben hated anyone looking down at him. "Of course she did. She's worried sick."

All the fear and hurt and rejection exploded in her stomach, a shrapnel bomb of emotion. She slammed her bottle down, braced her clenched fists, and leaned in. "What the devil were you doing, risking your house to buy a bigger boat?"

"Butt out, Piper," he growled.

"Not a chance. Just how much in debt are you?"

"I am not discussing it here." His clipped tone brooked no argument. "It's under control."

She slanted a glance to her right. Conversation had dwindled to a low grumble and clusters of people now craned their necks to catch a glimpse of the unfolding drama. Super. This little reunion would fuel the gossip mills for months.

Her attention returned to Ben. "Bollocks. When Shaye mentions late payments, foreclosure, and Mum offering to take out a second mortgage to save your ass, that tells me you *do not* have things under control."

"Shaye's got a big mouth."

"And you've got a fat head. Neither of which will save your house and Dad's business." She whipped around to glare at the now silent pub. Suddenly people discovered they had plenty to talk about, and the murmur of conversation and clink of glasses resumed.

Ben dropped his head back to grimace at the wood-paneled ceiling. "You've come a long way to rub salt in it." Fine lines fanned out from the corners of his eyes and he rubbed a palm over at least a week's worth of stubble.

She sighed and tugged her cap off, ran a quick hand through the flattened strands. Did he honestly believe she'd come to gloat? Temper vanishing, Piper squatted at the table edge and swallowed past the dry blockage in her throat. "I'm only here to help. I'll run the dive tours until your leg heals."

"It's not that simple. I don't just offer tours now. A lot of my business comes from cage dives. It's why I bought the bigger boat."

"Cage dives?"

"A shark cage. See the Stewart Island Great White sharks up close and personal. Loopies love it."

"Oh, Ben." Spidery tickles iced down her spine. "Not the sharks."

"Don't you go all holier-than-thou on me. While you've been up north living the dream I've done what I needed to survive."

Someone brushed against her, and Piper leaned for-ward.

"'Scuse me." Smitty's gap-toothed grin leered above a huge plate of fried fish and chips. "Good to see you again, lass." He winked and waddled off, stopping at the nearest group of men and muttering, "You fellas mind your own beeswax, ya hear?"

Piper lowered her gaze to the scuffed floor and took a deep breath. Old Smitty was the worst gossip of the lot, and even from his perch in the far corner, she'd bet a month's wages he'd been eavesdropping.

Liquid glugged into a glass and she looked up. "Thought you didn't drink that imported crap?"

"I'm not in a position to turn down a free beer when it's offered." Ben shifted in his seat and turned his face away to glower at the window.

Outside the wind had picked up, hammering sheets of rain against the glass in a blustery tantrum. She shivered, even though the temperature inside with so many bodies crammed together bordered on suffocating. "Listen, I've another idea we can try. When's your next tour?"

He took a sip of his beer and wrinkled his nose. "Got a shark dive booked this Wednesday—why? You gonna swim with the big fishies, little sis?"

Piper shot him a cocky smile. "I'm meaner than any-thing that cruises the ocean around here. So what time do we leave?"

"We?" He hacked out a laugh. "There's no we, Piper. Doc says I'm not allowed on a boat for at least five to six weeks, and I assume you haven't got a commercial skipper's license?"

Piper stood, rubbing her protesting thigh muscles with damp palms. License? Ah, no, she hadn't considered who would skipper Ben's boat. She just assumed he wouldn't be able to dive. "No. No license. What about one of your mates?"

"It's summer. No one has any spare hours to give me." He reached for the crutches braced on the other side of the table. "I told you, it's under control. We don't need you here. Go back to the city."

She lifted her chin, ignoring the small stab of hurt at the bitterness of his tone. "Not an option. So who's skippering for you?"

"Me," a voice grated directly behind her.

Her pulse exploded into chaos, but she controlled the tremble in her muscles as she half turned toward him. "Hello, West." She moderated her tone so it was chilled with absolute politeness.

His voice remained the same, but the boyishness there at twenty had vanished now West had nearly hit thirty. His shoulders were broader, the cut of his business shirt hinting at the shape of his chest beneath, and his dress pants sat low on lean hips. His dark brown hair, once unkempt in sync with Ben's, was stylishly trimmed and kept in line by some slick product. Bet the locals gave him hell about that.

Eyes the brittle blue of dried sea coral locked with hers. One assessing look shattered any doubt that he recalled each intense moment spent together when she was eighteen.

Bubbles of old, revived attraction fizzed through her veins, as potentially deadly as nitrogen collecting in her cells during a dive. Those feelings couldn't be allowed to multiply. A fizz could turn into a trickle, the trickle to a cascade, and the cascade to a torrent. She wouldn't go through the devastation of purging Ryan Westlake out of her system again.

Fool her once, and all that crap.

West smothered a grim smile as he scanned the length of her, from the leather biker jacket, down to black jeans emphasizing a pert ass, to grape-colored combat boots—a touch of pure Piper. Her shoulders stiffened to fence-post straight. So, she remembered more than just the sound of his voice.

Every cutting, snide comment he'd intended to use from the moment Ford had sidled into his office with a grunted, "Piper's back," evaporated into sea fog. He swallowed, unable to extract his gaze from her full mouth and creamy skin. Her hair, which in his rare poetic moments he'd thought of as burnished chestnut, should've flowed past her shoulders, but instead she'd cut it short, the fine strands curling in the humidity.

"You cut your hair." *Jeez, West, real smooth.*

She twisted a lock around her finger, before tucking it behind her ear. "Too many drunks tried to grab me by it."

He gripped the top of the nearest chair, then noticing his reaction, deliberately relaxed his hand again. What Piper chose to do with her life was irrelevant. "The perils of being a cop."

Her head swung toward Ben, who clattered and fumbled to get his crutches from behind the table.

West took a step closer, trying to block the faint per-fume of her skin from addling his brain even farther. "I take it you've volunteered to run the diving part of Ben's business." The rigid line of her backbone betrayed her tension.

Her arrival and plans to work would solve some of Ben's issues, but create a whole bunch of new ones for West. Back on the island, Piper became another pain-in-his-ass problem, a reminder of his youthful naivety. "So how does a cop plan to make nice to tourists and handle testosterone-fired guys on a shark cage dive?"

She slapped him with a deadpan stare. "I'll handle it fine. I know how to deal with pushy, arrogant men."

Score one for her. "Good for you, but Ben needs a qualified diver on his tours, not a hobbyist—"

"I'm a certified rescue diver *and* dive instructor. Probably more *qualified* for this than both of you combined," she snapped.

West pulled a fast grin before smothering it. Was she now? Color crept up underneath the collar of her jacket, an old telltale sign he'd done a great job of either unsettling her or pissing her off.

"A lot of qualifications for a simple officer of the law. You've been busy."

"Very busy." She turned to Ben, who had wrestled himself to his feet. "So who was your dive guide be-fore?"

At his sister's words Ben's face hardened into a stone mask. He could've warned her not to go there.

"No one you know." Ben's tone snipped the words into staccato bites. "And they left unexpectedly at the beginning of the season which is why I'm in this mess."

"Why did—" She paused, eyebrows drawn in a sharp "v" as she stared down a nearby table of snickering girls. Once they'd returned nervously to their drinks she switched her intense gut-clenching gaze back to West. "Can the three of us go to your dad's office and talk privately?"

"It's my office now, but sure. After you." West made a grand sweeping motion toward the bar. "We've also a small matter of reimbursement to discuss."

The idea had popped into his head on a flash of devilish inspiration. If Piper was determined to stay here and make him suffer with her close proximity, he could damn well ensure she was miserable too.

Her jaw dropped. "Reimbursement?"

"Everything has a price, including me."

Her gaze contained the lash of a stingray's barb, full of venom and almost as painful. Luckily she didn't have the ability to hurt him anymore with those beautiful hazel eyes.

Score one for him.

Ben made it across the pub to the polished wood bar before he stopped, leaning heavily on his crutches. "I'm exhausted and my ankle's throbbing like a bitch. Can't we hash the details out tomorrow?"

Piper shoved her fists into her leather jacket and sighed. "Go home then. We'll talk in the morning."

Ben crutch-hopped to the pub's front doors. The cunning bastard, playing on Piper's obvious concern. Pissed as a wet cat at her brother, she still knew when to push and when to leave him the hell alone. Pity that same savvy didn't apply to him.

West walked ahead down the hallway that led to the restrooms and also connected the pub and restaurant to the kitchen at the building's rear, not waiting to see if she followed. Flicking open his office door, which was just beyond the restrooms, he strode inside to sit behind his desk. Piper stalked in after him and slammed the door.

She ignored his gesture to sit and leaned against a file cabinet, a relic from when his dad, Bill, worked as Due South's manager. Probably just as well she didn't get comfy. He wanted her out before the crazy-good scent and sight of her made him say something stupid. Again.

"You've been running tours for Ben since he broke his ankle last week?" She tucked a strand of hair behind her ear.

"Only fishing charters and sightseeing." He shrugged, picking up a pen and clicking the nib down. "We can't run the cage dives without at least one qualified diver and a skipper aboard."

"Well, thank you for helping him."

"You don't need to thank me, we're a community here. We have each other's backs." He couldn't keep the bite of acid from searing through his voice.

"I'm sure Mum and Shaye have already thanked you enough."

"They have." He consciously relaxed his hands, re-placing the pen on his desk. "But the problem is we're short staffed and there's only so much Ben can do to take up the slack for me when I'm out on his boat."

She cocked her head, but remained silent.

"He's not a manager, I know he hates sitting behind my desk," West said. "But Shaye moves well between sous chef and the day to day running of the hotel."

"Shaye's a smart cookie."

No mistaking the pride in Piper's tone over her younger sister.

"We need you to help out."

"Ah. Kind of a 'you scratch my back, I scratch yours' scenario?"

"You always were a smart cookie."

Her nose crinkled like she'd smelt something bad. "You want me to wait tables like I did as a teenager?"

"No. We're trying to keep what customers we have, not scare them away by dumping water jugs over their heads."

Her eyes widened then narrowed to hard slits. "Hey, that was one time when a revolting old man shoved his hand up my skirt."

"I didn't say your reaction wasn't justified." He laced his fingers behind his neck and tilted his chair back. "But no. I don't want you as wait staff. You're needed in the kitchen—"

"Are you serious? You've choked down my attempts at cooking, right?" She pushed off from the file cabinet and paced the short distance to the opposite wall.

For a moment he just watched her, all long legs, stiff spine and bucket-loads of attitude. Gone was the pretty hazel-eyed girl who looked at him like he was every superhero rolled into one. Now she was fifty percent cop, fifty percent stranger.

"I thought you were here for Ben?"

"I am," she ground out between clenched teeth.

"Then if I'm prepared to reorganize my life to help out, don't you think scrubbing pots and stacking dishes is a small price to pay?"

She froze halfway back to the file cabinet. "What? I thought you wanted me to help Bill—with prep or something."

West barked out a laugh and smacked a hand on his desk. "You really think Dad will let you touch anything in his kitchen?"

The tiny darts of her gaze speared him from across the room.

"No. You're on kitchen-hand duty." He couldn't resist adding a tight grin. "Starting tonight since your sister's already done a full day's work and is out there now clearing tables."

"I'll happily do my share."

Happier if she could reach across the desk, rip off his arm and beat him to death with it judging by the razor edge in her voice.

"I'll ring through to the kitchen and let Dad know you're coming on board. Think you remember the way?"

"I remember." She spun one-eighty and headed for the door, bristly as a porcupine. He caught a glimpse of her flushed cheek as she stalked from the room and yanked the door shut.

Well, well. Looked like she remembered more than just the layout of Due South after all.

Piper studied the restaurant's double kitchen doors as if they led to the bowels of hell. And they may well, since she'd agreed to work for the devil himself. She blasted another glare down the short corridor to West's office and showed heroic restraint by not marching back to lodge her boot right where it would do permanent damage.

"Piper?"

She turned to see her sister coming out of the restaurant's staff entrance, sagging under a huge tray of dirty dishes, with wisps of long brown hair floating around her face.

"Ohmigod, it really is you. You came!"

"I told you I'd sort something out." Piper hurried toward her.

"I didn't think you'd ever come back after, well—" Shaye's voice trailed off to a whisper and her flush deepened. "I'm glad you're here."

"Let me get those." She avoided her sister's earnest green eyes and hauled the heavy tray out of Shaye's hands. "I'm gonna be stacking them from now on."

"What? Why? Ford said you were taking over the dive tours for Ben."

"Still faster than the speed of light, huh?"

"What is?"

"Gossip." Piper chuckled and shook her head. "Doesn't matter. Anyway, I'm the new kitchen-hand. It's one of West's conditions for skippering Ben's boat." She cocked her hip and prepared to bump the swing doors.

The door jerked open before she made contact. Bill Westlake scowled, his striped chef's cap askew and a spatula tucked into the band of his apron like a gun-slinger's .44. "Listen you two, the hallway ain't a place for chit-chat when my meals are getting cold. Shaye, run to table five. Piper, get your skinny backside in here, the pots won't scrub themselves." He disappeared back into the kitchen.

"He's still a grumpy old fella but his bark's worse than his bite." Shaye retied her ponytail with deft movements. "I'd better get back to work."

"Yeah. Buy you a beer later?"

"Long as it isn't that imported rubbish."

Piper choked back a laugh. "Oh, for Pete's sake."

"One more thing." Shaye frowned. "What were the other conditions West had for helping us?"

Something in her sister's tone made Piper squirm. "He didn't say. But I imagine cleaning the toilets will soon be added to my list of duties."

"Oh. Is that all?" Shaye sent her an astute look. "Well, thanks. I know being here isn't easy."

Piper nodded and nudged the doors open, her stomach once again tangling into snarls.

No one here knew what had happened between her and West just days before her father drowned, did they?

Chapter 2.

Not even two hours off the ferry and somehow Piper had ended up in Due South's kitchen. *Find your happy place.*

She submerged her hands into the dishwater and searched through food scraps for the pot scrub hidden somewhere in the voluminous sink. It was a little like a fingertip search, when a weapon or some piece of evidence the squad needed to retrieve lay at the bottom of a murky pond. Locating the rough sponge under the soaking roast pan, she hauled it from the depths.

"Got ya, ya little booger." She wiped the sheen of sweat off her brow with her forearm.

"Finished yet?" Bill bustled past. "Some of us have plans later tonight."

West's father ran his domain here the same way he once would have as a New Zealand army chef, with rigid discipline and a lot of barked orders. Every item shone ship-shape in Bill's kitchen—stainless counter-tops, fridge doors, and cookers. Not a speck of dust would dare land on one of his pots or assortment of utensils, which hung on precisely spaced hooks. Twice he'd returned a giant pot to her, wordlessly pointing at a miniscule trace of food left on the metal.

"Just about." Piper injected a cheerful tone into the words, resisting the desire to strangle him with the kitchen towel draped over her shoulder.

She plunged her dish-glove covered hands back into the water and dragged out the pan, attacking the glued on scraps of meat with the pot scrub like she was, well, scrubbing off the smirk West had worn earlier.

Bill's reaction hadn't been much better. Not a conversationalist, Bill's reticence suited her mood perfectly because she also had little to say to him. She knew where she stood with West's father. The man was direct, if nothing else.

West, on the other hand...

Piper crinkled her nose. No more wasted thoughts on West tonight. All she wanted right now was to be horizontal, preferably with something soft under her aching feet. She grabbed the pan and rinsed it under the hot tap, setting it aside on the draining board.

The swing doors blew open and her mother, Glenna, swept into the kitchen, towing West by one arm in her wake. "There she is! There's my girl!"

Glenna dismissed West with a wave of her peach-tipped nails and floated past the countertops, a wall of Chanel No. 5 preceding her.

"Hello, Mum." Piper peeled off the dish-gloves and stepped into her embrace, watching West over her mother's shoulder as he paused to talk to Bill.

He bared his teeth in a savage grin at something his father said and looked over.

"Piper, darling? Did you hear what I said?" Her mother pulled back, blocking West's stare and forcing her to refocus.

"Ah, sorry, I missed that last bit."

Glenna smoothed her cap of sleek auburn hair and sighed. "I said, 'It's wonderful to see you. How long are you planning to stay?'"

Aware of West and Bill standing across the room, Piper lowered her voice. "Mum, you know why I'm here, don't you?"

"Darling, I know nothing less than the catastrophic would bring you back to Oban." Glenna gave her a thin-lipped smile. "Shaye told me you'd arrived when she rang earlier. I would've been down sooner, but guests—always wanting one thing or another."

Piper glanced at her mother's clasped hands. The gold Claddagh wedding ring mirrored the one her father always wore. She cleared her throat, swallowing the memories before they overwhelmed her. "None of us are willing to let you use the house to clear Ben's debt—Ben's especially adamant. So I've come to help for about six weeks until his ankle's healed enough to skipper again. Dad wouldn't have wanted you to risk your home to keep his dive business operating."

"I'm grateful and very touched that you'd do this for your brother—stubborn as a mule though he is." Glenna squeezed her hand, her fingers a cool, soothing balm on her flushed skin. "Have you arranged for somewhere to stay?"

"Oh. I thought I could sleep in Shaye's old room."

"Darling, I'm sorry. I turned it into another paying room a couple of months ago and right now it's the busiest time of year for the B&B. I'm booked to the gills for the next two months." Glenna shrugged a shoulder under her chiffon blouse. "If you'd rung to say you were coming..."

She hadn't told *anyone* in Oban of her plans, be-cause up until the plane had left the runway in Welling-ton and turned toward the southern city of Invercargill, she had half-convinced herself she'd chicken out and change her mind.

"It's okay, Mum. I'll bunk in Ben's spare room, or with Shaye if she's got space—"

Glenna shook her head before Piper finished speaking. "Ben's rented his house out over the summer sea-son to bring in some extra cash—he's staying in West's downstairs room. Shaye's sharing a house with the new schoolteacher, Kezia, and Kezia's little girl, and good-ness, there's barely room to swing a cat in their tiny place."

She tapped one peach nail against her matching shade of lipstick and then clapped her hands. Piper respectfully resisted an eye roll. Her mum, ever the drama queen. "I've just thought of the perfect solution."

She whirled around in a swirl of chiffon and Chanel. "West, dear? A word, please?"

Piper's palms were damp, so she tucked them under her elbows.

Any idea, any perfect solution followed by West's name, couldn't turn out well.

Glenna beamed and gestured him over.

West slapped his father's shoulder and strode across the kitchen. "What's up?"

Behind Glenna, Piper looked like she was in the process of swallowing a lemon.

"We've a bit of a problem with where Piper's going to stay, but then I remembered your spare room." Glenna moved closer, and laid her hand on his forearm. His gaze jolted to Piper's, even as Glenna continued speaking. "—And though Ben's downstairs, I'm sure you could squeeze Piper in for a wee while?"

Piper. Just down the hall from his bedroom. The idea ranked up there with kicking himself in the balls or a self-inflicted root canal.

He glanced again at Piper, who if she opened that mouth any wider would start attracting insects. "I don't think—"

Piper blurted, "I'm not staying—"

West shoved his hands into his pockets and cleared his throat. "My office is in the spare room. It's not de-signed for someone to—"

"Pffft." Glenna patted his cheek, like he was still thirteen years old and offering a lazy-assed excuse of why he couldn't stay to help Ben stack firewood. "Listen to you, Ryan Westlake. I saw your office the other day and you've got that futon sofa-bed tucked in the corner. Piper doesn't need much room, do you darling?"

Piper uttered a strangled, "Mum!"

An out-of-control steamroller had nothing on Glenna Harland. "You, Ben and Piper were always thick as thieves growing up, weren't they Bill?"

Bill grunted in acknowledgement but West caught the undercurrent of humor in the clipped sound.

Piper finally found her voice. "I don't want to impose on West. I've brought my sleeping bag and I'll just find a spare bit of floor somewhere—"

"Don't be ridiculous. My daughter is not sleeping on the floor and you wouldn't be imposing on West, I'm sure." She turned back to him. "Right, dear?"

Like Piper, Glenna had piercing hazel eyes and he got the full intimidating force of them from *both* women. One woman demanding he accept her request, the other demanding he deny it. One woman had been like a mother to him when his had taken off with another man, and the other?

His back muscles knotted into steel barbs.

Going cold turkey off the drug that was Piper nine years ago, he opted not to put into words what she once meant to him.

But she meant nothing now. So really, after he'd moved past his initial knee-jerk reaction, Piper staying at his house temporarily would only be a minor irritation. Personally, he couldn't care less if she even warmed Smitty's bed at night. Except he'd feel a smidgeon of sympathy for the old fella.

So West hurled the ball back into Piper's court. "If she needs my futon, she's welcome to it."

He took an indulgent moment to wallow in Piper's poleaxed expression.

Piper sent West a look that could've shaved stubble off his smug face.

Sanctimonious prick.

He knew—of course he knew—her mother would give her the third degree if she insisted on finding somewhere else to sleep. And no doubt he presumed that she'd overreact. The old Piper, the wiseass teenager who couldn't control her temper, would've lost it. The new Piper, the seasoned police officer who'd learned to somewhat control her tendency to blurt out whatever popped into her head, would not.

So she closed her mouth with a snap and forced her lips to peel back into a smile. "Thank you. That's very kind."

"All settled then—and you'll both come for break-fast with Ben and Shaye for a family meeting." Glenna rubbed Piper's arm. "I'd best be off. Bill—?" Bill turned from where he was trying to slip out the back door. "Be a dear and close up for Ryan tonight, will you?" She blew him a kiss. "West can take Piper home. My poor baby's ready to drop."

"Righto." Bill gusted out a sigh and trudged back through the kitchen. "I'll nip into the pub and turf out the hardcore hangers-on."

Few could resist a direct request from Glenna. Ex-cept Piper, who had finally learned how after being away from her mother for so many years.

She whipped the towel off her shoulder. "I'll wipe these counters down."

"Don't be too long, you're looking decidedly peaky." With a toodle-oo wave, Glenna swept out the way she'd come—leaving her and West alone.

Piper's heart tapped out a little two-step routine.

West leaned against the stainless steel counter. "I'll finish up here and take you home. My bike's around the back."

A vision flashed into her mind of sitting precariously balanced on a mountain bike's handlebars while West pedaled madly behind. The bemused disbelief vanished when she remembered the old motorbike he'd slaved over as a teenager. "You still have the Suzuki 250?"

She put some distance between them by crossing the kitchen to slot the roasting pan back in its place under a countertop.

"No, I sold the Suzuki years ago. Got a BMW now."

"Really?"

"An R100-GS."

"Oh...nice." This conversation was so awkward-high-school that she expected to begin her next sentence with the word "like" and giggle uncontrollably.

Why was she acting like a dumbstruck teen when men dominated her everyday working environment? Some of them hot men—and men in *uniform*. Yet, for all the jokes her friends made about handcuffs and ba-tons, none of her fellow cops got under her skin with one sardonic glance like West had. "Look, give me directions to your place and I'll make my own way."

He raised both eyebrows but didn't shift from his casual stance. "It's almost eleven, and as Glenna said, 'You're looking peaky.' I'll take you home on my bike."

Sitting behind West, snuggled up against his back with her arms around his waist? Not going to happen. She ignored the lurch in her stomach and slowly dried her hands on the kitchen towel before draping it over a rail.

Piper untied her apron and tossed it into the hamper. "I'm a cop who's used to long hours and hard physical work whether I'm peaky or not. I'll walk. Just give me the directions. Please."

"Your call." His tone mild, West rattled off a series of lefts and rights.

"And where's the spare key? I don't want to get Ben out of bed to answer the door."

"It won't be locked. You're not in the city anymore, Piper."

"Right."

His lips curled into a half smile. "I'll probably beat you back anyway, but if not, my office is on the top floor, and the linen cupboard is in the hallway. Make yourself at home."

The beer she'd drunk earlier curdled at the thought.

Chapter 3.

"You're off your game, boy." Bill leaned in the doorway.

West looked up from behind his office desk, straightened, and slid the desk drawer shut. "All locked up?"

"Tighter than the Virgin Mary."

For the first time that evening, he really looked at his dad. Purple shadows bruised the crinkled skin under his eyes, and everything about him sagged, including the two woolen jerseys he wore, even though the temperature inside the pub was warm enough to be comfortable in only a shirt. "You look like hell. Did you stop to eat tonight?"

"That girl of yours bullied me into a sandwich. Didn't want anything else."

West sat forward with a frown. "I've told Shaye be-fore you're meant to—"

"—not Shaye. Piper."

"Oh." He aligned a pen next to the desk pad and straightened his stack of invoices. "I forgot to tell Piper to make sure you take a break. And she's not my girl."

Bill cocked a finger at him. "Waiting for that. As I said, since she waltzed back in the door, you've been off your game." He rubbed a hand through his white hair and yawned. "I am beat. Bloody old age."

"Go to bed. I'll look after the rest."

"Thought Glenna told you to drop the girl home?" Bill chuckled. "Though how the bleedin' hell she ended up staying at your place— should've seen your face, boy!"

"Ms. I'm-so-independent Harland declined a lift with me, saying she was quite capable of walking. She left about ten minutes ago."

Bill's gaze slid to the rain zigzagging down the office windows. "In this?"

"Bit of rain never killed anyone."

"True, true. She'll miss the turn to your road in the dark."

"More than likely."

Bill scratched the back of his head. "Ah well. As you say, bit of rain never hurts. Might cool that temper of hers."

West snorted and moved around the desk to collect his helmet. "Yeah. That'll happen. I'd better go find her."

West shooed Bill out the kitchen door in the direction of the tiny cottage he and his younger brother, Del, had grown up in on the corner of Due South's property. He'd have fobbed Piper off at his father's place if the cottage's second bedroom hadn't been stacked halfway to the ceiling with Bill's junk.

He changed into jeans, tugged on an ancient leather jacket, and headed outside. Temperamental weather was a fact of island life, something he was sure Piper had forgotten while living in the capital city.

Rain like automatic gunfire plinked onto his helmet as he strode to his bike, tucked away under a covered car-port. His plans of a quiet beer alone were screwed. The last thing he wanted tonight was to deal with a Harland temper tantrum. Why had he caved to Glenna's demands?

He straddled the bike and twisted the key. Revving the accelerator, West guided the bike onto the road and headed along the foreshore, tires hissing across the wet asphalt as he changed gears. He passed the wharf, where the streetlights abruptly ended. Surely a street savvy cop wouldn't walk off into the night without a flashlight? Or maybe it was Boy Scouts that were pre-pared for any eventuality. He sure as hell wasn't pre-pared for Piper. He swallowed thickly and concentrated on riding.

The bike's headlight illuminated the narrow lane leading to his place, and he stopped parallel to the en-trance. A gust of wind howled over the crest of the hill. Branches rattled and the rain hammered down so hard it bounced. West squinted through the trees to see whether his house lights were on. Nope. Which presumably meant she'd walked straight past. Piper was likely halfway to Horseshoe Bay, if she hadn't fallen into a ditch.

With a sigh, he continued on. Less than a minute later, a solitary figure appeared through the curtain of rain. Shoulders hunched, thumbs hooked into the straps of her backpack, Piper trudged single-mindedly toward him. He braked slowly and rolled to a halt, dropping his feet to the ground. Piper kept walking, head down. Either the driving rain had drowned out the sound of his bike or, knowing Piper, she'd chosen to ignore his presence.

At least she had the common sense to turn around and come back.

He pulled off his helmet as she drew alongside, and held it out to her. She froze beside him and kept her hands on the backpack straps, her mouth a pale, straight gash on her face.

Cold rain trickled down his neck and oozed inside his collar. The fingers on his left hand felt frozen to the handlebars with icy rivets. "For once in your bloody life don't argue—just get on."

Her face jerked toward his, but her eyes were hidden under the brim of her cap. The bike's engine rumbled in neutral and a peal of thunder cracked across the sky. Piper's lips opened but nothing came out. She took the helmet and moved out of his line of sight. Pretty certain she muttered a word ending with "hole" as she jammed the helmet on, West turned the bike toward home and waited. He forced his muscles to relax when she lightly touched his shoulder and swung on behind him.

The pretense didn't last once she settled into position, her wet denim-covered legs pressed against the outside of his thighs, her upper body forced close to his as the bulk of her backpack shifted her center of gravity forward. One hand clutched her cap in a death grip, the other snaked around his waist and settled lightly on his abs. His groin tightened and the crotch of his uncomfortably damp jeans squeezed like the denim had shrunk a size.

"Ready?" he gritted out.

The chin guard of the helmet clipped his shoulder blades as she nodded. He toed the bike into gear and released the clutch. The spread of her fingers across his stomach nearly caused the lever to slip from his grasp. Stalling like a kid with a learner's permit was not the impression he wanted to give.

West steadied his hand and let the clutch out slowly. Grit and small stones crunched under the tires as they gathered speed and headed back toward town. Thank-fully the rain tapered off to a wet drizzle so he could see where he was going.

When he turned into his lane and gunned it up the hill to his driveway, Piper's second hand joined the first as she clung to his torso, the firm mounds of her breasts mashing against his back.

He came to a complete stop in front of his garage. Piper leaped off the back like the seat of her pants was on fire. Fine by him. He hit the automatic roller door button in his pocket and walked the bike inside. Donny, the mad mutt, padded out of the shadows, panting and wet. By the time he'd nudged the kickstand down, Piper had the helmet off and was staring bug-eyed at his dog.

"Is that yours?" She let out a girlish squeak when Donny whipped his body around, sending water and slobber flying.

"Yep."

"What kind of dog is he? A miniature, balding Yeti?"

He studied her expression. Donny was a deal breaker, and if she he didn't care for him, tough. She could sleep in here. "Staffy boxer cross."

Donny strolled over to Piper and delicately sniffed her knee. Maybe he resembled a miniature bald Yeti, what with his missing ear, droopy jowls and mangy fur, but West's pal had manners. Piper slowly lowered her hand and let the dog transfer his snuffling to her knuckles. "He looks like he's been through the wars."

"He has."

"What's his name?" After receiving Donny's tongue swipe of approval, she stroked his head.

"Donny."

She crooked an eyebrow at him. "As in Donnie Wahlberg from New Kids on the Block?"

"You're kidding, right? Think I'd name my dog after someone in a boy band? No—it's short for Don Juan."

"Don Juan? You named this poor ugly creature—and no offence buddy," she crooned, scratching the dog's back while he shivered in delight, "—after Don Juan, the greatest fictional lover of all time?"

"Donny doesn't think he's ugly and the ladies appreciate him just fine."

"I suppose they see past his flaws." Piper shot him a pointed glance and strolled farther into his garage as if she owned the place. "This is quite the man cave." She placed the helmet on an empty spot on his workbench.

Tools and grease-smeared bike parts covered almost every available surface and he squashed an irrational urge to tell her to get the hell out of his garage. "You expected something else? A craft nook complete with scrapbooking supplies and knitting needles?"

Her nostrils flared and her hands returned to the straps of her backpack, gripping them until the skin across her knuckles turned a bloodless white. "I wasn't expecting anything." She huffed out a sigh.

"I know you don't want me here anymore than I want to be here, but surely we can be civil?"

Civil? They'd never been civil to each other in all the years they'd known each other, which was pretty much always. A memory flash of her with her ball dress rucked up above her waist, her long legs, lean and muscled from years of diving and playing sports wrapped around his hips. The hint of cheap champagne on her breath, the soft velvet of her skin, her bare breasts in his hands. He shoved the image ruthlessly aside—he wasn't touching a lit match to that powder keg. "Sure. I can do civil."

They walked out of the garage, and when he opened the front door and moved aside so she could enter first she said, "Thank you."

All very civil-like and it creeped him out. What kind of demonic game was she playing?

The door closed with a click and West rustled somewhere behind her.

What a nightmare this day had turned into.

A light blazed on and she blinked. They stood in a small entranceway with shoes and boots neatly aligned on the tiled floor, and jackets and other gear hanging on wall hooks beside another door.

West gestured with a thumb. "Ben's through there. If your brother wasn't so damn big he could've had the office while you slept down here."

"His feet stick off the end of the futon, huh?"

"Way off. The sofa is not made for guys. You should be okay."

Piper shucked off the backpack and dropped it to the floor, pressing her lips together to stop a groan of relief from escaping. She unlaced her boots and tugged them and her wet socks off. Looking up, she was level with a superbly taut butt as he bent to remove his boots. West's shirt rode up to reveal a strip of tanned back and the waistband of some Calvin Klein logoed underwear. Her tongue dried out. Her nerves fizzed, like someone had shot a caffeine bullet into her exhausted body.

Get your head in the game, Pipe. She thrust her gaze down to her pale toes and stood before he spotted her appreciative examination of his rear end.

"Hey—your bag's leaking," he said.

She glanced down at the water seeping out of the bottom of her backpack. Ah, crap.

"Here." He tossed her an old towel and snagged a strap, lifting her backpack as if it weighed nothing. "I'll take this upstairs."

"I can—"

"Civil, remember?"

"Right." She crouched down to wipe the tiled floor and was rewarded with another view of West's sublime rear as he disappeared up the stairs at the end of the entranceway. Fisher-the-Shrink hadn't done a thorough enough job picking around in her brain, because she was clearly certifiable.

Piper padded up the stairs into an open-plan family and dining room. Plain but comfortable-looking navy sofas and matching armchairs were positioned in front of accordion glass doors, which opened on to a full-length deck. Framed photographs of native birds hung on the pale walls and only a couple of coasters were stacked on the coffee table. The style was understated and functional, from the airy space of the lounge to the clean modern lines of the small kitchen and wooden dining table.

Where were the Harley Davidson posters, the stack of tatty bike magazines, and the piles of dirty sports gear? When she'd been the annoying little sister desperate to hang out with her brother and his cool friends, West lived in the cottage behind Due South with his parents. Later, he and Ben shared a tiny four-room house. But this wasn't a teenager's sloppy hangout; this was a man's home. West was no longer the carefree buddy from her childhood—and she'd best remember that when nostalgia and reality didn't mesh.

Her shoulders sagged under the weight of memories. Nostalgia sucked.

"I've put your bag in the bathroom, first door on your right." West appeared at her side with a stack of linen. "My office is the next room down. I'll find you some an extra blankets in a sec."

Piper blinked the dreamy rose-colored lens from her eyes. "Thanks."

He offered her a thick white towel. A faded tee shirt and a pair of drawstring shorts were folded on top. "Thought you might want a shower and something dry to change into."

"Oh—I don't need those."

"Did you use a plastic liner in your backpack?"

Know-it-all. "I forgot."

"Then everything will be soaked. You can throw your wet stuff in the dryer."

Her eyes widened. Wear West's *clothes?*

He hooked the tee shirt up with one finger and dangled it in front of her. "If it makes you uncomfortable..."

"No, not at all." Oh, she was way beyond uncomfortable. "Uh, I'll hit the shower now. I'm making a damp patch on your carpet."

Piper snatched the clothes and towel and marched into the bathroom.

Wrapped in the towel and finally warm after a decadently long time spent using up West's hot water sup-ply, Piper peeled open her backpack. Yup. Everything was drenched.

With a sigh she pulled on his shorts and picked up the tee shirt. The worn cotton slipped over her head, a shiver skating along her skin as she inhaled his scent. Sure, the tee shirt smelled of whatever laundry powder he preferred, but traces of something uniquely male, uniquely West, clung to the fabric. She slid her arms through the sleeves, letting the shirt caress her naked-ness. Her skin, where the shirt touched, felt covered in prickly heat, and her nipples hardened into tiny exclamation points.

Total overreaction girl, you're losing it.

She'd worn West's clothes before. At fifteen she kept his Red Hot Chili Peppers tee shirt because he'd never asked for it back. And so what if she still had the shirt stuffed in a bottom drawer back in Wellington? Or if sometimes she'd wear it to bed—but only because it was so comfortable, and hey, she still loved the Chilies.

Piper threw her wet clothes into the dryer and cracked open the bathroom door. The house was silent, except for a faint murmur of a TV or radio from the opposite end of the hallway. With any luck West would've gone to bed, since she'd hogged the bathroom for a good half hour. She tiptoed to the room West had indicated and rushed inside. A meticulously organized computer desk sat opposite the futon sofa—the futon which he'd made up with sheets and blankets while she'd been in the shower.

Propped against the pillows lay a hot water bottle.

She sat on the bed and picked it up. West gave her dry clothes, fixed her bed, and filled a hot water bottle, somehow remembering how her feet froze on cooler nights. But, she thought, he didn't want her anywhere near him.

Piper hugged the warmth of the rubber bottle and hoped the heat would nullify the tiny twinge in her chest.

***

West was woken by the now-familiar sound of thumps and snarled four-letter words as Ben crutch-hopped up his stairs.

Three fast raps on his door and a "Get your lazy ass out of bed," had West rolling onto his back with a pil-low jammed over his head, questioning why he hadn't killed Ben when he moved downstairs a couple of months ago. It'd been a long time since they'd shared a house. Now he knew why.

He lifted a pillow corner and squinted at the blurry hands on his watch. Six a.m. Jesus. Normally he was up at the butt-crack of dawn, but how many hours sleep had he got last night? Two? Three at the most. Torturous hours spent listening to the hum of the dryer and imagining Piper naked under his old shirt, then kicking himself for allowing his mind to roam down that dead end street again.

Yeah, he was a guy and all, and therefore his dick often controlled the direction of his thoughts. What he should've been doing was figuring out who he could unload his unwanted houseguest onto. But with only four hundred locals living full time on the island, and a lot of those locals running B&Bs or renting their in-vestment properties in the high tourist season, no one had a spare room.

"Coffee's ready. Move or I'll drink it all," came Ben's muffled yell from the kitchen.

West groaned, slid out of bed and walked to the French doors, which opened out onto the deck. Filaments of sunlight speared through the native bush surrounding his house and spilled like oiled silk over the flat surface of the bay below. Sunrise on another day in paradise. He tugged on some clothes and left his room, spotting the tousle-haired woman at the end of the hallway.

Piper. The metaphorical swarm of mosquitoes in his paradise.

She'd raided the dryer, dressed in her own clothes of cargo pants and a loose plaid shirt that skimmed over a breast-hugging tank top. And he tried, really tried, to ignore those breasts. It was far too early and he was far past his juvenile years of ogling a woman's rack at any opportunity. He nodded curtly and strolled into the living room.

Besides, he'd been there, done that. *Done her.*

Ben turned from the kitchen counter, his free hand clenched around the handles of two coffee mugs. With a graceless balletic spin on his good foot he placed them on the dining table. "Coffee's up—" His smile slipped as his glance slid from West to something a short distance behind. Ben straightened to his full height. "What's she doing here?"

Ben's suspicions as to where exactly Piper spent the night were etched on his wrinkled brow and stick-up-the-ass stiffness. West faked a yawn and slumped into a dining chair, his mind kicking into action. Did Ben honestly think he'd make a move on his sister on her first night back on the island? Because the idea of Ben figuring out he had a sexual history with Piper made him shudder.

Unwritten guy rule: You didn't screw your best ma-te's sister soon after her eighteenth birthday and then dump her like yesterday's leftovers.

West took a sip of his coffee, keeping his gaze on the steaming mug. "Sod off, Ben. Go bitch to your mother if you've a problem with Piper staying *in my office*—it was her idea."

Ben relaxed as he retrieved his crutches from their position against the kitchen counter and swung himself over to a chair. He picked up his cup and blew on it. "Touchy this morning, aren't you?"

"Now, now, boys." Piper swept into the kitchen heading straight for the coffee pot. "Let's get some caffeine in us before we have to face the Inquisitioner, aka Mum."

"What?" Ben said.

Piper scanned the row of cabinets above the counter and randomly opened one after another until she spotted the mugs. "You'd scurried away by the time Mum ordered us up to her place this morning." She snagged a cup and filled it.

Ben groaned. "All of us?"

"Yep."

"A family reunion at seven o'clock in the morning. Just great." Ben swirled the contents of his coffee cup as if the grounds might reveal a plausible excuse his mother would buy.

West flexed his fingers and bit back a groan. Sounded like a fun meal. Not.

Bad enough having his house invaded by Harlands, screw being trapped with four of them in a room at the same time. Not even Glenna's legendary cooked break-fast could tempt him. "Think I'll give it a miss. Family dramas are not my scene."

Piper leaned against the counter and slowly crossed one ankle over the other. Her steady, flat scrutiny made him wonder if this was the woman that apprehended criminals saw.

Cool. Centered. In control.

She snatched up the phone handset beside her and slid it across the table. It bumped against his coffee cup with a soft rattle. "Mum included you in that order dis-guised as an invitation. It's your call." Her voice was deceptively calm but beneath her even tone, flashes of temper sharpened the words. "You can ring to explain why you're not coming because I'm not making excuses for you."

Bugger. He could never say no to Glenna Harland. For that matter, he could never say no to Piper.

"Call it a miracle, but for once I agree with Piper."

West dragged his gaze from her and refocused on Ben.

"Since you're now part of the Save-Poor-Ben team, you should be there." Ben shoved his cup away and stood. "Just keep your head down, eat your breakfast, and agree with everything Mum says."

A dry chuckle escaped West. "You can tell you've been raised in a household of women. Jeez."

"Well, you and your bro hung around us long enough to know what it's like when you're outnumbered. You smile and wave to keep the women happy and then do whatever you need to do."

Piper threw up her hands. "Uh, hello? Female person right here."

Ben tucked the crutches under his arms. "Though in Piper's case you may want to cover your nuts if she catches you. I'll wait downstairs."

The clock ticked off monotonous seconds after Ben left the room.

"So. Are you coming...or not?" Piper crossed her arms, cleavage appearing at the motion.

Awareness clawed through his empty belly at the peaked outline of two nipples pressing against her top in the cool morning air. *Coming or not.* There would be no *coming* with Piper any time in his future. His dick twitched once in rebellion and he resisted the urge to adjust himself.

West shook his head and drained the remains of his coffee with a grimace. "I'll go. Give me twenty minutes to shower and shave."

"Better make it thirty—what, with you needing to fix your hair and all." A dimple winked in her cheek as she sashayed past.

West scraped a hand over his chin to mask the curl of his lips. That was the Piper he remembered. He blew out his cheeks in a harsh puff of air. Problem was, he remembered too much.

So it'd better be a cold shower.

Chapter 4.

A typical Harland family get-together, the peace lasted ten minutes after they arrived in her mother's kitchen.

Piper sat beside Shaye, who gave their brother the stink-eye across the kitchen table. Ben refused to contribute to the stilted conversation and continued to mainline his breakfast. West, seated next to him, hadn't glanced up since Glenna placed his plate in front of him.

Rearranging a cluster of grilled button mushrooms, Piper tried to pretend she was totally relaxed being in her old home. Other than a new coat of paint, everything had remained the same. Glenna's vast array of copper bottomed pots and pans hung from a ceiling rack, and fruit filled a carved kauri bowl on the island counter. Her mother flitted around like a hummingbird, refilling coffee cups and sneaking Ben and West extra sausages and slabs of buttered toast.

If she squinted, she could return to a time when her father sat at the head of the table, thumping his fist for emphasis, making them all jump as the crockery rattled. West and Ben would be outfitted in their rugby gear ready for their Saturday morning game, Shaye bent over one of her mother's recipe books or catching up on homework.

But those days had gone.

Her father was dead, her sister an independent twenty-four-year-old woman, and her brother and West no longer Piper's best friends.

Piper sipped her orange juice, the cool, familiar sweetness soothing on her tongue. "So, Ben. Tell me what happened and what we're up against."

Ben's fork stopped halfway to his mouth and he glanced over to West, looking for back-up. West carried on eating.

"I haven't been meeting my payments for nearly four months. Since October, when Jules and Curt took off," Ben said.

"The dive guides you mentioned last night?"

Her brother nodded. "I could've coped with one of them leaving, but not both. Gavin Reynolds didn't hesitate to take advantage of the situation by poaching my customers."

"Gav's a dickhead." Shaye sliced her knife across the remaining sausage on her plate with enough venom to cause sympathetic winces from both men.

Piper cut her sister a sidelong glance. Out of all the Harlands, Shaye was the most easy-going. She had a temper—holy crap, she had a temper—but you very rarely saw evidence of it and her usual sunny nature meant the locals loved her. What had Gav Reynolds done to warrant such a reaction?

"Agreed," Ben said. "He's always been a dickhead. But now the dickhead is a businessman who's never forgiven me for being blessed with the looks and charm he missed out on."

Shaye snorted. "More likely because you beat the crap out of him in high school."

"He had it coming."

Piper set her knife and fork down. Enough tiptoeing around. "You're four months behind in payments. Exactly how much do you owe the bank?"

It wasn't West's movement that caught her eye; it was the absolute absence of movement. He didn't look at her brother, just examined his plate with a neutral expression frozen in place.

Ben's knife squeaked on china as he sawed at a bacon rasher. Finally he looked up. "Thirty grand."

Piper's belly went into free fall and her hand jerked, knocking her fork off the table. Thirty grand? Ben owed thirty thousand dollars? "Are you screwing with me?"

Ben's silent gaze flipped her the bird.

"Piper, *please*." Her mother glided past to sit at the table head. The chair at the opposite end remained empty, a constant reminder of Michael Harland's absence.

"Sorry Mum, but Jesus, Ben! Why didn't you ask for help earlier?" She held up a hand. "No, no, don't tell me, I can guess—you were convinced you could crawl out of this financial shithole by yourself?"

"I would've sorted it."

"You're *such* a dumb-assed stubborn male."

Ben's shoulders hunched, his eyes narrowed slits. "I am not dumb."

Shaye, ever the peacemaker, touched Piper's shoulder. "We've had real crappy weather this summer and the tourists aren't coming. West has helped out when he could, but after Ben broke his leg—"

"What's done is done." Glenna angled the spout of her teapot over a delicate porcelain cup. She finished pouring and fixed them with a lethal stare. "We can throw blame around like monkeys hurling excrement, which gets everybody mucky and doesn't solve anything—"

Piper's mouth dropped.

"—or, we can work together to help extricate Ben from this *financial shithole*."

West lifted his coffee mug in a salute. "Well said, Mrs. H."

"Oh, shut up," said Piper.

"You big pile of monkey excrement," Shaye added with a snicker.

Glenna sighed theatrically.

Ben glared at Piper until Glenna reached over and pinched his arm. "Don't make me put you both in time-out."

"Fine." Ben dropped his knife onto his plate and leaned forward. "Piper, why don't you share one of your *wonderful* ideas of how to save me from financial ruin?"

"Ideas. Right." Piper ran damp hands down her thighs, her gaze darting to West.

He scraped his plate clean and leaned back in his chair, lacing his hands loosely over his flat stomach. Suddenly her ideas—actually, her only idea—didn't seem so wonderful. She grabbed a fistful of her cargo pants to center herself and blurted, "Romantic cruises."

Ben looked as though she'd suggested pole dancing lessons on his boat's mast. Except not being a sailboat, The Mollymawk didn't have a mast.

"For honeymooners or people celebrating anniversaries—or even marriage proposals." Piper continued, ignoring West's raised eyebrows. "We'd take them out in the morning, let them snorkel or dive in Paterson Inlet. Serve them a picnic lunch in one of the bays with local cuisine for dinner—provided by Shaye. Then they spend the night in The Mollymawk's double stateroom, which she tells me is lovely."

"Going at it like rabbits," Ben said.

West rocked his chair back on two legs and grinned. "Expensive way to get laid."

Smug bastard. "You're a sad, sad man, West. Some people like the idea of spoiling the person they love. Not everyone thinks romance is dead," Piper said.

"Do you?" he shot back.

Heck, yeah. Flowers and candy and whispered promises that vanished quicker than soap bubbles. Romance and sappy puppy love had no place in her world. "What I think isn't important. What's important is that for very little outlay we can charge big bucks and it's something no one else in Oban is offering."

West opened his mouth to speak, but the clink of Glenna's teaspoon against her teacup silenced him. "It's a brilliant idea. Shaye and I can do the meals, Piper and West will run the cruises and Ben, you'll handle the advertising and bookings. Once we're up and running I'm sure the whole thing will snowball. Since you've got Piper helping now, you'll pick up more shark dives too." Her mother turned to her. "You and West take The Mollymawk out this morning and get some location photos while the weather's good, then Ben can put the best shots up on his website."

Alone with West on Ben's boat? She wasn't ready. "Ah, Shaye, you're not starting work until ten. You come with us—I can never take a photo without sticking my finger in front of the lens."

Shaye gnawed her bottom lip, her gaze zipping to the left. "Sorry, I promised Kezia I'd watch Zoe for a couple of hours. I'm sure West can handle Mum's little digital." Her chair scraped against the wooden floor as she stood. "I'll meet you for lunch and bring Kez along—you'll like her."

Ben grunted and elbowed West. "And while you're out, you'd better show Ms. Romance here how to set up the shark cage. I booked five paying divers last night for Wednesday."

Piper bent to scoop up the fork she'd knocked to the floor, glad for a brief respite from West's intense scrutiny. Being alone with him worried her more than the idea of coming face to face with one of the ocean's largest predators. At least the Great Whites were forthright in their desires. They only wanted to eat you.

"I'll make sure Piper's clued up on how we roll."

She dismissed West's baiting tone and gritted her teeth. If she'd had a choice between a morning spent in West's company or the Great Whites—she'd opt for the sharks.

***

Later that morning Piper resisted the urge to poke her tongue out as West continued to shower scorn on her romantic cruise idea by saying *nothing*. He navigated The Mollymawk to each suggested location in Paterson Inlet and even set the camera up on a self-timer to take a few shots of them in their swimsuits pretending to snorkel side by side.

West offered no opinions, made no snide comments and in fact, he resembled a cardboard cutout at the boat's helm—gaze fixed on the horizon, wind tussling his hair. His perfectly-sculptured-with-product hair. Along with his perfectly sculptured jaw, perfectly sculptured biceps, and perfectly sculptured ass. Don't forget his perfectly sculptured ego. No, it wouldn't pay to forget that.

Fine. He could just play the chauffeur along for the ride.

"You all done?" he said.

"For now. I'll try to sweet talk our first guests into allowing their pictures to be used on the website. It'll attract more bookings."

West turned the boat in a wide circle and headed back in the direction they'd come from. "Assuming you get any bookings to start with."

"Yes, Mr. Positivity. Assuming we get any bookings." She sat on the helm seat and swiveled around to drape an arm over the backrest. West, at the wheel, continued practicing his thousand yard stare. Probably thought it made him look windswept and interesting.

Dammit, it did.

The Mollymawk motored out of Paterson Inlet and toward the open ocean. Fortunately, yesterday's wind had died down and the sea beneath them stirred in lazy ripples—so her stomach behaved.

Piper sucked in a deep breath. Even though she'd been out on the ocean many times, the air around Stewart Island was unique. Maybe it was the earthy green scent from the thousands of trees that covered the majority of the island's hilly landscape. Or maybe the uniqueness came from the countless varieties of birds that called Stewart Island home and that extra something in the breeze was the distant stench of bird crap. Cynicism often kept the ache of homesickness at bay when she sat on her postage-sized deck back in the city.

The Mollymawk powered down and the boat slowed.

She looked around. Oban was nowhere in sight. "Why have we stopped here?"

West cut the engine and brushed by her outstretched legs. "You've had your fun with the camera. Now it's time for real work."

"*Real* work?"

"The shark cage? Ben wants you to familiarize yourself, remember? Wetsuits are in the storage locker down below."

"Ben never said anything about going in the cage. He told you to show me how to operate it."

"Yeah, but I'm running these shark tours for the next six weeks, not Ben. You need to experience the shark cage before you take a tour." He paused in the wheelhouse doorway, his lips twitching once with sardonic humor. "It's okay to be a little nervous."

Which in West-speak translated to: It's okay to be a total pussy.

Hah. She wasn't nervous—nervous didn't begin to cover it. But she'd inform West of that, oh, in about *never*.

So she'd suck it up and get her butt in the water.

Piper puffed out her cheeks and with a gusty exhale slid off the helm chair and headed into a cabin to suit up.

Ten minutes later she stood on the stern's open deck, feeling exposed in a borrowed and ill-fitting black wetsuit. West was still checking equipment next to the shark cage poised at the boat's edge. His chin dipped as she drew alongside. Across the top of his dark sunglasses, his gaze skimmed her length and returned to the regulator cupped in his hands. Tugging a wrinkled bunch of neoprene out of her butt crack, Piper grimaced.

Sorry sweetie, without a bra cup size in double letters West's tongue's not hanging out over you.

His words nine years ago rose like a shipwrecked behemoth in her memory. "You're too stubborn, too tough, and too much one of the guys for my taste. There's nothing feminine about you. Sticking a party dress on doesn't make you any more of a woman."

She ruthlessly shoved the memory aside.

"You've used a surface air supply before?" he said.

"I'm familiar with it." *Familiar—huh!* She'd dived in rivers, tidal estuaries, and in her least pleasant experience, a fetid, pitch-black pond at the back of a farm. The share milker she'd been search for had taken a stroll after a hard night drinking at a mate's stag party. Paddling around in clear conditions with a surface air supply would be a lark in comparison.

"Good. Getting the cage in the water is the easy part. Dealing with first time divers, or divers who've never been this close to a real-life shark, isn't."

In between grunted instructions and the whine of machinery lowering the cage into the water, Piper asked, "Has Ben ever had any close calls with inexperienced divers?"

"Anyone who goes into the cage has to be a certified diver or, if not, the dive guide takes them on a ninety-minute theory and practical course for an extra fee. As long as they don't panic, there's little risk involved."

"And *have* people panicked?"

"Once or twice. Nothing major." He finished securing the cage to the boat, stooping to dip his fingers in the ocean. "Ah...just like bathwater."

Cords of ropey muscle in his exposed forearms drew her gaze. West had always been strong; he'd grown up hoisting beer crates and boxes of canned food in his dad's restaurant. Once his body had been so familiar she could've sketched every freckle, each scar. But the hard packed muscle farther up his arms and across his chest hadn't yet formed nine years ago. And the span of his shoulders seemed so much wider since the last time he'd given her a piggyback ride when they were horsing around as teenagers. Piper's hand itched to discover if his skin remained silky and hot-to-the-touch.

He glanced over his shoulder and she diverted her attention to the sky, fiddling with her wetsuit's pull tag.

"You scared? Want to pack up and call it a day?"

The thought of going in sent tiny stabbing pricks across her scalp. She let her gaze skim disdainfully over the cage, as if she often hopped into the territory of two-ton creatures with teeth sharper than Shaye's paring knives.

"Hardly. I grew up diving these waters too. I've seen the sharks." Safely aboard a boat—and never up close. Except for that one time, which she *would not think about now.*

His grin was as dangerous as what might lurk in the fathoms below. Almost as if he read her mind. "All right, then. It's simple. You get in before the paying guests and you help them into position. During the dive you'll signal me if there's a problem. Most importantly, you prevent any fool from sticking their cameras or limbs outside the cage."

"Got it."

"Normally I'd be attracting the sharks with some bait chunks, but today I didn't pack any. You only warrant a dry run, sorry."

"I'll survive the disappointment." Piper's voice came out smooth and even, not revealing the tremble gathering momentum in her knees.

Stepping to the boat's edge, she gazed into the water. Clear blue and sparkling, good visibility. If she'd paid for this opportunity she couldn't have picked better shark-viewing conditions.

"Into the floating metal lunch box, then," she muttered and tugged on the wetsuit hood.

West's snicker made it through the layer of neoprene. She pulled her mask into place and descended into the hole until her shoulders were submerged. Glad he found some humor in the situation, as right now it took all her years of training not to bolt back onto the boat. And not only because the sea was freakin' icy.

He laid out some air hose and handed her the regulator. "Ready?"

"Born ready."

With the regulator plugged in, she slipped under the surface. The frigid water slapped at her exposed cheeks as she glided farther into the cage, floating in a slow-motion semicircle.

The water was a pretty turquoise blue, darkening to azure under The Mollymawk's motionless propeller. Gentle waves buffeted her, shifting her neoprene slippered feet on the cage's mesh bottom. Her breath rasped in her ears, and she held the cage's handrail to keep steady.

Glancing up over her shoulder, the blurry shape of West leaned against the gunwale, watching. See, smartass? She was okay. She could totally do this. A smile formed behind her regulator and she faced forward again.

Dull grey cut through the turquoise right in front. Jagged teeth and scarred off-white flesh flashed away to the left. Metal shuddered under her fingers as the Great White's tail struck the cage. *Sonofa*— her heart whomped into triple time while her lungs squeezed shut.

Piper thrashed backward, her shoulder blades bumping the bars behind. Incomprehensible shouts overhead. A flurry of bubbles swarmed around her face as the reptilian part of her brain remembered to breathe, even as the mammal part wanted to curl into a ball to make the smallest possible target. Her fingers cinched on the hand rail again—a small miracle it didn't snap off at the weld.

Her gaze zeroed in on the shark cruising past; it was close enough that if she stuck her arm through the gap that allowed tourists to take photos, she'd touch the creature's battered dorsal fin.

A hollow banging sound above. Piper twisted her head up. West leaned over the boat edge with a fishing gaff in his hand. He tapped the cage again, held his other hand farther out so she could see his thumbs up signal. She returned his "come up now" gesture by showing him her back. Then she raised a hand, one digit extended from her fist.

It wasn't her thumb.

Give no quarter, show no weakness. Shark or no shark, bolting right now was not an option.

More shouting. This time she deciphered a few words—Piper, goddammit, and get-your-ass, before she tuned out.

Piper looked for the shark, but it had since disappeared into the gloom. The shifting of shadow and light and the motion of the water dampened down her pulse rate to almost normal.

No sharks. No dead bodies. Just the ocean she'd always loved.

Always *had* loved.

She was unsure what her feelings were toward it at the moment. Or toward the man above—and she couldn't avoid dealing with him for much longer.

Chapter 5

Once she estimated a good five minutes had passed since West threw up his hands and walked away, Piper swam over to the cage hole. Point made—she was no coward. Quitting because panic nipped at her heels was unacceptable. If she left the cage when West ordered, she'd find it twice as hard to go back in next time.

And really—a police diver losing it because of a big, dumb shark that *couldn't even get to her?* She confronted more danger patrolling the streets of Wellington city on a Friday night shift.

Breaking the surface, Piper spat out the regulator and pulled off her mask and hood. The sunshine striking her face after the chilly water was bliss. She climbed onto the boat and dropped her mask into the bin with the other spares.

West lounged on one of the cushioned benches, feet propped on an overturned fish bin, his fingers wrapped around an open bottle of Coke. He drank deeply, then placed the bottle on the table in front of him. "You done?"

"Yep." She sat on a plastic stool and peeled off the neoprene booties, wriggling her toes. "I can see why the loopies like it. It's an adrenaline rush."

"An adrenaline rush."

"Oh, yeah. Shark must've been a thirteen-footer."

"More like eleven." Sunglasses still covered his eyes and he kept them directed at the horizon, his thumb hooked all casual-like in the pocket of his shorts. As if the catching-some-rays act could convince her he wasn't seething on the inside.

Piper yanked on the wetsuit's pull tag, dragged the neoprene off her arms and chest, leaving it to flop down around her hips. Adjusting the straps of her swimsuit, she directed another covert glance at West. He still stared out to sea, but this time the twitch of his Adam's apple and the white-knuckled fingers around the bottle neck indicated an imminent blowout.

"Must've been my lucky day to see one without any bait." She stood and grabbed a towel off the nearby stack, rubbing it over her damp skin.

"Scared the crap out of you, didn't it?" He dropped his feet off the fish bin and slid the sunglasses to the top of his head.

Her temper sparked at the smirk coloring his gaze, fanning to flame by him being right. A more accurate description of her reaction was terrified-to-a-whisker-of-a-meltdown. And the shark's sudden appearance couldn't explain the sick apprehension that choked her before the dive. Not a comforting admission, when the ability to think clearly and cope under stress would affect her future career. "It startled me, at most."

"Startled? You leapt two feet backward— it was a wonder you didn't swallow your tongue."

"I wasn't expecting a shark to just *be there*, that's all. My reaction was completely understandable and no big deal."

West stood, muscles bunching under his thin tee shirt as he crossed his arms. "It could've been a big deal if you'd knocked the regulator out while you were panicking."

Trust West to select the one word guaranteed to trigger a response. Seabirds wheeled in the air currents, their cries slicing through the only other sounds—waves slapping against the hull and her teeth grinding together as she counted to ten. Counting didn't help.

Piper threw down the towel, balling her hands into fists. "I don't panic."

"You did that time, baby."

"Bull. Shit."

West edged around the table. "And your hissy-fit when I ordered you up? Childish, even for you."

Hissy-fit? Heat flamed her cheeks and spread, hazing her vision red, loosening her tongue. "After three-and-a-half grueling weeks on the Navy training course, a little thing like a shark or a lost regulator *would not* make me panic. I was in no danger, so your power trip was uncalled for."

"Just had to prove how big your balls were, didn't you?"

"I don't have to prove anything to you." She turned to make a grand exit to her cabin but West blocked her path, wrapping his fingers around her upper arm.

"You've got something to prove to everyone with that giant chip on your shoulder. But I'm not playing your juvenile pissing game again. Next time I signal you out of the water, you get out of the fucking water."

Piper gaped at West like he'd suddenly sprouted horns and a forked tail.

They always squabbled growing up—usually the kind that ended with someone getting dunked in the ocean—and the easy rivalry between her and her brother's mates had been a fun way to blow off steam.

That's what she expected this time. A nice, harmless shouting match that would bury the real reasons for her irritation. They would wind each other up, yell a bit and then everyone would feel better. But she hadn't anticipated the ice in West's blue eyes as they examined her without a glimmer of remembered affection.

She swallowed back a bitter dose of hurt. "Get your hands off me."

His palm burned her cool flesh, each finger branding a stripe on the soft skin of her inner arm. West moved closer, the few inches of height he had on her blocking out the sun. Hell, his size had less to do with blocking out the sun than just standing close to him. He dazzled her. And that alone made Piper want to punch him.

But she refused to shrink back, to allow him to see how his hand on her bare skin affected her. She latched onto her anger, pulling a memory from her days in police training college to reinforce it.

"More aggression!" her instructor bellowed at her when she'd participated in training exercises tackling suspects who were really other cops in jumpsuits. "You're a cop arresting a suspect who could have a concealed weapon. Don't give him a frickin' cuddle and kiss!"

More aggression, that's what she needed. Definitely not thoughts of cuddles and kisses with the man who hadn't blinked from examining her in the last ten seconds. She moistened her suddenly dry lips, and froze when something changed in his gaze at the flick of her tongue. Heat flared, heat that melted the ice of only a moment ago.

Piper narrowed her eyes so she wouldn't see his gaze track down to her lips again. Because she was mad, not thinking about the reasons why he might find her mouth interesting. "Remove your hand before I start breaking fingers."

Aggressive enough? Better than the alternative of, "Kiss me you crazy fool."

His smile was insolent as he slid his fingers along the sensitive underside of her arm, finally pulling them away. "I remember you begged me to touch you, once upon a time."

Yet another cringe-worthy moment in her past. "Aw, you still think about me sometimes? That's sweet. But that was before I became a stone cold bitch."

His eyebrows rose. Yeah, she'd heard the whispers after her father's memorial service when she'd stood at her mother's side, dry-eyed and stoic. More like catatonic with guilt and grief, but hey, that wasn't quite as juicy.

"You want to order me around at Due South, go ahead, if it makes you feel all alpha. But you don't get to tell me what to do in the water." She jabbed him in the chest. "And you sure as shit don't get to put your hands on me."

West wrapped his larger hand around hers, gently forcing her finger back into her fist. "Since being near me is so damn unbearable, why don't you hop on the next ferry and run back to the city. We'll all understand you just couldn't cut it. It's not like you haven't run before." His voice, smooth and slightly bored, could've been reciting an inventory list.

Piper's chin lifted, her treacherous heart hammering over and over against her breastbone. "I'm not leaving until my brother's home is safe. Deal with it."

West brushed her hand away from him as if the feel of her skin was repellent. So she stalked—if one could stalk on a shifting surface with neoprene jammed in one's butt cheeks—past him into The Mollymawk's galley.

***

Hadn't it been fun rowing Piper back ashore after mooring The Mollymawk? West snorted. Stony silence to the nth degree—like that wasn't a blessing. He dragged the dinghy up Halfmoon Bay beach while Piper sashayed off like the queen of the frickin' island.

Ben, who sat on a park bench overlooking the beach, didn't merit a word from his sister. She dropped the little digital camera in his lap and swept past, crossing the road to Due South. If she tipped her nose any higher the woman would trip over her bright green sneakers.

West finished pulling the dinghy out of the reach of the incoming tide and shoved the oars inside it.

"How did you piss her off this time?" Ben crutched his way over to the line of boulders separating grass from sand.

"I don't need to *do* anything to piss her off."

"Just being alive, hmm?"

Yeah. And being dumb enough to stop breathing when Piper was in the water with the shark—a visceral reaction of wanting her out of harm's way. He'd nearly dragged her out of the cage and made a fool of himself after she flipped him the bird. Later she'd displayed the same smugness as when they were kids, when Glenna would instruct him and Ben to, "Keep Piper with you and stay out of trouble." Inevitably they'd all fail to do the second part and Glenna would give them *the look*. A ball-shriveling look that made him want to kick Piper's ass for raising hell.

So this morning's episode had been a knee-jerk reaction. She hadn't been in any real danger. They'd dived with Piper's dad, Mike, for years. It wouldn't have been the first time she'd lost a regulator. Mike would knock it out of their mouths while teaching the three of them to scuba. "Be prepared for equipment failure or for something to go tits-up. You need to know what to do."

A lost regulator was no biggie. Yet he'd raised his voice, grabbed her arm, let Piper bait him, because it was easier than admitting she got to him. *Still* got to him. He nudged the blades of the oars farther into the dinghy and glared at the smirk on Ben's face.

West climbed over the boulders and punched his arm. "You owe me for putting up with your sister's crap."

How would he get through six more weeks? He already wanted to kill her. Kill her, but maybe do her first. He'd never claimed to be a gentleman where Piper was concerned.

Ben snickered. "Yeah, yeah. I'll hand over my first born child, pinky swear."

"Dickhead." West brushed past Ben, shoulder checking him before he slumped onto the park bench. He flung his head back to stare at the sky.

Muted thumps as Ben hopped over to sit next to him, his crutches clanking together as they rested against the wood slats. "Be nice to the cripple, man. Jeez, didn't your mother teach you any manners?"

"No. She left me to turn feral—and don't start with the yo' mama jokes."

"I'm sorry. You're having an *I miss my mummy* moment and I'm being insensitive—wanna hug it out?"

West extended an arm without turning his head and shoved. But a smile kicked up at the corner of his mouth when Ben recovered and shoved him right back. Ben was the only person on this island he would put up with this shit for.

They'd always been mates, always had the other's back. In his earliest memories, eight-year-old Ben punched one of the Reynolds boys when they teased West for playing the piano like a girl. He couldn't remember now if it were Gavin or his older brother, Seth. Most likely Gav, since he'd always been a nasty little prick, while Seth, at least, grew out of being a complete asshat.

"So," Ben said after a comfortable pause. "Piper gave you a bit of grief then?"

"She's a pain in the butt. A genetic trait, I reckon."

"You gonna say that around my mother?"

"I may be having a crappy day, which is turning into a crappier week, but I haven't got a death wish. Yet." West sat up and leaned forward, resting his forearms on his thighs.

"I know some good spots to hide your body if you want me to permanently end your misery."

West grunted.

"You told her to go home, didn't you?" Ben said.

"What makes you think that, Einstein?"

"Because I know you. And I know her being here has shoved a burr up your ass."

West trained his eyes on a group of kids racing across the beach, a sand-covered terrier hot on their heels. Back to that again. This morning Ben's reaction seemed a normal, big-brother deal. But now? Ben and West double dated with Piper and Erin at the girls' final school ball, but had Ben guessed he and Piper had been sleeping together for a few weeks before it? Or was he just fishing? Best mate or not, this was one conversation they weren't having.

"I don't care that Piper's back and I told her if she couldn't cut it, she should hop on the next ferry. You, on the other hand, have a cactus-sized burr up your ass about your sister, and have had for years."

Ben snorted. "There's nothing up my ass but the sun shining out of it, thanks."

"You resent her for becoming a cop when it was your dream."

The smile switched off and Ben's knuckles flared white around the crutch's hand grip. "More my old man's dream—and that dream's ancient history. I resent her for much more mature reasons now."

"Sure. Like coming back here to help you out?"

"You flipping sides now? You always had a soft spot for her."

West cleared his throat and stood. "Sod off. She's only here to rub your nose in her generous gesture, then she'll swan off back to the city."

"Exactly." Ben leaned back on the bench and crossed his ankle on top of his bulky cast. "So she's gone to buy a ferry ticket then?"

"No."

"You should've known better than to issue a challenge to Piper. She'll never leave now."

West glanced over at Due South. Piper, Shaye, Kezia, and Kezia's little girl, Zoe, walked through the doorway to one of the outside tables, talking and laughing.

"Yeah, she will."

As soon as things got tough—and they would—Piper would run. Just like she always did.

Only this time she wouldn't take his heart with her.

***

Piper entered Due South, her neck muscles knotted from the effort of not glancing over her shoulder at West and Ben still on the beach.

Touches of Shaye and her mother were everywhere in the restaurant. Ten years ago the dining room of Due South could've been labeled "shabby chic"—minus the "chic." Interior design didn't figure much in Bill Westlake's world and he hadn't changed anything since his wife left the island.

But now Piper saw Shaye's hand in the turquoise fish-themed watercolors on the whitewashed walls, the splashes of matching color in the woven flax flower arrangements. A smattering of late lunch diners lingered over their wine glasses and desserts—seated on elegant cane chairs that screamed her mother's taste. Wicker baskets stacked with firewood sat beside an open fire, ready to be lit when the temperature dropped.

Bill must've let her mother and sister go wild with the restaurant's décor, but he'd left the bar the same as it'd always been. A man cave.

A little girl of eight or nine kneeled on the sofa in front of the fireplace. Sitting beside her, a woman with a riot of espresso-brown curls read a newspaper. The girl peeked over the sofa back, watching her approach with twinkling dark eyes and a bold smile. Some of her foul mood evaporated and Piper grinned back. What a sweetheart!

Shaye leaned against the service counter talking to a young Maori woman with a tribal tattoo poking out from the sleeve of Due South's signature turquoise polo shirt. Shaye glanced at Piper's face as she slipped onto one of the wooden stools lining the counter and said to the younger woman, "Better start on a chocolate milkshake after you've taken those drinks out. Extra shot of syrup."

Piper slipped her sunglasses up onto her head. "What are we, twelve?"

"That scowl on your face tells me it's a chocolate emergency. Lani, make it two shakes when you're ready. We'll grab Kez and Zoe and sit outside."

The young woman fired Piper a quick look before scooping up the tray of drinks and scooting out from behind the counter. "On it."

"Lani? As in Lani Hohepa?" Piper whispered as the younger woman moved away. "She's like a little kid with freckles and posters of cute boy bands on her walls!"

"Hon, that was nine years ago. She can vote now. Drink. Have sex with hot guys like Kip, the bartender."

"Little Lani Hohepa is sleeping with your *bartender*?" Piper craned her neck around.

"No, you nut. But she could if she wanted to. Or if he did. He's a hard one to figure out. Anyway, I can see you're in a snit, but since we're eating with people who don't know you're loveable under that scary bad-cop persona, you can suck up some sugar and tell me later about what gigantic jerks West and Ben are. Come and meet the girls."

"I'm not in a snit. I don't do *snits*." Piper followed Shaye across the restaurant.

She was just indignant at West's behavior. Okay, so her one finger salute may have been a little uncalled for, but she was a dive cop, goddammit. She'd been in hairier situations. And she most certainly *did not* panic.

Shaye tapped the shoulder of the brunette with the newspaper. "Kez?"

The woman's dark gaze slid quickly past Shaye, her wide mouth splitting into a grin. Kezia folded the paper neatly and stood, her pretty floral dress floating around her knees.

"This is my sister Piper, down from Wellington," Shaye said. "Piper, my housemate and friend, Kezia Murphy. Her daughter Zoe's got her head in the toy box over there."

Without Shaye introducing the little girl, the relationship between the two was obvious. They both had the same hint of the Mediterranean in their bold features and olive skin. And while Zoe was too cute in her tee shirt, so yellow it stabbed her brain, her mother was a knockout. Something all the local penis owners in Oban would've spotted. She should've hated Kezia on sight for being everything she would never be—petite, feminine and sweet.

Then Kezia spoke, her voice slightly accented and with a natural soft rasp that would drive men wild. "If you need an accomplice to kick someone's boy-bits, I'm your girl."

Not so sweet. So maybe she could forgive her for being small, and curvy, and with a voice of a phone sex worker. "Got anyone in mind?"

"Whoever made you look like you wanted to spit nails when you walked in, *cara.*"

"That would be Shaye's boss. So I'll have to take a rain check."

"Ah, well. It'd be a shame to damage someone so pretty." Kezia pursed her lips thoughtfully. "We could hold him down while you muss up his hair."

"That'd teach him," said Shaye.

Piper laughed, but before she could speak a little voice interrupted. "I'm Zoe and I'm eight-and-a-half. Are you really a policeman?"

Kezia's daughter stood holding loosely on to her mother's arm.

"Hi, Zoe. I'm Piper, and I'm twenty-seven-and-a-third and yes I am a policeman—well, woman really."

"Cool." Zoe cocked her head, and chocolate brown curls bounced. Piper bit her lip to prevent a gooey "aww" from slipping out. "Do you have a gun?"

"Zoe!"

"Mamma—I'm just *asking*." She rolled her eyes in a theatrical fashion and turned back to Piper.

Piper patted her hip pockets and frowned. "Darn, I must've left my gun in my other shorts."

Zoe giggled, covering her cherubic lips with a small hand. Then her eyes widened and shifted to a serious confidentiality. "Did you know in America last year over thirty-one thousand people died from guns? *Thirty-one thousand!*"

Oh my God. She loved this kid already. "Really? That many?"

Piper tuned out the huff of laughter from Shaye and Kezia's muttered, "Sweet mother of God," followed the soft slap of palm meeting forehead.

Zoe nodded. "I read it on the internet."

The weight of the morning's tension oozed out of Piper's muscles. This was shaping up to be a fun lunch.

***

Conversation flowed under the blue-tinted shade of the sun umbrella while they enjoyed their lunch. West arrived at their table with a charming smile for Kezia, Zoe and Shaye, but his gaze switched to hooded and cool when it landed on Piper.

Kezia excused herself to go to the restroom while West and Shaye continued to talk shop. Zoe played on her mother's phone, and West turned away from Piper, excluding her from their conversation. Not that she gave a hoot about orders, or stock, or whatever else they continued to yatter on about. She had nothing to offer their discussion other than a barely masked yawn, because yeah, she was only the lowly kitchen-hand—and no offence to young Fraser whose job she'd taken over; he was a sweetie. Unlike his boss.

Piper bent over Zoe's shoulder and whispered, "I'm going to the bathroom too—you okay here with Mr. and Mrs. Boring?"

The girl giggled, but didn't look up from the screen. "Uh-huh."

Piper wound her way through the restaurant and went through the doorway leading to the public restrooms in the main hallway.

A concrete slab of a man had Kezia backed up against the hallway wall. He towered over her, meaty hands wedged on either side of her arms, preventing her escape. "How long are you going to use your dead husband and cancer kid as an excuse?"

Kezia's fingers curled claws in the crook of the guy's elbows, trying to force him away. Neither noticed Piper frozen in the doorway.

"Leave my husband and daughter out of it. They're not why I won't party with you, Gavin." Kezia's voice could've crushed ice. "Now, back off."

Gavin. Gav. Piper's mind made a quick foray back to age sixteen when Gav cornered her in Ford and Harley's bathroom at the twins' eighteenth birthday party. He'd followed her in, locked the door and tried to kiss her, ramming his slimy tongue into her mouth, grabbing one of her breasts. He missed having the tip of his tongue bitten off by millimeters. Then she kneed him in the nuts and went at him with the closest weapon at hand, which happened to be a toilet brush—but hey, those bristles could hurt if shoved somewhere with enough force. She only had time to smack him across his stricken face a few times before West and Ben, hearing the commotion, busted inside. Her heroes pissed themselves laughing at her makeshift club, but dragged Gavin outside and taught him a lesson about respect.

A combination of temper and training hustled Piper down the hall. She wanted to wrench Gav's arm up behind his back and bend his wrist at an angle cops affectionately dubbed the "chicken hold" until he screamed like a girl. Then maybe she could beat him senseless with the rolling pin Bill kept in his kitchen. Unfortunately, as an off-duty officer, the paperwork for manhandling Gav meant it wasn't worth the hassle. Pity. She'd really, *really* enjoy watching him scream.

"Cornering women in bathrooms still, Gavin? You're pathetic, you know that, right?"

Gavin started at the sound of her voice, but didn't move his arms. Joints in his beefy neck crackled as he swung his head to the side. "Piss off, Piper. This doesn't concern you."

"You're annoying my friend. That makes it my concern."

His lips pulled back in a sneer. "You don't have any friends. And I'm in the middle of inviting Kezia out for a drink."

Oban's newest primary school teacher may've look sweeter than a sprinkle-covered cupcake, but Gav risked his family jewels if the daggers shooting from Kezia's gaze were an indication. But Piper wouldn't risk his temper turning physical on the smaller woman.

"Sounds like she's not interested in what you've got to offer." Piper affected a bored note to her voice and dropped her gaze down to the crotch of Gav's jeans. A big guy like him wouldn't like the size of his tackle called into disrepute.

Gavin's chest expanded like a puffer fish and he finally removed his hands from the wall and turned to face her. "She's interested all right. She's just playing hard to get."

Kezia ducked around him and stood at Piper's side. "*She* isn't playing hard to get and *she* thinks you're a complete butthead."

"I'll second that assessment." Piper eased herself in front of Kezia, who'd be out of the line of fire should Gav do anything foolish. "Now, are you leaving, or do I need to go get a toilet brush?"

His thick neck flushed a coronary-inducing shade of lobster.

Maybe she'd pushed him too far. Then she remembered the sour stench of his breath and the stubby fingers squeezing her breast. Piper braced her feet and bared her teeth.

Bring it, butthead.

But like the blustery drunks she came in contact with on a daily basis, Gavin backed down once his bullying tactics failed to get him his desired result. "Stuck up bitches, the both of you." He stormed past and slammed the door open to the pub.

Kezia sagged against her, shaking. Piper slipped an arm around the smaller woman's shoulder and gave her a one-armed hug. "You okay? Tell me he hasn't tried something like this before."

She shook her head. "He's asked me out a few times and I've turned him down. He was more persistent today."

"Maybe you need to get Glenn involved."

"Glenn left years ago, so they tell me. Noah Daniels is the island's cop now and I don't think it's serious enough to call him." Kezia smiled, but her lips gave a telltale tremble.

"You should give West a heads-up—"

"Oh no—no!" Her curls danced wildly across her shoulders. "West has already told Gav to quit pestering me. If he finds out he's done it again he'll ban him from the pub—then Gav'll stir up more bad blood in the community. I'm pretty sure he'll leave me alone now."

Piper didn't believe it, but arguing seemed pointless. She studied Kezia's prettily flushed face and her chest that still heaved from delayed shock. Ms. Teacher had quite a pair of boobs on her and she didn't doubt West had noticed. No wonder he'd been keen to jump to her defense. "Up to you."

They looked at each other until Piper swallowed back a sigh, Gav's accusations and thinking of little Zoe with cancer tightening a compressing band around her chest. "I've heard you're a widow, but Zoe's got cancer?"

"Not anymore. She's in remission. I try to remind her that not everybody needs to know her medical history, but you've probably noticed that my girl loves to talk."

"Yeah, and I could tell right away Zoe's a tough cookie, too."

"She's had to be—dealing with leukemia and missing the love of her grandparents because they thought me a gold-digging bitch—" Kezia broke off, shoving shaky fingers under her armpits and hugging herself. "Sorry, I'm ranting. I don't usually dump my life story on people within minutes of meeting them. Gav's rattled me a little more than I thought."

"It's okay. I'm very dumpable."

"Thanks."

"My only regret is I should've rattled the prick for you—then afterwards you could've kicked him in his boy-bits."

"Next time?"

Piper pointed a finger at her. "If there is a next time you'll be talking with Noah Daniels."

Kezia pulled her shoulders back and smoothed down her dress. "Gotta get my mojo back before we go out again. What's with the toilet brush comment, anyway?"

"Invite me around for a beer sometime and I'll tell you."

"You're on." Kezia returned her smile, a genuine one this time, and casually slipped her arm through Piper's, like they really were friends or something.

Heck. How had that happened?

***

Piper spent the rest of the afternoon and evening elbow-deep in lemon and grease scented dishwater.

She'd pretty much decided her sister's career choice in the culinary industry sucked when Bill told her, "Go back to West's. You look like something Donny puked up on the rug."

After drying her prune-wrinkled hands, she snagged her lightweight hoodie off the hook by the back door. Forcing a friendly note into her voice she called out, "See you tomorrow, Bill."

She received a surly grunt in reply.

The temperature had dropped like the night before, but it wasn't raining. Piper tugged on the hoodie, glancing down at the soft whine from at her feet. Curled in his bed by the kitchen's back door, Donny looked up at her with a woe-is-me sheen in his eyes. When she held the dog's gaze, he began to shake.

"Poor baby." She squatted and scratched behind his remaining ear. "Did your mean old master leave you out here in the cold?"

"He's got fur so he's totally faking it." West's voice came from behind her in the open doorway.

"Jeez, will you stop sneaking up on me?" She sprung up and spun around. "It's not closing time—haven't you got your little empire to oversee?"

Donny clambered out of his basket and sidled over to West, his tail thwacking against her legs.

"I'll walk back with you. Dad's closing up tonight."

"For once," came Bill's disembodied shout from somewhere within the bowels of his kitchen. "You're a bleedin' workaholic. Always first in, last to leave. Ya must be coming down with something."

"Yeah, yeah, old man. Just lock up and keep out of trouble."

A muffled but audible, "I'm not the one headed for trouble, sonny-boy."

West shut the door on his father's continued grumbles. "Ready?"

Once again his proximity sent shivers rippling through her system. He had no idea about personal space, or maybe her awareness of him caused her to squirm like a gawky teenager again.

Should she insist she'd rather walk alone? She couldn't very well confess her plan to sneak back to his spare room to avoid another confrontation. Better to play it cool. But the woodsy-scented body heat rising from his long sleeve tee shirt, the way his jeans clung to every clingable bit of his lower body, and just the sheer, sexy bulk of him was almost enough to make her risk being rude. She spotted the gleam of his teeth in the semi-darkness. Almost, but not quite.

"Yep." She crossed her arms over her breasts, as her nipples pebbled under her hoodie. A natural consequence of the cool night air. Uh-huh.

"Let's go." He gestured for her to take the lead.

They rounded the side of Due South and headed along the empty road. Donny trotted ahead and paused frequently to sniff along the ground. Maybe they wouldn't end up snapping each other's head off again. Maybe they could remain civil. And since they were being civil, she'd ask him a *civil* question.

"How long has Gavin been after Kezia?"

Their footsteps echoed in sync on the asphalt, the hiss of small waves foaming along the beach to their right a watery complement. Finding their natural rhythm together had never been the problem.

West shoved his hands into his jean pockets and slowed his steps. "Why? Jealous he's not panting after you anymore?"

"Right." She snorted a laugh. "Like you're not a little bit green."

"Nah. Gav's not my type."

"But Kezia is." The words popped out of her in an explosive bubble. *Damn.*

"She's stunning, that's for sure."

Her pace sped up, cold slicking through her blood.

What had she expected? Someone as pretty and feminine as Kezia wouldn't catch his eye? That he'd been celibate for the past nine years? She sensed his gaze skim down her hoodie and the cargo pants, which scored an A for comfort and an easy D-minus for sex appeal. She'd never done pretty dresses or dainty heels, and up until West broke her heart it hadn't dawned on her that girly stuff may top his list of turn-ons. Piper's backbone straightened, each muscle contracting around her vertebrae a reminder of her resolve. Shaye and Kezia loved their girly stuff, but she would *never* be a girly-girl.

"You practicing speed walking here?" He lengthened his stride to keep up. "Or maybe a spot of jealousy yourself."

"You always did have a big ego to compensate for your small dick," she sniped, not letting up her pace.

"I don't recall you complaining about the size of my dick. You seemed pretty happy to get your hands on it."

Heat flashed through her. What their lovemaking lacked in sophistication was compensated for with passion and a deep connection. Well. *She had* experienced passion and a deep connection.

"Back then I had nothing to compare it to. I'm older and wiser now." And not dumb enough to get entangled with him a second time.

"And maybe we've both grown since then. I'll show you mine if you show me yours."

The grin in his tone said the bastard was laughing at her again. They both knew he only slept with her for convenience and curiosity—he'd clarified that nine years ago. So why tease her in a sexual way? To highlight the humiliation that she'd always been more into him than vice-versa? "I'm sure you'd rather show your dick to women who'll give it the adoration you so erroneously believe it deserves."

"My dick is quite adorable. Sure you don't want a peek?"

A clear picture popped into her mind. West in board shorts earlier in the day, the wind blowing the thin fabric against him, outlining his large—*hello, not going there.* "Can we not continue this asinine conversation? I'm surrounded at work by men who love talking about this sort of crap."

"We men do find it an endlessly fascinating topic."

"So I've discovered."

Past the last of the streetlamps, West produced a flashlight and switched it on. Donny, spotting the thin beam of light, loped back and trotted at West's heels. "Gav is interested in any female who hasn't twigged he's an asshole. There's not many left on the island."

"Puts me off his radar then—and Kezia thinks he's a butthead."

"Did something happen at your girls' lunch today?"

"Nothing we *girls* couldn't cope with. Kezia turned Gav down on a date and he didn't handle the rejection with diplomacy. It's no big deal."

"No big deal—just like you panicking in the cage was no big deal?"

"Are you always so contentious?" She slid him a sidelong glare, which probably got lost in the gathering dark. "I told you, I didn't panic."

"Because you've done three-and-a-half weeks training with the Navy."

Crap! He had listened to her tirade on The Mollymawk. Piper kept her jaw clamped shut and walked.

"Cat got your tongue, hmm?"

She hoped, even when hope was useless, that West would drop the subject. Like that'd happen.

"So why all this dive training? I thought you were just a cop?"

A beat passed while her brain sifted through frantic excuses. Nothing helpful caught and she sighed. "I am a cop."

"And?"

"And I'm a damn good cop."

He stopped. Right in the center of the road. Tipped his head to the side and folded his arms, the fingers on his right hand drumming a tattoo on his left bicep. Donny dropped his butt to the ground beside him and blinked accusingly at her too.

"I've read something before about the navy diving course. You're not an ordinary cop, you're a police diver."

Busted. And pointless denying it. But she fisted her hands on her hips and stared him down. She'd worked hard to earn her place on the squad. "Yeah, I am. The only female on the squad at the moment."

"Your family doesn't know about this, do they?"

"They don't need to know." She hesitated, thinking of her mother. "It would only hurt and worry them—you can't tell."

"Dammit, Pipe, it's not right." Her heart gave a pathetic hop at the sound of her old nickname on his tongue. "This kind of...work. It can't be good for you."

Murray O'Neill. The name of the seventeen-year-old she'd recovered at Lake Tikitapu. Her work. Murray's mother had wrapped her arms around Piper, thanking her for bringing her boy home. The woman's tears left damp patches on the stiff collar of her uniform shirt. Murray O'Neill built another brick in the wall of redemption she started constructing nine years ago. Not just work.

"I'm good at what I do."

"Why, of all areas you could specialize in, did you choose police diving? After what you went through with your dad..." He moved toward her, extending his hand.

Piper stepped back fast. No way. She'd rather he grab her in temper like this morning than touch her with big-brotherly gentleness. She didn't want his pity. Or his platonic caresses.

"I'm not talking about this. My career has nothing to do with you, or anyone else."

He dropped his arm and shoved his hand into the pocket of his jeans instead. "Still the original island who doesn't need anything from anyone."

"Precisely." Piper turned and walked away.

West was right. She didn't need anything from him or anyone else.

Especially him.

Chapter 6.

West glided through the pool, the liquid sensuality of the water flowing over his bare torso soothing the rough edges of the last few days. Everything felt better beneath the surface. Somehow the day to day problems faded when his focus concentrated on every precise movement, the slow thud of his heartbeat and the burn in his lungs.

One more fifty-foot length and he'd beat his personal record of seven, on one breath of air. He swept his arms forward again, pulled them back in one fluid motion, his body arrowing porpoise-like and perfectly aligned. He preferred the free immersion discipline of free-diving, descending vertically into the deep rather than coasting along horizontally, but since Ben was out of action as his safety diver, pool lengths would do for now.

The national free immersion championships at Lake Taupo were two months away and he needed to be prepared. Not just for the chance to take home the cash prize, but for the satisfaction of being the best in the country.

He touched the end of the pool and surfaced, resting his arms on the rough concrete edge and gulping in air. West pulled off his mask and checked his dive watch. Seven fifteen. He could spare a few more minutes in the pool before he needed to grab breakfast and head into Due South.

"Ford?"

His friend looked up from his Kindle and turned the device off. "Uh-huh?"

"You're a useless safety buddy, you know. I could've suffered a shallow water black out and you never would've noticed."

Ford tossed his trademark black dreadlocks over his shoulder and stood up from one of the spectator seats. "You pay peanuts, you get a bored monkey. And I would've noticed and gone all Baywatch on you."

"That's an unpleasant image. I'm just going to swim another couple of laps—you can head off now and go back to Star Trek or whatever trash you're reading."

"It's Isaac Asimov, you pleb." Ford tucked the Kindle under his arm and sauntered to the pool door, his flip flops slapping on the wet concrete. "Don't drown—unless your dad knows you owe me another meal on the house."

West left the mask on the pool's edge and dived back under, this time striking into a fast crawl stroke, plowing through the water's resistance. Two lengths turned to eight before a flicker of movement beside the pool snagged his attention. He raised his head, changing into a slow breaststroke.

Piper stood at the end of the pool, fists on hips, watching him with hooded eyes. They'd avoided each other since their heated discussion two nights before, but if he didn't know better he'd swear she was checking him out. West stood in the waist deep water and swiped a hand over his face. If her gaze contained a red dot laser, it would've tracked him from chest to groin. Oh, yeah, she was definitely checking him out.

"I drew the short straw to come find you."

He didn't speak, just followed the telltale shift of her irises as they continued to scan up and down his bare torso. She cleared her throat, her gaze veering off to the side of the pool.

"Ben and Shaye are meeting us at The Great Flat White for breakfast." She uttered a jittery laugh. "Erin's place—who would've thought she'd end up staying here."

"Not everyone finds living on the island unbearable."

West waded to the pool's edge and climbed out. He grabbed his towel from a spectator chair, hung it around his neck and rubbed his hair. When he turned back, his gaze dropped to Piper's long legs, once again encased in black denim. She wore her purple combat boots and a *Warning: If we're being chased by zombies I'm tripping you* tee shirt, which made him want to laugh. Oh, she'd trip someone all right. Most likely him.

She kept her distance, making an effort to keep her eyes fixed above the waistband of his Lycra training shorts. His cock twitched as her hazel gaze darted down again. The opportunity to tease was too good to resist.

"Like what you see?" He pitched his voice low and the reward was a faint tint of rose on Piper's cheekbones.

Her throat worked as she swallowed, but she met his gaze, affixing a smirk to her lips. "You must be very secure in your masculinity to parade around in those budgie smugglers."

"Oh, I'm very secure." He see-sawed the towel over his back. "And I'm happy to show you the rear view of my budgie smugglers—oh wait—you already saw it when you were *checking out my ass.*"

Instead of denying it, Piper barked out a belly laugh. "Oh puh-lease. Like I haven't seen your skinny butt a dozen times before."

"My butt is not skinny."

The cocky attitude returned and she bared her teeth. "How would you know what your butt looks like? Do you ogle yourself in the mirror while going at it doggy-style?"

Piper never bothered with little niceties, always straight for the jugular.

"I can't say that's quite my thing, but no woman's ever complained once she'd got her hands...or mouth...on it."

She certainly hadn't. West recalled one memorable occasion when Piper sunk her teeth into one cheek hard enough to leave tiny indents. She'd kissed it better though. Then moved those bewitching, pouty lips onto other parts of his anatomy.

"Low standards." Piper sniffed and walked to the door, looking back over her shoulder. "We got a couple of bookings for a romance cruise. We'll see you at Erin's in twenty."

She dropped a withering glance at his crotch. "And you might want to take a cold shower. Looks like your budgie's trying to escape."

Twenty minutes after taking Piper's advice and showering under a shrinkage-guaranteed temperature, West strolled into The Great Flat White café. He waved to Erin, her long, blonde plait swinging maniacally as she operated the enormous espresso machine. She flashed him a peace sign, which in Erin's world translated to a confirmation of his regular coffee order—a double-shot-flat white. He nodded, attention drawn to the corner table by the large picture window, which overlooked the ferry wharf.

Piper sat with her back to the view, across from her brother and sister. Shaye leaned into Ben and murmured something, and he gently nudged her arm and chuckled. Piper's gaze skipped between them, her lips pinched together, while under the table one purple boot tapped a jerky rhythm on the café's wooden floor. She looked away from the gentle ribbing going on between her siblings and pretended to study the laminated menu.

A sharp twinge hit him somewhere in the region of his heart. Piper considered herself the odd duck growing up, the one who never quite fitted in. Born the middle child, she'd been two years younger than him and Ben—and a girl, much to her annoyance—and most of the time they hadn't wanted her around. She was also three years older than Shaye and while her little sister was happy to be a mummy's girl, Piper gravitated toward her dad.

West quashed the feeling as he walked to the table. Likely the chest twinge was a misdirection of nerves from his stomach demanding breakfast.

He sat next to Piper, which she looked real cheerful about, and said to Ben, "You already ate a bowl of cereal at home."

Ben didn't bother to look up from the menu. "Yeah, but you know I hate that bran stuff you buy, it tastes like tree bark."

"It's good for you, keeps your ass in peak operational condition."

Shaye made a "T" sign with her hands. "Ewww. Too much information, dude."

West swiveled his head to the right with an evil grin. "We were just talking about asses, weren't we Piper?"

Her eyes tapered to annoyed slits but before she could retaliate, Erin arrived at the table with a tray of coffees.

"Right. Latte bowl with skinny milk for Shaye-Shaye. A long black for Ben, and West's usual..." Erin passed Piper's coffee over without looking directly at her. "And an Americano with hot milk on the side for you."

She placed a small jug of steaming milk on the table and whipped an order pad from her apron pocket. "Now, what can I get you all this morning?"

Erin noted their orders and hurried back behind the service counter.

"So, the new photos and blurb on the website did the trick?" West said, while Ben ripped open a tiny sugar packet. "Some loved-up couple keen for an overnighter?"

"Two couples, actually. Booked in for Saturday." *And I told you so, loser,* Piper's tone implied.

Ben scratched the scruffy stubble on his jaw. "Well, it's three couples now, *actually.*"

"Three? Wow, get out!" Shaye shoved Ben and nearly knocked him off his seat.

"Wait a minute. Three couples? When did this happen?" Piper didn't sound as enthusiastic as her sister.

"Got an e-mail last night. The original two couples are old friends and they've convinced some other friends to take a second honeymoon," Ben said.

Piper added milk to her coffee, frown lines appearing on her forehead. "But The Mollymawk's only got four cabins. We can't all fit."

Mathematics being one of his strong suits, West got it. He wasn't sure if he liked it, but he got it. A sidelong glance at Ben revealed Ben got it too.

"You and West will share the bunkroom for the night," Ben said.

"Hell no!" Piper snapped up straight, her chair skidding backward with a screech.

"It's just for one night." Ben stirred the sugar into his cup, keeping his gaze glued to the spoon's circles.

"I'm not sharing a room." Folding her arms, Piper shot West a baleful glare, but she wouldn't prolong the eye contact and switched her fierce gaze back to her brother.

Interesting that the lady protested with such vehemence. West angled toward her and waited for the fireworks.

Ben dropped his teaspoon on the table and huffed out a sigh. "Why? It's a bunkroom, Piper. It's not like you're sharing a bed, for the love of God."

She opened her mouth, clamped it shut again and remained silent. A miracle in itself. Though West couldn't blame her—thinking about sharing a bed with Piper kinda drained the intelligent cells right out of his brain.

"It'll just be like camping when we were kids," said Shaye in full peacekeeping mode. "Remember how we used to all take our sleeping bags and camp out on the beach around the campfire?"

"Fine." Piper affected an *I totally wasn't overreacting* shrug and picked up her cup. "But I'm kicking him out to the stern deck if he starts snoring."

Someone had their standard issue cop panties in a twist about spending the night in a shared space. Nice to know he wasn't the only one squirming. West took his first sip of coffee. "You bring earplugs then and I'll bring the marshmallows."

"No fires on my boat," grumped Ben.

West's grin widened at Piper's flushed cheeks. Oh, there'd be fire all right. Because things were heating up fast and like it or not, someone was gonna get burned.

And for the record?

This time it wouldn't be him.

***

"You're not planning anything I can't reheat in a pot, are you?" Piper leaned over Kezia's kitchen table later that morning, watching as Shaye flipped through a notebook of handwritten recipes. "Because cooking's not my thing."

"I'll keep it simple." Shaye continued to turn pages with one hand and scribble notes on the pad beside her with the other. "Blinis with smoked salmon for starters, that's easy. Now, a main. Hmm."

Piper wandered around the room. Kezia's place was a 1930s refurbished cottage—compact, yes, but also cozy and so, so Kezia. She admired the collection of brass knickknacks behind the flue on the bricks that ensconced the woodstove, wandered over to sniff at a delicate vase of sweet-pea, and studied the Zoe-created artworks pinned to a corkboard.

Kezia and her daughter were off on a play date.

Zoe had pulled a face when Piper asked about her friend before they left. "There are no girls my age around, so Mum said I have to make do with George. But he's not my friend, he's a *boy*. You can't be BFFs with a *boy*."

Thinking of West, Piper had agreed. Best friends forever? That hadn't worked out so well.

Sighing, she grabbed a pot mitt and lifted the kettle off the woodstove to make another coffee. Too much more caffeine and she'd be jittery enough to do or say something brainless. Like she nearly had at the pool.

"Like what you see?" West said, and she'd almost blurted out, "Baby I could eat you with a spoon."

Luckily, she picked her tongue up off the floor and did her pride a favor by cramming it back into her mouth. Strutting around in all that black Lycra, displaying all those sexy muscles and glistening, tanned skin...any woman under seventy would drool. Heck, even over seventy—she would swear the lavender-haired Mrs. Taylor batted her eyelashes when West personally served her her gin and tonic.

She poured the boiling water into her mug and stirred, staring out the window. Endless blue sky and variegated shades of green foliage dominated the island. Blue and green and very little else. No grey skyscrapers, no colorful billboards lining the motorway, no gold trolley buses trundling through city streets.

"You okay?"

Piper turned and leaned against the counter. "Sure. Just wool-gathering."

"About?"

Piper couldn't meet her sister's eyes. She still resisted asking for help. Hard enough setting aside her pride at work, but with family— family she deliberately estranged herself from—it went from awkward to excruciating. "If I can find someone to cover for you on Saturday, will you come on the cruise with us?"

Shaye dropped the pen and then snatched it up, rapidly clicking and unclicking the tiny button. "Piper..."

"Not for the whole time. Just to serve dinner to the guests and stay overnight." She hated the faint whine of desperation in her tone.

"I can't."

"I'm sure if we talked to West—"

"What is it with you and West, anyway?" Shaye hijacked her gaze. "The pair of you are like circling sharks, just waiting to attack each other."

Piper cradled her mug, relishing the heat on her chilled fingers. The tension between them was that noticeable? "We just seem to piss each other off. That's why I need you to come on this cruise and act as a buffer. Keep us from ruining the lovebirds' romantic weekend."

She dredged up a wan smile. Yeah, nothing would be more romantic on a second honeymoon than to see her and West emitting ferocious *I want to kill you* vibes the whole time. Or was it more *I want to shove your tonsils down your throat with my tongue and rip your clothes off* vibes?

Piper shook her head. Either way, this energy between them? Not good.

Shaye went to the fridge and pulled out a jug of orange juice, which shook briefly in her hands. "You're both grown-ups and you used to be friends. You'll just have to control your temper."

Right. Control. Because control was something she had in spades around West. It would be a lot easier controlling herself if Shaye came to smooth things over. "I really wouldn't ask unless—"

The jug clattered as Shaye almost dropped it on the table. "No, Pipe. I won't do it. I won't get on Ben's boat."

Whoa. Where had that come from? "You won't get on Ben's boat? Huh? Have I missed something here?"

Shaye steadied the jug with both hands and poured herself a glass of juice. "You missed the last nine years of my life."

Oookay. So there lay the truth, bald and ugly on the table.

And she deserved it.

Sure, she knew Shaye favored vintage clothes and that she probably still had a collection of Barbie dolls in her closet, because Shaye didn't like to let go of the things she loved. But, if asked, Piper wouldn't know how Shaye had coped living in Invercargill for two years while she got her hospitality diploma, or if the three dates that didn't turn into four with the real estate agent in Bluff were a disappointment or a relief. She didn't share Shaye's secret heart like she used to, when her sister would crawl into bed next to her and whisper the things that made her sad.

Piper edged over to the table and took a seat. "Sorry."

Shaye gave her a one shoulder shrug and sat sideways on her chair, keeping her body angled away. "I got used to not relying on you. I was old enough to understand the reasons why you left."

Piper winced, remembering the look on her sister's face two days after their father's memorial service when Piper loaded up a backpack and left Shaye and Glenna on the deck of their family home without a backward glance. "You were fifteen. A kid."

"I stopped being a kid the day Dad died."

"We all stopped being kids that day."

They sat quietly, listening through the open window to the whistles and squawks of a hungry kaka and the distant drone of a lawnmower. The coffee mug warmed her icy hands as she replayed her father's voice. "C'mon Pipe, don't be the Incredible Sulk. A dive'll do you good. Everything looks better underwater."

But that fateful morning was the exception. Nothing looked better. West had just dumped her and she was so in love with him she could barely construct a coherent sentence. Not a great candidate for a safety diver. She'd paid the ultimate price for that lack of concentration.

"I understood why you left."

Piper looked up from her mug. *No little sis, you have no idea what really happened that morning and why I left.* "Oh?"

"Staying in Oban was too hard with all the memories of Dad and some people weren't very kind. Plus, you knew you had to leave to join the police."

She found herself nodding. Job opportunities in Oban were scarce and the National Police College was located in Wellington. They were the standard party-lines she trotted out when questioned about her reasons for leaving Oban for the city.

"But that doesn't explain why you cut us out of your life like we were a bunch of inbred yokels you couldn't wait to get rid of."

"I didn't—"

Shaye whipped around, snatched a mandarin from the fruit bowl and fired it across the table.

Piper ducked to the side, the mandarin grazing her shoulder before it hit the counter and rolled into the sink. Dammit—her sister had a killer aim.

"Stuff you, Piper, you did. The odd phone call and weekend shopping trips with you in the city once a year doesn't count for much of a relationship."

"I didn't mean to cut you out."

"But you did. You weren't there for us when we needed you most." Shaye's eyes glistened. Crap, now look what she'd done. "I was fifteen—a kid, as you pointed out. Fifteen and forced to glue the pieces of Mum's life back together when she fucking fell apart."

Piper dropped her head into the palm of her hand. Tried to think of something that wouldn't make her sound any more like the selfish bitch she so obviously was. At eighteen she hadn't thought about what she'd dumped in Shaye's lap by taking off to live with her dad's aunt in Wellington. She'd just needed to get away from all the murmured accusations—and West. If it weren't for that knife aimed between her ribs, the decision to leave may have been different.

"I'm sorry, Shaye. Jesus. You never told me."

"Would it have made you come home?"

The Hello Kitty clock on the wall ticked off the seconds as Shaye swiped a finger beneath her eyes, smudging her mascara. She smoothed her ponytail and adjusted the collar of her pretty apple-green blouse. "Sorry about the mandarin."

"You missed my head, at least."

"If I'd been aiming for your head, I wouldn't have missed."

Piper barked out a laugh. "And the boat thing?"

"Getting on a boat stresses me out—big time. I avoid them when I can."

"Hon, you live on an island."

Shaye sent her a *duh* glare. "I cope with it, okay? I use the ferry all the time. Just so long as the boat ride doesn't involve going anywhere near divers or snorkelers or Paterson Inlet."

Paterson Inlet, where their father drowned. How could she continue to push Shaye in light of that revelation?

"Is there anything I can say, anything I can do, to show you how sorry I am?"

Shaye returned the jug to the fridge. She paused with the door open, turning her three-quarter-profile toward Piper. Even with raccoon circles under her eyes and her hair caught in a casual ponytail, Shaye epitomized the graceful beauty of a 1950s movie star. Piper's breath hitched, and for the first time in many years she ached for the sisters they used to be.

"Saying sorry is the easy part," Shaye said. "It's what you do now that's important, and you've come back to help. It's a start."

And it was a start discovering if the ties binding them as sisters were strong enough to repair the damage of neglect. They could forge a new relationship—assuming Shaye wanted her back in her life. And assuming a relationship could span the distance once she returned to Wellington.

Because after these six weeks?

She was outta here.

***

A light breeze skimmed across the ocean, and the clear water made sunglasses essential as the sun slipped out from behind the veil of cirrostratus cloud. Other than a case of sunburn and a temporarily misplaced contact lens, the trip was a success, with the two Great Whites who duly appeared both entertaining and scaring the crap out of their enthusiastic clients.

Piper packed away the last of the dive equipment and then kept herself busy in the galley. West could do the last round of schmoozing with the clients as they exited The Mollymawk onto the wharf. If she had to smile one last time for the camera, someone would sustain a Piper-inflicted injury. Not good for business.

Thank God the day was over. Once they motored back to The Mollymawk's mooring spot, escape would be imminent. If you could call working the evening shift in Due South's sweltering kitchen an escape.

Footsteps sounded behind her, the quick, purposeful tread alerting her to their owner. Heck, the tingle across her scalp told her West had entered the room. Like he discharged some weird static electricity and only she received a zap.

"Ben's on the wharf and he wants a rundown."

A rundown—more like checking she hadn't screwed up. Piper straightened. Might as well get it over with. "A quick one."

"Naturally. Dad'll have stacks of dishes waiting."

"Lucky me."

She followed West onto the wharf. Sitting on a bench facing the boats moored in Halfmoon Bay, Ben cut a striking solitary figure among the tourists strolling by. Piper rolled her eyes as they approached him. Ben probably set it up that way: the Heathcliff of Stewart Island. He certainly had the whole *don't approach me, I'm brooding* thing going on.

West peeled away and sat on a nearby wharf bollard, while she slid next to Ben, nudging his shoulder to rattle his cage a little. "So brother dearest, the loopies seemed happy with their experience, huh?"

His arm tensed and with a subtle shift he pulled away, instead of elbowing her back as he used to, and as he continued to do with Shaye.

The rejection smarted, but she pulled up her big girl panties and refused to be offended.

"West said you handled yourself." Ben continued to stare at the bay.

Waiting for violins to kick in, no doubt.

"I did better than handled myself. One of the guys talked of taking our romance cruise on his honeymoon because his fiancée's a shark nut—another possible booking."

Ben grunted, a sound she identified from years spent with other testosterone drenched males who couldn't concede a woman may have actually *done well.*

"And we have a group of seven booked for a full-day beginners scuba trip tomorrow, so it's a solid start." Piper's gaze snapped between Ben and West, both of them appearing unimpressed at her marketing abilities.

What was it with these two? Seriously? She still couldn't do *anything* right?

"You didn't scare the clients away, that's a bonus," Ben said.

Piper huffed out a sneering breath. "I never claimed to be a people person—that would be West." She angled her chin at him. "And since there are three females in the group tomorrow, why don't you use that smarmy charm of yours to take one of the dives?"

West stretched out his long legs, crossing his ankles. "Can't."

"Whaddya mean, can't? Why not?"

"That's your job. I wouldn't want to deprive the clients of all your skills that aren't being utilized in the backwater of Oban."

West got a warning glare, even though he didn't add anything further.

Ben sat forward. "Plus diving with scuba would interfere with West's training."

Training? What training? Ah—the pool laps. Her brow furrowed—how could that affect his ability to dive? "Swimming laps in the community pool is your training?"

"Nope." West hooked his thumbs into the edge of his shorts' pockets, fingers flexing and releasing. "I use the pool to practice dynamic apnea, because my safety diver mucked up my free immersion training by breaking his ankle."

Dynamic apnea.

Free immersion.

Terms she'd once been intimately familiar with when the three of them free-dived with her father. The discipline of a one breath dive to incredible depths without the benefit of scuba hadn't appealed to her, but West took to it like the proverbial duck to water. Michael's true prodigy.

But after all they'd been through, West continued to free-dive?

Blood napalmed through every artery, consuming her from the inside out. Piper lunged toward him before rational self-restraint could overrule her legs.

Past strangled vocal chords she gritted, "Free-diving?"

West stood, hands still hooked in his pockets, his eyes wary. "I'm training for the Lake Taupo Nationals."

The words wouldn't come. She couldn't verbalize the plummeting-elevator sensation in her gut at the idea of him training for the same competition that drove her father to his death. Her inner ear rang with an endless loop of "How could he? How *could* he?"

"You son of a bitch." She slapped both palms against his broad chest and shoved.

The plume spraying up as West hit the water gave her some satisfaction as she stomped away from the dock, ignoring the laughter following in her wake.

***

Piper stormed toward Due South, using the short walk to work off the need to punch something or someone. She refused to glance back over her shoulder to see if West had dragged his dripping carcass onto the wharf. Likely a cluster of sympathetic local women like Erin fussed over him, telling him what a dreadful cow she was and always had been. And he'd enjoy all the attention.

Piper marched faster.

Donny's head got a brief pat at the back door as she commiserated with him on the moronic owner he'd been saddled with. She sailed into Bill's kitchen, snatching her apron off the hook. Jamming it over her head, the neck loop caught on her ears. Tacky, ugly, Made-In-China apron.

Bill emerged from the cooler with an armful of carrots. "You get much hotter girl and your punk hair-do will catch fire. Then you'll need to take a dip like West."

Piper yanked the ties around her waist and knotted them. "Why am I not surprised you know about that."

"Because I'm all-seeing and all-knowing—and if you didn't want to cause an explosion in the gossip pool, you should've kept your hands off my boy." Bill placed the vegetables on the prep counter and moved to the stove.

"Your boy's an ass—" She caught herself, remembering he was the asshole's father. "Idiot."

"An ass-idiot? Don't believe I've heard anyone call him that before."

Piper glanced at Bill's slumped posture as he stirred a delicious smelling concoction in a large saucepan. "Well, he is one."

She moved past him and twisted on the hot water tap, adding a squirt of dishwashing detergent to the sink.

Behind her Bill sighed theatrically. "What'd he do this time?"

Piper whipped around to give him an earful on what an irresponsible, unfeeling and plain frustrating excuse for a human being his son was, when Bill's pasty face and hunched shoulders shoved aside her lingering temper.

Holy crap. Bill Westlake was not a well man.

She twisted the hot water tap off. "Remember when you said I looked like something Donny had vomited up on the carpet? Well, right now you look like the something that squeezes out his other end."

"Yeah, I'm feeling a bit crook today."

She could count on one hand the times Bill had taken a day off when she was a kid, and he never, ever admitted to being unwell. "Good grief. Did hell just freeze over?"

He snorted, coughed, and looked miserable. Piper stood alongside him, taking in the slight yellow discoloration of his skin and the way his apron bagged around his stomach. Maybe he didn't have much of a beer belly to start with—but given she'd had to nag him to stop for meals since she'd been back...

"I'm going to make an appointment with the doc for you and I'm guessing it probably isn't still Nigel."

"He left a couple of years ago."

"Sensible man," she muttered, and then louder, "So who's his replacement?"

"Joe Whelan, a young Irish lad. Number's the same. It's by the phone. But I don't need a bleedin' doctor. I'm just a bit off-color."

"Uh-huh." Piper gave him her mother's look, which she practiced and renamed as her *I'm a cop and I will kick your ass* glare. "You're *going* to see the doctor and don't make me drag your son into this. He's already in a foul mood."

"Hah. Like West can make me do something I don't want." He turned back to the stove and stirred his pot.

"No? Well, I can."

Bill uttered a couple of foul words he must've picked up in the army, followed by a cynical huffing noise.

Piper sauntered over and picked up the wall phone receiver. "I'll just give my mum a ring, shall I? Tell her to alert the church ladies that you're feeling poorly? They'll be down in their *droves* to fuss all over you."

Bill's shoulders hunched so high they touched the lobes of his reddened ears. "Anyone ever tell you you're a scheming bitch?"

Piper replaced the receiver with a grin. "I consider it an off day if someone doesn't."

"Make an appointment, then," Bill said, and slammed the lid on the saucepan.

Chapter 7.

West's shitty day just kept getting shittier.

As if being the laughing stock of Oban with Piper shoving him off the wharf wasn't enough, he'd arrived back at Due South to find his dad taking a sickie. So he had to juggle staff, which wouldn't have been a storm in a teacup except two of his waitresses were also home in bed with the flu. Which meant he'd run his ass off serving tables instead of bailing Piper up in a dark corner and finding out *what the hell was her problem.*

And now, with the kitchen closed for the night and things slowing down in the pub, he finally found a spare minute, only to discover the kitchen was deserted. She'd bailed.

Typical.

Striding into the pub, West caught Kip's eye behind the bar. "Bring a beer to my office when you get a moment."

Curious stares tracked his every movement—he'd never live the dive off the wharf down. He turned on his heel and walked out again. Half an hour till closing and he was gone. And if Piper was tucked up sound asleep? He'd take pleasure in disrupting her sweet dreams.

The lights were off when he arrived home an hour later. West stepped into the foyer and toed off his shoes, tempted to hammer on

Ben's door and wake him up too, since he'd caught him busting a gut as he climbed back onto the wharf. Ha-frickin-ha.

But, no. He and Piper had things to say that he didn't want Ben overhearing.

He climbed the stairs, turned on the lights, and headed to the back door to feed Donny. Not that the mutt needed an extra handful of dog biscuits since Piper started sneaking him kitchen leftovers. The dog biscuit bag by the back door had a note taped to it: *Wake me when you get in, no matter what time. We need to talk about Bill.*

That sucked the joy right out of jarring her awake. Not that he'd softened his ass-kicking stance just because she had some concern for his father.

Crazy, impulsive little witch.

He blew a stream of annoyed air out his nose and opened the biscuit bag, grabbing two. Donny shuffled from foot to foot on the back step, his tail a wagging blur as West opened the door and tossed him his supper.

"And don't think you're getting another later." Except he'd cave like wet cardboard when Donny started his soft whining.

"I'm such a pussy." He leaned against the closed door, slanting a look down the hallway. "And not just with the dog."

Walking the few steps to his office, West scrubbed his hand over his jaw. He didn't have the energy to deal with Piper tonight after all. Surely a case of the man flu wasn't enough to warrant a late night nag-session? He could think of a few things he'd rather do than challenge Piper to a verbal duel at midnight.

Like slide a hand up those long tanned thighs? Or crawl into her bed and plant a trail of hot, wet kisses from the indentation of her throat due south?

West leaned an arm against the door and dropped his forehead on his elbow. Christ Almighty. He needed to get a grip. Get a grip, and get laid with some pretty stranger *who wasn't Piper.*

The office door jerked inward and he stumbled forward, just about flattening Piper, who stood, squinting, in a white tank top and teeny-tiny shorts, her hair mussed and flattened on one side. The hallway light angled down, and the pajamas—if that's what they were—showed more skin than they covered.

West's gaze plummeted to her breasts. His cock woke up and completely sucked all the blood from his remaining brain cells. "Ah...what is that thing on your top?"

Piper looked down, made the unfortunate motion of straightening the knit fabric, which only emphasized the hardened buds of her nipples. "It's Animal, you know, from The Muppets."

She cut him a glance which said, "Why are we talking about pyjamas?" then her gaze lowered, skipping to a part of his anatomy that totally rebelled against the whole *I'm not interested in having wild monkey sex with you* plan his brain had settled on.

He bent closer, the hint of coconut from the conditioner she'd pinched from his shower curling into his nostrils. That, and the scent of mangoes on her skin, made him want to lap her up. Sweet as warmed honey. West reached out to see if the skin on her collarbone was as soft as he remembered.

Eyes widening, she turned away. "I'll just grab my robe."

He dropped his hand and clenched his fist. Resisted the temptation to pound it into his forehead to kick start his brain out of its adolescent lusting. *Hot things burn, Westy. Look at the pretty flames, but don't touch.*

She bent to pick up a pile of black fabric pooled on the floor, and his gaze fastened on the printed "A.N.I.M.A.L" across the bum of the shorts. The teeny, tiny shorts now riding up the crack of her deliciously-shaped ass. He wasn't sure, but he thought he groaned. Either way, he nearly swallowed his own goddamned tongue.

If she wore that get-up on their overnight cruise this weekend he was screwed—because he couldn't keep his hands off.

He needed to get the hell away from her. Now.

"I'll put the kettle on," West muttered and escaped to the kitchen.

Piper fastened her robe belt and shoved her feet into a pair of fluffy yellow slippers. Jeez, by the scandalized look on West's face, anyone would think she'd been sporting a skimpy Victoria's Secret babydoll, rather than cartoon printed shorts and a tank top. Maybe the kind of women he bedded *did wear* ridiculously expensive lingerie that made your butt look fat if you were anything over a size eight. She snorted and scraped fingers through a severe case of bed hair.

West looking at her half naked shouldn't make her insides feel all shivery and liquid—but it did.

She padded out to the kitchen, found him in front of the French doors, the kettle hissing on the stove. Their gazes connected briefly in the reflection, before she headed for the cabinets.

Piper snagged the last couple of mugs, her heart flip-flopping at the faded cartoon figures on one. A cluster of turkeys perched on a sad-faced elephant, and below, in a fancy font: *Don't let the turkeys get you down.*

West took the mugs from her limp fingers. "Tea?"

"You kept it." She'd bought the turkey mug for him thirteen years ago.

"I like it." He switched the kettle off when it began to wail. "So I kept it. Just like you kept my Chilies shirt to sleep in. You still got it?"

"No." She hoped he wouldn't hear the lie in her voice. "I swapped to Animal, remember?" And then *she remembered* his reaction to her choice of sleepwear. Her face ignited. Fair skin, bane of her life.

Piper opened the fridge door and poked her head inside. "Yeah, I'll have tea. You want milk?"

"Not if it's the no-fat-no-taste stuff you drink. I'd rather take it black."

"There's a surprise." The air wafting out from the fridge cooled the heat stinging her cheeks.

It'd lead him off the intended topic of Bill's health, but curiosity got the better of her. "I found that mug in a little gift shop in Bluff. I had to borrow five bucks off Shaye because as usual, I was broke, and she'd been saving her pocket money for a rainy day." Piper pulled out the bottle of regular milk and set it on the table, tracking him out of the corner of her eye.

West still wore work clothes—an untucked charcoal shirt with the sleeves rolled up to the elbows, and khaki pants. His bare feet were long and wide, tanned from hours outdoors, a contradiction to the more formal attire he wore while managing Due South. Most other men in Oban dressed in whatever they grabbed off the floor each morning, but West never liked doing what his peers expected. The little touches of professionalism made her think of the proud sixteen-year-old boy who wouldn't let anyone see how much he suffered when his family imploded.

"Right. It was just after Mum and Del left." His tone remained light, as if his mother running off with her American lover and taking his brother to live in L.A. wasn't important.

"I wanted to cheer you up. Because nothing anyone said would make you smile."

West dropped a teabag in each mug and snared her gaze. This time his eyes weren't the brittle shade of blue sea coral, but smoky blue and hooded. "You always knew how to make me smile."

She ducked her head. "By being a pain in your ass, and not leaving you alone to mope."

"Yep." He turned away to fill the mugs with boiling water and the moment was lost.

Piper sat at the table, rested her chin on the heel of her palm. "Do you still hear from your mum?"

The teaspoon clinked against china as West brewed the tea. The broad lines of his back shifted under his shirt as tension braced his shoulder blades. "I didn't speak to her for five years after she left." He barked a short, harsh laugh. "I figured if I refused to talk to her on the phone, she'd come back to us. Didn't work. She married Lionel, and had a new stepdaughter to cope with."

He dumped tea bags into the sink. "Anyway. She did come back to Oban for a few days for my twenty-first—ambushed me. Now she calls a couple of times a year on my birthday and at Christmas. She talks, I listen. I know she and Glenna still keep in touch."

"Well, they've been best friends since your mum first came out to New Zealand."

"Men don't do that sort of friendship. You walk away, cut your ties, and you're off their Christmas card list."

He would've scratched her name out of his address book back on the day he dumped her, then.

West carried their mugs over and sat in the opposite chair. "No sugar, right?" He handed her the plain blue mug, and took the turkey one for himself.

Impressed he remembered how she preferred her tea, she blinked. "No."

"Still sweet enough, huh?"

"I was never sweet."

"No, you weren't." He tempered the comment with a crooked grin which emphasized the fine lines around his eyes. He looked tired—dog tired—so she'd better get to the point. "I made Bill an appointment with the doctor tomorrow."

West's mug stopped halfway to his mouth. "He *let you* make a doctor's appointment?"

"I can be very persuasive. Plus, I threatened to sic the church ladies onto him if he refused to cooperate."

"Now why didn't I ever think of that?" West sipped his tea.

"I threatened him with you first, but it had no effect. He'll be pissed I'm even telling you about this." Piper wrapped her fingers around the mug's warmth and squeezed to keep her voice steady. "Your father's not a well man."

West's nose crinkled. "It's just the flu. Man flu as Shaye calls it. Take dose of *harden the hell up* and don't whine about it in the morning."

"Maybe it's the flu, but maybe it's something else. He's not eating properly and it looks like he's lost weight. Not to mention he's worse than a woman ducking into the bathroom every half an hour or so."

He studied her like a specimen in a petri dish. "You're really worried?"

Yes, she was—and he needn't look so insultingly surprised. Bill was a grouch and a slave driver, but she had a soft spot for the man who used to sneak her home-baked afghan cookies after a rough day at school.

"I just wanted you to know what's going on, so you can keep a check on him. It'd tick me off if your dad keeled over and I had to take on more prep stuff than I'm already doing. I hate cooking more than I hate dishes, so I know it'd give you great pleasure to make that part of your *reimbursement.*"

"Shaye's capable of running the kitchen solo for the next few days while Dad's not well." He tipped his chair back on two legs and sent her a smile hot enough to cause sunburn. "And I have other ideas of how you can repay me." His gaze zipped down to the v-neck of her robe which, judging by the cool air caressing her skin, gaped open.

Tugging the garment edges shut would only draw more attention to the hammering pulse at the base of her throat, so she kept her fingers clamped around the mug. "Oh? Since I'm already Bill's all-purpose drudge, how could you demean me more?"

"As I said, I've other ideas, but I'll save them for another time. Right now, explain why you pushed me off the dock."

Her stomach churned the tea she'd sipped into choppy waves. West. Free-diving for the Nationals. God. "Because you're a cocky asshole—and with dick for brains to boot." Piper stood and walked to the sink, pouring the steaming remains of her tea down the drain.

"And you've formed this opinion *because* I choose to free-dive."

She kept her back to him. "Actually I've known you're an asshole for a number of years."

The chair creaked as West rocked it back and forth. She wished it'd tip and drop him on his self-satisfied butt. She fussed at the sink, running hot water to flush the tea and rinse out her mug.

"I know what I'm doing. I'm not some amateur who's bought a mask and fins and decided to see how far he can dive. I've trained for years."

Piper twisted the water off so tightly it was a wonder the tap handle didn't crack off in her hand. "So did Dad."

"I'm not Michael."

She turned back. "The risks of free-diving, especially free immersion, are high. Dangerously high if you're pushing yourself."

"I know my limit. And the biggest risks in free-diving are caused by inexperience and the lack of a good buddy to make sure you don't suffer a shallow water blackout."

"Hello?—talking to a police diver. I know the risks. So you don't feel any urge to push the boundaries, to win the Nationals?"

"I have my own reasons for competing, and I know I *can* win."

His own reasons? To prove his balls were bigger than any of the other men at Lake Taupo? She snorted, crossing her arms with a slight shake of her head. "As I said, you're a cocky asshole. Which'll probably get you killed."

"Aw, baby. I didn't know you cared."

"I don't, other than in a professional capacity. I'm sick of pulling dead idiots from the water. Guys who think they're so invincible they don't need a lifejacket in an ill-equipped boat—the worst are those who bring innocent kiddies on board and don't bother fitting them with lifejackets either. Or fishermen who are so gung-ho trying to catch the big one they forget how unforgiving the ocean is." She clicked her teeth shut. Crap. She'd revealed much more than she intended.

"Sick of it, huh? So why do you continue to do it?"

"It's my job. I have to."

West lowered the chair onto four legs. "*Have* to?"

Blood pounded through her head, buzzed in her eardrums. "I told you the other day, I'm not discussing my career with you."

He crossed his ankles, his steady gaze pinning her in place against the counter. "Fair enough. Let's return to the subject of you worrying about my welfare. Was your overreaction at the wharf a desperate ploy for attention, like how you used to scare the bejesus out of Johnny Martin, hoping he'd chase you around the playground and try to kiss you?"

She stiffened, dumbstruck at the small crease of a smirk ghosting his lips. He thought she wanted his attention? Wanted *him*? Well, shamefully she'd started to, but damned if she'd let him know. "I was ten years old and I did not hope he'd kiss me! And FYI, I don't need to push you off the dock to get your attention. You've been all but panting after me since I arrived back."

West rocked back on his chair again, tilted his face to the ceiling and laughed. "Really? Who was eyeballing who in the pool the other morning?"

"I think your fancy swimming trunks showed the truth of *that* situation. You were the one sporting a hard-on then, and you were the one sporting a hard-on only minutes ago."

"I'm a guy, these things happen. It's nothing personal." He folded his arms, the thin cotton of his shirt pulling against the contoured outline of his chest, the muscles in his forearms standing out in stark relief. Not that she noticed or anything.

"You weren't my type then, and you sure aren't now," he said.

Nothing personal? Not his type? Well, no shit, Sherlock. But not being his "type" didn't stop his penis finding her attractive.

So, screw it—she'd call his bluff.

Piper strode to the table, fisted a handful of West's shirt, and tugged him forward so the feet of his balanced chair banged down on the floor. Bracing her free hand on the table behind her, she leaned in, keeping her eyes open to savor the flash of shock in his. She hesitated a breath away, drawing in the male smell of him. The remains of his cologne, a whisper of salt spray. Her fingers gripped his shirt, and the warmth of his chest pressed against her knuckles tingled like she'd grazed the side of a furnace. Always so hot, his fast metabolism used to drive her nuts.

Hot in more ways than one.

Piper dipped closer and pressed against warm and inflexible lips. Lips unwilling to part even a fraction to accommodate or welcome her.

Tough guy, huh? She nipped the slight swell of his bottom lip, and sucked gently— a trick which hadn't been in her armory of feminine wiles at an innocent eighteen. No response. Her face flamed again.

Suddenly it was waaay too hot in the kitchen.

Congrats, Pipe. You've just made a complete fool of yourself once again, pawing at the man who, let's be fair, warned you he wasn't interested.

With any luck New Zealand's propensity for earthquakes would kick in at this precise moment, cracking open a chasm beneath her feet which she could quietly slither into. She jerked her head back, but a large hand on her nape prevented her complete escape. West's other hand landed on her hip and squeezed, freezing her in an awkwardly bent position.

"Let me go." She tried to duck away, but his fingers snatched the soft toweling of her robe and held her still, like a kitten plucked up by the scruff of its neck.

"You grabbed me first, so you let go."

She unclenched her fingers from his shirt. "Now take your hands off me."

"But baby, you started this." The hand on her hip tugged her closer, her inner thighs brushing against the smooth fabric pulled taut over his long legs.

She tugged at the fingers on her hip, wriggling at the same time, desperate to escape. "And now I'm ending it."

"I'll decide where it ends," he said.

Her reflexes were wicked fast. As a police officer they needed to be. Moving fast could mean the difference between an arrest and a broken nose. Or a stint in hospital. So when West released her neck and yanked her robe open, plunged his hands inside and pulled on her hips until she tumbled onto his lap, she had plenty of time to react. Plenty of options to teach him to keep his hands to himself. She could've shoved him backwards. Kneed him in the nuts. Punched the Cheshire cat grin off his face. But instead her stony resistance melted, and she flowed onto him like lava.

His hands tugged the robe off her shoulders in quick, sure movements. She rested her weight on his rigid chest muscles, and shivered when his lips skimmed her collar bone. Hot, but not feathery light kisses blazed over her skin, and his teeth at the sensitive spot at the base of her throat nipped hard enough to blast any illusions of tenderness she might've had aside. This was lust, not desire. He wanted her, being pressed against his arousal left little doubt on that count. But the frost in his eyes as their gazes locked told her he didn't want to want her.

Even so, she couldn't stop from swaying forward until their lips were only inches apart. Her heartbeat soared, and her traitorous mouth parted in anticipation, yet she wouldn't close the remaining distance. "I'm not kissing you again."

"You're not?"

"No. You're not *my* type, either."

He angled his head and his breath, warm and tinged with the faint scent of the bergamot oil in his Earl Grey tea, caressed her cheek.

"Our radical deviation from type established, it still doesn't change this—" He bridged the gap, and his mouth settled on hers.

Resist! Resist him! The order welled up in Piper's brain in a fiery mantra. He resisted her kiss, she'd show him he didn't affect her in the slightest either. She resisted, and by resistance she meant keeping her lips together—until his tongue flickered along the seam of her mouth.

On her soft gasp he wielded his advantage and urged her to open farther, distracting her with his fingers sliding into her hair, positioning her exactly where he wanted. He played with her. Teased with kisses which retreated as soon as she capitulated and gave his questing tongue access. He caused her breath to hitch, her fingers to bunch into fists over his thudding heart. Bastard. But two could play this savage little game.

Piper linked her ankles around the chair back to keep their lower bodies aligned, one fluffy slipper falling off while she writhed on the hard ridge of his erection. Desperate craving swelled the tender flesh between her thighs as sensual heat scorched up from her core. She wanted him. Right now, right here, pride be damned.

Dropping her forearms from West's chest, Piper's breasts took their place. She took a second to luxuriate in his body shifting against her sensitized nipples. She shoved her fingers into West's hair either side of his ears and grabbed hold, dragging his lips back on hers. Bright lights exploded behind her eyelids as she shut them against the kaleidoscope of emotions fighting for dominance. Need. Lust. Anger.

This time the kiss West returned lacked teasing and playfulness. Harsh, demanding, his tongue dueled with hers. His hands left her hair, slid down her body and dived under the robe to grab her butt, shifting her impossibly closer as he angled his hips up. She wrenched away on a muffled groan, sucked his earlobe between her lips and bit down.

West surged out of the chair, her legs automatically clinging to his hips. He set her on the table edge and kissed her again, fitting himself between her thighs. Breaths backing up in her lungs, Piper couldn't get enough oxygen into her system. Every gasp she managed to suck in was all West. His scent filled her nose, the taste of him silky and hot. She couldn't breathe, couldn't find a trace of herself left in this woman who moaned and writhed against him.

Wrong, this was all so wrong.

She ripped her fingers from West's shoulders and flung her hands down, hoping to use the leverage of the table to push him away. Her left hand connected with a still warm object, toppled it. Hot tea splashed across her fingers, followed by a sharp crack as the mug hit the floor and shattered.

"Shit." West jerked back. His heel connected with his chair and sent it skidding. "Are you okay? Did it burn you?"

Piper glanced at the liquid splashed across the back of her hand, the slight sting seeping into her knuckles, the bee-stung heat radiating from her lips and the deeper sting prickling the inside of her chest.

Yeah, it burned all right. Her emotional control had turned to ashes.

"I'm fine." Nowhere near the realm of fine. Blood stampeded through her body, and every vein carrying it seemed to be on a direct route to her girly-bits. If he touched her again now, wrong or not, she might spontaneously combust. "I'm not burned."

Damp heat soaked into her thigh as the tea pooled over the table and pattered onto the floor. The turkey mug lay in half a dozen jagged pieces. She tipped herself forward to slide off the table—

"Wait." West's large hand spanned her knee. "You'll cut yourself."

"I'm not the one with bare feet," she said.

West turned and scooped her slipper off the floor. "Here, Cinderella." He shoved it on her foot, his eyes sparking blue fire. "Now you can flee the ball."

He stepped over the worst of the broken china to the row of cupboards under the sink, yanking one open and removing a roll of paper towels.

Piper hopped off the table and caught the roll he tossed. "I'm not running from you."

As she tore off a length of sheets she could've sworn she heard him mumble under his breath, "You will."

She picked up china shards and placed them on the table. West left the kitchen and reappeared at her side a few moments later wearing ancient flip-flops and carrying a dustpan and brush. "Here, hop out the way. I've got it."

She backed up a few steps and re-belted her robe. A delayed blush crept up her throat. Her breasts ached and she could still feel his hands molding and squeezing her butt. Good God, what had she been thinking? She hadn't been thinking—that was the problem.

West brushed tiny mug shards into the dustpan and sent her a sidelong glance that seemed to say *What? You still here?* reducing her to his mate's annoying little sister who didn't know when her company wasn't welcome any longer.

"I'm sorry about your mug." She twisted the robe's belt around and around her index finger.

"It's nothing." *Like you,* his tone implied. "Look, I can finish up in here. It's late, go back to bed." He carried the dustpan to the pantry and removed an old newspaper from a shelf inside.

"West—" The words to defend her actions, to lighten the moment and pretend the aftermath of their encounter didn't hurt because that kiss was wrong even if it'd felt *so damn right*—those words just snagged in a lump in her throat, and she fell silent.

"Just go to bed." He blinked slowly with a grimace. "Please."

She should've held her ground. Or prayed divine inspiration would supply a flippant parting shot to cover the discovery that the kiss meant far more to her than to him. But instead she fled.

Like Cinderella.

Only minus the stylish ball gown, and a Prince who thought she was worth chasing.

Chapter 8.

There was something downright disturbing about finding your mate with his ass stuck up in the air at six in the morning.

Ben crutch-hopped past West and his down-doggy-something-or-other pose on the living room floor.

"Point it in some other direction, will ya," he called over his shoulder as he entered the kitchen, moving to the coffee machine. "I just threw up in my mouth a little."

Jesus, his head hurt. Concentrating for hours hunched over his laptop last night, he'd tried to sort out more of his financial stuff. He'd heard West stomp up the stairs and then he must've flaked out cold—waking sometime after two, still at his desk. Made him wistful for the good old days when only a hangover caused him to feel like death in the morning. Not to mention his ankle throbbed like a bitch.

A whisper of bare feet on the yoga mat behind him as West shifted position. "You should join me. Maybe you'd end up with a tight ass like mine and actually get laid in the near future."

Ben snagged a container and dumped a few scoops of ground coffee into the belly of the beast. "Are you saying my butt's fat?"

"I'm saying you need a woman. A decent session of bumping uglies will improve the bitchy mood you've been in for weeks."

Ben turned, scoop in hand. West lunged into another ridiculous pose, like he was about to hurl an invisible javelin. "I'm not in a *bitchy mood*. Bitchy moods are a female thing." Ben glared at the grin on West's face. "Oh, don't go there, yoga-boy. Besides, I've had sex— didn't improve anything."

"Then you did it wrong. And sleeping with that scatty cow, Jules, four months ago doesn't count."

Jules must've agreed with that assessment, since she and Curt had not only taken off and left him in the lurch, but taken off as a cutesy couple. "I'm sick of holding one way conversations," she'd moaned at him that last day. "Curt *talks* to me, and he *listens* to my feelings."

Served that weasely little prick Curt right. Now he could put up with her two-hour monologues.

"Whatever. Not like there are many options around here." Ben hit the switch and the coffee machine kicked in with its soft hisses and pops.

"You're kidding. It's high summer—there are women all over the place."

West eased to the floor and did his cross-legged thing, resting his hands palm up on his knees and closing his eyes. The guys would've given him grief about doing yoga back when they all used to hang out as teenagers. But other than Ford and that prick Gav, all their other mates had left for greener pastures. And West swore yoga helped with his free-diving.

"Not my style." He grabbed two cups, hesitated, then reached for a third.

"Bro, you don't have a style. You're style*less* and verbally handicapped when it comes to women."

"Yeah? Well *your* style got you pushed off the wharf yesterday."

West grunted, but kept his eyes shut, inhaling until the outline of his ribs became prominent.

"Did you ream her out when you got home last night?"

West blew out a long, slow breath. "Nope. It was just a misunderstanding."

"So you kissed and made up then?"

An eye popped open for a split second and then snapped shut while West sucked down another lungful of air. He huffed that one out, angling his head down to contemplate his navel, or whatever he did while doing that weird breathing stuff.

"I called her out on her overreaction and she told me I had dick for brains for free-diving. Kind of a mutual agreement to drop the subject after that."

"Women never know when to drop the subject—that goes double for Piper."

"She doesn't have much to say to you. Now, shut up, I'm breathing here."

Piper's grim-lipped stance around him hadn't eased. His memories of his sister's nonstop chattering didn't mesh with the woman who'd shown up last week. Probably because every moment spent here with her family was a moment too many. Couldn't wait to get away; too bloody stubborn to leave. Or maybe her silence came about because she remembered the accusations he threw at her after their dad's death.

The coffee finished trickling into the pot and filled the kitchen with the unmistakable smell of decent java juice, one of the bonuses of hanging out at West's for the next few weeks until the summer season was over and he moved back into his house.

"Morning." Piper stood in the kitchen doorway, fully dressed, boots and all.

"Didn't take you long to smell the coffee."

She shrugged, ambled into the kitchen and grabbed the mug he offered. "I need it. West's bringing The Mollymawk to the wharf later so Mum and I can make sure it's outfitted properly for the weekend." Her gaze darted left to West, still cross-legged on his mat.

"Ahhh. A day spent with Mum fussing with bed sheets and folding facecloths into funny shapes, I can see why you—"

"What is he doing?"

Ben twisted his neck to follow her gaze. "Sitting like a preschooler and huffing like a steam engine."

"In his underwear?" Piper's voice rose half an octave on the last word, a flush of high color appearing on her cheekbones.

"Be thankful," he said in the driest tone he could muster. "Usually it's clothing optional."

"Up," West said after inhaling. "Yours," he completed on exhaling. "It's my house, my shorts—not *underwear*—and it's Pranayama, or yoga breathing for an ignoramus such as yourself."

Ben pulled the coffee carafe from the machine and poured a cup. "You just missed him doing his doggy-style pose. Quite fetching, really."

Piper darted a glance in West's direction and then a suspicious look at him, as if she couldn't quite believe he'd include her in their good-natured ragging. She shoved her mug out for Ben to fill. "I'm lucky I slept in then."

Ben waited until she raised the coffee to her lips and sipped. "Kissing up to West last night tired you out, hmm?"

Droplets flew in an arc as Piper choked and spluttered. Ben rescued the mug from her hand and leaned against the counter, his gaze skipping between his sister and West. Without sparing a glance at Piper who coughed up a lung over the sink, West rose, rolled up his mat, and said, "I'm hitting the pool for an hour."

Ben filled a glass with water and gave it to his gasping sister. Ah, bollocks, something was going on with West and Piper. Again.

***

Piper. Kiss-flushed, thighs spread, and moaning on his dining table. That was all he'd be thinking about on this romance cruise. He'd tasted her and now it made him want to pound the hell outta something.

West stepped from The Mollymawk's wheelhouse and gave a mock salute to Ben below on the wharf. Ben cast off the last rope and aimed his crutch, pretending to pull an invisible trigger. *Mate, if only you knew the images in my head you'd be reaching for the real McCoy.*

With a shake of his head, West retreated into the wheelhouse and navigated The Mollymawk away from the wharf, out into the choppy waves of Halfmoon Bay.

A short time later, footsteps tapped into the wheelhouse behind him. He kept one hand on the steering wheel and the other gripped on the throttle arm. That he could sense Piper's proximity now just smeared another layer of annoyance across his skin. He was far too aware of her. The mango scent of her skin and the throaty laugh she let loose whenever she thought he wasn't around. The whiplash along his nerves when their eyes met. Frickin' killed his concentration and kept him on edge.

And that smoking-hot kiss? He sucked in a breath and blew out his cheeks. Yeah. That murdered his concentration even more.

"They all settled in?" he asked.

"Yep." A glance at the window in front of him reflected Piper's tousle-haired image leaning against the doorway. "Couples one and two are keen to snorkel for a few hours before lunch. The husband of couple three wants to fish, while his wife plans to catch some rays and sneak admiring glances at your butt."

"What? She said that?"

Piper sauntered over and flopped onto the other helm seat, exposing a mile long length of leg that tempted him to lean over and run his hand along the silky skin.

"Not in so many words, but wife number three definitely checked you out."

Wife number three was attractive in a barracuda-ish type way, but Piper wouldn't mean the comment to be a compliment about his charming way with women. He sure didn't take it as one. "The woman's pushing fifty."

"Yeah, well, don't let her trap you in a dark corner is all I'm saying." She gazed out the window at the froth and spray kicked up by the boat's bow. The Mollymawk surged over another crest and Piper's hand gripped the seat under her leg.

"Ah, do you think the weather will hold?" she asked.

He braced himself at the wheel as the boat rocked down into a trough. "Once we're in the inlet it'll settle down, and the forecast was okay. Not great, but okay."

"Great would be better," Piper muttered, barely audible above the engine and rhythmic smack of waves on the hull.

West sneaked a sidelong glance. She had one arm wrapped around her middle, molding her shirt's soft fabric to her breasts, and the other hand cupped by her mouth, her teeth worrying the edge of a fingernail. What hid under her top—a plain sports bra, or something wickedly skimpy and trimmed in lace?

Jeez, West, stop thinking with your dick. He cleared his throat. "But no pressure or anything."

She looked at him then, hazel eyes darkening to cool green chips, like sea glass buffed to a matt surface. "It's not you my family's watching—they're waiting for me to stuff up in another epic fail."

"Nobody wants you to fail."

"They don't want me to fail. They just expect me to quit."

Funny that people might arrive at that conclusion. But not so funny when his heart jerked out of rhythm for a couple of beats. Like he cared if she left the island again. "People's expectations, huh? That sucks."

Her casual slouch on the seat unfolded until she sat bolt upright. "I'm not a quitter. I don't give up." She read the cynicism on his face and added, "Extreme circumstances nine years ago, West, and you know it. I didn't quit."

"Yeah, you did. You used Mike's death as an excuse to quit your family and leave Oban."

She winced, but her flat, cop eyes didn't shift away. "My father dying was not an excuse. I was leaving anyway. I had no reason to stay."

"There was every reason to stay. Your mother needed you. Your little sister needed you. Even Ben needed you, though he would've denied it." *I needed you.* Not that she could ever torture it out of him, not even with red-hot needles threatening his balls.

"Did *you* need me?" The bitterness in her tone hauled him up sharp. "No, dumb question. You didn't. You were glad to see me go."

Not glad—guilty. He'd tried to talk to her, to apologize for being such a wanker before her father died, but Piper refused to speak to him. So he'd done nothing, gave up, and let her go. And the night she left he drank himself into oblivion and woke the next morning on the bathroom floor covered in regurgitated whiskey. Yeah, he handled her departure real well.

He made a conscious effort to keep his brow smooth and his jaw relaxed. "Regardless of what happened between us—our teenage fumbling or whatever you want to call it—your family needed you here."

Piper lurched to her feet, her eyes wide and shiny. "Teenage *fumbling?* You think our *teenage fumbling* was the reason I left everything I loved, everyone I cared about, behind?"

Now he'd done it. Had he actually made her cry? "Piper—"

Her pale face looked like she was suffering a mixed-spirits hangover.

Shit. He hadn't meant to be so harsh, because he just didn't do harsh with women. Women made him laugh, made him lust, and sometimes made him crazy—but no one, other than Piper, rattled him enough to lose control of his tongue. She'd abandoned them all, but yeah, *ancient history*. And nothing that should bug him enough to dredge it all up again.

"Listen, I shouldn't have—"

"You, you—" she jabbed a finger at him, clapped a hand over her mouth, and bolted from the wheelhouse.

Not even the growl of The Mollymawk's engines could drown out the sound of Piper retching over the starboard side.

West shoved a hand through his hair and swore, easing back on the throttle.

Yep. He had a hell of a way with women.

***

Piper sprawled on her bunk bed with the crook of her elbow covering her face and her fingertips resting on an empty just-in-case bucket by her side. A soft knock at the door made her moan. Wife number three, who turned out to be a nurse, no doubt returning to check she hadn't choked to death on her own vomit. Though as West pointed out, no one died of seasickness.

There was always a first time, and the only consolation in this humiliating experience was she hadn't puked on his shoes.

The door creaked open. "You alive?"

Okay, now she wished she had, in fact, puked on his shoes.

"Go away, West. I'll be out in five minutes."

He ignored her and walked over to her bunk, draping something cool and moist across her brow. Another moan oozed between her lips. God that felt good!

"I take it back. You can stay and keep bringing me cold washcloths."

The mattress dipped as he sat by her knees. "So. A seasickness prone police diver, hmm?"

"Uh-huh. The squad thinks it's a hoot."

"Bet you don't throw up in front of them, though."

She waggled her head from side to side to indicate that no, she definitely didn't toss her cookies in front of the guys—when her stomach lurched again.

Oh, crap. She rolled onto her side fumbling for the bucket, but West already had it in position. Maybe she imagined it, hard to tell with her guts wringing the last of her breakfast out, but she could've sworn he rubbed her back as she heaved.

A small towel appeared under her nose.

"Here," his voice was oddly gentle. "Wipe your mouth."

"Thanks." She dabbed at her lips, blinked back tears, and squeezed the towel so hard the little cotton loops were sure to leave indentations on her palms. "You've done this before."

His low chuckle had her gripping the towel for entirely different reasons. "Your first drinking binge. Both our dads would've tanned your hide if they'd caught you that night."

Sinking back down into the mattress, Piper covered her face with her elbow again. "Luckily you found me."

A skinny sixteen-year-old girl hunched up at the outskirts of the beach bonfire because she'd decided to show West she wasn't a little girl anymore by drinking three bottles of beer in quick succession. That time she really did barf on his shoes.

"The first and only time you let me take care of you."

"I didn't want you to take care of me."

She'd wanted him to notice her as someone other than Ben's tomboy sister and one of the guys. She wanted him to kiss her under the star studded sky with the flickering flames shooting sparks high into the night. She wanted him to kiss her, instead of Brittany the petite blonde staying with her grandparents for the Christmas holidays.

"Because you can take care of yourself, right?" He laid the damp washcloth across her forehead again.

"Right."

"And you're not going to make a pass at me like you did back then?"

Oh Lord. Kill her now and spare the humiliation. He remembered that too? "I deny making a pass at you, Ryan Westlake. You'd had a few beers yourself, so your recall must be flawed."

"Nope. I remember the aftermath of your barf-fest well. You made drunken goo-goo eyes at me and tried dragging me in for a kiss."

She groaned and wrapped her other arm over her face. "Oh, God. I did, didn't I?"

"Totally. And Ben would've kicked your ass if you'd succeeded."

"And Brittany of the big boobs and French manicure would've gone for me too."

He patted her leg, leaving his warm palm on her calf. "You could've taken her."

"Damn straight, I could've." She sat up a little, resting back on her forearms, testing her stomach to see if anything else threatened to erupt. So far, nothing. "I must've seemed pretty pathetic—drunk, and trying to kiss you with gross vomit breath."

A muscle twitched in the corner of his mouth. "Actually, you shocked me. I couldn't understand why you wanted to kiss me."

Piper sat up farther and drew her knees to her chest, so his hand slid off her leg. His touch dizzied her senses more than the rhythmic rocking of the boat. "Like you didn't know I'd been crushing on you for ages."

"Believe it or not, I wasn't always so clued up on the mysterious hints women give."

"Well, I'm not such a cheap date now. I don't put out after only three beers."

His rich laughter filled the room and she smiled in spite of herself. It was the kind of laugh they used to share, back before the drunken kiss fail, back when they'd just been friends hanging out.

He stopped laughing and his gaze dropped, alighting on her lips. Suddenly conscious of her breath, Piper would've given a week's wages for a mint Tic-Tac. What was the protocol in this situation? The kind of situation where you've puked in a bucket held by the man who still turns your insides to jelly with only his laugh.

"I'm flattered you didn't kiss me in my kitchen the other night because you were drunk—" and before Piper could invent a blasé excuse or a sarcastic comeback, West continued, "—but we have guests suiting up to snorkel. Maybe you'd feel less queasy if you hopped in the water for a bit."

Floating face down under the water where no one could figure out the cool and collected cop wasn't actually all that cool, and with West around, *definitely* not collected—that sounded preferable to barfing in a bucket while he looked on. "Let them know I'll be up in ten. The show must go on."

"That's my girl." His warm fingers wrapped around her ankle and squeezed, then he stood and exited the cabin.

Piper swung her legs off the bunk and dropped her head into her palms, cursing her foolish, foolish heart for leaping into a wild calypso. Acting like the silly girl she'd been would not get her through the next five weeks, or even through the rest of the day.

Just because West briefly turned on the *I care about you, babe* charm in her moment of weakness, didn't mean she should jump to unfounded conclusions. She'd never been West's girl, even when at eighteen she'd been naïve enough to think that sex with him automatically labeled her as such. She'd been nothing more than a quick fling, an easy conquest, another chick he'd banged.

The only thing that kissing West proved was she was still too stupid to learn her lesson the first *and* second time around.

"Not aiming for third time lucky, pal." Piper staggered to the cabin door and locked it.

Now. If she could just stop thinking about the long night ahead, trapped in this cabin with him.

And how she would prevent herself from being stupid all over again.

***

Piper sliced strips of green pepper for the green salad with the focused attention of someone performing their first solo brain surgery.

Outside the galley, West's baritone rumble was cut into by wife number three's piercing giggle. "Oh, West, you're too much."

Wasn't he, though. Too much of everything decadent and yummy. An overindulgence she couldn't afford. She tossed the strips into the salad bowl, snatched up another pepper and pierced its glossy skin with her knife.

After West fixed the exhausted but happy couples their early evening cocktails, which they currently enjoyed on The Mollymawk's deck, he helped garnish the plate of smoked salmon blinis and carried the platter out.

Fortunately, the rest of the day had gone without a hitch. Couples one and two snorkeled their little butts off, while she thanked the gods her seasickness had abated once in the water. Later in the afternoon she buddied up with husband number three on the scuba dive, while his wife chattered non-stop to West back on-board.

Afterwards West sidled up to her and in a low-pitched voice, snarled, "Don't ever leave me alone with that woman again. She never, ever shuts up."

"Wiggles stories?" Piper whispered back.

Wiggles being the woman's spoiled Maltese terrier. Piper had managed to zone out from most of the Wiggles stories when Cynthia, aka wife number three, looked after her earlier.

"Did you know Wiggles has her own wardrobe?"

"She showed you her photos, didn't she?"

"I wanted to poke my eye out with one of those little cocktail umbrellas."

They grinned at each other.

God, his real smile, the genuine one she rarely got, made Piper want to lap him up like melted chocolate—the decadently expensive kind.

And he was out there now entertaining the three couples with his irresistible bartender charm.

"Salad greens, check. Peppers, check." Glancing down at her to-do list, Piper poked a finger at her sister's scrawl. "Cherry tomatoes." She yanked open the fridge and removed a small bowl. "Check. I've so got this."

"Got what?"

She spun back at the sound of West's voice. He carried a tray of glasses and set it on the outer counter of the galley, wisely staying out of her little triangle of space between the stove, sink, and fridge.

"Got everything under control." Piper blinked. "Refills already?" He nodded, and transferred the empty glasses to the counter top, along with the empty starter platter. "Wow. That was fast."

"They're hungry, happy, and starting to get horny."

Super. Nice to know that a group of fifty-somethings were getting in the mood for sex later that evening, while she would pass an uncomfortable eight hours on a narrow bunk in a tiny cabin with West. And definitely *not* having sex.

"Lucky Bluff oysters aren't in season," she muttered and returned to the chopping board, swiping the back of her hand across her forehead.

Was it just her, or had the kitchen become way too hot?

"They don't need an aphrodisiac, that's for sure. But I didn't take you for a prude."

He risked her wrath by moving around the counter and into her space, bending down to take out fresh wine glasses from the cabinet near her knees. His tee shirt rode up, baring a strip of tanned skin on his lower back.

What had she been thinking about yumminess? Would his skin be hot to the touch or cool from the brief swim he'd taken before cocktail hour? Would the scent of sea and salt and male pheromones transfer to her fingertips if she traced the bumps of his vertebrae?

Adjusting her grip on the knife, Piper studied the two avocados beside the board. Chopping a finger off while ogling a man she shouldn't be ogling wouldn't be a good look. She rolled her shoulders and instructed her pulse to drop the hyper act and return to normal.

"I had any prudishness stomped out of me after I started at police training college." She kept her voice breezy as she picked up an avocado and ran the blade around it lengthwise. "Men have dirty minds, male cops even more so."

"Intimidating for an eighteen-year-old." He placed another set of wine glasses on the counter and straightened.

"I was hardly an innocent," she said, and then realizing how it could be interpreted, tacked on, "I hung around with my big brother and his smut-brained friends."

West shook his head and moved to the fridge, his glutes flexing under his thin board shorts. *Oh, for Pete's sake.* Piper wrested the avocado halves open with a silent snarl and used a spoon to pry out the pit.

"We didn't always have smut on our minds." He selected another bottle of white wine and returned to the other side of the counter.

"No, there was fishing, diving, bikes, rugby, beer, and how to get more beer. That about covers the things you and the other guys gabbed about."

"Eavesdrop much?"

"All the time."

West's rough chuckle fired another bolt of some female chemical, designed solely to turn her on, straight to every damn erogenous zone.

"What else did you hear?" He peeled the foil off the wine bottle and looked at her expectantly, nothing but warm humor in his clear blue eyes.

Against her will, she found herself smiling back. "I heard about your bet with Ben that you could cop a feel of Lisa Cameron's boobs."

"Did you, now?" That earned her another sexy laugh. "I was fifteen and it was my first spectacular blow-out with a girl. She slapped my face."

Piper snorted. "I would've punched your lights out." She sliced the avocado into quarters. "And you've got me to thank for that slap—I told Lisa what you were up to."

West's eyes crinkled and he gusted out a full belly laugh. Gripping the edge of the counter he leaned forward until his face was only a foot away from hers. "You've got a mean streak, Piper. That slap cost me days of groveling to get back in Lisa's good books, and I never did get to touch her boobs." He paused, tilted his head, and deliberately directed his attention down to where her breasts pressed against her shirt. "So you owe me a feel of *your* boobs to make up for it."

Red alert. Red alert. Her next inhale stopped halfway down her lungs and her nipples budded into two hard points of *Ohmigod-yes-please*. She raised the tip of her chef's knife and pointed it at his nose. "Keep your hands to yourself, Westlake."

His gaze flared hot. "What if I don't want to?" He took two slow steps sideways, two steps closer to her. "What if I'm tired of playing your game of 'there's nothing going on here.'"

The knife in her hand swiveled to follow his cat-like movements. "I don't play games. And FYI there *is* nothing going on here. Nothing I'm interested in pursuing, anyway."

Another step and he rounded the corner, crowding her backward until her butt hit the counter. He rescued the knife from her shaking fingers, laid it on the chopping board, and left his hand resting there, effectively trapping her.

"Liar, liar, pants on fire," he murmured.

She shoved a hand against West's chest to stop him coming closer, but all that achieved was runaway tingles up her arm from the hard, hot muscles beneath his shirt. He leaned into her fingers and the rapid bump of his heartbeat throbbed against her palm. Close enough to see her own reflection in West's eyes, she froze when his pupils shrunk to tiny dots.

His nose twitched. "Something's burning."

Yeah, something was burning, all right. One more touch, one more second of him looking like he planned to do her on the kitchen counter and she would either catch fire or do something absurd like kiss him again.

"West." Hating the breathy quality in her voice, Piper sucked in a lungful of smoke-tainted air. *Smoke-tainted?* What the—?

She followed West's gaze to where a thin ribbon of steam mixed with smoke seeped out of the oven door. Shaye's carefully prepared meal was in that oven reheating. And now smoking.

The galley's smoke detector found its voice and screeched with gusto.

"The fish!" and then a second afterward she spotted the froth boiling over the pan on the stove, followed closely by a hiss and sputter as the lemon dill cream sauce sizzled down the sides and hit the element. "Oh, crap! The sauce!"

While she momentarily froze, West turned the stove off, shoved both hands into protective mitts, and yanked the pan from the oven. Steam, smoke and the stench of incinerated fish belched into the kitchen. The smoke detector continued at an even higher decibel to broadcast her cock-up to the world.

The galley door flung open and husband number three poked his face inside. "Everything okay in here?" He took one look at her stricken face and added, "Dang, is that our dinner?"

Yep, that was their dinner. Ruined. Absolutely annihilated.

West strode toward husband number three and the open door, trailing a plume of grey smoke behind him. Piper followed him, groaning as West chucked their guests' baked blue cod with skinny carrot thingies and spinach overboard.

With her luck? The Department of Conservation would have her up for poisoning the sea life. And then, Shaye would murder her for obliterating one of her culinary masterpieces.

Chapter 9.

Piper silently recited every foul word in her vocabulary, which thanks to nine years on the police force formed a substantial list.

How the hell would she fix this?

She couldn't offer green salad and cheese and crackers to guests who expected a luxurious three course meal. Fortunately, she hadn't destroyed the white chocolate mousse cooling in the fridge. Give her time, though, give her time...

"Oh, dear, what happened?" Wife number one appeared at her side, accompanied by her husband.

Piper massaged her temples and forced her lips to curl into a wry smile. "I had some trouble with my sister's reheating instructions. I'm afraid she's the domestic goddess in our family, not me."

Husband number one patted her shoulder. "My Janet's much the same, aren't you, love? Sticks to the 'keep-it-simple-stupid' philosophy or else everything turns to charcoal."

Janet slipped him a look that should've flash-fried his nuts to charcoal, while Piper debated rifling through The Mollymawk's cabinets in case she'd skipped over another gourmet meal in her haste. The couple moved away to watch the gannets circling overhead. She didn't like the birds' chances of a tasty snack if they were eyeing up Shaye's fish.

Husband number three wandered over with his refilled wine glass. "What's plan B then, ay? I'm starving."

Good to know he had his priorities straight. Would it be rude to snatch the glass out of his hand and gulp the rest herself?

"Plan B? Well..." Piper angled a sidelong glance at West who'd just finished scraping the crusty black remains out of the oven pan.

"How does fresh lobster and paua fritters cooked over a fire on the beach grab you?" West said.

"Brilliant." Husband number three wrapped an arm around his wife.

"We'll head a couple of beaches over to Kahurangi Bay where there's a good spot to catch lobsters. We'll take the dinghy and drop you off on the beach. The six of you can collect driftwood for the fire while Piper and I dive for seafood."

"Oooh a beach party, how wonderful! I love beach parties!" Wife number three's enthusiasm infected the others and the couples started chattering amongst themselves.

Piper grabbed West's arm and tugged him inside the galley.

"What? You don't like my idea?" he said as Piper shut the connecting door and leaned against it.

She shook her head. "It's great, thanks, but there's not enough air left in any of the couples' tanks for you to dive."

West continued through the small dining area into the galley and dumped the pan into the sink. "I won't be using a tank. You can, but I don't need to."

"Oh." She folded her arms and worried her bottom lip with her eye tooth. "You're going to free-dive."

"Why don't you call it 'spear-fishing' since the word free-dive pushes your buttons? Kahurangi's shallow with good visibility and we've both dived there many times."

None of which eased the knot of tension behind her breastbone. "You want me to be your buddy." She couldn't keep the flatness from her tone.

His eyebrow kicked up. "Don't dive alone, right?"

Rubbing at the tight spot did little to ease it when she thought of being West's buddy. "Right. Okay, let's go, then."

Thirty minutes later she and West trod water beside the anchored dinghy, while laughter from the beach drifted across the gentle swell of the bay. Suited up in wetsuits, fins, and masks, the neoprene couldn't keep the chill of the water from penetrating deep inside her.

Or maybe being West's safety diver brought on the ache that made her cold right down to the marrow. Because buddy was just another name for responsibility and he'd neatly maneuvered her into it while he "spear-fished." A responsibility she didn't want.

Piper had already collected half a dozen large-shelled paua while West snorkeled above, keeping her in his sights. She unhooked the mesh catch bag around her waist and dumped the molluscs into the dinghy.

"My turn." West pulled his mask into place again.

The words "be careful" were on the tip of her tongue but she gulped them back. She wouldn't give him the power of her worries.

You're okay. This is not the same situation as with Dad. The water's only thirty feet deep here at most. It'll be fine—he'll be fine.

Lots of self-talk that didn't slow her racing heart or the adrenaline slamming through her.

She nodded and popped in her regulator, not trusting herself to speak. West rolled onto his back and sucked in air, gulping like a fish to pack more into his lungs. Then with a smooth twisting movement he slipped under, barely rippling the surface.

Piper followed him down, bubbles trailing behind her. He moved through the water like one of the tiny fish who swirled around him in silvery shoals—effortless, at home. She kept her distance as he glided through the kelp forest to the rocky seabed. West's dive light flickered into cracks and crevices. His hand darted into a gap and emerged with a decent sized lobster, its legs flailing.

West gestured her toward him and she finned over, holding the catch bag open. He dropped the lobster inside and held up a finger, pointing back at the rock opening. Making a motion across her throat with her spare hand, she raised a questioning eyebrow. *Out of air?*

He shook his head and turned back to the rock, reappearing moments later with another struggling lobster. That one also stored, he gave her a thumbs up—returning to the surface. Mirroring the gesture she flutter-kicked away, feeling the drag of the catch bag in her hand, the movement and eddy of water flowing around her. She looked to the right, expecting to see West beside her. Nothing but air bubbles and a sleek kahawai swimming past.

West!

Her mind screamed, even as her body registered a shift in the water pressure behind her immediately followed by a sly pinch on her butt as West rose up, tapped the top of her head, and darted away—as only someone without a cumbersome tank could do.

Show-off. Long limbs curved and flexed as he propelled himself gracefully up to the sun, simple joy in every movement. It was more than showing off. West truly loved what he did and she accepted he'd never stop wanting the freedom found in the deep—like her father.

But that same illicit thrill could transform into a powerful drive. A drive which could prove fatal.

***

Piper finished digging a hole and tipped the scraps of lobster shells and legs into it. Couples one to three enjoyed their impromptu picnic and had taken a stroll to a cluster of exposed rocks at the end of the beach to watch the sun set. The sand slid between her fingers as she filled in the hole. Behind her West loaded the last of the gear back into the dinghy, ready for their return trip to The Mollymawk.

She sat back on her haunches. A gust of cool wind whipped a smattering of grit across her cheek and she brushed it away. Thank

God for West's quick thinking and the couples' willingness to see the dinner fiasco as a big adventure.

"Done?" West ambled toward her barefoot, those damn board shorts highlighting his—never mind.

Piper gave the mound one last pat, just in case the lobsters might reanimate and head for the surface. Zombie lobsters. Yeah, that'd take her mind off West's seriously hot body.

"Yep. You?" She cleared her throat as he sat beside her.

He stretched his long legs out in front and leaned back on his elbows. "For now."

She sat back too and crossed her ankles. Waves hissed, surging over the wet sand. The wind picked up and leaves cartwheeled across the beach. The repetitive call of a weka piped up in the distance.

"Was it so bad, diving with me today?" he asked.

Piper tilted her chin toward him, squinting as the dying rays of sun slanted into her eyes. Slight creases lined his forehead and his mouth was in a straight line.

"It was fine." She sighed and curled her toes. "I haven't buddied with a free-diver since my dad, and you freaked me out for a second when you disappeared."

"Ah. I'm sorry. I was a complete asshat. I didn't think."

Tugging her legs up to her chest, Piper rested her chin on a kneecap. "The only time I go into the ocean now is for work or training. There's little pleasure in it—other than knowing I'm doing my job. I've forgotten how to have fun in the water."

"The three of us used to have fun. Diving, spearfishing, races from the beach to your dad's boat."

"Yeah." Silvery waves and flashes of sunlight hit her brother's boat as it rolled gently in the swell. "Back when Ben didn't hate me. It feels like a lifetime ago."

"He doesn't hate you." There was a raw edge in his tone, like maybe he wanted to change the initial pronoun.

Wishful thinking.

"No, I suppose not. I'm channeling my mother's flair for the dramatic. Hate would require some emotion on Ben's part. He's indifferent."

"No one can remain indifferent to you for long."

Can you? Her fist clenched as a muscle worked in his jaw.

Ben's indifference hurt but West's hurt on a whole new level. Caring about what he thought was another painful illustration of her vulnerability where he was concerned. Piper hated that weakness in herself—and that wasn't dramatic, just truth.

"We'll see." She scrambled to her feet, brushing the sand from her legs.

West rose beside her in one fluid movement and touched her forearm. She started and he dropped his hand, shoving it into the pocket of his shorts.

"I want to ask you something." His gaze was steady and unblinking and as it lingered her stomach clenched in knots.

"Ask away."

"I want you to be my safety diver while I train for Nationals."

The words were a body blow, a battering onslaught that spun her thoughts so fast lightheadedness made her sway. Digging her toes into the sand as an anchor, Piper checked herself and schooled her features into a mask of polite interest that promised nothing. The same expression she adopted when one of her cop buddies was after a quick cash loan. "Really? And is this the final installment on the reimbursement you think I still owe?"

"It crossed my mind." His eyebrows drew together. "But I'm asking you because other than Ben, there's no one else I trust at my back."

"I'm flattered. But no thanks." She turned to walk away, but he came up behind her, his hands wrapping around her upper arms.

His chest brushed her shoulder blades and warm breath puffed against the curve of her ear. Goosebumps prickled across her skin as his fingers traced down her arms and linked their hands together. "Taking off again? You're becoming predictable."

"Sometimes being predictable will keep you alive." Her words came out choppy and Marilyn-Monroe-breathy. "You know what I think about the risks of free-diving."

"Without training, I'd agree. But I've been doing this for a long time and only a couple of years ago I did an intensive course in the Bahamas with world champions of the discipline. I know what I'm doing."

Yeah, he knew exactly what he was doing—murmuring in that seductive voice, which would normally have women whipping off their panties in two seconds flat. She was not one of those women. Yet she couldn't explain why she hadn't disentangled herself from his embrace. "It's still too dangerous."

"That's where your expertise comes in." He gripped her hands and moved in even closer, the front of his thighs brushing the backs of hers, her bottom settling into the cradle of his hips.

A flash of heat boiled through her at the contact. God, he was always a sly one at getting what he wanted. While other men would yell and demand, West was far craftier. He used his slick conversational skills and potent touch to talk a woman into thinking capitulation was her idea all along.

He pulled back fractionally and his stubble scratched the juncture of her neck and shoulder. She shivered, cursed herself for the weakness of wanting him to do it again.

"No. I can't."

His body aligned to hers from back to thigh, the hard curve of his biceps pressing against her arms. He cocooned her in the powerful heat which pumped off him, warming her chilled skin. He lifted their linked hands up and wrapped them, and his arms, around her waist. "You could keep me safe."

Her heart tripped and plummeted, taking her back to the early morning when she was eighteen, woken before dawn by her father yanking the covers off her tear-stained face saying, "Looks like it's you and me kid, because Ben didn't come home last night. Not that it matters. You'll keep me safe."

But she hadn't, had she?

"Don't ask me that! Dad asked me to keep him safe and he died." Her voice cracked on the last word and she threw herself forward, but strong arms pinned her.

"Christ, Piper."

She struggled, a feeble struggle that embarrassed her because, really, the strength of his arms around her was the only thing keeping her on her feet. She went limp and allowed him to gather her into the cradle of his chest. He turned her to face him and wrapped her in his arms, fitting her body flush against his, tucking her head under his jaw, where it had always fitted perfectly and somehow still did.

She breathed him in, the thud of his pulse a steady metronome. West's chest vibrated against her cheek as he murmured soothing words. Her eyes fluttered shut. *Just one moment.* His shirt smelled of the wine husband number three accidently spilled on him—that and the ever-present salt and the fainter traces of soap. *Just one more.* The scruff of his unshaven chin scraped against her temple. She clung limpet-like to the solid bulk of him while his fingers rubbed her upper back in small circles.

She wanted to suspend this moment forever.

And *that* jerked her back to her senses. Power and one-upmanship dominated the kiss they'd shared back in West's kitchen, but this hug was much more dangerous. This intimacy, these delicate tendrils of trust sprouting between them, they were the real threat.

"Is this about your dad? You can't still blame yourself for his death."

Yes, she could blame herself and did. But she also blamed *him.* The twenty-year-old Ryan Westlake who'd made her believe that he wanted her—loved her—and then took the love and trust she'd handed him and crushed it between calloused fingers. If she hadn't been grieving over a relationship that existed mainly in her own head, her father might still be alive.

She stiffened, and her fingers, which had curled into fists in the back of his tee shirt, creaked open.

"You were only eighteen. He should've known better than to take you out alone."

He was offering her the comfort of someone who had lost Michael too. But she wouldn't accept his comfort, because he didn't know exactly what happened that day.

"You're a trained police diver," he said. "You must be pretty good to make it on the squad. You're not that eighteen-year-old girl anymore."

She was definitely not that girl anymore. The girl who was so caught up, so ass-over-heels in love with him, that she'd destroyed her family.

Piper pulled back and met his gaze. Years of cop discipline prevented temper from spilling into her voice. "I'm more than pretty good."

"So, help me. Please."

Trained by the country's best through harrowing conditions, she'd succeeded where many had failed. She knew a hell of a lot more now than she did at eighteen. And she had no sappy, lovesick emotions to deal with this time.

Piper pried herself from the circle of West's arms and backed away. "Will you still dive if I say no?"

He rolled his eyes. "I've no death wish. I won't train in open water without a safety diver. But if I don't train then there's no way I'll be fit to compete at the Nationals and no way to help Ben."

What was he talking about? "How does your competing help Ben?"

"Stewart Island Dives is sponsoring me."

Her brother's company inherited from their father after he died. "But Ben has no money for sponsorship."

"Nope, not a bean. But if I win, he gets free publicity and a loan from me with the prize money."

"Hah. So competing in the Nationals is completely altruistic? You just want to help my brother out?" She couldn't stop her lip from curling and her stomach agitated queasily.

"I don't deny I want to win, but the publicity'll be good for him."

Yeah. And there was the crux. The one thing that could change her mind. The publicity and cash loan *would* be good—could make a huge difference in saving her brother's home, her father's business.

She slapped her hands on her hips. "Fine. But if I'm your safety diver, then I make the rules."

"Yes, ma'am."

Fat, wet droplets splattered on her scalp, then targeted her bare arms, her shoulders, her legs—Jeez, couldn't she ever cop a break? The clouds above Kahurangi Bay tore open. She squinched her eyes shut, the hands on her hips curling into fists.

In the distance came catcalls and squeals of laughter from the other couples. Rain hissed and pattered as it hit sea and sand, and the smell of brine grew stronger. A finger traced the curve of her cheek. Her eyes popped open. West closed the gap between them, his face wet, dark hair plastered against his head.

"You're pissed at me again." He tucked a dripping strand of hair behind her ear. "I don't know why I'm not surprised."

No way would she confess the thoughts playing through her head these last few minutes. "I'm not pissed at you. It's the rain—kind of a predictable end to this disastrous day."

"You never used to like things being predictable."

Yep, once she'd been the wild one. The impulsive, crazy girl always up for a dare, taking any opportunity to prove she was fit to be part of her brother's older, all male posse. And West? Well, West slipped easily into the role of an easy-going pal, patient and secretly protective of Ben's little sister. The sensible, practical one.

Her gaze dropped to the soft knit of his white tee shirt, soaked through now, transparent as it clung to the slight swell of his pecs and the jut of his small male nipples. Certain erogenous zones on her body started cranking out heat, unhampered by the cold rain.

"Sometimes predictable is safer. And regarding the weather, *which is what we're talking about,* predictable is preferable."

He ran a palm over his face and slicked back his dripping hair. "So if I kissed you now, would that make me predictable or *unpredictable?*"

"You're not kissing me at all. Not unless you want me to do some serious dental damage to your pretty-boy smile."

West stepped closer, she stepped back, but another flash of that pretty-boy smile stopped her from retreating any farther. He was teasing, toying with her emotions again. Their inexplicable attraction to each other was just a big joke. Well, har-de-har-har. She didn't feel like playing, but she wasn't going to run either.

"You want me to kiss you again. I know you do." His gaze purposely dropped and his grin expanded exponentially. "The evidence is right there, front and center, Officer Harland."

Goddamn misbehaving body parts. But she wouldn't draw more attention to them by folding her arms.

"In case it's escaped your amazing powers of observation," she raised her voice above the roar of the rain, "it's pissing down and about fifty-five degrees. I'm cold."

"Cold *and* a little turned on?" Once again he evaporated the distance between them, this time standing so close those wayward nipples of hers threatened to poke holes in his chest. "I bet you watched *The Notebook* and sighed dreamily when Ryan Gosling sucked face with Rachel McAdams in the rain."

"At least I didn't cry at the end of *The Lion King.*" She shoved at West's large hand which sneakily landed on her hip. "You big baby."

"Hey! We were kids."

His other hand grazed her arm and she slapped it away. "Well, we're not kids now, West, *so stop it.*"

The playful grin dropped off his face. His eyes went flinty, even as her breath hitched in her chest, like breathing air from a tank about to run dry.

"Go on, boy, plant one on her while you've got the chance!" husband number three's voice fog-horned from behind.

They jerked apart and looked at the three dripping wet couples splashing toward them. All three couples wore identical amused expressions.

Before she could react, West grabbed her, tipping her backward into a dramatic dip. Cool, firm lips pressed to hers for a count of two, but his eyes were the grey of gathering storm clouds, devoid of warmth. He levered her back to her feet, with the applause of their audience echoing around.

"Smile for the guests, *darling*," he gritted out.

After performing a mocking bow, he walked away.

***

West linked his hands behind his neck and wondered if counting back from a thousand in sevens would make his erection disappear. The mattress beneath him was as flexible as a wooden plank and the bunk itself certainly wasn't designed for a six-foot horny-as-hell male.

Please don't let her come out of the bathroom in those minuscule cartoon pajamas or I might embarrass myself here.

West groaned and shut his eyes against the blaze of moonlight shining through the cabin window. Piper could come out in sackcloth and ashes and he'd still want to strip her naked.

After their impromptu entertainment in front of their six guests earlier, all sorts of unwanted advice and innuendos bombarded them since their return to The Mollymawk. Unfortunately, the couples hadn't wanted to stay up late but instead retired to their separate cabins. Bugger for him and Piper once they ran out of chores—it meant they either had to make conversation or hit the sack. The oblivion of sleep sounded perfect, but he found himself offering Piper the use of the bathroom first.

The door clicked open and he couldn't resist a peek. Piper scurried through the doorway in long, loose pajama pants and a baggy, black tee shirt. The outfit, he assumed, her idea of non-sexy sleep attire. But he was a guy with a photographic memory of what curves hid under the loose fabric of her sleepwear.

"It's all yours." She slithered into her sleeping bag with a rustle— followed seconds later by the fzzzzt of the zipper being hauled up, all the way up.

Not taking any chances that I'll slide into it with you, are you, babe?

And the thought of trying to, really, *really* didn't help ease the ache of his cock pressed insistently against his jeans. Pathetic. Panting after her like Donny after one of the island's few unneutered bitches. He all but fell off the bunk bed in his haste to get into the bathroom.

Shoving his toothbrush into his mouth, West scrubbed at his teeth with enough force to scrape off enamel. This whole situation got crazier by the day. Bad enough to want Piper like he did, but the weird sense of intimacy, the jolt of *rightness*, that sucker punched him when he'd wrapped her in a bear hug—that was plain wrong. *Crazy* wrong.

He spat and rinsed. Not going there again. Not going there *ever* again. But, damn if he didn't want to storm back in the cabin all Neanderthal-like, peel that sleeping bag off her, and do her till she screamed his name.

West unbuttoned his jeans and prepared to wait until his hard-on went down enough to pee.

"C'mon, c'mon. You're not getting any action tonight," he muttered.

But unable to help himself, with thoughts of Piper's nipples jutting against the soft fabric of her tee shirt, he wrapped his fist around his throbbing cock.

Chapter 10.

West's head dropped back as his fist moved along himself in slow, achingly slow strokes.

"I want you to be my first," Piper said, meeting his gaze with fierce hazel eyes.

I want to be your only. The words he wanted to say but couldn't. She'd sprawled on his bed, her breasts bare, the nipples reddened like tiny strawberries from his suckling. Losing all imagined sophistication, he helped her out of her shorts and removed his jeans, nearly tripping over his own feet in the hurry to bury himself in her warm, tight depths. God, he wanted her and even the threat of Ben coming home to their flat early couldn't deter him from finally, finally making her his.

Thrusting into her, her slick wetness wrapped around him like a velvet-lined fist. She dug her nails into his ass and dragged him closer, even as he tried to pull away, terrified that he'd hurt her. Her teeth nipped his earlobe, her hissed-out breath brushing his cheek.

"Don't you dare stop now," she said.

His mouth found hers in the dark, claiming her, but cursing him to remember the taste of her forever.

He groaned through clenched teeth, his thumb spreading the moisture from the tip lengthwise, the pressure inside him building to volcanic levels as his palm moved faster and faster.

"West?" A soft knock on the bathroom door behind him. "Are you okay?"

Shit! His hand braced against the wall slipped and he stumbled toward the toilet bowl, gasping for breath.

"Are you sick?" Concern pitched Piper's voice higher than normal. "I heard you groaning."

Sick. That was it!

"Uh, yeah." He exhaled in a whoosh, his heart a kettle drum pounding in time with the throb of his cock. "Think I ate too many paua fritters—feel like I'm gonna hurl."

"Oh."

He caught her doubt in that one short syllable. How long had he been groaning? And what other sounds had she heard?

"You need anything?"

Just you baby, just you. Christ. He struggled to jam himself back into his boxers.

"No, I'm good." West splashed a handful of cold water on his face. Contemplated dumping a cup of it down his shorts to see if it would cool his aching balls off.

"Well. Okay. There's a roll of Quick-Eze in my bath bag if you need it."

Indigestion pills? Yeah, they wouldn't help—*how about a hand-job instead, babe?* Like that would happen.

"Thanks, I'll be fine. Go back to bed."

He waited, hands clamped either side of the sink to anchor himself in place, listening to Piper's soft footsteps and the final fzzzzt of the sleeping bag zipper sealing her away. Giving her a few more moments to settle, West cracked open the bathroom door and slunk into his bed.

***

Piper clutched her pillow like a life preserver, like she was floundering on the surface of a turbulent ocean. She remained in that stunned position for almost an hour.

Oh. My. God. West had been jerking off in the bathroom.

At first she hadn't been sure, had reacted out of genuine concern thinking he was sick. But after hearing the rawness of his voice— lightbulb moment! Did he honestly think the "I ate too many paua" excuse would cut it? What? Was she a complete innocent who didn't know the difference between a guy's *hanging over the porcelain throne about to puke groan*, and a guy's *this feels so good I'm about to come* groan?

Puh-lease.

And the worst of it? She'd stood outside that bathroom door for a moment with jellified knees and a growing damp patch in her pajama bottoms, wishing she could kick the door down and have her wicked way with him. She silenced a groan of her own by biting down on the fleshy web between her thumb and index finger. Crazy, sexually-frustrated tart.

Bastard knew she was attracted to him—okay, had gone beyond attraction and into the obsessively-craving-his-touch zone—so what was up with the sneaky bathroom masturbation? Her cotton pajama bottoms whispered together as she restlessly shifted her legs in the confines of the sleeping bag.

Hello? The snide little bitch inside her head piped up. *Are you for real? You dress in baggy tee shirts to disguise your teeny-tiny boobs, and combat boots to show what an ass-kicker you are. It's only now you wonder why West jerks off in the other room, imagining some dainty little thing in do-me heels and a g-string?*

Hot tears stung the corner of her eyes.

He was attracted to her but big-freaking-deal. She'd been attracted to guys who weren't her normal "type," had even slept with a couple, but she'd no intention of having a relationship with them. Just like West had no intention of having a relationship with her.

It's all about proximity and availability, kid. Don't delude yourself thinking it's anything more. And she wasn't going to change to please him. Been there, tried that, failed spectacularly.

But did she want a summer fling? To see if a quickie with West, now that she was a little older and wiser, would finally shut her yearning body up?

Maybe.

She could handle a fling. She had no ties, nothing to keep her in Oban once her duty was done. Nothing and no one.

So why did her family's faces float into her mind? Why did she see West in the sunshine with that half smile and his hair sticking up crazily on one side where he'd shoved his fingers through it? Why did she feel his arms around her still? And the burn in her throat as he stroked her hair and rested his hand briefly on the back of her neck?

She scrubbed away a tear slipping down her cheek and sucked a surreptitious breath in through her mouth—one sniff and West would guess what her snotty nose meant. Burrowing her face into the folds of the sleeping bag, Piper tried to tune out the soft breathing from the other bunk.

The only thing more humiliating than her tears would be to acknowledge that once again West had found a way under her protective armor.

***

Ten hours of frustration later, West followed Piper off the wharf to a corner table in Erin's café. Ben had beaten them and was about to tuck into a late breakfast of bacon and eggs.

West sat next to him. "How can you put so much cholesterol into your body day after day and still live?"

Piper slumped in the chair opposite.

"Erin'll disembowel you if she hears you talk about her food like that." Ben swallowed a forkful of eggs. "And what's your problem, anyway?"

"Nothing." He picked up a menu and snapped it open. "I just need a caffeine hit and not that instant swill, either."

Real coffee made from honest-to-God caffeine-rich beans that would psych him up—while the cause of him staying awake half the night sat across from him, examining her fingernails.

"You just missed your dad," Ben said. "Caught the early ferry with my mum. Off to Invercargill Hospital, aren't they?"

"Yep. Dad didn't want anyone going with him but once Glenna puts her mind to something..." West shrugged.

"She's worried about him, too." Piper straightened and picked up a menu. "And if he needs to go for more tests, Glenna will make sure he doesn't weasel out of them."

West scrubbed the heel of his palm along his thigh, remembering his father trying to be jovial as he told him about his blood test results—something was up with his kidneys and Doc Whelan was sending him to a renal specialist in Invercargill. "He's a tough old coot. He'll be fine."

"He will." Piper's cool stare melted. "There's nobody in Oban tougher than your dad."

The shard of ice, lodged in his gut from when Bill first confessed he'd been unwell for months, softened at her reaction.

Erin appeared at West's side, sliding a cup and saucer on the table in front of him. "Saw you coming and had Annie make your regular."

Piper lifted the menu in front of her face and their moment shattered.

West raised the cup and sniffed the intoxicating scent of his flat white. "This smells gooood. Marry me, Erin, and you can bring me coffee in bed every morning."

Erin laughed, flicking her plait over her shoulder. "I'm tempted to say yes just to see you squirm when I started shoving bridal magazines under your nose."

He glanced across to where Piper studied every option on the menu like she was cramming for an exam. A twitch in the corner of her lips was the only indication she listened to him pretend-flirt.

Erin moved to the end of the table and removed the order pad from her apron pocket. "Want anything?"

Piper lowered the menu and pinned Erin with her flat gaze. Fire kindled low in his belly. God, she was even hotter when she switched to Bad Cop mode.

"How about the same friendly service you offer your other paying customers instead of looking at me like week-old dog shit scraped off your size six ballet flats?"

The pen in Erin's hand clicked half a dozen times before she spoke, this time with a small shot of warmth in her tone. "I can't believe you still remember what shoe size I am."

"We stopped sharing shoes at twelve. You kept your little Chinese-lady bound feet while mine grew with the rest of me."

"Into a tall, skinny bitch."

Piper's mouth curved. "While you remained Hobbit sized."

"We've been friends since kindergarten."

"Yeah."

"You never called, never wrote." Erin's lip trembled once as she shoved her order pad back into her apron. "And you never said goodbye."

Join the club, honeybunch. West sipped his coffee and watched the women's byplay.

"I'm sorry, Erin," Piper said.

Ben dropped his head back toward the ceiling and clapped a hand to his forehead. "Look, can we bypass the *Thelma & Louise* reunion and fast-forward to the bit where you both realize you'll never be as hot as Geena Davis so you shut up and be friends again?"

Suddenly Ben ducked half under the table to clutch his shin.

"Hey! That hurt, Stubby," he grumbled, but West caught the hint of affection in the use of his sister's old nickname—and the sly trick he'd initiated by uniting the women against him instead of each other. "Lucky you missed my bad ankle."

"Did I?" Piper said. "Damn. I was aiming for it."

Erin tweaked Ben's ear. "That's for the Geena Davis comment." She glanced at Piper. "Americano with hot milk on the side?"

"Lovely."

After Erin scooted back behind the counter, Ben said, "So, how'd it go?"

West spotted Piper's quick glance in his direction, her lips forming a terse line.

"Good," she stretched the word out. "They all said they had a great time."

Ben rested his elbow on the table and propped up his chin. Piper shifted on her chair, placing the menu folder down and then picking it up again. The interrogator became the interrogated.

"Really?" Ben said. "Was the *great time* had before or after you were seasick and Mrs. Carter felt obliged to look after you? Or before or after you incinerated everyone's dinner?"

"They told you about that, huh?"

"They did." Ben's fingers drummed a short tattoo on his jaw. "Lucky for us they decided the seafood on the beach was a highlight, otherwise you would've totally screwed up the whole thing."

Piper leaned forward, scowling. "Like you expected me to."

Ben raised a palm, but said nothing.

Piper recoiled, her boots clomping to the floor as she sat bolt upright in her chair.

Keep out of it, West told himself. But no. It turned out where Piper was concerned he couldn't stop himself from riding in on his white charger. "You've got six satisfied customers now, Ben—so satisfied they're planning to tell a friend who's a travel writer to make a booking. Plus, they've agreed for us to use their photos for free publicity on your website— another of Piper's ideas."

"You just can't give me the benefit of the doubt, can you?" Piper flushed a pretty rose, her gaze never deviating from Ben's face. The gleam in her eye told him she wasn't *feeling* pretty. More like homicidal. "Yeah, I screwed up. But I have the balls to own it when I make a mistake."

Ouch, buddy. Direct hit.

Ben leaned back in his chair, the hard line of his jaw signaling his intention to freeze Piper from the conversation. If the café had been quieter they would've heard Ben's back teeth grind together. "It's easy to ask for forgiveness once the damage has been done, isn't it?"

The flush drained away from Piper's face, leaving the smattering of freckles on her cheekbones stark against her blanched skin. Her knuckles were whitened bumps as she gripped the edge of the table and stood. "Don't mistake my admission as asking for forgiveness."

She stalked to the counter calling out, "Erin? I'll have the coffee to go, thanks."

West waited exactly five seconds after the café door slammed. "You're too hard on her."

"If by 'hard' you mean I tell it like it is when she screws up a simple re-heatable dinner and is too proud to admit she gets seasick, then I'll wear it." Ben tore off a triangle of toast, swiped it in congealing egg yolk, and stuffed it into his mouth. "Ragging her about this will make her work twice as hard next time to get everything right."

"You were still a prick and I know you'd never come down on Shaye like that."

Ben swallowed his mouthful and chased it down with coffee. "Piper's solid, she can take some heat. And since when did you start siding with my sister? Since you started boning her?"

West's right hand curled into a fist, itching to plow into Ben's smirk. The last time the two of them scuffled he nearly broke Ben's nose with a solid right hook. They'd been fourteen and fighting over the affections of an older woman—Isabelle Collins, all of fifteen-and-a-half. West saw her first, Ben disagreed, and so they opted to settle the flirting rights with fists. Ben was bigger but West faster, and the matter done and dusted with Ben's bloody nose.

Having the gift of the gab saved West from a few fistfights, but he'd still beat the shit out of someone if he had to. And right now, for the first time in fifteen years, his blood pressure crept into the danger zone.

"Not that it's any of your business but I'm not sleeping with Piper."

"Not yet, ay?" Ben grabbed the other half of the toast and took a bite. Chewed thoughtfully, while meeting West's hot gaze with apathy. "I wouldn't if I were you."

"Suddenly you're the protective big brother? When you've just finished ripping her a new one. That's rich."

Ben stabbed a finger at him. "Stay away from her. I'm warning you."

"How touching. You're worried I'll break your sister's heart."

"You've got it wrong. I'm not worried about you breaking Piper's heart, or even you shagging her senseless—if easy sex was the only thing you wanted." Ben pushed his plate out of the way and rested on his folded arms. "But I know you. I've known you for a hell of a lot longer than she has and I can tell she's getting to you again. Mate, she'll cut your heart out and stomp all over it with her combat boots when she leaves—just like she did last time."

West's scalp itched. "You knew? About...last time?"

The slight lift of Ben's eyebrow screamed *duh* at him. He didn't know whether to be embarrassed or relieved. "Didn't think it was that obvious."

"When the life of the party turns into a monk for a year after a certain female leaves town, his mates notice."

"Yeah. Well, I'm not that hormonally challenged kid now. I can handle Piper."

"Sure you can. But don't kid yourself that after you've *handled* her, she'll stay." Ben studied him over the rim of his cup.

West lifted his gaze to the picture windows and the view of the wharf beyond. Piper leaned on the railing looking out into the bay, her hands cradling her takeout coffee, the toe of one boot kicking the heel of the other.

"I know it." West downed the dregs of his coffee, leaving his tongue coated in bitterness.

***

The estrogen in the women's changing room before the annual Waitangi Day touch rugby game was so rich Piper thought she'd either suffocate or start applying copious amounts of mascara—like one of her future teammates was doing.

"How did you talk me into this again?" she hissed in Shaye's ear as they entered the small prefab structure.

"A large dose of sisterly guilt." Shaye peeled Piper's claw-like hand off her elbow. "Come on, it'll be fun and the women's team needs you."

The team might need her for her gender and for numbers, but the body language of some of the women made it clear they didn't want her there.

Kezia, dressed like the other six women in black bike shorts and a hot pink, slim fitting tee shirt with *Bree's Kiwi Curios* screen printed on the front, looked up from lacing her rugby boots. "Piper, hey!"

"Hi, Kez."

"Zoe and I have hardly seen you since you got back from your romance tour." Kezia lifted her other foot onto the battered wooden bench and tugged on the laces.

Piper dropped her kitbag on the bench next to her. "Been keeping a low profile for the last week. We had a couple of dive tours and a fishing charter, too."

"And run off her feet while Bill's only working part time," Shaye said.

"West's a slave driver, hmm?" Erin offered a sharp smile from her position by the shoulder-high windows overlooking Oban's sports field.

"That man can order me around his bedroom any time," said a brunette with a set of ripped biceps, her nose so close to the window that a patch of fog had formed. "Wow. There's some seriously fine man-flesh parading around out there in the mud."

Shaye chuckled. "Piper, that's Tarryn O'Dell—she's the new Department of Conservation worker."

"Heard about you, but nice to meetcha anyway," Tarryn said by way of greeting, softening the statement with a grin.

Piper smiled back warily. "Likewise."

Shaye walked past her, farther into the room. "And you know Lani—" at the other end of the bench Lani raised a hand and continued to bop silently to the tinny music pumping from her earbuds—"and you'd remember Bree and Holly." Neither of whom bothered to look away from the sink mirrors since she'd stepped inside.

Shaye cut her an embarrassed glance and Piper knew her sister would be having words with Holly later. The slender woman with the fuchsia streak in her sable colored hair fussed with her fringe. Currently working in Oban's grocery store and moonlighting as a hairdresser, Holly had been Shaye's bestie since primary school, and was still loyal to a fault.

Holly partially turned with a clipped, "Hi," before resuming her grooming.

Bree, the third member of Piper's schoolgirl cronies, continued to apply another coat of mascara, her parted, gloss-slicked lips reflected in the mirror. Only Queen Bee would think to touch up her make-up before getting down and dirty on a rugby field.

Un-freaking-believable.

Bree's mascara wand made a sharp click as she jabbed it back into the tube. Smoothing non-existent wrinkles in her pink tee shirt, she turned and leaned against the sink.

"So kind of you to take time out of your busy schedule to help our little team."

Honestly. There were half a dozen snarky remarks she could choose from to remind Bree she was just the biggest fish in a teeny-tiny pond, but the déjà vu of high school struck her right on the funny bone.

"Happy to help—so long as you're not planning to reenact the shower scene from *Carrie* where you start hurling sanitary products at me."

Mouths dropped, and a couple of women made choked snorting noises. Bree uttered a sharp bark of laughter before moving to the center bench and snatching up a pink shirt. "I'm glad to see you haven't lost your good taste in humor." She tossed the shirt over Lani's and Kezia's heads.

Piper snagged the shirt with one hand. "And I'm glad to see you still insist on picking a color that appeals to the six-year-old princess trapped inside you."

Bree raised an immaculately shaped brow. "Since my business is sponsoring the women's team uniform, I got to choose the color."

"Such a sophisticated choice."

That almost forced a genuine smile out of her. "Are you still fast on your feet, Piper? Or has your bum gotten fat after years of coffee and donut stakeouts?"

"Think you've been watching too many cop shows." Erin rose on tiptoes to angle a better view out the window. "Now, take our local lawman, Noah, out there—nothing wrong with his bum *at all*, not from where I stand."

Holly raced to the window and elbowed Erin over. "Praise Jesus—he's doing lunges now!"

"I bags full body tackling him," Tarryn said.

"Nobody tackles anybody," Bree said. "That's why it's called 'touch' rugby."

The other three women who weren't ogling ignored Bree and made a beeline for the window. Piper stripped off her tee shirt and slid her arms into the sleeves of the pink monstrosity.

"Oooh... are there any bits we *can't* touch?" Kezia said, turning back to give Piper a quick wink. "And can someone explain why we have to wear bike shorts, while the guys wear ordinary rugby shorts?"

"Men don't look good in Lycra hot pants, Kez." Shaye had given up on the cluster of women by the window and climbed onto the bench for a better view.

"West does," Piper said.

Ohhhh...crap. A total brain-edit-fail moment.

Piper stretched the tee shirt over her head. Maybe no one heard amongst all the lusting noises. Pink knit fabric, probably close to the shade of her burning face, slid past her nose as she looked up to seven pairs of unblinking eyes.

"Really?" Holly said, with an utterly evil grin. "*How good?*"

Piper's disgustingly accurate memory did a u-turn back to West rising out of the pool in those snug training shorts. Or West wearing nothing but his yoga pants.

Her face flamed hotter as she hauled the tee shirt down over her sports bra. "Aren't we meant to be out on the field by now? They're all waiting for us."

"Piper and West sittin' in a tree, k-i-s-s-i-n—" Piper shoved Shaye off the bench.

Various other lewd comments were directed Piper's way before Bree silenced them with three sharp claps and an imperious voice. "Ladies? We have a game to win—out, out, out!" She hustled the others from the changing room with a pointed look back at Piper, leaving her alone with Shaye.

Piper clapped her hands over her face and sat down on the bench.

"Bet you wish they had thrown tampons," Shaye said.

"God, yeah."

"Your face is *very* red."

"Thank you for that insightful observation, dear sister. Now leave me to my humiliation." Piper unzipped her kitbag and dragged out the spare pair of rugby boots Shaye loaned her.

Shaye sat down next to her and laid a cool palm on her leg as Piper slid her foot into the cleated boot and started lacing. "You like West, huh? Like him *a lot.*"

"You've come to that conclusion on the basis that I said he looked good in Lycra?" Did her tone sound incredulous? Probably not enough to fool Shaye.

"I came to that conclusion because you sometimes use snooty words when you're covering something up. And because I've seen the way you look at him when you think no one's watching."

"Shaye—"

"Have you slept with him yet?"

Piper gawped.

"That's a no then. Well, have you kissed him?"

"What makes you think I kissed *him?* Maybe he kissed me!" Then her brain caught up and she stopped in the middle of lacing her boot. "Oh, for Pete's sake."

Shaye giggled. "For a hardened police officer, you're surprisingly easy to interrogate."

"I'm not hardened." Hardened on the outside, maybe. If only she could harden herself on the inside, where it mattered.

"Most of the girls think you are."

"I bet most of the girls think a lot of things about me right now." Piper dropped her elbows to her knees and rested her forehead in her cupped palms.

"Yep, and they'll expect to hear all the deets at the beach bonfire tonight."

"I'm not going."

"Course you are."

"No." Piper lifted her head. "I'm not. A group of women who'd gain orgasmic pleasure witnessing my ongoing humiliation at the Westlakes' annual bonfire after this morning's slip of the tongue, are not people I'd voluntarily hang out with."

"You've got some weird ideas about your friends, sis."

"They're not my friends."

"Yeah, they are. And the ones you don't know could be, if you'd let them."

"Puh-lease, Pollyanna."

Shaye shrugged and squeezed Piper's knee. "You're coming tonight, Pipe, or I'll tell everyone you're crushing on West and want to have his babies."

Piper hoped the glare she turned on her sister disguised the lurching thump of her heart. "You're such a brat."

"Agreed. Now let's go chase some good-looking men around a muddy field."

***

Muddy hair, muddy face, and mud plastering his shorts and top to his skin. Twenty minutes into the game and all was good with the world.

West swiped a hand across his forehead as a light rain began to fall. A bloom of multi-colored umbrellas sprouted up at the sidelines. He glanced to the other end of the field where the women's team clustered in a circle, his gaze automatically honing in on Piper's rangy, thoroughly mud-covered form. The guys' team was at a serious disadvantage with six hot females in tight, wet clothing running around. Or maybe he was the only one distracted by a certain hot female.

He dragged his gaze away from the curve of Piper's ass as she bent down to re-lace her boot, and glared at the huddle of men around him.

"Right. Kip and Joe, you're on the bench until the last ten minutes, then we'll sub you in to win this thing."

Opposite him, Gav Reynolds spat on the trampled grass. "Women are kicking our sorry asses out there."

"Would help if you'd stop getting so many penalties," Ford said.

Gav swore, his Due South team shirt straining over his puffed-out chest.

Ford's dad, Rob, grunted and shook his head. "Chill, Gav."

Ben, complete with his plastic bag-covered cast and crutches, elbowed farther into the group from where he'd watched the game on the sidelines. "The ref's already threatened to send you off for misconduct, Gav, so stop acting like such a douche and leave Kezia and Piper alone."

Gav swung toward Ben. "What business is it of yours?"

"It's my sister and her friend you're gunning for." Ben refused to budge.

So even Ben noticed Gav's amped-up aggression toward the two women—accidently shoving Piper out of the way, taking the term "touch" to mean grabbing Kezia's ass. And it hadn't escaped his attention that Piper kept heckling Gav, putting herself between him and Kezia. Like a rodeo clown distracting a pissed off bull.

The ref's whistle blew a long continuous blast. End of half-time break.

"Watch your step, Reynolds," was all West said as they jogged onto the field—when what really burned on his tongue was, "Touch Piper again and you'll be pissing blood for a week."

"Bunch of pussy-whipped little girls." Gav moved to his position as left wing on the sideline.

West walked onto the field, spectators clapping and bellowing advice. Blocking out the rush of super-heated testosterone that made him want to punch something until his knuckles were bloody, West looked down the opposite end of the field where Piper jogged in place, calling out last minute instructions to her teammates.

A short whistle blast pierced the air and they were off.

The women flew across the grass toward them, determination to make it to the men's try line etched in the stubborn set of their jaws. Gav homed in on Kezia, who had the ball, his teeth bared. Pumping his arms faster, West charged after him, until he was close enough to spot Piper coming up on Kezia's left side, her gaze also rooted to Gav's murderous expression.

"To your left, Kez," Piper shouted and to Kezia's credit she didn't hesitate, tossing the ball left in a textbook on-the-fly pass. Piper caught the ball and put on a burst of speed— straight toward Gav.

It happened so fast, so smoothly, that if he hadn't watched with such vested interest in the son-of-a-bitch now targeting *his woman*, he would've missed it. Piper feinted left and immediately changed direction and ducked right, intending to dodge past Gav. Gav, having wised up to her modus operandi, didn't fall for it and slammed his body right, his elbow connecting with Piper's stomach and knocking her clear off her feet.

The ref's whistle shrieked, the crowd roared, and voices shouted all around him.

A red haze blurred his vision as he covered the last few feet to where Gav smirked down at Piper, who curled on her side in the mud. West dived, hammering Gav in a full body tackle.

Kill him. He'd bloody kill him.

Chapter 11

Rough arms pulled him up, and blood, bitter and warm, flooded his mouth. Voices hollered his name—Ford, Joe, and Noah—and someone pinned his arms so he couldn't swing at Gav again.

Noah's deep growl finally penetrated beyond the rasp of his labored breathing. "Don't turn this from fisticuffs into an assault, West. I don't want to arrest you."

He glared at Gav, hauled to his feet by Rob, Kip, and even West's skinny dish-hand, Fraser, who looked a little grossed out at the blood pouring from Gav's flattened nose. His gaze flew to where he'd last seen Piper, curled in the mud. She sat a short distance away with her head drooping between her bent knees, arms wrapped around her stomach. Kezia and Shaye crouched at her side, the other four women in a unified circle behind them, shooting venomous glances at Gav.

West rolled his shoulders to loosen his wire-taut muscles and met Noah's gaze. "I'm done."

Joe released West's right arm and slapped him on the back. "Jaysus, that's a killer right hook you've got there. Knuckles okay?"

"I'll live, Doc." West flexed his hands but didn't bother looking at them. "Have you checked out Piper?"

"The prick hit her like a Mac truck," Ford said from West's other side, he too letting go of his arm and thumping West's back. "He was due a good hiding anyway."

"Now you've got yourself under control, I'll check the state of her, but it seems your lady's just winded." Joe walked over to the cluster of women.

If his jaw, knuckles, and stomach—where Gav got in a couple of lucky punches—hadn't throbbed like a mother, West might've had the energy to correct the doctor.

Piper was not his *lady*. Or his girl, his woman, or his frickin' girlfriend.

He didn't know what she was. But seeing Reynold's plow into Piper smashed open a floodgate of protectiveness and, okay, he confessed, a gut-clawing possessiveness.

The referee appeared in front of them, red-faced and harried. "The other bloke's gone off field already, but sorry, mate, you're out too."

West raised his palms. "No worries. Just let me make sure the lady he hit is okay."

The ref nodded. "Couple of minutes, then."

Around him the crowd murmured and a few people pointed over his shoulder, wide-eyed and whispering, but West blocked the rising chatter of voices and strode toward Piper. Spotting her mud-covered legs and the crown of her short hair sticking up in wet spikes, the urge to scoop her up and cradle her into his chest kicked his heart into a mad gallop.

Her head lifted, those clear hazel eyes zeroing in on his. Could she see what he thought? How much he wanted her, how deep she undermined every wall of resistance he threw up? He froze, locked in place. Before he could take another step, a hand grabbed his forearm. He started, so caught up in his single-minded purpose to reach Piper he'd been unaware of anyone else nearby.

"Ryan."

There were only two people who ever called him Ryan and only one of them still held the flat, monotone drawl of a Californian accent.

His head whipped around. "Ma? What the hell are you doing here?"

Steady blue eyes looked back at him. Eyes that hadn't changed, although his mother's rosy skin had wrinkles, and her hair—in his memory glossy brown and falling in waves to her waist—now cut in a sensible bob, streaked with fine threads of dulled silver. "We need to talk, Ryan."

Tension ratcheted up his spine. Holy hell—his father! What would he think of Claire's sudden presence back in Oban? Adding a heart attack to Bill's kidney issues when he came face to face with his ex-wife wasn't something West wanted to contemplate. "You need to leave before Dad finds out you're here."

"Bill already knows I'm here. I went straight to him when I got off the ferry this morning. I'm not leaving and the three of us need to talk."

He raked a hand through his hair. This had turned into his year for women showing up unwanted and refusing to bloody leave. "I'm busy—right in the middle of a rugby game in case you hadn't noticed."

His ma cut him a sharp glance. "Looks to me your game was over the moment you pounded the Reynolds boy."

"He's not a boy, he's a hundred kilo wanker who slammed into my—" dammit, she was not his woman, would *never* be his "—into Piper."

Why had his brain fixated on this when his mother, who he hadn't seen since he was twenty-one, stood two feet away? And, what—Bill *knew* she was here?

His father lumbered across the field toward them, a thunderous expression on his face. This just kept getting better. A frickin' Westlake reunion. "Don't tell me Del is here too."

"No, Del's still in LA, but..." His mother's voice trailed off the same instant he sensed Piper behind him.

Sidestepping, West shook his head at them, trying to find some relief from the pressure crushing his skull, the adrenalized blood surging through his system. He needed to get away from his prodigal mother and the curious stares of the locals, away from the pain his father must be suffering at seeing Claire again, but most of all, away from Piper, quietly watching him while the walls closed in.

"I can't deal with you at the moment. Give me a break, all right?" He raised a hand, his bones feeling like they'd been hollowed out and filled with lead. "Just give me a break."

Without meeting Piper's eyes again he spun around and jogged off the field, pretending he wasn't doing exactly what he always accused Piper of—running away.

***

Piper stormed up to West's house, his mother's tears fresh in her mind. She'd come to look after Bill, Claire had told her after West stormed off. And while Piper understood why West wouldn't be happy to see his mother—honestly—shouting at her and stomping off the pitch?

Assuring Claire she'd talk some sense into West, or at least, calm him down enough to listen to reason, she left the field five minutes after his departure. She hadn't even stopped to change out of her rugby gear. She paused in West's downstairs hallway, toeing off her boots. Well, too bad about the trail of mud across West's floor.

She climbed the stairs and pushed open his bedroom door, the splash and hiss of his en suite shower the only sound in the stillness. A quick, curious glance around the masculine pewter and white color-schemed room revealed no surprises, but the polished walnut piano beside the French doors tugged a gasp from her chest. Claire's piano— he still had it. And from the exposed keyboard and scatter of sheet music on top, it wasn't just decoration. He still played. But not since she became an unwelcome houseguest.

"Hey," she shouted. "I wanna talk to you."

"Leave me alone, Piper," West's voice rose above the running water.

He hadn't told her to "piss off" or "stop bitching at me and go back to the city." Progress, right?

"Not this time." Catching West in the shower meant she'd have a captive audience.

Knowing he wouldn't have locked it, Piper walked inside and shut the door behind her. In her imagined scenario, the steam-filled room would modestly conceal West in the shower cubicle while she talked.

She hadn't taken into account an extractor fan. No steamed-up mirrors, no fogged-up shower glass, just the whirr of the fan and the hiss of the water. Plus the tanned and very bare length of West's body. She froze beside the door and gripped the doorknob, her heart hurtling into her throat.

Thank God he faced away from her. The sight of his toned ass turned her breathing into an asthmatic wheeze. She debated a quick, quiet exit, but tossed that idea out—West was on the back foot here, since she had clothes on. Besides, the tension etched across the muscles of his back indicated he knew she was already inside.

Just keep it above neck level, say what you need to say, and get out.

She cleared her throat. "That was a crappy way to talk to your mother. You made her cry."

West pulled his head out of the spray and scrubbed water off his face. "The woman cries at a drop of a hat. It goes with her artistic temperament."

Then he turned.

Holy guacamole. Piper nearly wrenched the doorknob off the door. Her brain must've missed the memo to keep her eyes above West's neck because, hello—nicely shaped pecs, washboard flat abs, corded thigh muscles...and then her gaze skipped straight back up to his, er, expanding interest.

"True, buhht..." Her tongue unfurled to her knees when West rubbed a bar of soap over his chest, never taking his direct, blue gaze from her.

"So you barged in here to tell me I was rude to my mother?" Water sprayed over his shoulder, running down his body. His soapy hand slid from pecs to the trail of dark hair low on his belly. A happy, happy trail indeed.

"Well, I..." She licked dry lips, looked at anything other than where his hand headed, and found her mud-flecked, crimson-cheeked reflection instead.

So much for West's awkwardness at being butt naked—she was the one exposed and vulnerable. Her excuses for being there suddenly seemed lame. Under the circumstances maybe his reaction to Claire was understandable, and though she told his mother she'd talk to him, nothing was so important the conversation couldn't wait until *after* West had finished being all wet and hot and naked.

The creak of the shower door made her jump.

"Piper?" His voice, low and loaded with seduction, blazed through her.

West left the shower, water cascading off him and onto the tiled floor. She averted her gaze and turned her back, yanking on the doorknob again. It slipped through her damp fingers.

"Is this really about my mother or did you barge in here for something else?"

The spicy scent of his shower gel curled around her and the heat of his skin singed the fine hairs on the back of her arm, but still she grappled with the stubborn doorknob.

"Like because you're very, very muddy," he said.

His breath touched the back of her neck, droplets of water falling on her shoulder. "There's a clean spot here, I think."

A thumb traced the sensitive skin behind one ear and her vision blurred.

"And another here." Warm lips trailed along the curve where the cords of her neck met her shoulder.

"But on the whole—" his hand snaked around her waist, fingers spread wide across her lower belly.

Hot shivers arrowed through her pelvis and struck their target.

"—You're a dirty girl who should hit the shower—" he pressed her hips back against his body, shifting so his erection wedged intimately between her Lyrca-covered cheeks "—with me."

West untangled her fingers from the doorknob and lacing them with his own, drew them behind her body to rest on his thigh. His lips closed over an earlobe, teeth gently grazing the small fleshy edge. A protest turned into a moan when his fingers moved from her belly to gently roll a nipple through the fabric of her top. Her hips jerked back in reflex and this time it was him who moaned, his breath a harsh pant in her ear. His body shifted to one side and he wrapped her palm around a part of his anatomy, which grew larger in her hand as her grip tightened.

"God." He slid his fingers out from hers, but she couldn't seem to let go.

She should peel her hand from his slick, satiny skin and not continue to stroke her thumb up and down. Take her hand off his body and get the hell out of this situation. Yet her weak limbs refused to fight as his breathing, ragged and harsh, puffed against her nape.

"Piper...I need you."

Those four words transfixed her because in this moment, when things hurtled out of control for them both, he needed her to be his anchor.

And she needed him.

"Shower. Now." She gasped when his hand slid under her tee shirt.

West scooped her off her feet and transplanted her there before she could change her mind.

The pink tee shirt splattered on the floor outside the shower, closely followed by her Lycra shorts, and black sports bra, leaving her in only a tiny black thong. West backed her into the shower corner and kneeled before her, drawing the scrap of fabric down her legs and stopping to kiss a pair of freckles just below her pubic bone. His gaze when it returned to hers was hot and intimate, but this couldn't be anything other than the two of them taking the physical release they needed.

"You played rugby in a thong?" The stubble on his chin rasped along her inner thigh, his breath teasing the sensitive flesh hidden by soft curls. Her knees went gelatinous, and leaning against the glass cubicle she prayed they'd hold her weight.

"No panty line."

"Mmm. I noticed." His forefinger and thumb ran down the "v" of her sex, gently spreading the folds apart.

Her hands clutched at West's shoulders and she swore it was the lack of oxygen in such a small space that gave her voice a sex-kitten breathiness. "You're such a pervert."

"Baby, you've no idea." He rubbed a knuckle against her inner lips, carefully avoiding the swollen bundle of nerves, which cried out for his attention.

Hips thrusting forward, a moan escaped from deep inside. "Please."

He stroked the very tip of his tongue to her core and at the same instant slid two fingers inside her. Little stars flashed behind her closed lids. If he got her any hotter she'd melt into a pool of goo and be lost down the drain.

"Feels good, huh?" He pulled back slightly to support her butt with one hand as she sagged against the shower wall.

"Feels okay." She transferred her grip from his shoulder to his dripping hair. "But maybe I should clean up. I'm still covered in mud." And because if he didn't remove those slowly thrusting fingers, she would come in the next two minutes.

West's low rumble of amusement sent flickers of molten heat into her womb. He leaned in to nip her thigh.

"Trust me, Pipe, this bit isn't." And he buried his face between her legs, making a liar out of her in less than half her estimated time.

Piper tasted of musk and the sweetest, earthiest honey. Her juices on West's lips addled his brain and throbbed all the way down to his straining cock, which begged for the opportunity to swap places with his tongue. Her little mews of pleasure vied for dominance over the hiss of falling water. He'd waited half a lifetime to taste her and even though her hand fisted in his hair hard enough to leave a bald patch, nothing would pull his mouth away.

She convulsed around his fingers, moaning his name over and over. West stood, pinning her to the wall to keep her from a boneless slide to the shower floor. Kissing her again, the knowledge she would taste herself on his tongue almost undid his resolve not to come like a horny teenager on his first sexual encounter. Need roared through him at her dazed look when he gently rolled the pebbled bud of her nipple before sliding his palm over her soft flesh.

God, she was so damn beautiful.

Piper's eyes fluttered half shut and she hooked a leg around his hip. Her hand snaked between their slippery flesh, found him and stroked, her thumb circling the pearl of moisture that wasn't from the spray. She tugged him closer, angling her pelvis so he nudged intimately against her.

"Wait—condom." With a groan West eased her back, dropping his head to suckle on the nipple he'd toyed with. "Don't move. I'm not finished with you yet."

"I hope not."

Pure male satisfaction zipped through him at Piper's shaky voice.

He stepped out of the shower, dripping rivers of water across the floor into his bedroom. Sliding open the drawer in his nightstand, he spied the small, rectangular, and unopened box. Bingo.

While his impatient fingers scrabbled over the cellophane wrapping, other sounds penetrated the lust-fog in his brain. A car engine turning into his driveway. Donny's joyful greeting bark. A car door slamming and Ben's voice shouting, "See ya, Ford."

Shit, shit, shit!

West dived back into the bathroom, caught a glimpse of Piper stroking soap over the swell of her ass and groaned. "Ben's here."

She looked over her shoulder with huge eyes. "What? *Here* here?"

"Downstairs, here. Ford just dropped him off."

"Oh, crap. He'll likely come up to check on you—"

"Exactly. I'll divert his attention while you swap bathrooms."

Piper twisted the shower mixer and the water cut off.

"But what about you? What about your...?" she waved in the direction of his cock, left splendidly and uselessly waving in the breeze.

"I think your brother's arrival will take care of that." He cast one last longing look at the bubbles sliding over her bare breasts, snatched a towel from the rail and exited the room.

Fuckity, fuckity, fuck. He wanted her so much he thought his head would explode.

Drying his body in four swipes of the towel he hauled on a pair of shorts, just as Ben rattled around in the downstairs hallway.

"You better not have hogged all that hot water, West. I know how you are in the shower."

Blown away was how he'd been in the shower. Blown away and about to have the hottest sex of his life.

So the last thing he'd do before he died of sexual frustration was to kill his best friend.

***

Horniness and desperation destroyed any sensitivity and understanding as West contemplated sorting his parents out.

He strode down the hill toward Due South, Donny trotting at his heels with a dumb, gleeful expression on his ugly mug. Good for Donny. Donny wasn't sexually frustrated because Piper disappeared into his office and wouldn't come out, and her big lug of a brother had settled in for the afternoon at the kitchen table doing accounts.

At least the rain had eased off, the sun deigning to make an appearance. His steps slowed as he approached the beachfront. Toddlers paddled in the gentle surf. Girls sprawled on beach towels, and guys played with a Frisbee, or tossed rugby balls back and forth.

A woman in oversized sunglasses and a red bikini gave him a once over, her lips curling in silent invitation. He could take her up on it, find his release at her B&B or hotel room. Scraps of spandex hugged her full breasts and even from this distance, the outlines of her nipples jutted through the thin fabric.

He thought of the perfect handful of Piper's breasts and turned away. He didn't want a nameless woman to perform a perfunctory twenty-minute sex act with. He wanted the connection he'd had with Piper. A bone-deep, all-consuming, block-out-the-world connection that transformed what they'd done in the shower from sex act to something else. Making love.

They walked to Bill's place, Donny making a half-assed attempt to chase a seagull before brushing up against West's leg with an inquiring stare.

"Yeah, listen to me." West scratched the dog's head. "What would I know about making love? It's just sex. Sex with someone you know is better than with a stranger, right?"

And why ask his dog for an opinion? Jesus, he was totally losing it. Time to pack those thoughts into a mental locker and bolt it shut.

He tapped on Bill's open front door and without waiting for a reply, walked inside. "Yo, anyone home?"

Once, the front hallway had been scented with lemon furniture polish and the mysterious bowls of dried leaves his mother religiously changed every few months. Nowadays the hallway leading to the kitchen at the back of the house stunk of damp wool and sweaty shoes.

Except today it didn't.

Today no balled-up old socks lay scattered in corners, no shoes piled around an empty plastic crate, and no dirty mugs remained on the kitchen table as he entered the room. The drapes were flung wide open and sunshine poured inside—highlighting the absence of dust that usually coated the cabinetry. Chugging, spinning noises came from the tiny laundry off the kitchen.

His mother, stationed at the kitchen sink, held up a mug with one pink rubber-gloved hand, looking for stains to banish, no doubt.

"Ah, there you are, Ryan," she said, like she'd just returned from a quick trip to Oban's grocery store down the road, instead of thirteen years spent in L.A. "I wondered when you'd show up. Feel better after a shower?"

An image of Piper riding the crest of her orgasm flickered into his mind, but he caught it and stuffed it back into the same mental locker. "Sure."

Claire placed the mug on the drying rack and peeled off the rubber gloves. She must've caught him staring, as she said, "Bill's never liked housework even though he keeps his workplace spotless, so I came prepared."

"I can see that."

She came around the edge of the counter and before he could move out of the way her warm fingers gently probed his temple.

"Ow—hey." He jerked away from her touch.

She tutted, but didn't reach for his face again. "You've a cut there. I'll just get my first aid—"

"Claire." His tone halted her in mid-turn.

She glanced back at him over her shoulder. Deep grooves bracketed her mouth as her lips pinched together. Hell, when had his mother gotten old? He prepared to gentle his voice and explain that he didn't need her to fuss, when she cut in first.

"I forget you're all grown up. You don't need Band-Aids and a bit of candy to make it better now."

They studied each other for a moment before Claire sighed and waved a hand to the door leading off the kitchen. "Your dad's just having a rest. I'll make tea."

West sat staring out the window to the tiny yard, then back to the empty spot at the dining table opposite where Del had fired green peas at his head in a silent but violent war. Dad or Ma often caught them at it and half the time joined in the battle.

That hadn't happened much in the last few years before his mother and brother left. Dinners were terse blocks of time where his parents instructed him or Del to, "Ask your mother to pass the butter," or "Tell your father about your weekend plans." And if the two of them weren't in a snubbing phase, there were shouting matches followed by his mother's tears and his father's stoicism.

Claire placed a steaming mug on the table and then a plate of chocolate chip biscuits.

He looked up, incredulous. "You baked biscuits. *Already*"

She shrugged. "I'm American, and a mom. We bake and clean house in times of stress."

West snagged one, dunked it in his mug and bit off half. "Bill probably shouldn't be eating these."

"No. That's why I've boxed up the rest for you to take home." While he worked through his second biscuit, she added, "I could never understand why you'd ruin a good cookie by sticking it in hot tea."

"It's a Kiwi thing, like gumboots, and the All Blacks. And we call them *biscuits*, not cookies."

"Well, blow me down, ay? Good onya mate, I'd best remember that while I'm here," she said in a terrible attempt at a Kiwi accent.

West swiped the last biscuit off the plate. "Talk like that at the pub and someone'll stick you on the next ferry."

Humor drained from her gaze as she studied him across the table. "Like you, Ryan?"

He tipped his chair back on two legs, part of him waiting to see whether she'd swat him on the kneecaps like she once used to. Dragging both hands down his stubble-roughened jaw, he tried to assemble his thoughts into coherency after a blast of mixed emotions cartwheeled through him by sitting there eating her damn cookies.

"Why are you here, Ma?"

Instead of answering, she rested her arms on the table. "What has Bill told you about his health?"

"That the specialist's said his kidneys aren't working too well."

"It's worse than that." Her voice was gentle. "Bill needs dialysis treatment—once a week to start with—and we need to look into the possibility of finding a donor in the future."

Bill Westlake, tough as a dried out pot roast, the one constant in his life, the man who'd never given up on him throughout his revolting teenage years, who made him manager when he was twenty-five so he'd be his own boss—*his dad* was sick enough to need a kidney transplant?

His chair banged down on all four feet and he swore viciously.

"So. To answer your question, that's why I'm here."

"To donate a frickin' kidney?"

"I'll get tested to see if I'm a match, but since I'm not a blood relative, the odds are slim. I'm here to look after him—and to help out at the hotel if I can."

"You didn't have to travel thousands of miles. I'll see to Bill. You have a life back in LA."

Claire's face crumpled and she dropped her gaze. "Not much of a life since Lionel died."

Ah, hell. What was he supposed to say? Sorry for the loss of the man you dumped me and Dad for? He'd never met Lionel or Lionel's daughter, Carly, his unknown stepsister. On his one trip to LA in his early twenties, he'd battled to re-establish some kind of relationship with Del, but he refused to make contact with his mother and her new family.

West braced for the histrionics. "Yeah, that must've been hard."

But his mother remained dry-eyed and sipped her tea. "Yes, it was. I looked after Lionel until the end and when Glenna phoned me to tell me how sick Bill was...I had to come. I needed a break from all the memories in LA and I couldn't lose another husband."

"He's your ex-husband."

"And a good man and right now he needs me."

"He needed you *then*." West nailed her with a jab of his finger as his gut took him back to the day he awkwardly hugged his mother and Del goodbye at Oban's tiny airport. "But you shed your husband and eldest kid like a fucking pair of out of fashion shoes thirteen years ago. We don't need your bleeding-heart pity now."

"Enough, West," Bill said from the kitchen doorway. He plopped onto the seat next to Claire with a gusty sigh. "Don't talk to your mother like that. We settled our differences years ago and her being here is none of your business."

"Your health makes it my business. You're head chef and Shaye's not ready to step into your shoes."

Bill thumped a fist on the table and glowered. "She won't have to, boy, because I can still work part-time on the days I'm not travelling to the hospital. And stop talking about me like you're about to shop for a bleeding casket—I'm not dead yet."

Both of his parents mirrored each other's folded arms and scowls. Since when did Bill side with the woman who'd walked out on him? *On them?*

West stood. "Well, if you're staying, I'll take your bags up to my place. You can have my room and I'll take the sofa until we can figure something out."

Bill and his mother shared a glance.

"Your mother's in the hotel at the moment, but once I get some of the lads in to clear some of the piles of junk from the spare room, she'll sleep there." Bill said.

"What? You're letting her move back in?"

"It'll be easier for me to keep an eye on him," Claire said.

West was about to accuse his father of not just losing his kidney function but his *goddamned mind*, when Bill raised a bushy white eyebrow and said, "So, what's going on with you and the Harland girl, ay?"

West folded his arms and looked down his nose, giving his brain a chance to catch up and his tongue to unfreeze. "What has Piper got to do with anything?"

"She's living with you, isn't she?" Claire shifted in her seat to lean closer to Bill. He nudged her with an elbow.

"Piper's temporarily staying in my office—and we're just friends."

Bill snorted, rolling his head toward Claire with a wink. "Friends. Is that what folks call it now?"

West hooked a finger in the neck of his tee shirt and pulled the strangling thing away from his throat. "Don't wink at her—there's no 'it' to be calling—and even if there were an 'it' between me and Piper, we were talking about the completely different situation with you and Ma."

Babbling like a woman.

Yeah, what an effective tool to convince his parents he wasn't making a complete fool of himself over Piper. Jeez.

He ran a hand over the warm skin of his face, cringed, and gathered up the container of cookies sitting on the counter.

"Ryan," his mother said to his back. "I don't believe I've ever seen you blush."

Blushing? He wasn't blushing. It was summer and this kitchen had no air-conditioning. "I haven't got time for this. I've got work."

With as much dignity as he could muster, West tucked the container under one arm and exited the kitchen. Unfortunately, the heat of his skin didn't affect his ears ability to pick up Bill's chuckle and parting comment, "Yep, that boy's ass-over-tea-kettle for the Harland girl."

And his mother's thoughtful, "Well, you never get over your first love, do you?"

Chapter 12.

Piper's face, hot as slapped sunburn, wouldn't return to normal.

She'd have to hide in her room indefinitely, calculating dry dive statistics to keep her brain from playing a visual loop of West's naked body. Man, that out-of-this-world orgasm must've ruptured a few brain cells, because dive statistics just weren't working.

Off-key singing drifted out of the kitchen and the piercing trill of the phone was cut off by her brother's impatient, "Yep?"

How would she ever look Ben in the eye without him guessing what she'd been up to with his best mate? How could she ever look West in the eye? She'd thrown herself at him, and if it weren't for Ben's terrible timing she'd be in West's bed right now.

Doing stuff.

Stuff that flamed her face again when thinking about what stuff they could've been doing.

Incredible orgasm or not, her body still ached for West's touch. She was hollow, craving the sensation of his body moving against hers, *inside* hers. But allowing these desires to multiply did nothing to stem the cold little voice asking, *Are you sure West wanted you? Or were you just a convenient alternative to him jerking off in the bathroom again?*

Piper studied her distorted reflection in the office window. Wild spiked hair, because she hadn't thought to run a comb through it yet. A pair of rumpled knee-length shorts. Her tee shirt pulled over damp skin and clinging to her half-an-apple-sized breasts.

She snatched her comb off the desk and dragged it through her hair, the scratch of its teeth on her scalp a welcome distraction from the sick feeling flooding her stomach.

What had West thought when he'd touched her breasts? Was she still too boyish and angular for him? Had he compared her to the more well-endowed women he'd slept with? Women who weren't still shaped like a kid's pencil-drawn stick figure.

God. No wonder he'd made no effort to get rid of Ben and had rushed from the house.

Two sharp taps on her door.

"Piper? You ever coming out?" The words contained a smidgen of anxiety—a Ben-ish way of checking she wasn't hurt.

She opened the door. "I was resting. My stomach's still a bit sore."

Ben leaned against the hallway wall, keeping his weight on his good leg. "Gav's not the most popular guy around town at the moment."

"And West's hailed as a hero, righteously defending the poor city girl who took a tumble. I could've dealt with the great dickless wonder once I'd caught my breath."

Ben's unflinching brown-eyed gaze nailed hers. "West's actions weren't about defending some random girl on the opposite team."

"Sure they were." Piper crossed her arms up high, tucking her fingertips under her arms. "If it'd been Shaye or one of the other women Gav had gone after, he would've done the same."

Ben snorted. "You see him lay into Ford when he accidently tripped Holly? Or even Gav the first few times he shoved Kezia?" Ben's voice roughened on the last example, an undercurrent in the tone of his words. "He went after Gav like a psycho, because Gav hurt what he considers his."

Her fingers curled into fists, knuckles stabbing into her armpits. Oh Lord, Ben had picked up the sexual tension throbbing between her and West after all. Surely he hadn't guessed everything though?

"West has no claim on me and vice-versa." She angled herself to slip past him.

Ben moved forward, blocking her exit with a hand on either side of the doorway. "Then perhaps you should clarify that? Make sure he understands you're still leaving in less than a month's time—that you're only a temporary distraction."

Piper's heart, only moments ago leaping at the thought of West's male possessiveness, plunged to the floor, a leaden weight. "He knows. But thanks so much for your concern."

"I am concerned—for both of you. Tell me you'd give up your life in Wellington to stay here with West in the 'dead-zone' as you called it, in the place where Dad died—"

"Dad's got nothing to do with this—"

"No?" Ben's bulk towered over her in the doorway as her shoulders hunched. "Then why is it you've been here almost three weeks and you've never once visited his memorial."

"How do you know whether I've been up there or not?"

"Have you?"

She shook her head, blinking away the image of an engraved plaque set in a rock pile at Oban's cemetery. River rocks, smooth and speckled grey, a cairn marking empty ground because her father's body had never been recovered.

"You're right," she said after a strained moment passed. "But speculating about whether I could, or would, live on Stewart Island again is irrelevant, because I am only a temporary distraction for West. There's nothing between us except a knee-jerk attraction, no more serious than all the other one-nighters I imagine you both indulge in."

"And if you think you deserve that from West, it's another reason you should keep your distance."

Piper stood in front of him, drilled a sharp finger into his chest. "What if he's a temporary distraction for me, too? What if I just want hot, uncomplicated sex with West to take my mind off the boredom of being here?"

Ben recoiled with a grimace. "Jeez, Stubby. Too much information."

Pressing her advantage, she gently shoved him so she could exit the room. "You brought it up. And get over yourself—I'm not a twenty-seven-year-old virgin, and this isn't the Dark Ages. I can have sex with anyone I like."

"So, go have it with someone other than West. There's plenty of other guys in Oban." He jerked back and smacked his forehead. "What am I telling you? Just save everyone the anxiety and keep your legs crossed until you're back in Wellington."

"Yeah, that'll help."

Ben sighed and leaned against the wall again, tipping his head back until it thunked against it. "I'm not telling you what to do and I'm not going all big-brother-ish on your ass—well, maybe a little. But picking up where you and West left off nine years ago is a ridiculous idea—and stop gawking, I've always known you two have a history—so you're fooling yourself if you think you can do the friends-with-benefits thing and walk away without one or both of you getting fucked up."

Like she'd been left fucked up last time. But if Ben knew it, who else did? Piper swallowed the thorny lump in her throat. "You know, I think that's the most you've said to me in one conversation since I've been back. If you weren't so immune to genuine warm emotion, I'd think you actually cared."

"Hmmph." Their gazes clashed, but Ben kept his lips tucked together in a hard line. Finally he pushed himself away from the wall. "That was Mum on the phone before. She wants you to stop up there and deliver a casserole to Bill and Claire."

"Great. Another golden opportunity to be given the third degree," she grumbled.

"It's all part and parcel of being in the Harland family. And like it or not, you're part of this family."

"It sure doesn't feel like it most days."

"Feelings have sweet stuff-all to do with fact, as Dad would've said." Ben limped away to the kitchen, his voice drifting back out through the open doorway. "Sucks to be on the other side of the two-way glass, ay, Constable Harland? Wait till Mum hits her stride. You'll beg for the thumb-screws."

Her brother spoke the God-honest truth.

Piper tugged on her cap and headed to her mother's, ostensibly for the casserole but aka The Oban Inquisition.

***

Piper knocked on the back door of her mother's house and entered to find her bustling around in her kitchen.

"Darling, I've told you, you don't need to knock."

"Habit, otherwise my mind starts thinking it's B and E."

"Breaking and entering? Ooh, did I get it right?" Her mother rinsed a pile of peeled potatoes in the sink. "I watch that reality police show sometimes. It's so exciting."

If you didn't take into account the daily drudge of paperwork, drunks, verbal abuse, paperwork, the mundaneness of checkpoints, juveniles who knew enough about their rights to be a pain in the rear, and paperwork—yeah, it could appear her life was full of car chases, drug busts, and foot races with bad guys.

But why disillusion her mum? "You got it—" she said with a quick smile. "B and E, breaking and entering."

"This is your home too—you don't have to worry about *B* and *E*. You're always welcome." Glenna sent a keen glance in her direction as she lined up the washed potatoes next to the chopping board.

Piper moved farther into her mother's lair, leaning on the island counter in front of her. "So, the Westlakes' casserole?"

"All in due time. Take a seat." She nodded at the three bar stools by Piper's legs. "I've got to boil and mash these spuds for the cottage pie, then a quick bake in the oven at three hundred and fifty—" Glenna caught Piper's eyes glazing over and chuckled. "Or gas mark 4 if you're on The Mollymawk."

"Still going on about it, are you?" Piper slumped on one of the barstools. "I'll never live it down."

"Not likely." Glenna slid a knife from the rack and picked up a potato. "Luckily your knight in shining armor saved the day, hmm?" She leveled a *you may as well tell me now* stare at Piper and chopped the first potato in half without glancing down.

How her mother could multi-task interrogating while controlling a lethal instrument was a skill to be envied. Unless she was the one being interrogated. But Piper had experienced many variations of her mother's fishing techniques growing up, so she replied with a neutral, "Wasn't it, though?"

"Ryan's a good man."

And would she disagree? Not a chance.

Piper affixed a bland expression on her face. "Yes. And it's generous of him to help Ben out."

"Hmmph." Chop, chop. One potato quartered. "Kind, also, to let you stay so long with him."

"Very kind," she agreed.

Chop. "And you're being a thoughtful guest?"

"Yep."

"You're not leaving your stuff around? No make-up cluttering the bathroom vanity or bras drying over the towel rail?"

Chop. Chop.

Like Piper's boring B-cup sports bras would incite a lustful response from West. "No, Mum, I'm keeping my underwear out of sight."

Glenna's mascara-slicked lashes lowered as her gaze turned speculative. *Oh, here we go.* Bringing out the big guns from under her sweet apron with the embroidered flowers on the pocket.

"I see the way you look at him."

She could plead ignorance and ask, "What way?" but she didn't know if she had enough of her mother's acting talent to pull it off with a straight face. Safer to remain silent.

"It's the same way you looked at him way back then." Glenna picked up another potato and positioned it on the board, resting the knife along its length. She paused and looked down at the utensil in her hands. "You look at West the same way I looked at Michael when we were young. He was my first love too, you know."

"Mum." Piper slid off the barstool and moved around the counter.

Her hand hovered an inch from her mother's shoulder and she tried to push past the blockage in her mind and go in for a bear hug. But she saw him there—her dad—in the same position, his big, broad shoulders filling the kitchen, Glenna's laughter as he tugged her into his arms, running his stubbled jaw along her neck, kissing her soundly.

In the years since her father's death she'd never once heard Glenna say his name. She always referred to him as "your father," or "my husband," or "Mr. Harland."

Never "Michael."

Glenna dropped the knife and caught Piper's hovering hand, pressing the back of Piper's fingers to her flushed cheeks. "I spotted this thing between you and Ryan before either of you did, so don't look so surprised."

Piper moistened her lips. "You did?"

Her mother nodded, squeezing Piper's hand. "Here, you finish these, I'm shaking."

"Sure." She patted Glenna's shoulder. "Why don't you pour us a glass of wine?"

"Before three in the afternoon?"

"After the day I've had, Mum, I think we can risk moving Happy Hour forward a little."

"Chardonnay, then?"

"Perfect."

While her mother poured the wine, Piper chopped potatoes and transferred them into a pot.

Glenna slipped onto a barstool and slid a glass of wine across the counter. "You were fifteen."

Piper looked up from filling the pot with water. "What?"

"When West noticed you weren't just Ben's little sister anymore." She leaned forward, lacing her fingers under her chin. "It was on one of those picnics we used to go on to Kahurangi Bay. Your father—I mean, Michael—insisted on bringing a bunch of Ben's friends along for a seafood feast. Do you remember that day?"

Actually, she'd blocked it from her mind, stomping it underfoot when they'd taken the three couples to Kahurangi Bay. The day Glenna mentioned, *that day*, should come with its own disclaimer: Piper's most mortifying moment. Ever.

She took a *big* swallow of wine. "I remember."

"You were wearing that cute little bikini and you just had to compete with the boys who were diving off the top of Michael's boat—"

"Mum—"

"And you can't have knotted the top's ties properly—"

"—that, and I had absolutely no boobs to keep the top in place. Gawd."

The memory yawned open—standing on top of the highest point of her dad's boat, looking down into the clear water, droplets sparkling in the sun as the group of teenagers dog paddled and frolicked below. West staring up at her, the grin on his face making her shiver, making her feel warm in places that should've been cold from the water below.

"Watch me!" she shouted and propelled herself off the cabin into a cannonball, hoping to splash a tidal wave of water over West and the other boys.

She had.

Only, losing her bikini top in the process hadn't been part of the plan. The others hooted and whistled, while West swam over, told her to hold on to the boat's ladder while he clambered on-board and grabbed the nearest tee shirt, which happened to be his Chilies one.

"Well, *boobs* or not, I saw the way he looked after you that day, the way he looked at you."

Piper transferred the pot to her mother's stove and turned on the element. "I think we've established that West is a kind man, that he used to be a kind boy."

Glenna shook her head, the gold hoops in her ears swaying. "He wasn't just being kind that day. You were so embarrassed you never noticed."

"So, how did he look at me then, Mum?"

"Like you were his."

The blossom of warmth in her chest solidified into a hot throb. Once she'd thought that too. She'd thought they'd belonged together. That West would one day own Due South and she'd help her dad and Ben run dive tours. They'd get married under the colorful blooms of a fuchsia tree and tell their future kids about how their mum and dad started off as mates, and ended up as soul-mates.

The hero-worshiping dreams of true love, as seen through the eyes of a fifteen-year-old. A wildly gullible fifteen-year-old, as it turned out.

"And he's looking at you that way again." Glenna raised her wine-glass at her. "Point in case, the way he went after Gav today."

"I've already had this conversation with Ben. West just did the macho guy thing and you're both reading way too much into it." Wiping her hands on the kitchen towel, Piper picked up her wineglass.

"And whatever happened back when we were teenagers is ancient history.

"So something *did* happen back then."

Crap. Once again she'd underestimated her mother's sneakiness. She took another swallow of wine, wondered what the reaction would be if she drained the whole glass and poured another.

"You used to tell me everything," Glenna sighed. "How Johnny Martin screamed like a girl when you scared him. How Jake Cummins promised to write you when his family left Oban and how he never did."

Piper forced out a laugh. "Oh puh-lease, Mum. I was like twelve— naturally I told you everything."

And she'd continued over the years to tell her mother about the Johnny Martins and the Jake Cummins clones that came and went in her life. The terrible blind date who thought her being a cop meant she'd get his traffic violations wiped. The funny, and sometimes plain weird, anecdotes from her job that her mum enjoyed. She populated her phone calls with these kinds of stories.

"You didn't tell me how West broke your heart just before Michael died."

Piper lowered her glass to the counter with shaky hands. "How did you know that?"

"Puh-lease, as you say. I am your mother. You think I didn't notice when you'd been crying all night? That I didn't notice West stopped coming by the house?"

"Did Dad know that we were, ah, more than friends?"

"I don't think so."

"I'm surprised you didn't tell him."

Glenna rotated the wineglass stem between her fingers. "Your father had other things going on at the time."

"His preoccupation with the free-diving Nationals?"

"Yes. That was certainly on his mind."

Piper remained silent, but the one question she'd never found the courage to ask burned on her tongue. "Mum." She lifted her gaze to see her mother watching her with shiny eyes. God. But if she didn't ask now, she never would. "Before I left Oban you told me that you and Dad had an argument, and that you went to the Komeke's late that night and slept in their spare room."

Her mother nodded, continuing to fiddle with the stem of her glass.

"A year later at the inquest you told the court you argued over finances. That he accused you of spending too much money on your little fripperies."

Her mother nodded again.

Piper kept her voice pitched low and even. "You lied at that inquest, didn't you?"

A fat teardrop spilled over her lashes. "I—I—" Her chest hitched, snatching the rest of her words away as more tears fell.

"Dad never once complained about the money you spent. I remember he always told you to splurge on something nice for yourself."

Her mother sniffed. "He was a generous man."

"What did you really fight about, then?"

Glenna drained the last of her wine and shoved the glass away. "His diving. His blasted free-diving. Oh, it was an awful, *terrible* argument, and I—" her mother's voice cracked "—I told him, 'You're too old and foolish to still be doing this.' The look on his face, darling, I just crushed him."

Piper's breath evaporated, imagining her proud and stubborn father's reaction to *that* accusation. "Jesus, Mum."

With legs filled with jelly, Piper stumbled to the dining table and slumped into a chair. Her fingers splayed over her breastbone, tried to keep her heart from pulsating right out of her chest. "So you left Dad?"

What had her father thought as they'd chugged through the cool morning fog into Paterson Inlet to his favorite diving spot? After a massive fight with his wife, he still chose to free-dive?

Scratching around the edges of her memories, she unearthed some discrepancies which before now she couldn't explain. He'd seemed quieter that morning, subdued and lock-jawed—she assumed his unusual surliness was due to her mood turning his sour. Could his focus, split between his wife and the need to concentrate, be part cause of her dad's fatal dive? It didn't excuse her culpability, but she now had a possible explanation for what may have gone wrong.

Glenna hiccoughed, slid off the stool and came to sit next to her. "We needed time apart so we could talk things through when we were calmer. I came home the next morning, and found you both gone."

"But you and Dad never fought."

"Of course we did." Glenna retrieved a tissue from the pocket of her apron and delicately blew her nose. "All couples disagree, especially when you have the Harland temper to contend with. Michael and I learned to disagree quietly."

Piper sat glued in place at the table, studying the pattern of the wood grain. "You never told me."

"I never told anyone. No one needed to know that I'd tried to shame such a proud man into changing because I was petrified of losing him." She flung up a hand and shrugged. "And what use afterwards, when the love of my life had gone? So I've lived with the bitter words of our last argument every day for the past nine years and I've learned to make my peace with them."

Piper looked up. "He loved you and he knew you loved him. He would've known it was a silly fight, that you'd be back in the morning."

Glenna's gaze cut away from her and she drew in her lower lip with her teeth, her fingers twisting the tissue into a little ball. "Yes." She laid her hand over Piper's. "And he loved you kids too. He'd have been so proud of you all."

Her father would've been proud of Shaye, pursuing her dream of becoming Due South's head chef, and of Ben, for taking over the family dive business, even with this major setback.

But, her?

Following in his footsteps, becoming a cop whether he wanted her to or not. And taking it farther, fighting the odds to become a police diver so that other families wouldn't face a memorial stone that sat on bare earth, no body beneath.

Would he be proud of her? *Maybe.*

But maybe he would've cursed his middle child who left him to float away from his wife and family because she was so brokenhearted she forgot to check her dive watch at a critical moment.

Glenna squeezed her hand. "Well, that's enough doom and gloom, don't you think? We were talking about you and West."

"Right. Me and West." Piper shifted on the hard dining chair.

Changing the topic back to West seemed less painful than their shared grief, though no more resolvable, at least in her mind. "It won't work between us. His life is here in Oban, mine is back in Wellington—I'm a cop, remember?"

"Pffft." Glenna flapped her hand. "You're a woman first *and* you have strong feelings for him—" She held up a finger when Piper tried to object. "Uh-uh, I know you do and I'm not asking you to tell me about them, just be aware Oban does have a police presence here. Or I'm sure Ben would love to have his sister as a business partner—should you ever get weary of B and E shenanigans."

Her mother was seriously suggesting she stay? Transfer to the Oban police department or partner up with Ben? Exactly how much wine had Glenna drunk?

"Mum, the island's not big enough to support two full-time officers and I don't think Noah Daniels has any plans to move on. And as for Ben..." Piper's voice trailed off and she raked a hand through her hair.

She couldn't say Ben still blamed her for their father's death, not without her mother cornering him to try and smooth things over. "We don't see eye to eye. I can't see how we could ever work together."

Glenna chuckled and then surprised her by leaning over to give Piper a smacking kiss on her cheek. "Can't see, can't see. Of course you can't see how it could work between you and West, or how to bridge the gap between you and your brother. You're like your dad in some ways; you're blind to what's important. Sometimes your heart sees more than your eyes, my darling."

"Sounds like something out of a cheesy Hallmark card." West's name mentioned alongside the words "strong" and "feelings" caused a funny flutter in her belly. She'd pretend it was a wine buzz.

"Doesn't make them any less true." Glenna stood up and smoothed Piper's hair. "Now, how about we have a little cooking lesson? You don't want to make the same mistake twice now, do you?"

"No, I certainly don't." Piper followed her mother back into the kitchen.

Did she have feelings for West? Her mind skittered away, but she forced it back to impartially examine the question. Feelings? *Strong* feelings, even? Did she want something more than the casual sex she'd mentioned to Ben? Could she be with West and then a few weeks later hitch on her backpack and hop on board the ferry without a backward glance?

Piper tuned out Glenna's running commentary on oven temperatures and the difference between baking and grilling.

You don't want to make the same mistake twice.

But which had been her mistake the first time? Falling in love with West, or walking away from him without a fight?

And which mistake was she at risk of making *this time*?

***

Dragged, not kicking but definitely disagreeing, to the Waitangi Day beach party later that evening, Piper was sandwiched between Erin and Bree on a blanket overlooking the bonfire. Kezia sat in front of her, using Piper's shins as a backrest while they watched Zoe and a few other kids finish an enthusiastic game of cricket. Holly and Shaye disappeared into the crowd to the picnic tables set up with soda, juice and snacks.

"So, now your baby sister's gone, tell us desperate old spinsters when you're going to make a move on you-know-who?" Erin said from her left.

"Watch who you call old and desperate," Bree said on her right.

"And I'm not a spinster. I'm a widow. Widow trumps spinster." Kezia jerked upright, cupping her hands around her mouth, "Hey, George wasn't out, ref!"

Ben, farther along the beach and nominated informal referee because of his cast, raised a crutch and shook his head.

"What is *wrong* with your brother's eyesight?"

"Don't give her a chance to change the subject, Kez, she's a wily one." Bree nudged Piper's ribs.

Piper's nose crinkled. "Wily? Haven't you vultures picked off enough raw meat from my bones yet?"

Between the five women they'd wheedled out the basics. Yes, she was single. Yes, she thought West was hot. And yes, it was kinda sweet he'd gone all me-caveman-you-my-woman at the game earlier. No, that didn't mean they were bumping uglies. And no, there was absolutely no sign of wedding bells. She personally vowed to disembowel anyone who suggested a whiff of the opposite within West's hearing.

Kezia reclined back on her legs again. "Ah, yes. Piper's a tough cookie, but we'll work on that, won't we, girls?"

"I volunteer to beat it out of her," Erin said.

"The only thing you beat with any success, short-ass, is egg whites." Piper closed her eyes and enjoyed the last rays of sunlight kissing her lids, the other women's friendly ribbing warming her more than she cared to say.

"Mamma, Mamma!" Zoe spilled onto the blanket with them, a tumble of limbs with a ring of tomato sauce around her lips from the barbecued sausages earlier. "Ben says I'm a real good batter and he was impressed at how far I can whack the ball."

"Fantastic, *bella*." Kezia stroked Zoe's dark curls.

"Think he'd come to school and teach us how to play better?"

"Oh." Kezia's hand stilled on her daughter's head. "I'm not sure about that."

"I'll talk to him, Zoe," Piper said. "I'm sure he'll be happy to once his ankle's better." Or the Harland women would make his life unbearable until he agreed.

"Awesome," Zoe said. "Look, there's Ford and Mr. Komeke with their guitars."

"And Laurie with his harmonica." Erin stood and brushed sand from her shorts. "On your feet girls, the entertainment's about to start—let's get our boogie on."

"What's a boogie?" Zoe stage-whispered in her mother's ear as Bree and Erin strolled toward the bonfire.

"It's dancing, you know—" Kezia stood, slapped a hand on her hip and finished with a *Saturday Night Fever* flourish.

Zoe giggled, briefly clapping her palms over her eyes. "Oh, *Mamma!* Nobody dances like that anymore—and anyway, I want to dance with Ben."

"*Bella*, I don't think Ben will be dancing, with his sore foot."

Zoe bounced to her feet and took off toward the bonfire, tossing over her shoulder, "I'm gonna ask West, then."

"You coming?" Kezia turned back to her, a half-smile still on her face.

Piper wrapped her arms around her knees. "I'll just enjoy the music from here. Dancing's not my thing."

Kezia hesitated. "I'll keep you company, then."

Piper shook her head. "No way. You go and keep a cat fight from starting—your girl's already herded up all the good-looking men to dance with."

"Oh, Lord." Kezia looked over at her daughter, who was indeed in the midst of West, Noah, and Joe.

Ford, Rob, and Laurie played an old bluesy classic and couples drifted onto the hard-packed sand, their silhouettes swaying in the firelight. A little girl danced with a man in a white shirt, her fingers clutching the ropy muscles of his forearms as he spun her giggling around the makeshift dance floor.

West, dancing with Zoe, scooping her up in a spin, the girl's arms wrapped around his neck. The sight sprung around her heart like a velvet-lined bear trap and her eyes teared up. Piper chewed her lip until the bitter taste of copper filled her mouth.

Kezia sat back down and without drawing attention to the two of them, slid her hand into Piper's. "You can trust me, Piper. You know it. So spill."

Piper watched them a moment longer before she spoke. "When I left here at eighteen, I thought I was pregnant. My period was late, I felt nauseous, and so I bought one of those home pregnancy tests."

"Was it positive?"

Piper shook her head, swiped at a stray tear on her cheek. "No, and that's the crazy thing because part of me wanted it to be. To have something of him that he couldn't just throw away, like he'd thrown away us."

"You thought you were pregnant with...West's baby?"

Piper nodded.

"And if you had been, that child would've been around Kezia's age now?"

Piper nodded again.

"Aw, hon. I'm sorry. But at eighteen..." Kezia squeezed her hand hard.

"I know. It would've been a total disaster. I wasn't ready to be a mum."

"And now?"

"Now if I want a kid, I should probably just look for an anonymous donor."

Zoe's high-pitched voice counting off steps carried on the breeze. She and West shuffled forward and back, left and right, the man curved protectively over her when she stumbled, patiently starting over once she regained her footing.

"That's bollocks. Look at West now—he's so good with Zoe. He'll make a great dad," Kezia said.

He'd make a great dad all right, just not in the loving family she'd once envisioned having. West would one day find a nice, voluptuous Oban woman to settle down with. They would have cute, chubby babies. She wanted to scratch that imaginary woman's eyeballs out and hurl them in the bonfire.

"To someone else's kids, sure, because he and I don't have a relationship." The words sounded stale and overused, even to her.

"Yeah, you do."

Piper couldn't see Kezia's eye roll, but she heard it.

"Crap. I suppose we do. I'm not sure what kind of *relationship* it is though, just that it's temporary—so, not one that will involve procreation."

"Uh-huh." Kezia's voice oozed skepticism. "Well, West's staring at you like he wants to *procreate* right now. Like he's planning to add you to his list of favorite foods."

Piper's gaze jerked up. West strode toward them and his gaze zeroed in on her face.

"That's a sucky metaphor, for someone who calls herself a teacher," Piper muttered from the corner of her suddenly dry mouth.

Kezia pulled her hand out from under Piper's and leaned in close. "Science is more my thing, hon—and even I can spot the chemistry between you two a mile off."

With a wink, Kezia stood, waved at West and took off to the drinks table where Zoe was attempting to wheedle another cup of soda.

West stood in front of her, sandy feet poking out of faded blue jeans, his hair tousled by the light breeze.

Sex appeal in spades.

Piper wanted to launch herself off the blanket and tangle around him like seaweed.

He extended a hand, tomato sauce fingerprints dotting his rolled up shirt sleeves. Before she could think twice, she placed her palm in his firm grip. He tugged her to her feet, not releasing her hand as they faced each other in the flickering light of the bonfire.

"Dance with me?" The rough tone of his voice translated the words to, "Have scorching hot sex with me?"

"Ah..." Her pulse spiked into an uneven rhythm at the soft sweep of his thumb over her knuckles. Tingles buzzed along the new highway formed from the nerves in her hand straight to her girly-bits.

"West, my man." Ben appeared at West's shoulder and gave him a hearty back slap. "You're not copping out on our traditional poker game tonight, are you?"

Piper tried to tug her hand away, but West gripped harder, sending more of those electric tingles skittering along that highway.

"Actually—" West said.

"Don't be a piker now." Joe appeared on his other side, bumping West's arm with his fist. "Bill warned me about you, he did."

West finally released her fingers and Piper stepped back. Tingle time officially over. But her body still hummed like a tuning fork with anticipation.

"I'm pretty hammered after the game—hey!" West snarled, flicking Ben's hand away when he patted his head.

Ben chuckled. "Aww, you poor lamb. But Doc here will provide smelling salts at the poker game in case you swoon from the agony."

"Did someone say poker game?" Kip ambled over, two teenage girls in micro board shorts trailing after him, at what they likely thought was a discreet distance. He stopped, and the girls tittered behind cupped hands. "I'm in. What time?"

"In an hour, at West's place," Ben said.

"Why does it have to be my place?" West sent her a look of apologetic frustration, telling her an hour wasn't long enough for what he had in mind.

"Because you're the boss. See you in sixty." Kip strode away, his teenage posse falling in behind.

"I'll let Noah know we're still on." With a nod at Piper, Joe wandered off in the direction of the bonfire.

"I might've forgotten and had plans," West gritted between clenched teeth.

Ben smirked, knowing exactly what plans he'd interrupted. "Poker beats any other plans you made, right Piper? You play poker with your cop buddies back in the city?"

Piper cleared her throat, swallowing the thickness gathered there from the touch of West's hand. "Not any more. I whipped their butts one too many times. But I'm game to take your money, brother dearest."

West's mouth curved in a grin that sling-shot another load of tingles south. But there'd be no shower scene replay tonight and West's rueful smile confirmed it. Maybe it was a good thing. Maybe it was the sensible thing and Ben was right. She should keep her legs crossed.

"But you're not a guy," Ben said.

"That is true." West's gaze dropped to her breasts before they returned to her face, his gaze smoldering. "Piper's definitely *not* a guy."

Her toes curled into the damp sand, legs aching to metaphorically uncross—aching to wrap around West's hips so she could grind against him. Damn him and his sexy voice that told her without words he wanted the same thing.

Ben grunted. "God's sake, West. Can't Joe give you a shot for those hormones?"

"Scared I'll fleece you, Benny-boy?" Piper cocked her chin at her brother. "We could play with jellybeans like we used to, if you'd prefer."

"Men don't play with jellybeans," Ben said.

She widened her eyes. "Nuts then? I'm sure you've some *nuts* somewhere?"

"Unlikely," West said.

Ben laughed, and for the first time the sound was laced with nothing but good humor. "Still a feisty thing, aren't you?"

"Feisty enough to empty your wallet."

"We'll see." He hop-turned on his crutch. "I better ask Shaye to play too, or we'll never hear the end of it. Oh—and West?"

West's intense gaze wrenched away from hers. "What?"

"Go and rustle up some nuts for the game, ay?"

West swore under his breath and the look he sent her before he turned away nearly set her just in case I get lucky a second time underwear on fire.

Chapter 13

West rose at dawn, sat at his piano, and hammered out Chopsticks. Since Ben's bedroom was underneath his, he hoped the bastard had the mother of all hangovers and each chord throbbed like a blister in his brain.

They'd played hand after hand of poker until four in the morning. Shaye left at one, Piper quit with her winnings at half two and disappeared into her room, and the rest of the guys staggered off just before four. Only Ben remained a little longer, giving him the stink-eye before he limped downstairs. Like West still planned to have swinging-from-chandeliers monkey sex with Piper the moment Ben's back was turned.

Tempting. But what he had in mind for Piper wasn't a quick tumble in his bed. Oh, no. When he got Piper beneath him he intended her to be panting his name and he doubted she'd be keen on a screaming orgasm if Ben listened below.

West's fingers moved over the smooth keys, sliding from Chopsticks into Chopin. He sighed as the melody wound around him, the notes unknotting the ropy tension in his shoulders. He should thank Claire for all the time she put into teaching him to play, but he'd chew his own hand off first. Over the years she never once asked about her beloved piano. Out of sight, out of mind. A bit like him and Bill.

A soft thud at his bedroom door before it swung open. His fingers stilled as Piper walked in with two coffee mugs, her hair in random wet spikes and her robe knotted around her waist. She smelled like mangoes and his conditioner again. West curled his fingers into fists so he wouldn't do something dumb—like haul her onto his lap.

"Don't stop, it was amazing." She placed one steaming mug on a small table beside the piano and cradled the other to her chest, standing by his bench seat.

He shifted along and patted the empty space. "Sit with me, then. And thanks." He nodded at the coffee.

After placing her drink next to his, she perched on the edge of the bench, keeping plenty of air between them. "I don't want to get in your way."

"You're not. Come closer."

Piper scooted over so the soft toweling of her robe pressed against his bare bicep. A pretty flush crept up her cheeks as her gaze zipped down to the open waist of his jeans he'd tugged on and forgotten to button.

"I can put on a shirt...if you want."

"No. I'm good." Her voice came out a little strangled.

West's gut dipped into a barrel roll. Piper drove him to the edge of madness as her usual ass-kicking self. But being vulnerable?

She slayed him.

"Play for me?" she said, her voice a whisper, a caress.

He wrenched his gaze away and started to play, cursing every now and then when his fingers hit a sour note. Nerves. Anyone would think he was soloing at Carnegie Hall.

West never played for the rare women he brought back to his room—though a few had asked. He smiled at their sly innuendos about the skill of his fingers and shook his head. Music revealed too much.

And yet he didn't hesitate when Piper asked. Because she knew his soul and all its scars, and wore her own hidden under a mask of bravado. Or was it just the tinkling ivories weaving silly fantasies in his head?

Each time his right hand swept across the keyboard, their arms brushed, awareness sparking the hairs to attention along his skin. He switched from classical to jazz, allowing the conflicting emotions to ooze out through his fingertips as they stroked the haunting notes of Kosma's "Autumn Leaves." When the last chord drifted away, his bare foot slid off the pedal and he turned his head. Piper stared wide-eyed at his fingers, a solitary tear tracking down her cheek.

"Jesus, Pipe." He reached for her but she slid off the bench seat too fast, standing a safe distance away.

Her palm rested against her breastbone, her fingers spread across her throat. He'd caught her off guard and something inside him softened. He ached to sweep her into his arms and take her to bed— brush the tears off her face and make her forget everything but her own name. And maybe that, too.

But not now, not like this.

"Was it me, or the music?"

"Both," her voice quavered. "I didn't know you could play like that—it was the most beautiful thing I've ever heard, and you...you're beautiful." She wrapped her arms around her waist.

"Thanks. Though I'd prefer to be called hot, or manly. God-like or generously-endowed, even better." He swiveled to face her, the boulder on his chest falling away at the small curve her lips. "But I'll take 'beautiful,' because it's better than *cute*."

"Cute, huh?" She scrubbed the last teardrop off her face. "You were cute, deadly cute, you know—back when you were five and sitting on that same piano bench in your little Superman tee shirt and teeny-tiny sandals."

He groaned. "Ma showed you that photo?"

Piper grinned, and this time her eyes creased in humor too. How had he ever labeled her smile as sweet yet sexy? It was wicked—pure wickedness with lashings of black leather and a riding crop.

"Your mother showed me more than just the piano one when I was growing up. There was baby Ryan having a bath, toddler Ryan on his potty wearing only his red gumboots, and I believe there's even one of an older Ryan streaking butt-naked along the beach at Horseshoe Bay."

Jeez. Thanks Ma for snatching away his illusion of mystique amongst Oban's eligible females. How many other people had seen Claire's dirty little stash? "Hopefully there were none of me as a teenager."

"Given your penchant for nudity, it's fortunate there weren't."

Another evil, evil grin. Her tears had evaporated, but he remained curious at her reaction. So, instead of taking the bait of a verbal sparring match, he stood, and sipped his coffee.

Her gaze zipped to the door and he pictured the cogs and gears of her mind grinding as she thought of her next quip before darting away. Because bantering was easier than talking. He should know, he'd been a bartender longer than a manager. Keep the smartass comments popping back and forth and no one got to dig below the surface.

"Why the tears, Piper?"

Her mouth flat-lined, the last curve of her lips disappearing. "What? I'm so tough I can't get girly once in a while over a movie or a piece of music?"

He cocked his head at the thread of bitterness in her tone, an icy sludge settling low in his stomach. Back then he'd fed her some line like that. Too tough, too stubborn, too boyish. And it had all been bullshit—except perhaps the stubborn part.

But he'd pulled the other two words from the air in desperation because, at twenty, he had no clue how to tell Piper he loved her. That he was terrified she'd leave for the city and never want to come back. His cowardice hurt her—and right before Michael drowned. No wonder she hated him.

West rubbed a hand over his face. "You're not so tough."

"Yeah, I am." Her lower lip trembled and she tucked her hands up higher under her armpits.

"You don't have to be, not around me."

A bitter laugh slipped through her lips. "Of all the people I need to be tough around, you're number one. You shattered me once—" She shook her head and grimaced. "You won't slip past my guard a second time."

An apology burned on his tongue, but he swallowed it. If he said those two little words, Piper wouldn't hesitate to plunge a scalpel in to try and dissect his motivations.

West rolled his shoulders to try and ease the stiffness bunching the muscles across his back. "Listen, it's a nice sunny morning. How about we go fishing?"

Piper's eyebrows winged up like he'd suggested she join him for a yoga session. Or maybe strip poker. "Fishing?"

"We'll take my little run-around out, like we used to." Rubbing a hand down the back of his neck, West met her wide-eyed stare. "When we were friends."

"We're not friends, West."

He shrugged and gave her a lopsided grin. "Fake it till you make it?"

When she said nothing, he added, "C'mon, Pipe. You and me, the screaming gulls, and a couple of rods. It'll be fun. We both could use some fun."

After a moment she uncrossed her arms. "You used to sulk when I caught the biggest fish."

"Hey, I wasn't sulking. I was quietly resigned because I knew you'd boast all over town and do that crazy happy dance." He leaned an elbow on the piano top and scanned the length of her, from the tips of her purple painted toenails, to her hair, which had dried into an interesting just-been-tumbled-between-the-sheets style. "I'd pay cash to see you do those jiggley dance moves again, baby."

"In your dreams, Westlake." With lips twitching to keep a smile at bay, Piper grabbed her mug and made a fast exit.

West drained the rest of his coffee and shut the piano lid. The thing was, now she'd reminded him of the way her body looked under those jeans and baggy tee shirts she favored, he would dream of her tonight. And every night until he managed to get his hands—and mouth—back on her.

***

"See? No sulking," West said.

Behind her sunglasses, Piper kept her eyes closed and stretched out her bare legs. The sun warmed her skin and the cool sea spray tickled as it splashed over the hull. West's boat, the thirteen-foot-long "Daisy," skimmed across the bay and headed around the tree-lined coast. Fortunately, she hadn't suffered the humiliation of puking over the side.

Yet.

Being this close to West without resorting to tart one-liners threw her off kilter. She vowed before leaving Halfmoon Bay to keep her cool and play the we're-just-friends game, like West wanted. Except it hadn't worked out well. Hyper-aware in the small space of his fishing boat, every move he made impacted her. Even while they waited for the fish to bite in amicable silence, not a moment passed when she didn't think about him. And her thoughts were far from platonic.

"And the reason why we're heading to another fishing spot around the coast?" She raised her voice over the rumble of the motor.

"Gotta give a man another chance to reel in a kahawai as big as yours." Wind ruffled West's hair and his grin stretched as wide as the horizon.

Goosebumps prickled along her arms.

So in over her head. She'd been smacked in the face with that certainty this morning after listening to him play. My God, talk about Killing Me Softly. Sneaky bastard. And trust West to have such a classy trick to seduce women.

Her mind travelled back to the previous day—West pulling her into the shower, taking her to heaven regardless of her weak protestations.

Dammit. West didn't need to trick a woman into his bed.

Piper focused her gaze on the coast, the tree line giving way to another long, sandy beach dotted with—"West!"

She lurched to her feet and West pulled down the throttle arm, the little craft slowing.

"Oh, Christ. I see them," he said.

Piper's pulse leaped as she counted the haphazard line of charcoal-colored bodies scattered along the sand, the small waves hissing onto the beach barely reaching their large, triangular tail flukes.

Twenty-six stranded and helpless whales. Pilot whales, by their resemblance to giant dolphins.

West guided the boat closer. "They're still alive. Some, anyway."

Piper grabbed the plastic bin storing the fish they'd caught, dumped the contents at her feet and chucked a couple of smaller plastic buckets inside. "I'll swim ashore and start wetting them down. You go for help."

She kicked off her sandals and tossed them into the bin. When she looked up, West stood right beside her, his face grim. He slid one rough palm along her nape and tugged her in, his lips feathering over hers with restrained fire.

"Be careful around them," he said pulling back. "I'll be as fast as I can."

She nodded like a marionette, the brief taste of him lingering on her lips. Wrenching her gaze from his mouth, she dropped the bin overboard and dived after it, the cold slash of the ocean on her skin distracting her from the urge to reel West in for another, hotter kiss.

Nearly an hour later, Piper's arms ached from lugging bucket after bucket to the twelve whales that still lived. The back of her neck stung as she hauled more water up the beach. She couldn't imagine the pain these poor creatures were in and if their skin dried out the results were a lot more serious than sunburn.

She poured the contents of the first bucket over the whale, carefully avoiding its blowhole, and bent down to meet its small black eye. "It's okay, buddy, I've got you."

Running a hand over the creature's massive flank, she grabbed the second bucket and tipped her head back to glare at the sky. Why couldn't it have poured today? Stewart Island was notorious for its four-seasons-in-one-day climate and high annual rainfall—surely on the one day it would be welcome, the island could cooperate?

From the distance, yet growing louder, drifted the growl of engines. Piper upended her bucket over the whale and jogged back to the water's edge. A fleet of boats appeared around the rocky tip of the bay—dinghies with outboard motors, larger fishing boats, and bringing up the rear, The Mollymawk—all of them filled to capacity. More volunteers on their way, thank God.

Tarryn, the new Department of Conservation worker, jumped off the first dinghy to arrive. She scanned the line of whales, some still now, as she waded onto the beach.

Expecting a blunt request for details followed by a string of orders, Piper was shocked when Tarryn grabbed her in a quick hug. "You're doing an amazing job."

Piper didn't have time to mumble more than, "Thanks," when dinghies and people and supplies descended into organized chaos across the sand.

Hours blended into a sweaty, salty blur as countless people, both locals and loopies, toiled under the sun to keep the whales hydrated. Her mother, sister, and Erin worked together on the whale next to the one she, West, and Ben claimed responsibility for. Piper had no energy to even raise an eyebrow when Ben arrived with the second wave of volunteers, a rubbish bag taped around his cast and a *don't give me any grief* scowl on his face. Everyone worked as a team and they needed each and every person if there was any hope of refloating the last nine whales on the incoming tide.

Piper spotted a duo of strangers walking amongst the crowd. The male had a monstrous camcorder on his shoulder, the blonde woman at his side held her flippy skirt down with one hand and clutched a microphone in the other. A national TV crew—just what they needed underfoot. She rolled her eyes when the woman squealed, drawing her knee up as a whale splashed a flipper in the trench dug around its body. Squatting by her whale, Piper smoothed her hand over its rounded head and murmured encouragement.

"Whale-whispering now, Pipe?" Ben hefted another bucket and poured the contents along the animal's back.

"The whale's still a better conversationalist than you."

She stood and the TV duo was directly opposite, camcorder trained on her no doubt sweaty and sunburnt face. Super. Then she looked closer at the woman, whose make-up-gunked lashes popped wide open.

Oh, hell, no. Not her!

The woman elbowed her companion in the ribs and thrust a microphone in Piper's face. "Constable Harland, isn't it? Are you here in an official capacity?"

Since when did a police diver—and Ms. Charlotte Cooper knew her occupation since she interviewed Piper after she joined the squad—officiate at a whale stranding? Piper sensed, rather than saw, her family tracking their exchange, so she kept her reply polite. "No, I'm off duty. Just helping, with everyone else."

"How fortunate you were here." Charlotte offered a piranha-like smile and with a quick hand-signal to her partner, turned to face the camera.

"Along with the many locals who have turned out to save these majestic creatures of the deep is Piper Harland," the woman's voice projected magnificently in the sudden silence. "Constable Harland is a member of the New Zealand Police National Dive Squad and the first woman to join this male-dominated and highly exclusive team of professionals—"

Piper zoned out from the rest of Charlotte's monologue, blood surfing past her eardrums in a deafening roar.

Oh, crap.

Her neck twisted in stiff increments. Shaye and her mother stood side by side, gripping each other's hands, their eyes unblinking with shock. Next to her, Ben's curled lip and furrowed brow was what she'd expect if she switched allegiance from the New Zealand All Blacks to the Australian Wallabies. Baffled disgust summed it up.

"What's she on about, Piper?" he hissed in her ear. "You're just a cop."

She lurched backward and her shoulders bumped into warm solidness, rough hands wrapping around her upper arms and squeezing. *West.* Right there to assume the role of her backbone since hers liquefied to jelly.

Piper never wanted her family to find out this way—had never intended them to find out at all. After Charlotte Cooper shoved a camera in her face the first time, she'd been prepared to spill her secret. But the reporter's interview was edited to a ten-second slot and overshadowed by the victim the squad had searched for at the time. When no one mentioned it, Piper decided to keep that part of her career under wraps. The likelihood of her appearing on camera again seemed small—police divers weren't a glamorous bunch like homicide cops—and really, who wanted to hear about people who rooted around underwater for corpses?

Now that omission came back to bite her on the ass.

"Ms. Harland, does it faze you working with all these dead things—" Charlotte startled when the whale between them blew air out of its spout "—or are you so hardened by facing death every day you feel nothing?"

Piper's breath hitched in her chest, her lungs compressing into two hard pebbles. She stared at the reporter, at the man with the camcorder's indifferent black eye trained on her, and thoughts emptied from her head.

"As you mentioned earlier, *Constable Harland* is a professional," West's voice, steady and calm, spoke from behind her. "But if you're implying police divers don't have hearts or feel compassion, then *you're* not doing *your* job professionally."

Charlotte's mouth clamped shut and she made a cutting motion to her cameraman. When he hoisted the camcorder off his shoulder, her eyes pinched into slits and she slapped her hands on her hips. "I only suggested that for you, *Constable Harland,* death doesn't hold the same meaning as it does to the general public."

Piper's mind returned to the morning her father drowned. The rush of emotions thundering through her brain, clawing out her heart, after she'd finned through the depths and glimpsed her father's face. When she'd seen his open mouth and the lack of bubbles, she'd known—intimately known—death.

"You're wrong," Piper croaked through salt-encrusted lips. "Death holds the same meaning for everyone. It's grief, and loss, and devastation. It's no less meaningful for those of us who face it every day. We're not hardened by death, we're *strengthened* by it—because in order to do what we do over and over again, it's only knowing we help the deceased's friends and family that makes our job bearable." She cleared her throat, suddenly aware of the murmurs growing louder around her.

"Somebody give this chick a soapbox." Charlotte nudged her cameraman again, but he moved aside, shaking his head.

"Watch what you say about my sister, lady," Ben growled.

"Yeah, back off, blondie." Ford's voice sounded nothing like his usual laid-back self.

"We don't like outsiders insulting one of our own." Erin stepped closer to Piper, looking like she wanted to crack something together and not a pair of eggs.

Her mother and Shaye stood beside Ben, Glenna shooting the infamous Harland death-glare at the reporter. On her other side and gathered around her and West were Ford and Erin, plus more she couldn't quite see.

Standing with her. Standing *for* her.

"I'm just doing my job." Charlotte's gaze slid sideways searching for backup from her cameraman, but her co-worker had abandoned her, trotting along the beach toward another group of whales. She hugged the microphone close to her chest and edged away.

Glenna strode forward, a warrior queen resplendent in sand-covered shorts and a jaunty bandana tied around her forehead. "Young lady, I'm proud of my daughter and your mean-spiritedness isn't welcome."

Her mother's voice was regal, but Piper didn't miss the cutting edge below the polite.

Glenna clicked her fingers in dismissal as Charlotte turned to flee. "Run along now dear. I think you're better suited to covering flower shows and squabbling politicians."

"Now that snooty cow's been put in her place, back to work people," Erin said as Charlotte speed-walked to her cameraman, her floaty and ridiculous skirt whipping around her legs.

West dropped his hands from her arms and her whole body felt bereft and cold without his quiet strength keeping her upright.

Eyes sad below the cheery red bandana, Glenna said, "Family meeting later—you too, West, since your guilty expression tells me Piper's little bombshell was no surprise."

"Police *diver*. Bloody hell." Ben tapped her arm with his fist and limped away.

"Mum..." Piper reached out a hand.

Glenna grabbed it and squeezed. "I meant what I said. I am proud of you, though I expect an explanation once we get these beasties back in the water."

West handed her an empty bucket after her mother bustled off. "You okay?"

She nodded without making eye contact and headed down to the water. Small waves bubbled over her toes, doing little to cool the heat scorching her face. A heat not caused by the sting of sunburn. Piper blinked to keep the tears at bay.

They stuck up for her—Ford and Erin, West and her mother, and even Ben. She'd somehow become one of their own again and her sense of alienation remained only as a reflection of her insecurities.

It touched her unbearably.

Piper filled the bucket. But what should she do about it? She'd carved out a life for herself in Wellington, earning the respect of her colleagues and considering herself settled. Settled, huh? Then how come a short time on the island had undermined everything?

It wasn't just coming home that rocked her foundations. Oh, no.

It was West. West had revealed the unpalatable truth.

He'd gotten to her again. Big time.

Piper started back up the beach. He wielded a spade, sand flying as he dug around the whale's body, calling orders to the other volunteers with humor and an easy tone. Taking charge of his little corner of the world, but in a way each person felt part of his team and strove to give their best. West stopped digging long enough to tug the hem of his shirt up to wipe his brow, exposing the hard planes of his stomach. He winked when he turned his head and caught her staring.

She'd never been shot on duty—never stabbed while wearing her protective vest—yet one glimpse of West's smile as he continued watching her punched with brutal force into her chest. Much like she imagined the slam of bullets would feel. Her heart kicked into a harsh, uneven rhythm and her shaking fingers slipped on the bucket's handle.

Oh, dear God. Dead woman walking.

Could she really be strong enough to leave him a second time?

Chapter 14.

Somewhere in the blue-green ocean heading away from Stewart Island swam five lucky-to-be-alive pilot whales, refloated on the tide by weary, yet jubilant, volunteers.

The joy of saving five of the twenty-six whales had drained away to sheer exhaustion and Piper slumped at her mother's kitchen table, her forehead pressed to the cool wood. Shaye and Ben encircled her, while West helped Glenna carry over cans of soda from the fridge.

"West, there's some aloe gel in the top cabinet. Could you fetch it for Piper—the back of her neck's awfully pink," her mother said.

A cabinet door opened and clicked closed again. Piper kept her eyes shut. "Touch my lobster-fried body and I'll rip your face off."

"Yeah, yeah," West replied.

A cap unscrewed and a squirt of cool gel splattered onto the back of her neck. Piper yelped, but as his fingertips spread the aloe across her skin she sighed in relief. His fingers were blissful, even if the skin he touched sizzled like it'd lost a round with a blowtorch.

"I expect you can reach any other bits without my help." West pulled his hand away and Ben snorted.

Piper lifted her forehead from the table and sat upright. Glenna pushed a Coke into her hand and its icy touch centered her. She popped the tab and drank. Best get this drama out of the way and break the simmering tension in the room.

But before she could launch into her hastily prepared explanation, Shaye said, "How can you do it? How can you look for dead people— *dead bodies*—after what happened to Dad?" Tears clogged her sister's throat.

"It's my job. It's what I'm trained to do." She looked at Shaye, begging her to understand. "They're not just bodies. They're somebody's son or sister or—" a deep breath forced air into her lungs, allowing her voice to appear firm and calm "—or father."

"Why you didn't tell us, darling?" her mother said.

Ben folded his arms, nailing her to the chair with a raised eyebrow.

"The last thing I wanted was to upset you all, to bring up painful memories, so I decided to keep that part of my life separate." Piper slanted a look at West.

He, too, sat in identical fashion to her brother, his only outward sign of tension the flicker of his fingers tapping a backbeat on his upper arm.

"You keep all the important parts of your life separate," Ben said. "It's no surprise you didn't give Mum and Shaye the full picture."

"I was trying to protect them."

"You were protecting yourself. You didn't want to defend your job choice."

"I don't have to defend my job—not to Mum and Shaye, and definitely not to you." Her core body temperature amped up. "My life, my decisions, and my choice whether to share them with people I knew wouldn't understand."

"Oh, I understand, all right." Ben's eyes sparked cold fire.

"Ben!" Glenna rapped her knuckles on the table and glared at her son. "Let your sister speak." She turned to Piper. "I'd like to hear from the beginning about the process you went through."

So, in hesitant steps, Piper described the years of intensive training put in to try and make the squad. Bit by bit, her sister and mother's stiff posture softened as she told them of the overwhelming reaction of the families when they brought a loved one home. She explained how body recovery made up only one part of her work and how she enjoyed the challenge and camaraderie of a tight-knit team. Throughout all the questions Piper fielded from Shaye and her mother, Ben and West remained silent.

"And being a police diver makes you happy?" her mother asked.

West leaned forward. A lock of hair tumbled onto his forehead and she remembered that morning—the lightness in her chest as they listened to the sigh of the ocean, the breeze ruffling their hair, the simple joy of it all.

Did being a police diver make her happy? Piper swallowed the automatic response of, "Yes, of course it does," because it didn't make her happy anymore. Now it was what she did, and what she had to do, in order to live with who she'd been nine years ago. But telling that to her family and West wasn't an option.

So she gave the same half truthful answer she'd given West.

"I'm good at what I do. There's a lot of personal satisfaction in being a squad member." Like knowing that even though she was a "girl" she could make it in a man's world. "That makes me happy."

"Hmmmph." Ben crushed his soda can.

"Yoo-hoo, anybody home?" A warbly voice from outside the back door interrupted any further comments.

Without waiting for an invitation, the back door swung open and Mrs. Taylor swept inside, her pale lavender hair-do matching the large flowers on her dress and the ribbon tied around her walking stick.

"Do come in, Betsy," Glenna said as the older woman clumped over in her orthopaedic shoes to the table, batting her powdery lavender eyelids at West.

"West, how delightful to see you, dear," she said, the sarcasm in Glenna's voice apparently flowing over her pristinely curled head.

Ben stumbled off his chair and hopped aside. "Have a seat, Mrs. Taylor."

"Oh, aren't you a gentleman! Glenna, such charming boys." She sat, edging the chair a little closer to West.

"Cold drink, Mrs. Taylor?" said Ben.

"Yes please, it's been a busy day, hasn't it?" She patted West's knee with a gnarled hand resplendent with rings.

Piper sipped her Coke. Heaven forbid the old dear fall off Oban's wharf—she'd sink like a proverbial stone.

"I'll get you one." West tried to slither off his chair, but Ben blocked him in.

"Wouldn't hear of it." He grinned at West, no doubt noticing that Mrs. Taylor's hand still rested on West's bare knee. "I'll fetch it. Lemonade in a glass?"

"That'd be grand, dear." Mrs. Taylor smiled, revealing a scary set of false teeth. "Now, Glenna. I have something exciting to tell you."

Piper and Shaye exchanged glances, Shaye's dimples appearing in the effort to keep a straight face. Unless you were part of Mrs. Taylor's church ladies, or walked around with a dangly appendage between your legs, you didn't warrant much attention in Betsy-Taylor-world.

Piper leaned back in her chair, crossing an ankle over her knee. Mrs. Taylor's arrival got her off the hook and she'd enjoy watching Ben and West squirm under her attention. Speaking of her attention— Piper nearly sucked soda into her lungs as Mrs. Taylor's fingernails shifted higher up West's thigh. West's bulging eyes and *I have a branch up my butt* clench of his teeth could be mistaken for that of a man suffering from lockjaw, but he refrained from shoving the woman's hand from his leg and shuddering.

Glenna made a polite noise in the back of her throat.

"Right as we speak, the ladies and I are organizing a ball and charity auction, and your Ben will be the recipient of all the funds we raise." Mrs. Taylor removed her hand from West's leg and rested it on the curved handle of her walking stick, bracing herself for the outburst of expected praise.

"Oh." Her mother looked stunned. "That's very kind of you, Betsy. But I think that's a little extravagant."

"I can't accept that kind of help, Mrs. Taylor, but thanks," said Ben from the kitchen.

Mrs. Taylor's penciled-on eyebrows twitched inward. "Nonsense. We don't want you losing your home because you're in a bit of a fix, do we, dear?" She wagged a finger at Ben.

"Well, no, but—"

"It's a great idea," Shaye interrupted, as Ben placed a glass of lemonade in front of Mrs. Taylor. "You need all the help you can get."

"Mum—" said Ben, placing a hand on their mother's shoulder.

She shook her head. "Darling, you're running out of time and even though you've got more bookings, you're not out of hot water yet. Think of all the years you've helped other people with fundraising. Consider it a community loan."

"Hell." Ben's shoulders slumped and he moved over to the hutch dresser to snatch up a coaster.

"Oh, it'll be such fun. We'll have a band, and a buffet, and we'll tart the community center up till it sparkles." Mrs. Taylor thumped her cane on the floor. "And wait till you see how much money your boy here will bring in at the bachelor auction."

"Bachelor auction?" Every gaze in the room leaped to Ben, who froze halfway back from the dresser with the coaster in his hand.

Forget about the cat that caught the canary—Mrs. Taylor was the cat that brought down an albatross. "Ooh, we've had lots of local women tell my ladies it'll be a popular and financially worthwhile event."

"I bet they did." Shaye nudged Piper's ankle under the table.

"Auctioned for what?" Ben spluttered.

"Shotgun marriage? Personal love slave?" Piper suggested.

Ben hurled a venomous glance in her direction, which made her grin like a crazy woman.

"Oh, dear, nothing like that." Mrs. Taylor frowned. "No, no. The winning bidder will get a complimentary dinner at Due South with her bachelor and some charming conversation and companionship. No hanky-panky stuff *at all.*"

West tipped his chair back on two legs, locking his hands behind his neck. "I think it's a great idea, but expecting Ben to make charming conversation with a woman? Good luck with that, Mrs. T."

Ben Frisbee'd the coaster at him, but West continued laughing his butt off until her brother stormed into the kitchen.

"I'm *so* glad you approve." Mrs. Taylor's sugary tone could bring on a diabetic attack.

Piper uncrossed her ankle, leaning forward to get a closer view of the punch line.

"And isn't it fortunate that *you're* such a smooth talker, West dear, since your name is also on the auction list."

That shut him right up.

But even as she laughed alongside Shaye and Ben, a kernel of jealousy unfurled and smoldered in her stomach.

Piper didn't want to share West with anyone, good cause or not.

***

The next day, after a queen's wave from Mrs. Taylor in the bar, West snarled under his breath and went to check on the kitchen staff.

Bullied into a bachelor auction by a seventy-one-year-old harridan, how pathetic was that? Jesus, he needed to grow a pair. At least Ben, Ford, Kip, Joe, and Noah suffered the same fate. And to add to his complaints Piper was avoiding him and Ben made a nuisance of himself whenever he tried to wrangle a moment alone with her.

Plus, his training schedule was screwed up by all the erupting drama. They had another romance over-nighter with only one couple tomorrow. He intended to find—make that bloody enforce—an opportunity to dive.

West pushed through the double kitchen doors into somebody-just-shoot-me chaos. As usual, he sought Piper out first. Her bare arms were elbow-deep in dishwater, her cheeks a pretty pink from the steamy kitchen heat. At the sound of the doors hissing open she glanced up. Sexual voltage arced between them, her gaze dissolving from bored to white-hot in seconds.

Not the only frustrated one in the room.

Shaye streaked out of the walk-in pantry with her arms full of vegetables. "I need that pan—like five minutes ago. Hurry the hell up!"

"Yes, commander." Piper pulled a saucepan from the sink, whipping the kitchen towel off her shoulder.

West glanced to the far corner of the room by the back door where Bill had taken to sitting in a chair during the meal service, bellowing orders at Shaye when he deemed necessary. Today Bill didn't appear to be paying any attention to his frantic protégé, choosing instead to make goo-goo eyes at his ex-wife, who stood at his side, her hand resting on his shoulder.

How cozy.

West flexed his fingers, the knuckles cracking. Less than three days back on the island and the widow Gatlin already wove her sticky web—and his father was jumping in it with both feet. Like a brainless blowfly.

"West." A wet hand clasped his forearm and he looked down at Piper's frowning face. She tugged. "Pantry—now."

He followed Piper into the pantry, unable to prevent his gaze dropping to the pert twitch of her ass under snug black jeans. The sight momentarily distracted him from his annoyance at Bill's belly-up capitulation.

"Aren't you hot in those jeans?" he said, as Piper ducked around him to shut the door. "It's like a sauna in there."

She leaned against it, watching him. "I didn't invite you in here to discuss my clothes."

Normally she wore a full length apron, but today she'd donned a chef's half apron, knotted around her slim hips and hiding nothing of her upper torso. Fascinated with the trickle of sweat disappearing under the "v" neck of her *CSI: Can't Stand Idiots* tee shirt, West braced his palms against the door on either side of her shoulders. "Perhaps we *should* discuss them."

Piper's gaze lowered and her breathing accelerated, the rapid movement of her chest freeing a second droplet of sweat. Her nipples puckered under the soft knit fabric and West wanted to drag his mouth down to those sensitive peaks.

Instant hard-on.

"The Due South polo-shirt, right?" Her swallow was a dry click in the small, enclosed space. "No one sees me back here and it's not like I'm really part of the staff—"

West traced a slow finger from the dent in her throat to the "v" of her shirt, stopping when he met the resistance of her bra. Her heartbeat thudded under his fingertip.

"I was thinking more along the lines of some short-shorts instead of jeans. Mix it up a little." Removing his finger from her neckline, he brushed his hand down her ribs then gently gripped her hip. Her breathing ceased for a moment—if his other hand wasn't holding her in place would she bolt?

Time to find out.

"You've got the hottest legs, Pipe." He released her hip and stroked his knuckles partway down her thigh.

Piper didn't move but she didn't meet his gaze either, her focus off to the right, like she opted to study the row of cans on the wall shelf.

"I want to see more of them. Preferably when they're bare and wrapped around my hips."

A soft moan escaped from her lips and her head thunked back on the door. He hardened further. He'd do her against the pantry door right now if she made another noise like that. He leaned in to kiss her—just a little kiss, maybe sneak in some tongue if he played it right—when a splayed hand, still damp with dishwater, clamped across his mouth and shoved.

"Not the time or place," Piper rasped. "Your parents are right outside."

Damn. He was all riled up and she'd nearly melted in his arms. A couple of wet and wild kisses would take the edge off. She did that lip licking thing and he nearly kissed her anyway—even though her hazel eyes sparked a warning: *touch me and I'll ensure you walk funny for the rest of the day.*

"Pipe." He delivered his best c'mon-baby smolder.

"Your mother is on the other side of this door, West—your *mother.* Do you need more of an incentive to keep your lips to yourself?" She darted under his arm and fled to the chest freezer at the end of the pantry—in case the threat of his parents catching him with his tongue down the dish-hand's throat wasn't enough to make him behave.

West shoved his hands into the pockets of his business pants, pulling them away from his groin—which still hadn't received the update that hot sex in Due South's pantry wasn't a go. They watched each other, wary as two cats squaring off for a backyard battle. He waited until his pulse settled back into a halfway normal rhythm before speaking.

"So why did you drag me in here?"

Piper folded her arms. "I saw the way you looked at Bill and Claire, like you were about to chew them both out."

Exactly what he'd been about to do.

Not that he'd admit it. And thinking of the sappy look on his dad's face—anything other than a scowl on Bill's face was sappy—his annoyance spilled over. "I should chew them both out, her especially—taking advantage of a sick old man who's not thinking straight."

Piper dismissed him with a toss of her head. "There's nothing wrong with your father's mind, and how is Claire uprooting herself to come look after him taking advantage?"

"I don't know, yet," he said. "But she's up to something. Fussing and fawning over him. Making him smile, for God's sake."

"They still care about each other, West, and it shows." She moved across the pantry and stood toe to toe with him, gently drilling a finger into his chest. "That's what's bugging you, isn't it?"

West wrapped his hand around hers, pressing her palm flat. "She walked out thirteen years ago. She can't just waltz back in and act like she didn't abandon him."

Abandon them both.

"I know you and Bill are close, but whatever's going on with him and Claire is not your business."

Piper's fingers curled on his chest and sent shivers skittering over his skin. She stared up at him, stared until he was half convinced her intense gaze peeled back his protective layers until every secret inside him split open to her scrutiny.

Could she see the unhealed scars of the boy he'd been? The boy who'd thought himself too old for tears, yet cried for his mother and little brother, hating every moment of his weakness. Piper's sympathy rolled over him like a soft blanket, but it suffocated him, made him want to push her away.

Again.

Sympathy was a blink away from pity and he couldn't stand the idea of her pitying him.

"My business or not, I don't have to like it, and I don't want to see my father devastated when she goes back to LA." He removed her hand from his shirt and let it drop.

"It doesn't sound like LA's where she wants to be at the moment."

"She made her bed."

Piper huffed out a sigh and dragged her fingers through her hair, leaving the strands in short spikes, which he itched to smooth down. He forced the impulse away by grabbing the door handle.

"Haven't you ever had to make a choice where there were no good outcomes?" she said. "Where no matter what you did, someone got hurt?"

West thought of the morning he'd broken it off with her and the night two days after Michael died when he'd tried to take it back. Piper had stared at his face for five solid seconds before quietly closing the door. He thought of her in the rain at Michael's memorial up on the cemetery hill, standing a short distance apart from her family. Of Piper wearing her backpack and walking to the ferry. And him, hiding in the shadows, not saying a word. Making a choice to let her go.

"Yeah."

"Then cut your parents some slack."

He nodded. Who was he to judge Bill when he stood on the precipice of making the same mistake with Piper?

So he said, "Back to work," and flung open the pantry door, stepping through it before Piper could see that mistake written all over his face.

***

With the honeymoon couple out of the way for three hours on a deserted beach toting a picnic lunch, Piper tugged on her wetsuit and cursed a blue streak.

Yeah, she'd kinda agreed to be West's safety diver. Okay, she *had* agreed, as long as he followed her rules—but agreeing to a theoretical situation was one thing. It was another to arrive at a sheltered cove in Paterson Inlet and have him announce his intention to dive.

And it was another matter entirely when West emerged from his cabin in a painted-on silver and black wetsuit. With a normal wetsuit, some areas, some *things*, were left to the imagination. Not so much with a free-diving wetsuit. Thinner and super-stretchy, the material clung to every inch of his body bar his feet and head.

Every. Single. Inch.

West looking so damn hot wasn't a bad thing, though. It distracted her from the heavy slab of fear constricting her chest at the thought of him free-diving. She scuttled into her cabin to change before she did something really dumb, like offer to adjust his fancy outfit with her lips.

She zipped up her wetsuit and faced the mirror.

C'mon Pipe, get it together.

She was a highly trained professional with hundreds of hours of experience under her weight belt. She wasn't eighteen, West wasn't her dad, everything would be fine.

"A cakewalk," she told her reflection.

Her pale face stared back at her, unconvinced. A small vein pulsed in her temple and she raised a shaky hand to press a fingertip against it.

A rap of knuckles on her cabin door. "Let's go, daylight's wasting."

Piper took a last look in the mirror before she walked out of the cabin, punched a smirking West in the bicep, and headed for the equipment locker.

She was okay, dammit.

Thirty minutes later and sixteen feet below the surface, West's silhouetted legs churned lazily above her by the anchor line as he prepared to dive. He'd use the line to guide himself down to the predetermined depth of ninety-eight feet, then follow it back up to the surface. Her job was to track his ascent and react quickly if he displayed any signs of a shallow water blackout.

The draw from her regulator rasped in her ear as she breathed and the chill of the water pressed in on all sides. But still, she remained steady—on task and in control.

In one smooth action, West folded at the waist and glided down in a series of calculated but graceful motions, like ballet executed underwater. He didn't acknowledge her as he dropped below her position, so focused on each precise movement of his arms and legs.

But no more focused than she was on him. Piper's gaze didn't deviate off his streamlined body. West's legs flexed again in a frog kick and then returned to complement the straight line of his torso. He held his arms relaxed at his sides, negative buoyancy now causing him to fall weightlessly into the deep. Hypnotic to watch, the power of it combined with the memories of her father training, stung her eyes.

Visibility closed around him and he slipped from her view. Now the hard part—trusting he'd return. She checked her dive watch again. Counted off the seconds. Talked herself out of diving down another thirty feet after him. Checked her watch again.

By now West would've reversed direction at the end of the line, no longer falling, but reliant on pure muscle and determination to propel him upward. But things often went wrong in the ascent. Push the body too hard and air-hungry lungs would suck the oxygen right out of a person's blood—then buh-bye consciousness.

West reappeared out of the murky dark, his black swim-capped head arrowing smoothly through the water, not too slow, not too fast. She finned closer, close enough to make eye contact for those last crucial moments. His gaze fixed on hers as they swam in parallel synchronization. No emotion filtered through his steady gaze, his mind turned inward to master his lungs' crippling need for air.

With a short distance to go, bubbles exploded around his face, obscuring his mask and catapulting her heart into frantic overdrive. West's body arched as his head broke the surface, but almost immediately he sank back under, and plummeted—straight into Piper's arms.

No time for panic. No time for accusations. Only response, action, training.

She hauled West to the surface, supporting him under his arms and twisting him awkwardly onto his back.

She yanked her regulator out and tugged off his nose clip. "C'mon, West. C'mon now." Piper blew gently across his face and patted his cheek.

Ice blue eyes popped open and he coughed, blinked, and swore. After a short pause he tore off his mask and rolled over until he trod water beside her. His brow creased and he shook his head, water flicking off his face in tiny droplets. "Pipe?"

You blacked out. You could've died.

The words crowded her throat but wouldn't form out loud. She labored even to breathe, just gawking at him with her vocal chords frozen.

"Pipe?" He wheezed, sucked in more air. "Shit." Gasp. "You okay?"

That should've been her line, but she couldn't say a damn thing, transfixed by West's face, the rise and fall of his chest as he sucked in air.

Piper's lungs refused to work smoothly. Her father's face, grey and motionless with water spilling from his slack mouth, superimposed over West's. No longer West's fancy black and silver suit beneath her fingertips, but Dad's. Dad's bulk, as she battled to keep his head above water. Dad's eyes, that didn't blink when she tore off his mask, when she blew on his stubbled cheeks. When she sobbed his name over and over and over.

She had to get out of the water. Now.

She clamped her trembling lips shut and swam the short distance to the boat's ladder. Splashes from behind and he shouted her name, a string of four-letter words chasing it. Her arm muscles had the same tensile strength as overcooked pasta as Piper hauled herself aboard. Nearly there, nearly there.

More water sluiced onto the deck as West climbed up the ladder after her. "Hey—"

She kneeled on the deck and stripped off her inflatable vest and tank.

"Talk to me, please." He crouched beside her.

Piper kept her head down and unclipped her weight belt, letting it fall off her waist. She still couldn't look at him—didn't trust herself to speak. One glance at those baby blues and she'd lose what little control she had left.

Her cabin, that's where she needed to go. A place where she wouldn't use the dive knife strapped to her thigh to take West's head off. Yeah, after a hot shower, her temper, primed by a mix of the adrenalin and terror flooding her system, would dissipate enough for her to have a rational conversation.

Piper lurched forward on hands and knees, intending to use the short bench seat to drag herself up onto unsteady legs.

"Piper, listen to me—" West's hand closed around her ankle.

She slapped out at him with a growl that choked her in its ferocity. His grip tightened, and suddenly she was screaming at him.

Screaming like a banshee hyped up on meth.

Chapter 15.

He'd blown it. But when she tried to walk away from him again? All bets were off.

He lunged for her ankle and suddenly it was all on—Piper shouting, punching, and snarling.

Her elbow connected with his ribs. Goddammit, she was strong. He winced, ducked from a fist that would've cost him a front tooth had it landed. Her flailing hadn't caused any major damage, as much as it would've enraged her if she'd any inkling of his thoughts. West didn't want her to hurt herself, so he pulled rank and flipped her onto her back, pinning her with his additional weight and bulk.

"Enough." He snatched up her wrists and stretched them above her head.

Piper continued to wriggle, inciting a predictable effect on a certain part of his anatomy.

Impeccable timing, West. As usual.

But with her breasts mashed against his chest and her hips bucking as she attempted to throw him off, his cock didn't care that an erection was not only inappropriate but potentially dangerous.

Her hips stilled mid arch, cradling the length of him. God, terrible timing or not, it was good to be this close to her. Breathing in ragged pants, Piper kept her face turned away.

West lowered his forehead, resting it against the wet spikes of her hair. "Stop fighting for one second and *listen*."

Her jaw worked as she spoke through clenched teeth. "Get. Off. Me."

"No." Blood rushed in his ears, his head pounding as he racked his brains for a way to apologize. But everything he came up with made him sound like a selfish prick for putting her in this situation. Of course—he was a selfish prick.

His lips brushed her temple. She tasted of salt and sun lotion. "I'm not ready to let you go yet."

She twisted her head, the motion nudging his lips away. Hazel eyes, almost green now with bright fury, clashed with his. "I'm a cop. I know how to hurt you."

"Yeah, I figured that."

And he'd figured that, one, he'd earned her knee in his nuts and, two, it couldn't hurt more than the pain he'd caused by reminding her of Michael's death. They were at a stalemate. Neither could look away. The intensity built in his chest to a living, clawing thing until he had to either kiss her or let her go.

Her breath hissed out and she rolled her head to the side, the harsh lines of her jaw relaxing. Whether it was a temporary truce, or a trick to lull him into exposing his vulnerable nuts, he didn't know. He released her wrists, propping his weight onto his elbows so he didn't squash her on the deck. She rotated her wrists and flexed her fingers, bringing her arms back over her head and resting her palms on his biceps, pushing against him. He didn't budge, so her fingers stayed there, splayed on his skin like petals. The stiff tendons in her neck softened and she swallowed, but he didn't for a second believe she wasn't still pissed.

"You could've died, moron," she said.

"You've downgraded me from asshole to moron. That's something."

Her eyelids lowered, the inky black lashes forming tiny clumps from the seawater. Nails dug into his upper arms hard enough to leave dents. "I'll rephrase that—you're an asshole and a moron."

"A moron for free-diving?"

"Clever-clogs, aren't you?"

"And an asshole for scaring you."

She said nothing, switched to her slightly-bored game face. Except he'd seen glimpses of the Piper behind the game face. The Piper who managed to sneak lunch into his office when he wasn't looking, because he'd forgotten to get his own. He'd seen that Piper again at the bonfire—the naked yearning on her face as he danced with Zoe. The Piper who cried while he played the piano and the Piper who held back tears when she realized the community had reclaimed her.

His chest squeezed as his heart turned a slow summersault. He used the back of his fingers to stroke the smooth skin of her jaw. "I'm sorry I scared you, baby."

Piper's lower lip quivered and he grappled with the need to kiss the tremor away.

"It took me right back there. Back to that morning."

West's gut hollowed, then filled with cold, hard stones. Piper's dad treated him like a second son, but he would've given West a solid ass-kicking for putting his girl through a nightmare—again. "I wish I'd been there for you—wish I'd been there *instead* of you."

How many times after seeing Piper that day, wrapped in a blanket on Old Smitty's boat, fighting to escape the men who'd half carried her onto the wharf, had he thought that? He'd never forget her soul-wrenching cries, begging to return to the inlet to keep searching for her father.

But it wasn't until over a year later when he'd accompanied the Harland family to the formal coronial inquest that he heard the details of his mentor's death. Piper delivered her verbal evidence in a wooden tone, never acknowledging his presence at the back of the courtroom.

Not that he blamed her for hating him, because he'd hated himself for allowing the sight of her, so damn lovely even in her starched cop uniform, to affect him.

"But you weren't there and because of the way things ended—" she paused, pressing her lips together, "—I couldn't ask my best friend to come out that morning, since my brother wasn't around."

West shut his eyes and her words stabbed at him, tiny needles piercing his heart.

"I stayed home the night before. I didn't go out with Ben and the guys—" he said.

She went rigid beneath him, her whole body stiffening to ironing-board straight. Looked like it was news to her.

"—but I understand why you didn't call me, because I didn't deserve to be your best friend." He opened his eyes to find she'd closed hers.

Her chin dipped a fraction in acknowledgement, before she turned her head to the side again.

"Get off me," she whispered. "Please."

West eased up and rolled aside. Piper scuttled backward and used the bench to haul herself to her feet.

"I'm sorry," he said.

She stumbled to the door and the look she sent back over her shoulder hollowed him out. He'd failed as her lover, but what killed him was failing as her friend.

***

"Oh-god-oh-god-yeahlikethat-oh."

Piper lay like a tomb effigy on her bed and pretended the couple in the next cabin weren't going at it like proverbial bunny rabbits. Make that a tomb effigy with a pillow clamped over her face.

She heaved out another long-suffering sigh. God, they really were two enthusiastic love birds. But somehow she and West got through the rest of the day without snarling at each other in front of them.

Now everyone had retired to their cabins and the night settled to stillness. Still except for the slosh of waves against the hull, the odd rasping call from nocturnal kiwi digging for sandhoppers on Kahurangi Bay beach, and the sexual Olympics next door.

She'd insisted on West taking the double stateroom earlier, rather than have him curled like a prawn on the single bunk. Super illustration of the cost of being a soft touch, because on the other side of The Mollymawk West drifted into blissful slumber while her lullaby—*Oh-God-oh-God-oh-God*—made her want to puncture her ear drums. Or take a cold shower. Or a swim.

Piper sat up and swung her legs over the edge of the bunk. Swim it would be. Maybe the shock of cold water would clear her mushy brain. Ever since West blacked out on his dive she'd vacillated between the urge to kill him and bang his brains out—because she was so *fucking grateful* he didn't die.

And the shock of West not being with Ben and the guys the morning her father drowned? She always assumed he'd been out partying—since his heart wasn't broken into teeny-tiny pieces. He'd flipped her assumptions on their head with that little grenade of information. Not that it changed anything.

Piper stripped out of her pajamas and pulled on a swimsuit. So— quick swim, a run along the beach, and back to the boat for chamomile tea. By that stage the honeymooners should be sexually satisfied and fast asleep.

Piper crept into the galley and eased through the door onto the deck. A crescent moon hung suspended overhead, surrounded by the diamond-pierced velvet of the night sky. No big city lights to fade the stars into oblivion, no rumble of traffic to dilute the peace of waves meeting the sand. Just a gentle breeze scented with brine and the shifting of the hull under her bare feet.

She sucked in a deep breath, stilled when her night vision kicked in. A dark silhouette tucked into a corner drank from a bottle.

"Couldn't sleep?" West said.

The huskiness of his voice licked sudden warmth under the small, but modest, barrier of her swimsuit. "Looks that way."

A low chuckle in the darkness. "Honeymooners?"

"Yep."

Easier than confessing the honeymooners were but a fraction of the reason for her restlessness. Add to the mix a dollop of sexual frustration, stir in a combination of guilt and anger, season it with her rapidly diminishing days on the island, and you had a big bowl of Piper-on-the-edge. "I'm going to take a swim."

West placed the bottle on the table beside him and stood, the glimmer of moonlight illuminating the smooth, kissable skin across his chest and shoulders, the pair of board shorts that hung low on his hips. "Think it'll help?"

Help her stop thinking about him? Unlikely.

"Better than a sleeping pill." Piper hustled to the end of the deck and climbed onto the ladder.

"Need a buddy, Pipe?"

"No."

Her toes dipped into the water, and goosebumps rippled up her legs. Freezing freakin' water—all the better to snuff out the dangerous heat swirling through her limbs.

"It's dangerous to swim alone."

"I'll risk it," she said, and dived into the water.

Swimming toward the line of foamy white breakers, Piper let the cold shock her into concentrating on nothing more than the rhythm of her strokes. Wading onto the beach, she shivered as the air knifed into her. She glanced back at The Mollymawk and long arms lazily slicing through the water.

Damn the man.

Yeah, like he wouldn't follow. If she hadn't wanted West's company, she would've high-tailed it back to her cabin the instant she'd seen him in the shadows.

Didn't mean she'd make it easy for him.

Piper ran for the cluster of rocks exposed by the low tide. Once around them, the next bay opened up to a long stretch of beach out of sight of The Mollymawk.

She had a good head start, but even still, his footsteps behind her came surprisingly quick. West, like his brother Del, had always been fast on his feet, beating the other island boys in a footrace as kids.

Slowing as she reached the rocks, Piper risked a glance over her shoulder. Sixty feet away jogged a tall, lean silhouette. Not in any hurry, West's arms pumped with no visible effort. He intended to wear her down like a cat waiting for a mouse to keel over from terrified exhaustion.

Hah.

Piper put on a burst of speed, streaking past the last of the rocks, flying over the beach, splashing through the tiny waves and suddenly laughing, laughing like a loon, at how incredible it felt to run down a deserted beach at midnight.

"I can do this all night, West. You won't wear me out," she yelled.

"Not trying to," his mild voice came right behind her.

"Shit!" She lost her rhythm and stumbled to a fast march. "Don't you ever get tired of scaring the hell out of me?"

"Can't help my panther-like reflexes." West loped alongside her. "And I like the view from back there."

She bet her freezing ass he did. Piper slid a hand down to her butt to check the thin nylon hadn't ridden up too high. So far, so good.

Her fast march slowed to a brisk walk, and then a stroll. He wasn't going to be shaken off by her power-walking. She crossed her arms over her breasts in case West's panther-like reflexes extended to superior night vision. Her night vision uncovered cords of muscle contracting in his upper arms as he moved, a bare, wet physique, which gleamed almost white in the monochromatic landscape, and board shorts clinging to the long line of his thighs. And Lord, he smelled good. Salty, a little sweaty, and with a boatload of male pheromones on top of that. Good enough that she pinched her lower lip with her teeth to stop from leaning over and taking a bite.

"It's good to hear you laugh, Pipe, to see you happy." He moved closer as they walked, his arm brushing against hers.

Prickles of awareness skated along her nerve endings from the brief contact.

"I'm not happy." Turned on a little, but definitely not happy. "I'm in a pissy girl mood, so for your own safety you should u-turn now."

Before she jumped his bones right on the sand and shocked any stray kiwi still in the vicinity.

"Ah." He made no move to turn away.

They kept walking and when he tried to link their hands, he laughed as she slapped his fingers away with a, "hmmph," and a muttered, "Pissy, remember?"

"You can't scare me off with your moods, you know. I've survived them all," he said. "Besides, you're a lot more fun now than at eighteen."

"Fun? How am I more fun now?"

She thought of her life as it had been up until a few weeks ago. Days blurring, filled with work or squad call outs, brief outings with friends who weren't cops, more work, raiding the shelves of the massive public library for something to do on those long nights alone, and then back to work. Sparse time in her schedule for fun.

"Well, you're more fun to play with."

Heat shimmered along her cheekbones and detoured south to parts that didn't need to get any hotter. "Oh, shut up."

He chuckled. "There's the added challenge now of knowing you can kick my ass if I cheat."

"So you'll cheat to win, huh?"

"I'll use any means necessary to win."

Her breasts ached at the smoky tone in his voice, like he'd reached out and rolled her nipples between his fingertips.

"We're not playing a game."

"Then what do you call this series of steps we've been dancing to since you got back?" He tugged a short strand of her hair, but let go before she could flick his hand off. "I step toward you, you back off. You blindside me and I knock you off kilter. Isn't this all a game, Pipe?"

Not to her. Not anymore.

But would she tell West her emotions had been roped into this game, where nobody could win and the best she could hope for was a painful draw?

No. Damn. Way.

"Sure." She forced a casual laugh, but it sounded ragged and a little desperate in her ears.

West stopped on a dime and she snapped to a halt beside him, the tension between them a bungee cord. The light atmosphere, the undertone of flirtatious humor, vanished. She stepped back and a wave swirled around her ankles, her toes digging for purchase in the shifting sand.

Eyes glittering dangerously in the starlight, West closed the gap and caught her wrist, dragging her flush against him. "So, let's play."

Skin to skin, her brain short circuited. The only reply she uttered when his lips crushed hers was a soft moan. Nothing in the demanding pressure indicated playfulness. No teasing nibbles or caresses, no introductory *this is just the appetizer* kind of kiss. He kissed with full-throttled focus—a furious order for surrender. Her surrender.

Piper's body flamed to life, from her parted lips, to her toes curled in the sand, to the dampness of her center, each vying for dominance. West's tongue slipped into her mouth, deepening the kiss and stoking the fire higher and higher. She drowned in the taste of him—warmth, sea salt, pure heaven. Heaven mixed with the yeasty bitterness of beer.

Her last date, so many weeks ago she'd almost lost count, tasted of peppermint mouthwash when she'd kissed him goodnight. Like other men she'd gone out with he favored suits, the city nightlife, and sixty-buck bottles of wine. Yet none of those guys revved her engines as much as a shorts-wearing island man who drank beer. They didn't challenge her in the sack, didn't care if she only gave as much intimacy as she was comfortable with.

Bottom line—those men weren't West.

Because West, while easy-going on the outside, would never let her get away with holding back. He wasn't satisfied with half measures and she wanted a man to fight with her, fight for her. She wanted a man who would sometimes let her lead and at other times say, "the hell with this" and take what he wanted.

Like West took what he wanted now.

One hand threaded through her hair, his other gripped her hip, pulling her against his arousal. Piper swayed under the power of the kiss, shifting onto her toes so she could grind against the delicious length of him. The hand in her hair left to cup one butt cheek and she looped her arms around his neck. West broke the kiss long enough to growl, "Jump," as he shifted her lower body higher. Piper jumped, her legs wrapping around his hips.

The play of muscles bunching across his shoulders tempted her. She inhaled the scent of sea and the faintest whisper of spicy cologne as she traced her lips over silky skin. West carried her a few strides away from the waves, dipping his fingers under the leg-line of her swimsuit. His touch whiplashed fire through her, forcing out another moan that she muffled by sinking her teeth into the column of his neck.

"Down, baby." He breathed delicious warmth into her ear while clutching her butt with those strong, sure hands.

"Sorry, I don't usually bite, I, ahhh—" She lost her train of thought when he nipped her earlobe, lapping the tiny hurt with his tongue.

"No, I literally mean, hop down." His stubbled chin rubbed along her jaw, his lips curving against her cheek. "I've got both hands full of you and while that feels amazing, I need my hands free for other things."

Other things.

Piper's girly-bits liked that idea. A lot.

Unhooking her ankles, she slid down his legs, loving the rough brush of his hairs on her thighs. He claimed her mouth again as she touched the ground and her hands snaked around to grab his butt. How long had she wanted to get her hands on it? Forever. Piper dug her fingers into firm muscles and made like a limpet.

"God, I love your ass." She tasted salt when she nipped his neck again, then trailed hot kisses up his throat.

"You've ogled it enough over the last few weeks."

"Guilty."

He caught her chin, took her lips in another knee-jellifying kiss. West lowered her onto her back, wedging himself into the juncture of her thighs. The sand, damp and cool, was forgotten. His weight covered her, the furnace heat of him warmed her, and the hard lines of his body—and, ohmigod, especially one part of his body—all conspired to momentarily distract her from the grittiness beneath her skin.

"I've never had sex on a beach before," she gasped, when his hands, now free, peeled the swimsuit off her shoulders, exposing her breasts to the night air.

He paused, and even though starlight dulled the color of his eyes to a pewter grey, she couldn't miss the desire in them.

"Tell me to stop right now, or you're about to." The ragged edge to his voice confirmed he meant it.

He dropped his head and sucked her nipple into his mouth. His tongue teased and tormented the sensitive bud until her nails dug into his shoulder, her hips thrusting up to meet his.

Jeez, the man really was a cheat.

Panting, Piper slid her fingers into his hair and jerked his head back, her breast slipping from his mouth with a soft pop.

She groaned, wanting nothing more than to let him continue his sweet torture. "West, we haven't—you know, *got anything.*"

Starlight or not, his white teeth flashed in an unmistakable grin as his hand fumbled at his hip. His shorts rustled and with a flourish he produced an oblong strip of foil, which gleamed in said starlight.

A belly laugh escaped and she slapped his shoulder—hard. "You've got condoms in your pocket? Were you hoping to get lucky?"

"I'm a guy—lucky's my middle name." He angled his body so his erection pressed against her core. "I won't believe it if you say you're not grateful for my foresight."

Piper snaked a hand between their damp flesh and tilted her hips, sliding her fingers beneath the waistband of his shorts to wrap around him. Rewarded with a startled groan that vibrated through his body into hers, she continued to stroke him. West rose up and supported his weight on his forearms, allowing her hand to trace farther down his length and cup his balls, pulled close to his body with arousal. Hard, hot, and satiny smooth—nothing had ever felt so wonderful against her skin.

His brow creased with concentration, his breathing choppy. West's hand wrapped around her wrist, stilling it.

"Baby, I can't take much more of that."

"Sure you can." Piper fondled the head of his cock, ensuring her thumb rubbed over the ridges slooowly.

He moaned again and jerked his hips so her hand slipped out of his shorts. "No, you witch, I can't."

West reared back and stripped off the rest of her swimsuit. He stood, tossing it aside and removing his shorts. What a sight he made in the glimmer of the crescent moon. He stole her breath, captured it in his calloused hands. She wanted to run her lips over every inch of him.

A crinkle as he ripped open the foil square for a condom. She would've offered to help, except at some point in the last minute her muscle control deserted her. So hot for his touch it was a minor miracle the sand beneath her hadn't melted into glass.

He dropped his shorts to the sand and lay on top of them, pulling her astride his hips. Piper pinned his biceps down and bent to lick his nipple, causing him to gasp most satisfactorily.

"Feels good, huh?" Wondered if he remembered saying the same thing to her in the shower—after he'd driven her half out of her mind.

"Feels okay." His chuckle came out strangled when she rocked her slickness along his hard length and sucked his nipple between her lips.

"Okay, okay—it feels amazing."

She tortured his other nipple with her tongue, lapping up the taste of him, salty and sweet, as addictive as the decadent combination of peanut butter and dark chocolate. But yummier, *much* yummier.

His fingers kneaded her bottom, his hips grinding his cock into the moist seam of her until her thighs squeezed together with the unbearable sensations. She forced herself to straighten.

"You've no idea how much I want to touch you." West's voice was rough, edgy. "But I hadn't thought through the logistics of this being our first time. Bloody sand."

Piper huffed out a laugh. Leaning forward again, she angled her body so the tip of his cock nudged at her swollen entrance. Sinking down an inch, the thickness of him inside her was so good she blissed out for a couple of seconds. Piper raised her hips until he started to slip out.

"Shall we stop, then?" she whispered.

And, sincerely, she'd have to kill him if he agreed.

A hand clasped her hip, fingers spread wide, preventing her from moving farther. "Only if you want me to flip you over and hammer you until sand ends up where sand shouldn't go."

His voice sent another volley of shivers skimming down her vertebrae. Oh, how she wanted this man to hammer her. Hammer her over and over, to the moon and back, until she couldn't remember her own name.

Piper sucked in a breath, fixed her gaze on West's face and sank down. Delicious friction dragged a moan from her, a moan lost inside West's mouth as he kissed her again, the fullness of him inside her body completing the circle. She rotated her hips, her core rubbing over the base of his cock. Not as satisfying as those long, piano-playing fingers of West's, but still...

She braced herself against West's chest, his heartbeat a jackhammer under her palms. She rode him, every rolling thrust of her hips taking him in deeper. He filled her, completed her, and owned her in that moment. West loosened his grip on her hips and she linked their fingers together, using his strength to move herself faster, harder, driving them both closer into the flames. She arched her pelvis back, biting her lip as the connection threatened to leave her in a begging puddle of lust.

West thrust his hips again and again, driving her up and over the edge. And then she wasn't thinking, just surfing the pleasure cascading though her, sensuous ripples becoming rolling breakers as the orgasm slammed ashore. She dug her nails into his shoulders and held on as the spasms contracted so powerfully she expected to be turned inside out. West's cock throbbed inside her as he climaxed and growled her name.

Collapsing forward onto him, Piper's breasts mushed against his pecs. West wrapped an arm over her, pinning her to him. After a moment the pressure eased and his hand drifted to her waist, tracing soft circles on her rapidly cooling skin. Cheek pressed to his collarbone, nose against his throat, Piper fought to catch her breath instead of sucking in more of his delectable scent, an impossible task because he surrounded and overwhelmed her. Still as intimately joined together as two human beings could be, every damn inch of him, inside her and beneath her, touched her right down to her soul.

It felt perfect, he felt perfect.

Her brain mocked her with every slow swirl of West's hand.

Lust? Yeah, right.

***

West wasn't a cuddler. And he really didn't like women invading his space, snoring in his ear when he wanted to sleep.

So why didn't he peel Piper's naked limbs off his body and engage in a tuck and roll maneuver to ease her onto the other side of the double bed?

He sprawled on his back, Piper's cheek pressed to the spot where only minutes ago his heart nearly erupted out of his chest. One long leg draped over his thigh and her arm was a dead weight across his stomach. Slow breaths puffed against his skin and twice she'd given a soft, snorting sigh as she relaxed even further, melting into him like warm syrup.

And speaking of melting—making love with her the second time back in his cabin annihilated any remaining brain cells left from their beach encounter.

His fingers feathered over the sweet curve of her ass and she muttered something, shifting her knee higher—any higher and he'd wake her for round three.

He couldn't get enough.

After their sandy exuberance on the beach, which had simultaneously whet his appetite and frustrated the bejesus out of him because he couldn't touch her the way he wanted, they'd swum back to The Mollymawk. West then decided that unless one of the local Great

Whites went all *Jaws* on them and attacked the boat, they were headed straight to the shower and then his bed, so he could bury himself in her over and over.

Mission accomplished.

His normal mode of operation from this point—the afterglow—was to either kiss the woman goodbye and disappear from her hotel room slash rented accommodation, or if she indicated she'd like him to stay, he'd put up with cuddling for a short period until she became sleepy enough for him to ease her over.

But nothing was normal about making love with Piper. Starting with the fact his brain kept supplying the words "making love" instead of the usual four-letter descriptions. He'd made love to Piper. Not screwed her, or shagged her, or joined her in the act of sexual intercourse. He'd loved her with his hands, with his mouth, with his body—and gave her every part of himself.

Except his heart.

That was off limits.

Piper stirred, tilting her chin up. He couldn't see her face clearly, but he knew she was awake.

"West?" she said after a moment.

He'd been drawing her in so tight against his body that she'd woken. "Go back to sleep, Pipe."

He reached over with the arm that wasn't prickling with pins and needles and ran the back of his knuckles down her cheek.

"It'll be dawn soon. I should go back to my room." Piper's leg brushed across his as she arched her back, preparing to pull away.

His hand that traced down her cheek made a rapid drop south, landing on her knee and pinning her in place. "Stay with me."

Suddenly it seemed important he didn't lose the little bubble of warmth surrounding them under the covers. Even the small gap she'd put between them was a chasm filled with dead air. He needed her, needed the skin on skin, her hair tickling his neck, the smell of apples from her shampoo. "Please."

A chill prickled across his shoulders as he sensed her trying to gauge his expression in the dark. Piper inched back into the crook of his arms and her hand settled on his chest, one finger tracing consecutive circles on his skin. He tucked her even closer to his side and angled his face so he could inhale the scent of her hair again.

One by one her muscles relaxed, until she slumped bonelessly against him once more, her breasts mashed against his ribcage, the brush of her sex rubbing on his thigh when she moved. The pins and needles were totally worth it.

And when she started to make those soft, snorting sighs again he closed his eyes, a smile creasing his lips.

Turns out he was a cuddler after all.

Chapter 16.

Piper emerged from the bathroom in a pair of dressy, black pants and a glittery, off-the-shoulder tunic top. She'd snatched the clothes off a rack when her sister and the whole female gang dragged her along on a shopping trip to Invercargill three days ago.

"What happened to that cute cocktail dress we all decided on? You can't wear that to the ball tonight." Shaye, with one hand on the hip of her vintage gown, tapped a dangerous tempo on her bedroom floor with a lethal-looking stiletto.

"*You all* decided on it. I changed my mind and got this instead. There's nothing wrong with it." Piper couldn't keep a note of irritation from her voice.

She didn't even want to go to the ball—not after her last experience at one—and what was wrong with her outfit? It was eveningwear. The top had *sequins*, for God's sake.

"Please tell me you're not planning to wear your combat boots."

"Why not? Someone needs to kick the men falling at your feet out of the way, once you and Kez make your grand entrance."

"Flattery doesn't change the fact you're wearing butt-ugly pants and an old-granny top, Piper Marie Harland."

Piper twisted in front of the full length mirror, checking out her reflection. "Hey, these butt-ugly pants and granny top set me back over a hundred bucks."

But, yeah, she had to concede Mrs. Taylor would covet her outfit if the top was lavender instead of salmon pink.

Shaye huffed, and jabbed a dangly earring through a lobe. "I don't know how we can be related. Honestly, do you think West's jaw is gonna hit the floor when he sees you in that outfit?"

It'd been a week since she and West made love for the first time and she hadn't slept on the futon since. He wouldn't allow it—told her that one way or another they'd spend their nights together, either in his big roomy bed, or squished together on the office futon.

"Your choice," he'd said.

But really, there'd been no choice at all, because the only place she wanted to be was in his bed, wrapped in his arms. And did she think too intently about that admission? Not on your life.

"Well, if he can't accept me as I—" A sharp rap of knuckles on Shaye's bedroom door cut Piper off.

The door swung inward and Glenna marched in, her dark-sienna evening dress swirling around her legs. "Hello, darlings. How are we going?"

Arms full of pale sea-green fabric, Glenna beamed at Shaye and said, "Gorgeous as always, baby."

Her stare switched to Piper, scanning her from head to toe. Her lips formed a pained moue. "No, darling. Just no."

Glenna spread the yards of fabric draped over her arms onto Shaye's bed, revealing a chiffon gown with intricate beading on the one shoulder strap that crossed diagonally from the bodice to the low cut back. "You'll wear this."

Piper recognized the garment immediately. "Mum—I can't."

An old album held a photo of her mother in that dress, worn to the first dance Glenna and Michael attended. Her mother used to whisper to her and Shaye, as they sat on the sofa flipping over the heavy black pages, that the photo was taken the night she fell in love with their father.

"You have my coloring and you're the same size as I used to be, way back when. You'll look exquisite."

"It's your special dress. I just can't."

And she couldn't open herself up to the hurtful memories of facing West across another dance floor in a pretty dress. Much safer to arrive incognito, and let all the other women dazzle.

Her mother's gaze went dreamy and Piper could almost see her mind travelling back over the years to the church hall, Michael's arm tucked around her waist, his smiling face half turned into her hair.

"Please, don't argue. Wear it for me. Don't hide under those dowdy clothes thinking they'll protect you from a broken heart. He sees you, darling, West sees you anyway. Give him something more than those awful black pants and this—" her mother scowled as she pinched the loose sleeve of the tunic top between her fingers "—as a memory. You'll knock him straight out of his socks, mark my words."

Beaten by a pro at emotional warfare, Piper knew when to give in. Sighing, she reached down to finger the slippery-soft fabric of the dress. "All right. I'll try it on. No promises."

"Brilliant." Glenna clapped her hands and swung around to Shaye, sidling out of the room. "Shaye? Have you still got those silver-sling backs? They'll go divinely with the dress."

Shaye blinked, her glossy lips forming an "o."

"But Piper was going to wear those, Mum." She pointed to the corner of the room, her mouth morphing into an impish smile after Glenna whirled in a flurry of skirts.

"Her purple boots? Over my dead body."

"Shaye thought it'd be a fashion statement. Kinda goth and thumbing-my-nose-at-convention, all rolled into one." Piper grinned back at her sister, warmth spreading through her when Shaye poked out her tongue.

Glenna tutted and then laughed. "You girls. The pair of you will drive some poor men batty one day."

"Piper's *already* driven West batty." Shaye snickered, and then squealed when a small cushion from her bed sailed across the room and smacked the doorframe beside her. She ducked outside the room, poking her head around the frame long enough to make kissy noises. "Piper *lurvs* him—he's ever so dreamy."

"Shove off, twerp." Piper fired another cushion and it bounced off the door on the opposite side of the hallway.

Her aim was way off, thanks to the shakiness in her upper arms. Shaye laughed again, her heels clicking along the floor.

Love? *In lurv?* Nuh-uh. Not possible, no way, no how.

She barely liked West most of the time, because he was just another irritating pain-in-her-ass male. Sure, the fantastic sex each night somewhat made up for it—the man was an orgasm-giving machine. But, if she added to the "love scale" the fact that beneath his slick exterior beat the soft heart of a man who'd rearrange his life to help a friend...if she added the way he helped out in menial kitchen prep so that his father rested enough...well, the scale tipped dangerously into the little-red-hearts zone.

But he still pissed her off and he never, ever remembered to leave the toilet seat down in his en suite bathroom.

That alone took *lurv* out of the realm of possibility.

The door opposite opened and Zoe's head popped out. "Mum!" she hollered. "Someone's throwing pillows! How come I can't throw pillows?"

"Piper, stop throwing things and get ready! Thirty minutes and counting, woman!" Kezia's muffled voice came through the wall next door.

Trust Shaye to choose a bossy housemate with x-ray vision.

Piper turned back to her mother's Cheshire cat smile. "I'm *not* in love with him, so do *not* get that look on your face."

She gathered up the dress and stormed out of Shaye's room, stomping down the hallway into the bathroom. Leaning against the back of the bathroom door she smoothed the dress's soft skirt against her face.

Lying to her mother. Tsk, tsk.

"Not lying." She dragged the granny top off, squinting at her reflection with a twist of her lips.

"I am not in love with that insufferable man." Her mirror image stared back with flushed cheeks and a telltale sparkle in her eyes.

No, she wasn't in love with Ryan Westlake.

But she sure as hell was sliding down the slippery slope toward it.

***

At the entrance to Oban's community hall Ben waited, and itched. From the open doors behind him laughter and conversation drifted out, along with the smell of crispy sausage rolls, and the odd sound-system feedback as technicians made last minute adjustments. Mrs. Taylor had informed him his first job of the evening was to greet people at the door. If *that* wasn't bad enough, he had to wear a suit.

A suit, for Christ's sake. He didn't even own a suit.

Last week he made a simpleton's mistake of mentioning this to Mrs. Taylor and she offered him one of her dead husband's God-awful checkered things. When he turned her down she smirked and suggested he take a trip to Invercargill to hire one.

So now he stood on the community hall's verandah like a funeral director with a crowbar jammed up his ass, in a jacket half a size too small which pulled across his shoulders.

He itched all over and beneath the cast his ankle drove him nuts too. And as for the flaming starched collar of the shirt that threatened to asphyxiate him...

From the parking lot behind the corner of the hall rolled a smoky laugh. Ben forgot the irritable spot under his cast.

Kezia.

He straightened his shoulders, scowling at the tug of the wool jacket. Bad enough he'd catch grief from the guys tonight, not to mention the heckles from his sisters, but Kezia? She confounded him with her sheer sunny nature and refusal to take his coolness as a personal affront. Thank God that as the local primary school teacher, their paths didn't cross often. If he wanted to hang out with his baby sister, he didn't visit when Kezia and Zoe were home.

But it wasn't Kezia who appeared around the corner first; it was Piper. And, good God Almighty, his mother must've conned her into wearing a dress. The grin spread across his face before he could stop it. West would stroke out when he caught a glimpse of Piper all fancied up.

She caught his look and stabbed a finger. "Not one word, Benjamin Harland."

He looked her up and down while she teetered toward him in some wicked looking heels. Shaye or Kezia, since they were into that girly crap, must've held her down and piled goopy stuff to her eyes and lips, then swiped something through her hair to make it sit in a sleek, shiny cap around her face.

"Not. One. Word." Piper climbed the verandah's two stairs, Shaye behind her with a smug expression, and Kezia bringing up the rear.

He'd been about to say something lame like she looked nice, but at her fierce stare he shrugged. Whatever. She'd get the compliment soon enough with West panting over her.

He swept his hand to the side. "Ladies."

"Come on, Piper. Don't start in on each other," Shaye said.

The three women moved toward the open hall doors.

Kezia paused and looked over her shoulder. "Shoot, I left my wrap back in the van. I'll meet you in there." She turned away and walked back toward him.

He developed a sudden interest in the construction of the hand rail above the stairs. A spicy, exotic scent drifted into his nose, tickling his senses and causing the tips of his ears to burn.

"Ben?" Kezia's voice, a sensual stroke along his skin, came from right beside him.

He looked down, way down—God, she was tiny—into smoldering chocolate-colored eyes. Ben offered a rumbly grunt, since his vocal chords failed when she smiled.

"If you turn that frown upside down it'll result in the ladies paying a higher price for the chance to *have* you for a night."

He shoved his fists into the pockets of his suit pants, which in direct contradiction to the jacket were half a size too big. Just as well, since the thought of *Kezia* having him for a night stirred things below his waist that he didn't care for anyone to see.

"I'll remember that." His voice came out gruff and clipped with an unintentional edge of annoyance.

Small white teeth flashed under gloss-slicked lips before she turned away, moving with an easy grace down the stairs, the silky red dress clinging to the lush curves of her very fine ass. An ass he couldn't pull his gaze from as she sashayed around the corner.

Nope. Not taking his hands out of his pants pockets any time soon, since they hid one mother of a hard-on.

A couple of minutes ticked by while he got his dick under control, kicking himself the whole time for being such a jerk when Kezia had only tried to...well, he didn't understand *what* the sultry smile and soft, suggestive words were about.

Ben glanced around. The street alongside the community hall remained deserted. He didn't want to ruin the start of Kezia's evening by sounding like the world's grumpiest jackass, so he'd go mutter an apology.

Limping down the stairs, he set off along the sidewalk, a couple of different apology scenarios scrolling through his brain. Apologizing to women wasn't his strong suit. *Talking* to a woman like Kezia, who for some unknown reason made him feel like one of the eight-year-olds in her class, wasn't his strong suit.

Ben strode into the parking lot, his gaze tracking across the concrete until he spotted the bulky outline of Due South's courtesy van in the far corner. He didn't spot Kezia at first, but zeroed in on the dark-haired man on the opposite side of the van. The man leaned on the van's panel with his hands spread apart, his head dipped down, a snarl twisting his mouth.

Reynolds.

Then a glimpse of a woman's pale fist thumping Gav's shoulder, before his hand snatched her wrist away and shoved. The back of the woman's head hit the van with a dull thunk, followed by a familiar husky voice cursing in Italian—Kezia's voice.

That sonofabitch.

Broken ankle notwithstanding, Ben ran, hurtling around the van and hauling Gav backward by his shirt. Gav choked and sputtered as the collar tightened around his neck and buttons pinged off, but he managed to swing a sloppy left hook. Ben dodged easily and Gav staggered, tripping over his feet.

"The fuck's your problem, Harland?" Gav righted himself, puffing out his chest and glowering.

Gav was drunk. Stinking drunk and mean with it. Terrific.

Measuring Gav's agitation, Ben said to Kezia, who looked more murderous than teary-eyed, "You okay? Did he hurt you?"

"No, he didn't hurt me."

While he could hear the fury in Kezia's voice she kept her distance, backing up a few steps. Smart cookie.

"But the bastard ambushed and pawed me when I climbed out of the van."

Ben stilled, even as his blood pressure rocketed into the danger zone, blood pulsing through his skull like his head was about to explode off his shoulders. "He put his hands on you?"

"Yes." The single word, almost a whisper, slipped from her glossy lips.

"We were just talking, you stuck-up, frigid bitch."

"Don't speak to the lady like that." Considering his internal temperature, he had no clue where the ice coating his words came from.

Gav lurched toward him, his eyes dark chips of built-up resentment. "Piss off, cripple. This is none of your business."

Cripple or not, the prick had touched her and now a messy conclusion was unavoidable.

Gav aimed a kick at Ben's broken ankle, broadcasting his intention by wobbling onto his left leg. His balance sucked, thanks to the Jack Daniel's fumes wafting off him.

Ben swiveled to avoid the ill-timed kick and grabbed Gav's wrist to pull him farther off balance. Stepping slightly behind him, he delivered a blow with his elbow to the side of Gav's jaw. His annoyance spiked at the hiss of his hundred-dollar hired suit tearing at the seams, so he added a knee to the gut.

Gav folded like a bad poker hand. But even scrabbling on the concrete, he had to have the last word.

"Not. Lady...Whores," Gav wheezed, blood trickling down his chin from where Ben's elbow had split the corner of his lip. "Her and...your sisters."

Righteous anger detonated into rage. Ben pulled back a fist to teach the bastard a life lesson when a small but strong hand gripped his forearm. He glanced down—Kezia at his side again, with that unfathomable gaze trained on his.

"Don't, Ben. The pathetic worm's not worth it."

"No one calls you, or my sisters, whores." Like his father, his temper proved hard to ignite, but once provoked beyond tolerance and the fuse caught fire, it was a hell of a thing to put out before an explosion.

"He can call us anything he likes." Kezia tugged on his arm with both hands. "And then he can repeat it to Noah Daniels when I press sexual assault charges."

Ben sucked in a breath. The scent of her perfume broke through the urge to add more bloody splotches to Gav's white dress shirt. He took a step back and looked at his hand, forcing his fingers to relax. He breathed some more. God, she smelled amazing. "Well. That's something."

Gav rolled over onto his hands and knees and vomited. Ben considered planting his cast on Gav's ass and toppling him into it. Later. Maybe later he'd pay him another visit; the last time he "visited" him after the Waitangi Day game he'd told Gav he'd end up with both arms in casts if he touched one of his sisters again. Gav didn't comprehend the threat extended to other women in Ben's orbit.

"Escort me back to the ball?" Kezia slid her fingers up his forearm to tuck into the crook of his elbow. "And you may want to take the jacket off, it's almost in shreds. You look like The Incredible Hulk after a night on the town."

"Not Dr. Bruce Banner?"

"Definitely The Hulk," she said. "You've got some muscles there." She patted his bicep and gazed up at him.

The last of his temper fizzled, the hairs on his arm standing to attention.

"But he's the green one." Kezia dipped her chin at Gav who slumped like a beached starfish on the parking lot, groaning.

Aware of the warmth of her at his side, Ben guided her around Gav's prone form. Kezia paused and trod on Gav's hand. He let out a tea-kettle whistle and yanked at his hand trapped under her dainty stiletto.

"Whoops. My bad." Without another glance, she stepped off again. "Ready?"

"Remind me never to cross you, Ms. Murphy," Ben said as they strolled out of the parking lot.

She laughed, and temper had nothing to do with the heat that abruptly roared through him.

When they reached the verandah, Kezia slipped her hand from his elbow and straightened the lapel of his ruined jacket. Her fingers wrapped around his tie and pulled, his head dipping closer to magnetic dark eyes a man could lose his mind in.

She rose on tip-toe, brushing a whisper-soft kiss across his cheek. "Thank you for being all big-brotherly on my behalf."

For once, Ben wished he had West's skill for easy conversation. A witty remark, a casual comment to smooth this awkwardness over. Something. Because he couldn't blurt out that he now wasn't thinking of her in a brotherly way at all.

He hooked a finger inside his too-tight collar and cleared his throat. "Ah. You're welcome."

Christ. What a jackass.

Releasing his tie, Kezia smiled, and disappeared into the crowded hall.

***

As part of free-diving training, West learned that on a deep dive his lungs compacted to the size of two oranges. That was nothing compared to the pressure compressing every oxygen molecule in his lungs at the sight of Piper across the crowded hall.

Her dress floated around her, the pale green fabric contrasting with her tanned skin and glossy hair. But it wasn't the way her eyes sparkled, or the heels which made her legs look a mile long, or even the seductive slick of her painted lips.

Piper glowed, from the inside out. She lit up the hall with enough energy to power Oban through many cold, winter nights. While she'd always been beautiful, tonight—tonight Piper looked incredible.

West dodged through the crowd to claim her before anyone else could and the tingles racing out from his heart meant one of two things. Either he was about to suffer a heart attack, or the barricades he'd erected to prevent himself from falling in love with her had yielded without a whimper.

Refracted light from the disco ball sparkled over Piper's face as she angled her chin toward his father, laughing up at him when he touched her arm.

Oh, yeah, one small step away from catastrophe, one not-so-giant leap from hitting that one-way, slippery slope.

The band started with a catchy number and couples flowed out onto the dance floor. Piper patted his father's arm and gestured to Claire, who stood on her other side talking to Shaye. Piper mouthed something and with an aw-shucks shrug Bill tapped Claire's shoulder.

West ignored the soft smile his mother returned as she took Bill's elbow and allowed him to guide her onto the floor.

He had other issues. Like Kip, his about-to-be-fired barman, honing in on Piper with the determination of a Great White after a seal.

Not that Piper was a seal, but dammit, she was *his*.

West caught Kip's eye and threatened disembowelment with a single glance. Kip grinned, not at all perturbed, and changed direction to swoop toward Shaye instead.

West slipped behind Piper and set his hands on her waist. "Hey, there."

She stiffened, then melted into him as he planted a kiss on the crescent of skin behind her ear. With her little ass snugged into his crotch, and her skin sprayed with something delicious and citrusy, dancing with Piper would be less scandalous to the group of octogenarians clustered in the seating areas than dragging her off to a dark corner.

"Dance with me?" he said, his mouth by the shell of her ear to counter the music volume. It also presented the opportunity to take her lobe between his teeth for a gentle nip.

She shivered, and pressed so intimately together, the muscles in her bottom contracted as she reacted to both his action and suggestion.

"West..." Her voice was a hesitant breath on his jaw as she turned toward him. "I don't dance."

"I won't step on your toes this time. Promise."

A soft laugh tempted him to kiss her right then and to hell with it. "You didn't step on my toes last time. You were too slick for that, even then."

He captured her hand and feathered a kiss on her knuckles. "Give me another chance, Pipe."

Piper glanced over her other shoulder at Mrs. Taylor and her cohorts, who pretended not to watch, but did. Her gaze, hooded and unreadable, met his again. "I could encourage your reputation as a lady's man before the bidding war starts."

"That's right. You'll be helping Ben by dancing with me."

Her lips curved. "One dance, Westlake."

Freeing her hand from his grasp, Piper slipped it behind his neck and tugged his ear close to her mouth. "And if your hand goes anywhere near my ass like it did the last time we danced, I'll nail your nuts to the wall with one of my five-inch heeled sandals."

"Baby, I love it when you go all 'cop' on me." He led her out onto the dance floor.

West got five dances with her in the end, and would've kept her trapped flush against him for another if she hadn't mentioned the charity auction was about to start.

"There'll be a catfight if you go onstage like this," she whispered, while rotating the cradle of her hips against his erection.

Judging there was a low risk of emasculation, he palmed her sweet bottom before whispering back, "Just don't tear your dress while you're fighting them off me, hmm?"

He pressed a chaste kiss to her forehead. A chaste kiss, or else take advantage of the space beneath the buffet to ravish her. Not much of a choice.

"I'll try to restrain myself once women start throwing their panties," she said.

West chuckled. "Good. And don't dance with anyone else while I'm gone, or you may have to arrest me—you're mine tonight."

The look she cut him from those gorgeous hazel eyes was a mix of indignation and confusion.

It warmed him as he walked away. Once again he'd caught her off her guard.

***

"God, that woman's scary." Piper leaned back in her chair and shuddered. "I almost feel sorry for them. *Almost.*"

Sandwiched between Shaye and Kezia, she watched Oban's last two eligible bachelors herded onto the stage by a voraciously smiling Mrs. Taylor. Possums caught in a hunter's spotlight with a .22 rifle couldn't look more stunned than Ben and West.

Shaye snickered. Kezia smiled into her wine glass.

"They love the attention, Piper, don't you worry." Erin twisted a lock of blonde hair around her finger from her seat across the table.

"Well, Kip certainly did," Shaye said. "All those flexing muscles, and Mrs. T. copping a feel of his biceps."

"She never lets an opportunity pass her by, that's for sure," Erin said.

"Shaye-girl, you paid two hundred bucks to take Kip on a date you'll end up cooking for. What a sucker." Tarryn, looking amazing in a burnt-orange dress that showed off curves Piper would flip to the dark side for, grabbed another handful of pretzels.

"Hey! Holly paid three-fifty for Ford and we all know how *that* date will turn out, since Ford talks even less than Ben—and that's saying something. She's the sucker. I'm planning to have a fun night out with a hot guy." Shaye glared at Tarryn, who shrugged amicably.

"My date's hot too and I could listen to that sexy Irish brogue of his for hours—oh, wait, I *will* get to listen to that sexy brogue for hours." Tarryn raised her beer bottle.

"Tarryn's gonna play doctors with Joe, oh yeah!" Erin snorted and nearly choked on her carrot stick.

Tarryn pointed the neck of her bottle at Erin. "Like you're not intending to play good cop, bad cop with the *I'm too sexy for my rugby shorts* Noah Daniels?"

"Bust-ed," Erin said.

The interplay around their table only captured half of Piper's attention. Kezia, clutching her wine glass and shifting frequent glances to the hall entrance, seemed unusually quiet.

Piper nudged her with an elbow. "You okay? You seem a little off, tonight."

"Not many men left to choose from, Kez. It's slim pickings now," Tarryn said.

"I'm fine. And I'm playing the young widow card tonight, so no dates for me." Kezia tossed back her curls but her smile appeared forced, her usually lush mouth thin and pinched closed.

"Spoilsport," Tarryn said, but with no real heat. "So that leaves you, Piper. Make your play, girl—and since one of those remaining hunks is your brother..."

Shaye edged her chair closer and leaned in. "I hear Bree's gunning for West. So, are you going to let your man hook up with one of those desperate hussies in front?" She jabbed her thumb toward the tables set up by the stage where Bree, Holly, and some other local woman sized up the talent.

Piper started to say the whole *West isn't my man thing* and then stopped.

The idea of Bree—who, okay, wasn't a total bitch—cozied up with West, made her want to snarl. And the desire to snarl meant one thing.

Crap. West was so her man.

If only for another two weeks.

Mrs. Taylor grabbed West's hand and towed him to the front of the stage.

"Now then, who here doesn't recognize this fine specimen of a man?" Mrs. Taylor said into the microphone, and without a bat of her lavender eyelids, she smacked West on the ass.

West jumped, his charming smile slipping as a chorus of wolf-whistles and hoots of laughter echoed around the hall. His wild gaze scanned the crowd, searching her out. Piper raised her wineglass at him in a sympathetic toast.

"That's right, ladies, this is Ryan Westlake. Ryan's our local hotelier, so he has a steady job and he's quite the catch of the day—" Mrs. Taylor paused to glare at Ford, Joe, and Noah, the worst of the hecklers now they'd been auctioned off. "Doesn't he scrub up well? Six feet of pure feminine fantasy up for auction tonight. Who'll give me fifty dollars?"

Bree's paddle jumped into the air.

Shaye giggled. "Feminine fantasy? OMG."

Piper's gaze swept back to West, all six feet of him. His black wool dinner jacket outlined broad shoulders and skimmed down in a pleasing "v" to his hips. With his jaw clean shaven and his blue eyes sparking fire now the hecklers had pissed him off—well, hello sailor.

Piper squirmed on her seat.

If she'd pegged the man as dangerously good-looking in blue jeans and a tee shirt, then wearing a formal suit with an honest-to-goodness bow tie?

Lethal, baby. *Lethal.*

And it appeared she wasn't the only one to notice.

Fifty dollars leaped to seventy by a redheaded loopie on the other side of the hall, topped by Bree again at a hundred, then another blonde at the front table. The bids came thick and fast: one-twenty, one-fifty, two hundred, two-fifty—

"C'mon Piper, bid!" Shaye hissed in her ear. "I'll give you a hundred. Call it an early birthday present."

"That redhead's already thinking dirty thoughts about stripping West out of that tux—look at the way she's leering at his butt," said Erin. "I'll spot you another hundred."

"And a hundred from me. Stick your paddle up, woman," said Tarryn.

Shaye grabbed Piper's arm and forced it up, yelling, "Three hundred."

Bree swiveled in her chair and gave Piper a thumbs up sign—she'd stopped raising her paddle back in the mid-hundreds.

The redhead wasn't keen to let it go. "Three-fifty."

The other blonde shook her head and laid her paddle on the table.

The crowded gave a collective "Oooooh."

"We'll see about that." Kezia yanked Piper's paddle hand off her knee and into the sky. "Five hundred," she hollered.

West's eyes bugged open.

Mrs. Taylor chortled into the microphone. "Dear oh dear...seems our Piper's staking a claim, ladies, unless anyone wants to pip her at the post?"

There were no takers.

"Sold," crowed Mrs. Taylor with a wink in Piper's direction.

Good Lord. The girls had bought her a date with West for a whopping amount of cash. Warmed by their show of solidarity and the thought of West wining and dining her in his James Bond attire—and didn't that amp her temperature up—Piper accepted congratulatory hugs from around the table.

West exited the stage as Ben reluctantly shuffled forward.

"Our last auction is a teensy bit different," Mrs. Taylor said in the microphone, while Ben scowled at West who'd joined the other men in front. "Seems our Ben has a secret admirer who's given me a private bid—a very *large* bid, in order to secure a special evening alone with this hunk." Mrs. Taylor paused, her gaze slicing through the crowd to ensure she had their undivided attention.

She did. And still she eked out every moment of drama until the crowd leaned forward in anticipation.

"The private bid is for two thousand dollars. Anyone care to make a better offer?"

Stunned silence reigned for two seconds before voices exploded in chaos.

Two-freaking-thousand?

Piper's throat glued shut, thick with emotion. Only one person could've afforded a bid like that. While Shaye and the girls squealed with excitement, Piper turned to the woman beside her.

Kezia tucked a curl behind her ear and sighed. "Your brother's a good man."

"He won't accept your money, Kez," Piper whispered. "He's too damn proud."

"He won't know where it's from unless the secret bidder comes forward to claim her prize and I've no intention of doing that."

"So why are you doing this for him—for us? Why now?"

"Because he helped me out tonight and I owe him. I owe him and I don't like that debt hanging over me."

Piper's eyes narrowed. "Really."

"I'll tell you about it tomorrow. Let's not ruin the rest of the evening."

"He'll figure out it's you. Ben might look like a big, mute lug, but he's no dummy."

"I know, but he has no choice but to accept it—time's run out, hasn't it?" Kezia said gently.

Yep. Time had run out for Ben.

And for her.

Thanks to the generous contributions tonight, Ben's debt would soon be paid, but the hourglass had flipped—and the days she could legitimately stay in Oban were trickling away. Ben's cast was due to come off next week and she'd received three when-are-you-getting-your-butt-back e-mails from members of her squad.

Piper's skin prickled. West watched her from the front of the stage, his gaze speculative, his mouth drawn in a terse line. Had he come to the same conclusion?

She didn't want to leave. She had to leave.

The words hammered through her brain with the same painful throb as her heartbeat.

Piper looked away first, for once not caring at the show of weakness.

West hadn't given any indication he wanted her to stay. They'd kept their conversations light, distracting each other with smoking-hot sex to avoid the one bald fact carved in granite.

She was leaving.

Time had nearly run out for them.

Chapter 17.

"If I fall out and wreck Mum's dress, you do realize she'll skin you alive?" Piper dropped her hand over the side of the dinghy and let the cool water bubble over her fingertips.

"So don't lean out so far, and you won't fall, dummy." West didn't break the rhythm of his strokes as he rowed them out to The Mollymawk.

"Dummy?" Piper kicked West's shin, conveniently bare since his suit pants were rolled up to his knees. "This was your idea, numbskull. I would've shagged you senseless back at your place, without coming all the way out here."

West laughed, the sound spilling out over the night's stillness. She grinned back at him, loving the way his teasing and the whispery breeze ruffling her hair soothed her earlier nerves.

After that one awkward moment at the charity auction, the rest of the evening passed in a blur. West whispered in her ear that he'd made other plans and at eleven they sneaked out a side entrance. Once on the beach she kicked off her heels while he hauled Ben's dinghy to the water's edge.

"Such a way with words, Pipe. How could a man resist you shagging him senseless?"

Piper adjusted the flowing skirt of her dress, piling it on top of her thighs so it wouldn't trail in the murky seawater puddle below. West's gaze tracked up her bare leg. Apparently he wasn't opposed to unconsciousness via multiple orgasms tonight. Her nipples puckered against the dress's silky lining.

She hunched under West's dinner jacket, which he'd draped over her shoulders after she mentioned the chill out on the water. The scent of his jacket, all spicy cologne with heady undertones of hot male, tempted her to bury her nose in the collar. Pride kept her from snuffling it like a bloodhound.

"You did. For quite a while." Piper linked her fingers and cupped them around a knee.

West continued to row, strong strokes that pulled his white shirt tight across his chest and biceps. Piper tried not to gawp. Tried and failed.

"I wanted to be the good guy." He paused, the oars trailing in the water as the dinghy bobbed along. "I didn't want you to get hurt when you—never mind. I just don't want you hurt."

"Right." Cuz his Piper-immunity was up to date. He could worry about protecting her tender romantic feelings, since *he didn't share them*. How selfless.

"We both know this is temporary," he said.

This. Whatever the hell *this* was.

Was *this* her curling toes when he kissed her hard and fast before releasing her with a grin that promised more later, much more? Was *this* the ache in her belly when she dared to contemplate life without Ryan Westlake in it again?

They drew alongside The Mollymawk and Piper took a deep breath. She could continue to snip at West, or somehow let go and just embrace the now.

"Yeah, I know the score." She placed a hand on his knee. "And I don't want to ruin tonight. It's been perfect so far."

He squeezed her fingers, his eyes as dark and unreadable as the fathoms below. "I wanted it to be."

He helped her onboard.

West guided her to the main stateroom, his hand splayed on her lower back. He brushed his hands down her forearms under his dinner jacket and gave her a teasing kiss, pulling back before she could twine her arms around him.

"Close your eyes and relax. I won't be long."

Piper obeyed and leaned against the wall.

The stateroom door whispered open and shut. Wood creaked as he moved inside the room. West had gone to some effort. Would he go the red roses and champagne route? Or the beer and satellite TV, casual and chummily-relaxed route? The door opened and she caught the flicker of candlelight before squinching her left eye shut again. Not TV and beer.

He stood in front of her, and even without the sense of sight every single atom and molecule in her body leaped to attention. She'd know him blind, deaf, or in a straitjacket. West was part of her DNA. It took extraordinary willpower to keep her arms tucked under his jacket, when she wanted to rip off his fancy shirt so she could taste him from stomach to sternum.

A finger traced a lingering path down her cheekbone and along her bottom lip. It dropped off her chin, continuing south until it rested against the wildly bumping pulse at the base of her throat.

"Cheater." He threaded his fingers through her hair.

Cheater, liar, fornicator—he could call her anything as long as her punishment involved some part of his body touching hers.

"You can look now."

Her lids flickered open. Blue eyes darkened by the languid pools of his pupils gazed back only inches away. Piper closed the distance and pressed her mouth to his, sighing as the power of it dragged her under.

West broke the kiss after a few seconds, sensuously nibbling her lower lip as he pulled back.

"Come with me." He extended his hand, and without hesitation, she took it.

Kissing West made her so ditsy that if he suggested a dip in Halfmoon Bay as foreplay, she'd be out of her dress and in the harbor's freezing water in no time.

West opened the stateroom door and led her inside. Tea-light candles dotted around the room spilled golden patches of light across the cherry wood flooring. Lush green stalks topped with distinctive violet blue flowers were scattered over the wood.

"Periwinkles?"

West let go of her hand and shoved his fingers into his hair, rumpling the smooth strands into bed-head sexy.

His shoulders drooped and he huffed out a sheepish sigh. "I know, they're weeds. I planned to steal a few roses from Mrs. Taylor's garden, but she'd figure out who snatched them and hunt me down."

He'd gotten her flowers. Not just filched some roses or had a bouquet delivered with an easy mouse click.

No. West had gone into the hills above Oban and picked her wild flowers.

"West, they're beautiful."

"You're beautiful."

Piper looked up at the sound of his gravelly voice. Her bare toes curled on the wooden floor. She could say nothing to that, her vocal chords frozen solid. He'd never once told her she was beautiful. In the last week he'd shown her with his hands, with his mouth, and with his body, but he'd never spoken the words out loud.

West closed the gap between them. "I lied, that night."

That night. The heat of it still stung like a fresh burn, branded in her memory. The night of her school ball when West told her they were done. That everything that happened between them was a mistake.

Piper bit down on the inside of her cheek. She would not—*would not*—be one of those women who sniveled and flapped their hands to fend off girly tears.

"I spent half the evening with my hands stuffed in the pockets of my rented suit, trying to keep my hands off you—or to stop from embarrassing myself—since I just about came in my boxers when I saw you in that dress."

The prickly stiffness in her spine eased. She'd wondered why West kept his hands hidden, miserably assuming he didn't want to be at her graduating ball. He'd been so quiet that afternoon when the four of them boarded the ferry to the mainland—Ben who gallantly escorted Erin to their ball, and her and West.

Piper pulled West's jacket closer around her shoulders. "I hadn't worn a dress in years. I felt like I was in drag."

He shook his head. "You were stunning. And clichéd as it sounds, you took my breath away."

"I had hardly any boobs to speak of and I wobbled like a baby giraffe in my new black pumps." Pulse thrumming thickly, Piper looked down at the floor. "You were right, I wasn't much of a woman. I couldn't believe you wanted me—a tomboy playing dress-up."

"I wanted you long before then." His fingers caressed her chin, tilting it so she met his eyes. "And, God, I'm so, so sorry for what I said. You were every bit a woman—a gorgeous, dazzling woman—and I didn't deserve you. You should've kneed me in the nuts for what I said."

She stilled his fingers sliding along her jaw with a trembling hand. "So why did you say those things?"

His gaze darkened and shuttered. "Because I knew you well enough to slash at your Achilles' heel. You'd hate me afterwards, and hating me was the only way you'd leave Oban to follow your dream of becoming a cop."

Piper sucked in a breath to disagree, but he was right. At eighteen she'd wanted to be a cop, but her head had been stuffed with romantic daydreams of West and living happily-ever-after on Oban. She wouldn't have left him and when their teenage affair petered out. She would've stayed, pining.

"I hated you for a long time." Her voice emerged as a hoarse whisper.

Yeah, she'd hated him. Hated him in the way consuming love can flip one-eighty degrees. But, oh, how she wished she could let go of that hate, after it'd gotten its poisonous claws into her. How she yearned for icy indifference to replace the heart that bled every time her mother or sister mentioned West's name.

"Well, I deserved it. I was an immature little shit."

"Yes. Yes, you were."

He eased his jacket off her shoulders, tossing it over a nearby chair. He pulled her into his arms. "Well, tonight I want to give you a different memory of an after-ball event."

"Event, huh? Well, that's raised my expectations." Piper rose on the balls of her feet to rub her lips along his jaw.

The stubble along his chin prickled against her sensitized skin. Delicious prickles accompanied by little darts of pain. Because tonight would only be another static snapshot to paste in her mental scrapbook. Nothing lasting, nothing ongoing. Just a pretty memory to overwrite the ugliness of the past.

Well, beggars couldn't be choosers and all that crap. When she boarded the ferry for the last time she'd cram this pretty memory into the ragged hole left in her chest.

West slid a hand up her back, tugging experimentally on her dress's zipper. "You weren't kidding about your mum's attachment to this dress, were you?"

She rotated her shoulders and he obliged by sliding the pull-tab down a few inches. "It's vintage. So we'd better get it off, stat."

Pressing a kiss onto the base of her neck, he murmured, "We're not rushing anything tonight, baby. No matter how much you beg."

He showed her how torturously slow he could move by stripping the dress off her bit by bit, kissing and tasting each inch of exposed skin until she stood naked in front of him, bar her panties. West swept her up into his arms, his sheer upper body strength making her feel small and delicate cradled against his chest. Not often a five-foot-ten woman had a man go all *An Officer and a Gentleman* on her. At least, not this woman.

And it wasn't every day she got the butterfly-dancing sensation in her belly of stepping off a precipice into something from which she had no hope of escaping.

West laid Piper on the bed and stood upright again. Candlelight traced swirling patterns over her creamy, naked body—naked except for her skimpy red panties. With fingers that weren't quite under control he struggled to get his miniscule shirt buttons undone.

Piper crawled over to the edge of the mattress. Coordination would come a lot easier if he could stop watching the sweet sway of her breasts.

"I want to do that for you." She hooked a finger in the waistband of his pants and reeled him in.

Brushing his hands away, Piper undid two more buttons, pausing to run the tip of her tongue over his nipple.

"God, I love how you taste," she murmured as she made quick work of the other buttons and pushed his shirt open.

Her gaze tracked from his chest to the bulge in his pants.

"And I can't wait to get my hands—and mouth—on you." She raked fingernails gently over his abs and he couldn't repress a sharp shiver of pleasure when her fingers once again slipped under the waistband of his pants. One finger found him beneath his boxers and stroked around his head with a touch that had his cock jumping.

Yeah, but then they'd both go up in flames. They generated some amazing frickin' heat between them—one shared look and minutes later he'd be buried inside her, her moans in his ear as he drove them over the edge.

But tonight was different. Tonight was all about her.

West peeled her hands out of his boxers. "You're gonna have to wait for that, baby."

With a smoky laugh, Piper eased back on her haunches. "I'm very impatient."

"Always in such a rush." West stripped the shirt off his shoulders, letting it fall to the floor. "When getting there is half the fun."

"That wasn't your philosophy two days ago when you did me on your desk during a coffee break." Piper lay back on the bed and ran her big toe down his straining erection, her smile feral.

He caught her foot and walked forward until her knee bent. Then he traced moist kisses from her ankle to the join of her inner thigh.

"Behave." He closed his teeth on the muscle that trembled under her skin.

Fingernails dug into his shoulder. "I'll be good. Get naked though, okay?"

"Not just yet." West blew across the damp trail on her leg and outlined the "v" of her sex with one finger, before pulling back, satisfied with her moan of protest.

Moving farther onto the mattress, he settled into the cradle of her hips and pinned her wrists above her head. He kissed her, keeping the touch of his tongue to hers lazy and sensual. When he judged every protest was out of her system, he rolled to the side and plucked a little silver foil wrapped object from the nightstand and quickly un-wrapped it.

Piper jerked at the sound. "I thought you wanted to take it slo—" the slight note of indignation was cut off when he slid the unwrapped Hershey's Kiss into her mouth. Her lips closed and he could've sworn her eyes rolled up in her head.

"Chocolate." She made a low orgasmic sound as she rolled the morsel around.

What was with women and chocolate? Maybe this wasn't one of his better ideas. He'd hoped to hear those sounds exclusively when she came—again.

Then Piper opened her eyes to half-mast. "You are so getting lucky tonight, Westlake."

"I've more where that came from, but you have to earn it."

And he proceeded to introduce her to the rules of his game, one by one.

He devoured her mouth until neither of them could breathe without gasping, suckled and kissed her breasts until she moaned his name, laved his tongue down to the line of her panties, and then stopped. Rewarded her with another dose of chocolate.

She swore a blue streak before he shut her up by popping another Kiss into her mouth.

"You're a teasing bastard," she groaned around the chocolate.

"Yep." West stripped her panties off. "One chocolate left, Pipe."

He leaned down and kissed her again, loving the taste of chocolate and the tang that was uniquely Piper. "And you'll have to work for it."

Licking his way down her delectable body, he paused only long enough to shuck off his pants and boxers, returning to kneel between her thighs.

"I want to touch you," she said.

"You do touch me."

Piper's hands glided up to his chest, her thumbs stroking his nipples before sliding down to trace the line of hair below his belly button.

His breathing snagged. "God, you have no idea how you touch me."

West slid down her body, positioning his mouth right where he wanted to be. His fingers unfurled the delicate pink folds in front of him and he wrestled with the temptation to bury his lips there. He could make her come hard in minutes, but as he'd told her, there'd be no rushing tonight.

West took his time, delighting in the soft, musky smell of her, the velvet taste of her arousal as he circled his tongue over the bundle of nerves at her core.

Women could keep their chocolate. He'd take the heaven between Piper's legs any day.

"Please, West." It wasn't the first time she'd pleaded.

He licked her again and slid two fingers inside. Piper moaned and he pinned her to the bed with his free hand to keep her writhing hips in position.

"Like that, huh?" His cock pulsed, wanting desperately to replace his fingers as her inner muscles contracted. Seconds later, Piper cried out, her body jerking hard under his hands.

West rolled on a condom and joined her, not giving Piper a chance to come down from her high before he thrust into her. Slick sweetness encased him as he palmed the curve of her ass and lifted her so he could drive deeper.

God, she felt incredible.

"West—"

His name a shattered gasp on her lips he pulled back, teasing his cock at her swollen entrance until he had her undivided attention. Hazel eyes dueled with his, alternately begging and then demanding he take them over that last obstacle.

Not yet.

He stretched her arms over her head once more and explored her mouth with confident strokes of his tongue, at the same time sliding his hips forward.

Tight, hot, and his.

He trailed kisses along her jaw. "Watch me, baby. Don't shut me out."

With slow, steady thrusts, West moved within her. The tension built layer upon layer, exquisite friction that inflamed every inch of him until his balls were about to explode from the pressure of holding back one mother of an orgasm. Liquid heat beneath him, Piper urged him faster, but he wouldn't be rushed.

He released Piper's wrists, cupping her face in his hands and keeping their gazes entwined.

"Why are you torturing me?" She shut her eyes and writhed beneath him, which did some erotic things to his trapped cock.

West nibbled her bottom lip, touched her closed lids with gentle fingers. "No cheating. Keep them open and I'll give you what you want."

Silky black lashes flickered open. "I want you."

Not enough. Not nearly enough.

Because she owned him now, each disconnected part of his heart made whole by her claiming. There was no retreat, so he didn't hold anything back. Frustration, need, desire, denial, desperation.

Love.

Everything he had inside, he gave to her. Trapped by her soul-filled eyes, West let go, trusting instinct and emotion to carry them both home.

Piper drew her legs higher around his hips as he thrust into her, another languid pulse of pleasure spiralling outward from her core.

West rolled them over until she sat astride him, then reared up so she was seated impaled in his lap—eye to eye, nose to nose, mouth to mouth. He cupped her jaw and kissed her again, pulling back a fraction so that when he breathed out, she sipped his breath into her lungs. He surrounded her, completed and filled her.

And it was his absolute focus as he moved gently within her that stirred the first flutters of another orgasm deep inside. How could she hold on to her resolve, when to look at his face emptied everything out of herself, except him?

When he gave her that killer smile, and said "Come with me, baby," she quit fighting the inevitable. West asked for her heart and she handed it over without a murmur of protest. But could he see it? Could he tell by their visual connection she'd taken that last step and fallen in love with him?

Before Piper could figure it out, the staggering wave of her second climax slammed into her. She cried out West's name, letting his endless blue eyes take her into the abyss.

***

No wandering hands or lingering kisses woke West the next morning.

Instead, the growl of an outboard motor and a male voice hollering his name snatched him from a very pleasant dream. He'd been about to do Piper on his kitchen table, so being woken by someone requesting to board The Mollymawk pissed him off no end.

What pissed him off more was the tangle of naked limbs sprawled across his body shifting away as Piper woke. She stumbled out of bed, taking the sheet with her, leaving him bare assed, his good-morning-sunshine hard-on waving.

She wound the sheet around her body and tucked the ends in the notch made by some delectable cleavage. Catching his gaze on her breasts, Piper hiked the sheet higher.

"Well?" she said in that snitty tone he'd come to adore. "It's not like I can get Mum's dress on before our visitor boards."

He stretched, satisfied at the way Piper's gaze honed in on a certain part of his anatomy. If he hadn't recognized Noah's voice and figured the cop wouldn't be paying them an early visit to congratulate him on being one of the studs at the auction last night, he would've stormed out of the stateroom and told Noah to take a hike.

Footsteps squeaked in the hallway followed by a sharp rap on their door. "You in there, West?"

Since he and Noah and Ben were mates, Noah didn't feel the need to adhere to the concept of receiving permission in order to trespass his cop-ass all over Ben's boat.

"Yeah, hang on, Noah. Let me get some pants on, for Christ's sake." West rolled off the bed, sending Piper, who'd abandoned the sheet for his shirt, a sorrowful look.

Acres of velvety skin disappeared under his shirt as she buttoned it up. Damn. Twenty minutes and he could have her twined around him, panting and screaming his name again.

A pregnant pause from outside the door and a muffled rumble as Noah cleared his throat. "I'm sorry to wake you too, Piper."

A blush rose from below the collar of his shirt, staining Piper's neck a rosy pink.

"Crap," she mouthed.

Did she really think anyone left on Oban didn't know the score after last night's bidding war?

"It's fine, Noah," Piper called out, while half bent over and flinging periwinkle stalks aside.

His shirt crept farther up her thighs as she ducked down to peer under a chair. God, what a sight. West scooped up the scrap of red lace from beside the bed and dangled it under her nose before holding it high out of her reach. "Looking for these?"

Piper tickled his ribs until he relented and dropped her panties. She snatched them up before they hit the floor, hurling a look that could crack the eggs he'd planned to make her for breakfast. "You're a funny guy, Westlake."

"Baby, I live to make you laugh."

"Get your pants on and go see what Noah wants." She turned away—but not before he'd caught a glimpse of curving lips.

West grinned back and yanked on his rumpled suit pants. "Yes, dear."

"Bite me," came the muttered reply, as Piper vanished into the tiny en suite and slammed the door.

West stepped outside their room. Noah, dressed in his police blues, leaned against the opposite wall. He spoke into his phone, harsh lines carved into his forehead.

Something serious had happened and here West was, underdressed for the occasion.

Noah disconnected and met West's gaze. "I'll buy you a beer in apology later, mate, but this is important. I need to speak to Piper too."

West's stomach dropped to his knees and he sucked in a harsh breath. "Did something happen to her family?" he murmured, with a quick glance over his shoulder.

Noah shook his head. "Nothing like that. They're fine—they're all fine."

West held up a finger. "Then give me a minute to grab her some spare clothes. She's not a morning person and she won't be happy to greet you in her current get-up."

Noah sent him a crooked smile. "Don't get distracted."

Ten minutes later they found Noah on the aft studying the filler cap of The Mollymawk's fuel tank. Piper had swapped his shirt for the spare tee shirt and shorts she kept in the single cabin.

Noah's expression had Piper's gaze flat-lining into pure, concentrated cop. "Tell us."

"We've got a missing person. Gavin Reynolds."

"And you're here because...?" West said.

Noah directed his next words at Piper. "Gav had a run-in with your brother last night before the ball. Kezia provided me with a statement that Gav inappropriately touched her in the parking lot. Ben found them and intervened."

"Son of a bitch," Piper hissed.

Son of a bitch, all right. West gritted his teeth and focused his gaze on the sea. Good thing Gav was missing, because when he woke up with a hangover under some tree he'd be the center of a shit-storm of hurt. He and Ben would see to that—and it sounded like Ben had already given him lesson number one.

"By 'intervened,' you mean Ben beat the shit out of him," said West.

"In a manner of speaking." Noah shoved his hands into his uniform pants. "Gav's mate, Trent, contacted me early this morning. Told me Gav planned to row out to The Mollymawk last night and dump sugar in the tank. He sat in the park and watched Gav in his dinghy head off at around ten, and then passed out on the bench. He didn't see him make it to the boat and when he woke at sunrise, the dinghy hadn't been returned to its usual spot." Noah paused, rocking back on his heels. "And we all know how anal Gav is about his 'spot.'"

"Understatement." A slow curl of unease wound through West's body. "Trent went to his house?"

"Yeah. Gav wasn't there."

"The dickhead could've contacted you before Gav went out on his revenge mission." Piper walked over to the gas tank and bent over for a closer look. "You've already organized a house to house?"

Noah nodded. "No sign of him yet. Thought I'd better check The Mollymawk to see if he'd made it out here."

"We arrived at about half-eleven last night and everything was locked up," West said. "We didn't see any sign of Gav's dinghy when we rowed out."

Noah ran through more questions, ending with a thorough examination of the gas tank, which didn't appear to have been tampered with.

"Ben said Gav was drunk, reeking of Jack Daniel's. He likely didn't make it this—" Noah's phone trilled Bob Marley's "Bad Boys." He answered, listened, and then quick-fired instructions. Disconnecting with an, "On it," Noah swore. "Old Smitty's just called it in. He found Gav's dinghy drifting about a mile offshore."

"No Gav?" Piper said.

"No Gav," Noah agreed. He shoved the phone back into his pocket. "Right. I've got to go back to base and coordinate with Search and Rescue and organize the locals so they aren't buzzing aimlessly all over the bays." He glanced at Piper. "I know you're not on duty, but can you contact the dive squad and put them on alert?"

Piper's lips thinned into a pale line, but she nodded. "I'll get on it."

West hooked an arm around her shoulders. "Count us in with the water search, Noah. We'll take my Daisy."

"Thanks."

Once Noah left, West tugged Piper into his arms. For a few moments, her body strained against his, but then she relented, threading her arms around his waist and holding on.

With anyone else he'd come up with platitudes like, "Maybe Gav swam back to shore," or "Perhaps Trent got it wrong." He stroked a hand over her hair, felt the shudder sweep through her. But Piper knew better than anyone the likelihood of finding Gavin-the-bloody-idiot Reynolds alive.

Chapter 18.

A cool breeze ruffled Piper's damp hair as the launch chugged to the next search area. She squinted past her boss's shoulder into the darkening sky. Sunset was an hour away and this would be their last dive of the day.

The Police Dive Squad had arrived this morning, after yesterday's land and sea search failed to locate Gav. Locals scoured the bays and beaches for hours, grim-lipped with the knowledge the ocean's low temperatures meant Gav's survival would be a major miracle.

Piper had greeted her buddies at the airfield and drove them to Oban's tiny police station for their first briefing. A cluster of locals watched as the five men climbed out of the borrowed van and Oban's one official police utility vehicle. Everyone knew when police divers hit town, the search switched from locate and rescue, to body retrieval. If they could even find him.

Her hands hadn't stopped trembling since she first donned her wetsuit earlier.

"You okay for the last shift, Piper?" Tom leaned back on the bench and took a swig from his water bottle.

Had he missed her shaking hands each time she'd resurfaced? Did he buy her "freaking cold water" explanation? Maybe.

Piper slicked back her hair and shrugged. "Totally. I don't know if Buck can handle another one though—looks like he's been hitting the KFC while I've been away." She jabbed her elbow into the rock-solid abs of the officer slouched next to her.

"You'll keep, girlie." David "Buck" Rogers, a six-foot something Maori, lifted his mirrored shades long enough to send her a wink.

Laughter and good-natured heckling erupted around her. She'd missed her guys—Buck, Paulie, Mac, Trigger, and even Tom. The five of them—half of their squad remained in Wellington in case another call came in—had worked through some awful cases together. While none of them would claim to be world-class divers, they prided themselves in their ability to get the job done as a team.

Ten minutes later Piper dived with Buck and Trigger at her side. The wind had picked up, stirring sand and sediment through the water, so visibility was iffy. All part of the job—it was a rare day when the squad could claim the luxury of ideal conditions.

Piper finned toward the sea bed. Their last grid search would take place in water fifty feet deep and according to Tom's calculations, if they didn't find Gav before the tides turned again, the recovery odds grew even slimmer. Piper didn't want to be the one to relay this fact to Peter Reynolds, who still scoured the beaches hoping to find his son alive.

Foveaux Strait had taken many lives and sometimes the dead never returned from her volatile depths, her father a classic example.

Piper thrust that thought from her mind. Thinking of her dad's death was almost a knee-jerk reaction, given what she was now doing in this stretch of ocean. In her time on the squad she'd never been assigned to a recovery operation farther south than Invercargill. She imagined that Tom, who knew her history since he'd been one of the divers searching for Michael Harland, had engineered that.

When she met him at the airfield he'd given her the look. The *are you up to this kid* look. And she'd nodded, knowing before he even requested her assistance what he'd planned.

She could do this. She'd *trained* to do this. She just had to focus.

Steadying her breathing, she continued to sink into the murky depths.

Piper reached the sea floor, her fins stirring up even more silt. Visibility? What visibility. This dive would be like looking for a needle in a haystack, or finding *Where's Waldo?*—every sarcastic cliché she could think of to distract her mind from what she was doing: hoping to discover the body of a man she'd known since childhood.

Time became meaningless as Piper worked the grid. She relied solely on her sense of touch, because outside her mask swirling eddies of sand and silt clouded what little vision she had in the light of her dive torch. The currents buffeted her, the harsh rasp of her breathing and the blood soughing past her eardrums the only sounds.

Her right hand, sweeping in a slow arc, nudged something solid. She moved her left hand to join the right and it skimmed over the distinctive shape of a foot. Moving closer, Piper squinted through the haze. She didn't need the visual confirmation, but the ghostly flicker of a white shirt in the light of her torch confirmed it anyway. She'd found Gav.

With three sharp tugs of her swim-line, Piper signaled that the victim had been located. Tears pricked in the corners of her lids and she kept them back by sheer will, but the icy clutch of panic waited for a sliver of opportunity to rip years of training from her grasp.

Sucking air like she was down to her final few ounces, she whipped her head around at a flash of black to her left. It was only Trigger and Buck finning to her side, but the loaded bolt of adrenaline blazing through her system made her want to vomit.

She gripped the torch, the handle ridges jabbing into her palm even through the layer of neoprene.

She had to get out of there, before millions of tons of seawater crushed her to a pulp.

Her movements jerky, Piper floundered and grabbed Buck's arm, signaling with her other hand that something was wrong. She owed it to her team to let them know—this time she'd swallow her pride.

Buck took one look at her, and after ascertaining her equipment functioned correctly, gave her a thumbs up instruction to ascend. She didn't consider arguing.

Trigger indicated he'd stay with the victim until a fresh diver could be sent down and Buck signaled on the swim-line to let Tom know divers were heading up. Buck watched her like a mother cat as they finned toward the surface, and the solidarity of his presence along with his paw-like grip on her hand acted like a shot of sedative. At the safety stop, she returned his querying "okay?" with an almost honest "okay" signal of her own.

But the cavernous churning in her stomach signaled a truth she didn't want to accept.

She couldn't do this job anymore.

***

Piper had been sequestered in Oban's tiny police station for hours. And West was prepared to wait until she'd finished all her official crap, even if it meant sitting out here on his bike for another hour. Or two.

He'd spoken briefly to her earlier back at the wharf when she'd returned with her grim-faced squad after delivering Gav's body to the undertaker on the mainland. One look at Piper's gaunt face and West wanted to hold her and kiss her until those hazel eyes lost their defeated look. Something other than finding Gav happened out there. But she denied it, squeezing his hand and telling him she needed to accompany her squad back to the station.

She walked away, surrounded by her cop buddies. One of the men—a big Maori bastard with a crew cut and the posture that came with military training—popped him the assessing eyeball as he walked past, glued protectively to Piper's side.

West refused to let the big guy intimidate him. *Yeah, you look after her, mate.* Because he knew Piper belonged with them. A fact slammed home when the man bent and murmured something in her ear and she offered him a weak smile.

She should be with her squad. Not here with him, stuck in the place she once described as the Greenbelt of Hell. Yet, he'd asked his parents to close for the night and brought his bike to wait for her—so she wouldn't have to walk alone in the dark.

West scrubbed a hand down his face, his fingers rasping against two days' growth of stubble. He was pathetic. Fucked up in love with a woman who was leaving in a week's time—and he'd known it from the start.

The station door opened and Piper walked onto the small deck, warm light from inside spilling onto her, bringing out the auburn highlights in her hair. She was dressed once more in black jeans and combat boots and his heart give a little flip as she jogged down the steps and walked over to him. West jammed his helmet on. God, he'd be spouting love sonnets at her in a second.

He held out the second helmet. "You gonna argue this time?"

Piper shook her head and took the helmet, shadows masking her features. "Take me on a ride somewhere, West. I don't want to go...back, not just yet."

His jaw tensed under the helmet's chin guard. A little hesitation before the word "back." Couldn't she say the word "home," or perhaps she didn't feel it. His place, *him*—well, neither of them were home to Piper.

West twisted the key hard and thumbed the starter button. The bike's engine roared to life. Piper tugged on the helmet and climbed on. Her arms slid around his waist, her thighs snug against his. One of her hands stroked his abs before stilling, clenching onto the thin fabric of his shirt. He gunned the bike and pulled away, picking up speed as they hit the long strip of road to Oban's tiny airfield.

They rode in silence and each time they leaned into a curve Piper hugged him tighter, her breasts pressed into his back. It near killed him when her chest hitched, the jerk followed by a stealthy sniffing sound.

Goddammit to hell.

West drove onto the tiny airstrip, abandoned and empty after the last flight left for the mainland hours ago. He killed the bike engine and hauled off his helmet. Behind him, Piper climbed off and placed her helmet on the ground. She stalked away, swiping her fingers across her cheeks. West kicked the bike stand down and went after her.

He came up from behind and touched her shoulder, then stroked his hands down her folded arms. "Talk to me."

Piper's lips pinched shut, her chin pointed along the runway, the breeze ruffling her hair as it raced down the wide clearing.

"I found him," she said.

"I'm sorry—" He tried wrapping his arms around her but she ducked out of the way and whirled, holding up her hand.

"Gavin Reynolds was a complete prick, but still, it's irrelevant how I felt about him. Once the water claimed him, he was my responsibility." Her chest heaved and the hand she'd extended shook. "Mine. And I let him down, and worse, I let my team down."

She swiped her wrist beneath her nose and refolded her arms. "I panicked, West. I panicked when I touched his foot and if it hadn't been for Buck and Trigger, I could've got into serious trouble."

Icy tentacles wrapped around his guts and squeezed. He could've lost her. The bends could've claimed her, or worse. "Fuck."

"Yeah, and it's not the first time it's happened." She cut him a glance. "I lied when I said the shark didn't scare me—that I didn't panic."

"I kinda figured."

She snuffled out a watery laugh, wiped her cheeks again. "Yeah, well, an incident happened before I came south. A teenager drowned while water-skiing in Lake Tikitapu."

"I heard about that on the news. Were you one of the divers who found him?"

"Yep."

West closed the distance between them. Tears glittered and spilled over her lashes.

"I was *the* diver who found him. And I saw something in him that resembled you at the same age. I nearly lost it."

This time when he laid gentle hands on her, she didn't pull away. "You're solid, Piper. You reacted by the book when I blacked out and I think you're selling yourself short."

She sighed and ran a trembling hand through her hair. "Yeah? Well, maybe I am, because what else is there for me?"

West cupped Piper's nape and she fell forward, burying her face in the crook of his neck. Her arms slid around his waist and clung.

Me. He wrapped himself around her as she wept. *I'm here for you. I've always been here.*

But the greasy chill inching down his spine told him he wasn't enough. Not nearly enough.

***

The tendons in Piper's neck protested as she walked away from the graveside service at Oban's cemetery. Behind her, Peter Reynolds and Gav's older brother, Seth, remained at the open grave. She peeked over her shoulder once again at the two men, silhouetted against the churning pewter clouds. The smaller figure hunched in grief, while the other stood to attention, his arm awkwardly positioned around the older man's shoulders.

Five days had passed since her squad returned to Wellington, leaving with casual but pointed assurances they'd see her in a week. She waved them off with a smile that wouldn't have fooled anyone. But she made it through Gav's service—thank you, God, because she *hated* funerals—and hadn't once given in to the temptation to glance at her father's memorial.

She held on to her mother's arm as she and West helped Glenna navigate the damp, slippery grass.

"Such a terrible waste." Glenna dabbed her nose with a tissue and stuffed it into her jacket pocket as they reached Ben.

Her brother grunted and folded his arms, leaning back against Due South's courtesy van. Piper sent him a warning stink-eye. While Gav hadn't been the most popular man in town, Glenna suggested it would be more sensitive to his family if Ben remained by the parked cars.

Over the past few days gossip had sprouted wings and flapped from front porch to back, house to house. But while her brother received a few sidelong glances, no one dared accuse him of anything. People chose to gloss over the fact the deceased had been a bully who'd planned to vandalize a half-a-million-dollar boat, and instead lamented the loss of a hardworking, authentic bloke.

Glenna patted Piper's hand. "I'm sure Peter and Seth are very grateful to you for bringing Gavin home, darling."

"At least Piper gave the *Reynolds* a body to bury," Ben muttered, as he opened the passenger door of Due South's courtesy van for Glenna.

Piper's feet, in borrowed kitten heels—since combat boots or sneakers didn't seem appropriate for a funeral—glued themselves to the asphalt. Her stomach lurched to her throat as if the ground had started to roll like the Strait on a rough day.

"Benjamin Michael Harland." Glenna whirled, her voice chipped ice, the tone all three Harland siblings had been terrified of as kids. "Everyone in the van, right now. Since there's no privacy at my place, family meeting at West's."

"Asshat," Shaye hissed as Ben climbed into the van ahead of Piper. "Look what you've done—*another* family meeting."

West flicked Piper a questioning look as he slid the van door shut, but she just shook her head. She'd accused herself of everything Ben thought or tactlessly said out loud. She just wanted this awful day over with.

Glenna was a demon matriarch when she got her mad on. Ordered into West's living room, the four of them sat when told and kept their mouths wired shut as instructed.

"That was an insensitive thing to say." Glenna stopped pacing and stood in front of Ben, who was slumped into an armchair. "I can't believe you'd imply Piper was in some way to blame for us not getting Michael back."

Curled into one sofa corner, Piper massaged her forehead. "It's okay, Mum, it doesn't bother me."

"No, it's not okay." Her mother fixed Ben with a loaded gaze.

"Who should we blame for Dad's death, then?" Ben laced his fingers together. "You, for not being there that morning to stop him? Shaye, for sleeping through the whole thing? Me, for being out drinking with my mates? Yeah, I blame all of us too. But Piper's not innocent—" He tossed his head in her direction. "She could've refused to go out diving with Dad that morning. He wouldn't have gone alone."

Glenna sunk onto the other sofa next to Shaye, her rigid posture suddenly dissolving into that of a much older woman. "Not while he was sober, no."

Piper's gaze flipped to Ben, then back to her mother. "Dad didn't drink. He couldn't with his cholesterol medication."

"Your father never took cholesterol medication. He used the idea of needing medication as a cover for not drinking alcohol," Glenna said.

Piper's heartbeat went from a plod into an out-of-control sprint. "But he was always at the pub."

"Drinking ginger ale. Or lemonade. He never touched alcohol, even though he caught a bit of grief for it at times."

"Why, Mum?" Piper tried to swallow the words back—to keep her mother from speaking the harsh truth written in her tired eyes and down-turned mouth.

"Your father once had a problem with alcohol, but he'd been sober for more than fifteen years when he died."

"A problem? Like an alcoholic?" Piper recoiled back into the cushions.

West slipped out of his chair and sat on the sofa arm beside her. The warmth of his hand on her shoulder steadied her.

"He didn't like to label himself that, but yes, as a younger man he was an alcoholic and it shamed him terribly. He drank to cope with the demands of being a city cop. That's why he moved to the island, for a fresh start. He told me he quit drinking the day we met." Her lip quivered once then steadied. "By the time we got married he hadn't had a drink—said he hadn't *needed* a drink—in a year. I promised him then that so long as he kept his vow to remain sober we need never mention it again. You know your father and how much he prided himself on being a man of his word, of how much self-discipline in free-diving and in life meant to him."

Glenna sighed and sent Ben another look. "So if you want to blame anyone, blame him and then blame me. We kept a secret from you kids far too long when it should've been out in the open."

"Sounds like you kept a lot of secrets," Ben said sourly. "Were you telling the truth about arguing over finances that night?"

Glenna shook her head, her lips pinching so tightly that harsh grooves cut canyons around her mouth. "I was ashamed to admit what we really fought about—his free-diving. I accused him of being old and foolish, and then I gave him an ultimatum—'Quit the Nationals or I'll divorce you.'" She paused to blot her eyes with her tissue.

"Oh, God." Piper sank back into the sofa. "You threatened to divorce him?"

Glenna exhaled a shuddery sigh. "At the time I truly meant it. I was just so terrified of losing him."

"So you went to the Komekes' after dropping that bombshell on him." Ben's voice was as stiff as new cardboard.

"He refused to discuss it any farther and froze me out. I decided we'd be better to have some time apart to think."

"By then it was too late," Ben said.

Glenna nodded and pulled a fresh tissue from her pocket. "It wasn't until Shaye and I cleaned out his office two months after his death that we discovered a half empty bottle of whiskey hidden at the back of the closet. I couldn't speak, couldn't *breathe*, when I realized Michael had likely started drinking after I left that night." She pressed the back of her fingers to her lips.

"I saw him." Shaye toed off her heels and tucked her legs up onto the sofa.

In the maelstrom of emotion whirling between her, Ben and Glenna, Piper had forgotten Shaye. Icy prickles swept down Piper's spine. "Shaye?"

"I got up for a drink of water and Dad was sitting at the kitchen table in the dark—he scared the crap out of me. He had a tumbler in his hand—" Shaye paused to scrub the heel of her palm across her cheeks. "He apologized for frightening me and told me to get my water and go back to bed."

"You couldn't tell the difference between a glass of water and a glass of booze?" Ben said.

"She was fifteen," Glenna snapped. "And it was dark."

"So you knew?" Ben said to Shaye, lurching out of the armchair. "You knew he'd been drinking *something* that night and you never said anything to the police, or to Mum?"

"The police asked me where I'd been all night and I told them the truth—in my room! I didn't think seeing Dad in the kitchen was important." Shaye hugged herself. "How was I to know he wasn't just thirsty, like me? Then Mum and I found the whiskey bottle and we figured it out."

Glenna straightened her spine. "I decided it would do no good for the gossipmongers to find out about Michael's problem. Nothing would bring him back or make his death any easier to bear. So I made Shaye promise we'd keep his secret."

Ben limp-stomped to the picture windows facing the ocean and turned his back on them. "All these years I've blamed myself, blamed Piper for agreeing to go out alone with him, and it turns out our father was an irresponsible drunk."

"He wasn't irrespon—" Piper said.

"Don't dive drunk or on drugs—wasn't that rule number two or three in that damn litany he taught us? Christ." Ben whipped around, the cords of his neck stark either side of his bobbing Adam's apple. "Didn't he stop to think if something went wrong his teenage daughter would have to deal with it? Irresponsible bastard."

Glenna flinched and Shaye covered her face with her hands.

"Don't talk about him that way." Piper scrambled to her feet, her nails cutting into her clenched fists. "You don't know what Dad thought. He made a mistake and he paid for it with his life."

"Well, you've paid for it too." Ben threw up his hands and stormed out of the living room, clomping down the stairs and slamming the front door.

"He's right," West said behind her.

She whirled to find his intense blue stare stripping her of all her defenses.

"You've carried this burden for nine years and it's eating you from the inside out. Time to let it go, babe."

The guilt was a cold weight in her chest, but unlike a diving belt she couldn't just press a button and have it drop away.

"West's right, darling." Glenna touched her arm. "And I'm sorry for being so self-absorbed I never realized how much your father's death still affected you."

Piper forced a smile to her lips. "I just need some space to get my head around this." She patted her mother's hand, on the outside trying to look as if she'd pulled herself together, while on the inside her whole belief system crumbled.

Alcohol still in her dad's system impairing his judgment, emotionally distracted by relationship difficulties, and pushed by innate competitiveness to prove himself. If she examined the facts objectively she came to a simple conclusion. Diver error was the cause of her father's death. *She wasn't entirely to blame.* But it still *felt* like it.

"Well, don't take too much time," Shaye said with a sniff. "You're heading back to the city at the end of the week." Her sister switched her red-rimmed gaze between Piper and West. "Or maybe not."

Piper sank back onto the sofa. Clouds scudded past outside and the same light wind blowing them across the horizon shook tree leaves in a continuous rustle against West's house. Donny padded onto the deck and slumped down, rolling onto his back as a hint for someone inside to rub his belly.

And West said nothing. Not. A. Thing.

Not a, "Like hell the love of my life is leaving a second time," or, "Piper won't be going back to the city alone because I can't live without her." Not even a, "I'm hoping to convince Piper to stay longer so we can continue bonking our brains out every night."

"I hope you and Ben can clear the air before you go," said Glenna. "And he's not the only one you need to sort things with."

Her mother glared at West who still stood behind her. Fabric rustled and she imagined he folded his arms and gave Glenna a stare right back.

Piper linked her fingers on her lap and squeezed. "We've got one more shark dive booked before I leave on the Saturday morning ferry. Back to the grind on Monday. My holiday's over and I've got a job to do."

"Speaking of jobs," West said. "They're expecting me back at the pub to help at Gavin's wake. I'd better get going."

Rough fingertips closed on her earlobe and tugged gently. "You'll be okay?"

Piper turned to West and forced her lips to hold the fake smile she'd slapped on. "Sure. I'll get changed and wander down to help Bill and Claire in the kitchen."

Piper focused on the bridge of his nose, pretending to make eye contact.

Because damned if she'd let him see her soul raked to shreds at his indifference.

Chapter 19.

The four mates making up the tour group on her last shark cage dive were weenies.

But they were paying weenies.

A banker, a sales rep, a real estate agent and some computer something-or-another hotshot. All out to prove they were real men by strutting around with their wetsuits peeled to the waist to show off their real manly chests. All laughing and shoving each other as they descended into the cage, and all going strangely still when the first Great White appeared out of the gloom.

Piper floated at the far end of the cage, making sure the real-men's masks hadn't fogged up or their air lines tangled. So far two sharks had visited. One, a huge mature female with a ragged dorsal fin she'd nicknamed Shabby Sally, and the second, a juvenile male she hadn't seen before.

The female glided by, regal and powerful—eying them with her beady black eye as she swept past with lazy tail sweeps. After dives, their clients often gushed about how beautiful these creatures were. But to Piper? *Oh, hey, look, a tank with teeth.* Not beautiful. Majestic, impressive, memorable—she conceded. But an animal with a one ton bite capable of chomping off a limb if you were dumb enough to poke it out of the cage didn't deserve "beautiful" as an adjective.

She tapped the guy next to her on the shoulder and positioned her gloved fingers into an "okay" sign. Eyes wide behind his mask, Raymond-the-banker didn't appear to require an adult diaper just yet. She bent forward to check on the other three men and a grey blur exploded into her peripheral vision.

A shark's conical shaped snout jammed into the horizontal gap of the cage, its body whipping and shuddering. Her heart bolted into a gallop and she jerked back. *Crap!*

Pandemonium erupted as the four real men panicked. Raymond flailed backward, ripping the regulator from her mouth in an eruption of bubbles. Keeping her lips sealed, Piper swept her hand through the chaos to relocate her regulator, but good ol' Raymond still thrashed around like a total spaz keeping it from her reach. *Double crap!*

Two of his mates vamoosed out of the cage and the other cowered in the back corner. The juvenile shark, smaller and more agile than the female, twisted forward wedging its bullet-like head and toothy maw farther into the gap. The Great White might give her a case of the screaming heebies, but its bulk couldn't squeeze through solid steel. At least, she hoped not. But West couldn't raise the cage with two terrified clients and one instructor with no freakin' air, all while a two-thousand-pound teenage shark had a hissy-fit, half in it.

Sudden motion to her right. A foam of bubbles cleared as legs clad in black board shorts, followed by West's bare chest and grim face, appeared in the cage beside her. He held a fishing gaff in one hand and moved to her side, using the top bars of the cage to steady himself as the shark struggled. Whether it still wanted to eat them or had changed its mind and was trying to free itself, she didn't know. But West seemed unconcerned that Jaws attacked only inches away.

Real man number three in the cage corner unfroze and floundered up the boat ladder. Piper recovered the regulator and shoved it back in her mouth, sucking in great gulps of air. Raymond-the-banker looked near to a coronary episode, so with a meaningful glance at West they each grabbed a wrist and stilled his flailing arms.

She dragged the regulator from her lips and held it out to West, who just rolled his eyes behind the face mask. Yeah, got it. Free-divers didn't need bottled air—show off. She patted the banker's arm, willing him with her intense stare to *calm the hell down.*

West turned in a tight circle and aimed the blunt wooden end of the gaff at the shark's head. A couple of well-aimed jabs to the gills and a smack across the snout made the shark fight more. The cage vibrated and clanked, while above, voices shouted in hollow booms.

Piper sucked in another gulp of air and although her heart still thudded in a quickstep, the sick, spilling-over feeling of panic didn't follow. Though the Great White's razor-sharp teeth flashed close to her face, her concern was directed toward the trembling banker hiding behind her. And West. West who jumped into the cage with only a fishing gaff and a face mask.

West jabbed the creature again and it wrenched away from the cage in a flurry of white water, disappearing into the murky gloom. West turned back toward them, since he'd placed his body between her and the shark, and gestured to the ladder. This time she didn't argue. Raymond-the-banker didn't need to be told twice either.

Fifteen minutes after West shook off the backslaps and hails of, "You're a bloody legend, mate," from the real men, he cornered her in the galley.

"You okay?" He placed his hands either side of her hips, trapping her back against the counter.

No doubt he meant: *You're not going to wig out on me, are you?*

"I'm fine." She tried to shove one of his arms away, but his muscled forearm under her palm wouldn't budge.

He raised an eyebrow and she sighed. "I am, West. A little shaky, but I'm not about to hyperventilate or bawl my way through a box of Kleenex."

"That's my girl." West shifted his hand to her hip, squeezed. "Tough as nails."

"Speak for yourself, Westlake. Your four groupies out there are hailing you as the Kiwi version of Bear Grylls and Steve Irwin rolled into one."

"Would've looked bad if I'd stayed on the boat squealing with the other two guys."

Piper squirmed when West's other hand dropped to her hip and then slid around to cup her bottom.

"Squealing, huh?" she said.

"Like little girls."

"I suppose I'm grateful you showed up when you did."

"Well, your banker may have drowned himself with clumsiness before the shark decided his skinny ass wasn't worth the bother."

"So you didn't jump in to save me?"

He stared at her thoughtfully. "This is one of those female trick questions, isn't it? Damned if I do, damned if I don't."

"Answer the question."

"I wouldn't let anything happen to you, Pipe, but I also knew you could hold your own. Consider me your backup shark wrangler."

"You're still my hero." She meant the words to come out with a heavy note of sarcasm, but as West's lips grazed a sensitive spot under her jaw, they instead sounded breathy and soft.

West hauled her into a bone-crushing hug. Piper clung back, burying her face in his throat. His pulse hammered so fast it bumped against her lips. She kissed the throbbing bump and closed her eyes. The hard length of him warmed her from chest to knees and she inhaled eau de West, the salty, earthy scent of his skin.

He'd saved her, and not just from the shark. West believed in her like no one else ever had. He'd jumped in the cage not because he doubted her ability, but as an equal partner. Once, she'd been devastated when West called her tough. Now the look in his eyes told her that "tough" in his vocabulary translated to "hot."

But would that be enough to warm her on all the empty nights yawning in her future after this weekend?

***

Piper walked into The Great Flat White café, the grumble of The Mollymawk's engine receding as it chugged toward the marker buoys in Halfmoon Bay behind her. West would lay anchor and meet them inside for a brief rundown before they headed to Due South for another evening shift. Though greasy dishwater appealed a lot more than suffering through Ben's teasing about "Piper-shaped shark bait."

West radioed in earlier to let Ben know their clients were safe, and the four real men bragged the whole way back. Their city friends would no doubt hear a modified version of events—one in which they were cool and heroic. She hoped it would boost Ben's business.

"No shark jokes." She sat at Ben's table and pinched a French fry off his plate. "I heard every variation on the way in."

Ben's lips twitched, the only indication of amusement since his brown eyes remained steady. "You're okay?"

"It was a freaky fluke. No harm, no foul." She finished the French fry and stole another. "The shark was probably more unhinged than me."

"Could you climb into the cage again?"

Piper upended the tomato sauce bottle over Ben's plate, the thick red sauce oozing onto the white porcelain. "Are you implying I'm a wuss because some dumbass shark got disoriented and thought we were dinner?"

"You're the bravest woman I know."

Piper froze, her half-eaten fry hovering between Ben's plate and her mouth, fat red globules dripping onto the table. Had lightning struck, or had The Rapture started?

"Did you just pay me a compliment?"

"I'm serious. And I need to know, could you take another tour into the cage?"

Nibbling on the fry, Piper leaned back in her chair and crossed her ankles. Could she do it? Even with a lost regulator and a big-ass shark snapping its jaws in her face, she'd remained focused. *She hadn't panicked.*

"Yeah, I could." For some reason sharks no longer worried her as much as the thought of coming across another drowning victim. "Have you got another booking this week?"

Ben shook his head. "So, are you still planning to board that ferry on Saturday?"

She'd reached across the table for another fry when Ben's words killed her appetite. She dropped her hand, her fingers clenched. "Already bought and paid for my ticket. Plus the connecting flight from Invercargill to Wellington."

"Back to police headquarters. The guys miss you, huh?"

"They do." She blew out a breath. "But I'm going to resign from the squad."

Ben's gaze shifted to the windows opening out toward the harbor. In the distance The Mollymawk bobbed on the swells with a circle of gulls wheeling overhead. A tiny figure moved around on deck.

"Your decision, but you should be proud of what you've achieved." Ben's voice dropped. "Because we're all proud of you."

"Thanks," she managed before her throat clamped shut.

He leaned forward, his large hand covering her fist. The unexpected touch turned the lump in her throat to a boulder. "I've been a sorry excuse for a brother and you know apologies aren't my thing, but I'm sorry. For everything."

She blinked and looked down at their hands.

"So I'm asking you for time to make up for being such a jerk all these years. You don't have to go back, Pipe. Stay, and work with me."

"As your safety diver?"

"And to run your weekend shagging cruises, which, yeah, yeah, have turned out to be wildly popular. I also thought we could offer more comprehensive learn-to-dive training courses—that way, you could spare your squad some work."

"You want me to work for you?"

"Nope. I want you as my partner."

So much swirled around in her head, her palms sweaty at the idea of staying and working with Ben, that she repeated his words like an imbecile. "Be your *partner?*"

His brow creased and he rapped two knuckles against her forehead. "Didn't I just say that?"

She swatted his hand away and he grinned. They were good now. Or, on the way to being good.

Studying his face, she said, "I'll have to think about it."

Ben turned his head toward the window and she followed his gaze. Out in the harbor West rowed the dinghy back to shore. Pressure, like boiling magma, bubbled in her belly and seared her lungs.

Ben offered her a way back to her roots, a way back to herself—if she could admit these last six weeks diving recreationally were the happiest she'd spent in the water for years.

"Will you tell him?"

Her gaze darted back to Ben's face at the tone in his voice. "Tell him what?"

"Tell him you're considering staying? You ripped his heart out last time you left."

"*I* ripped *his* heart out?"

"At first I thought West was just busted up about Dad dying, like me. Then I caught him with your photo—and twigged to why he was a basket case for months."

"But *he* dumped *me.*"

Ben barked a harsh laugh. "No kidding?"

"He told me I meant nothing more to him than a quick summer screw."

Ben winced and shook his head. "I really didn't need to know that. But still, you believed him?"

"Yeah I believed him—he was very *believable.*"

"Maybe I should step outside and kick his sorry ass for treating you like that."

"Yeah, that'll help."

Ben leveled a piercing Harland stare at her. "What'll help is if the two of you stop dancing around the flaming obvious."

Piper snorted.

"You're in love with him," said Ben. "And he's in love with you. If you both weren't so bloody proud and tied up in knots, you'd tell each other and be done with it."

She jerked upright. God, were her feelings for West so transparent that even her *I don't talk about girly emotions* brother felt compelled to point them out?

"I'm not in love—" Realizing how loud her voice had become, Piper stopped and sucked in a breath before continuing in an octave lower. "We both knew our relationship was casual, temporary at best. And this is so not a topic I'm discussing with you."

She stood, and her chair screeched on the wooden floor. "I've got kitchen duty with Bill."

Ben grinned up at her, all smirky and smug, flapping his elbows and making a clucking sound. "Running away, my little feathered sister?"

Piper bared her teeth. "Well, I could spare another five minutes to grill you about *your* sex life."

Ben's smile faded and he folded his arms. "Not going there."

"And you call me chicken," Piper threw over her shoulder as she walked away from him and stepped outside into a brisk sea breeze.

Piper hustled her butt off the wharf and along the road to Due South. In the distance West drew closer to shore in the dinghy. She walked faster. Coming face to face with him right now? *Such* a bad idea. Not when she felt so vulnerable, her heart having finally rolled over to expose its soft underbelly.

Was Ben right? Was she really in love with him—a forever-kind of in love with him? And if so, did she dare deliver her heart into West's hands again?

***

West opened sleepy eyes to find an empty bed. Normally he woke before Piper, wrapped around her like a pretzel. Last night they'd worn each other out, the intensity of their lovemaking a silent illustration of time slipping away. West kicked off the sheets and pulled on discarded jeans and a shirt.

He padded through the house, the first burnished rays breaking over the harbor and spilling through the windows. Piper wasn't in the office surfing the net or in the kitchen brewing their morning coffee. He glanced outside. Donny's tail and half of his body wagged as he ambled down the driveway.

West slipped on a pair of battered sneakers and followed his dog, finding Piper picking flowers at the property edge. Nothing too odd, except dawn was way too early for flower arranging, and today was their last morning to cuddle, aka fool around. Tomorrow Piper would hop on the Stewart Island ferry and out of his life.

Piper turned, clutching a fist of battered-looking daisies.

"Oh. You're up." She tucked in her lips and kept her eyes downcast. Like that would hide her tear-wet cheeks and reddened lids.

Donny scooted over and plopped down on her feet, leaning his head against her knee and whining. Piper was a total sucker for his mutt's woe-is-me act, but this morning she didn't even glance at him. Something was wrong.

"So you're...trimming the shrubbery?" he said.

"I'm going up to Dad's memorial and I wanted to take something." She gave a half shrug and waggled the makeshift bouquet. "Pretty sad specimens, aren't they?"

"He wouldn't have minded."

"No. I don't suppose he would've."

West canted his head. Piper had grown from mischievous kid, to awkward teenager, into an amazing, courageous, and beautiful woman. More than anything he wanted to watch her grow into a feisty old lady who'd continue to stick her freezing cold feet on him every night of their long, long lives together.

He wanted to tell her that, but he wouldn't use her emotions and vulnerability to convince her to give up the career she'd fought so hard for in Wellington. How could he ask her to give up something she loved? Something that gave her an identity and purpose?

He shoved his fists into the front pockets of his jeans, bracing his spine for an argument. "I'd like to come with you."

She gently nudged Donny off her feet. "Okay."

That was it? No thunder and lighting and barbed comebacks? West upgraded something wrong, to something very, very wrong.

They walked the winding road to the cemetery with Donny trotting at their feet, the trill of a tui fluttering from flax bush to tree ringing through the still morning air. Michael Harland's memorial stood away from the other graves, in a section Glenna had purchased after he died. Glenna intended to be buried beside the memorial she told West once, even though the sea had stolen her soul-mate and never returned his body.

And as far as he knew, Piper hadn't returned to this spot since the day she left Oban.

Piper stood in front of the memorial, a pyramid-shaped stack of river rocks, Michael's name and dates inscribed on a plaque at the base. To one side lay a browning rose stalk, the petals long blown away by the sea wind rippling across the grass.

A rose from Glenna's garden.

Every Sunday morning Glenna walked past his road to the cemetery. Would he ever feel that same dedication, that unswerving love and loyalty for a woman? Piper dipped into his line of vision as she laid her daisies on the other side of the cairn. Yeah, he felt it all right.

The real question—would he ever feel it for anyone but her? A resounding *no.*

She straightened, crossed one arm over her belly and used the other hand to cover her mouth as she stared at the stones. He stood at her side, his hands forming fists in his jeans pockets while he debated hauling her in for a hug. Muscles bunched in her jaw and then released as she huffed out a sigh.

"You heard what happened that morning, at the inquest." They were alone, but her voice only just rose above the twittering birds hopping around the headstones. "How I found my dad on the seabed and dragged him up. How I tried to resuscitate him, how I knew he'd gone. And then how I couldn't get his body onboard the boat by myself, so I had to let him go." Piper smeared a runaway tear off her cheek.

"What I didn't tell the inquest was of my own cowardice. While I was trying to get Dad onto the boat, I glimpsed a shark—" She glanced at him, but before he could hold her gaze it skipped to the trees encircling the cemetery. "One of the big bastards, I think—"

Bloody hell. He and Ben had all but forced her back into the water with them.

West called himself every foul name he could think of. "I'm sorry—"

Piper patted his arm and he winced at the brotherly touch. His game plan didn't include being relegated back to the role of her old friend, but he hadn't a clue how to stop her pulling farther and farther away from him.

"It's okay. I was stuck there in the water, trying to hold onto Dad. The weather closed in and a shark was somewhere below. I've never been so terrified."

"God, Pipe—you weren't a coward. There was no way you could wrestle a man who outweighed you by over a hundred pounds onto that boat, and only a crazy person would remain in the water with a

Great White. I don't know how you went through that and stayed sane. No wonder you freaked out that first time."

Piper swallowed. "Yeah, but it's strange. I'm not terrified of them anymore. The sharks are what they are and I don't blame them."

"You blame yourself, though."

"Oh, yeah." The pain emblazoned in her words drilled him as mercilessly as her gaze when it swung back to his. "I was moping over you, West. I'd cried myself sick the night before, and all I could think of while I waited for my dad to hurry up and finish his dive was what I could do to change your mind. Maybe if I somehow transformed myself into a hot chick with big tits and a curvy ass, you'd want me again." She snorted out a bitter laugh, which *just killed him.*

"I didn't see my dad struggle. I didn't see him reach the end of the guideline—" Piper's voice rose to fingernail-on-blackboard level. "I didn't see him get into difficulties, because all I could see—" she nailed him with a finger in the center of his chest "—was you, and how much I *fucking loved you.*"

West recoiled. Each word, each jab of her finger punched like a nail gun. Piper had loved him. But what had that love turned into when she lost her father? She'd carried the weight of her father's death on her conscience for all those years, linking it to her old feelings for him. How could she bear to touch him? How could she stand making love to him? How could she even look at him, when he shared just as much culpability in Michael's death?

He opened his mouth to speak, though God knew what could fall out to make things better—but she interrupted. "Please, don't say you're sorry again."

Right. That limited his options. So West buttoned it, his heart rending into useless shreds when Piper sank down in the dewy grass, a sob escaping from somewhere deep inside her.

"Daddy, I'm sorry. I'm so, so sorry I screwed up." She squeezed the words out in a croak as she traced her father's etched name with a fingertip. "But you screwed up too and somehow I've got to believe you've forgiven me, so I can forgive myself."

West dropped to his knees at Piper's side and tugged her into his lap, fully expecting an elbow to the ribs or a fist in his nuts. Instead, she wrapped herself around him and clung. He bowed his head, his arms full of warm, weeping woman. At least she trusted him to hold her while she grieved. Piper burrowed into him, her face pressed to his neck, tears soaking into his collar while he smoothed his palm over her shuddering back.

When her sobs finally tapered off to sniffles, West brushed back her fringe and looked at her face. Even puffy-eyed and blotchy with emotion, her loveliness still smacked him upside the head every time. "It's a lot to ask, but can you ever forgive me? If you blame anyone for that day, it should be me."

Her brow creased and her fingers slid into his hair, caressing his scalp until they suddenly gripped his nape. "I realized sometime in these last six weeks that I'd already forgiven you—that I needed to take ownership of my feelings for you back then."

Bittersweet relief coursed through him. "Honey, if you can forgive me, surely you can forgive yourself? Your father never held a grudge in his life longer than ten minutes. How could you think he'd blame you when he broke so many of his own fundamental rules?"

She sniffed, loud and long. "I've carried this guilt with me for so long, I don't know how to stop."

"Leave it here. Leave it right here with these stones." His eyes stung. Must be the sea spray.

She sighed, and laid her head back on his shoulder. "He waved at me before he dived, you know. I remember the whiskers on his face, the glitter of his wedding ring in the sunlight. He'd been quiet all the way out on the boat, but as soon as he hit the water he started to smile again."

He stroked her hair. "He loved to dive and he loved sharing that with the three of us."

"I'll never stop missing him."

"No, none of us will. But it's time to see his death through a different lens."

"Yeah." She pulled back to look at him, choking out a wry laugh. "I sure could've used some of your wisdom while I fixated on all the 'if onlys' over the years."

"There are so many, huh? But the biggest is—" he grazed a thumb across her cheekbone "—if only I hadn't taken the easy way out and broken things off before you could leave me."

"I wouldn't have left you."

His forehead touched hers and he breathed her in. "I know."

And as unavoidable as a jab to the throat, there lay the problem. He swallowed, though the spit in his mouth had turned to ash. Piper would've stayed with him and eventually become restless and miserable. All those years ago she didn't know what she'd be missing. Now, she had a whole other life in the city. A life with different friends, a challenging job, and men who could offer her more than being a pub owner's wife.

Wife? That was outta left field.

Wind stirred her hair, blowing strands of it up to tickle his jaw. He cradled her face, loving her silky skin under his fingertips—couldn't imagine not touching her a week from now.

She sighed, her breath puffing softly against his chin. "West?"

Piper, becoming his wife. So, was he really going there? "Mmm?"

Her spine stiffened, vertebrae by vertebrae under his arm and she leaned back, her expression guarded. After a short hesitation she said, "Will you still dive at Lake Taupo?"

Piper's question derailed his thought train, currently chugging along the one-way-track to commitment-land. "Oh. Um, yeah. I've already got Ben on board as one safety diver and I hoped you'd agree to be my second..."

Piper's eyes popped open wide and her fingers hooked like cat's claws in his shirt. "You can't ask me that."

His glance skipped to the memorial. "Well, I hadn't planned to ask you here—"

"No, no, no—here or anywhere, the answer's no. After what I just told you, after you blacked out on me only a few weeks ago, *how can you still compete?*" She wrenched away and nearly kneed him in the nuts as she scrambled to her feet.

"Whoa, hang on. You've seen me still training every morning at the pool and never said a word."

She whirled on him. "What *word* could I have said? Is there anything I could say to stop you competing in the Nationals?"

His stomach plummeted like he'd descended a flight of darkened stairs, miscounted and stepped off into the void. West stood, every nerve, sinew, and muscle thrumming with tension. Stop him? Piper wanted to stop him from the one thing he loved, the thing that gave him an identity and a purpose?

"This is important to me, Piper. I've worked too hard to quit free-diving because you don't approve."

Color drained from her flushed cheeks. "I'm not asking you to quit free-diving. But competitive apnea has a lot more risks than if you just enjoy spearfishing or diving without a tank on your back." She stalked over to him, her chest heaving. "You'll push yourself to win, I *know* you will—and I won't watch anyone else I care about kill themselves for a *sport*."

Piper shoved both palms against his chest, which rocked him back a little on his heels. They glared at each other, gasping like marathon runners. When she uttered a sound suspiciously like the snarl of a small cornered animal and went in for another shove, West grabbed her wrists.

"This isn't about me, it's about your dad. *But I'm not your father.* I'm not fifty years old or an ex-alcoholic on a bender. I'm not going to die!"

She cringed away from him, her eyes haunted. "Maybe not, but you're wrong. It is about you—it's about you, and me, and if there can be an 'us' that lasts longer than tomorrow."

Fire broiled in his veins, taking every lick of oxygen with it until it reached flashover point in his mind. He threw down her wrists and jerked away. "Are you giving me an ultimatum? Is that it? Give up your dream, West, or there is no 'us'?"

Talk about your frickin' irony.

He'd worried he couldn't ask her to sacrifice her job and the dive squad to be with him. Yet Piper would manipulate his feelings for her? Would use her power over him to try and snatch something vital from his grasp, just to ease her fears?

"Haven't you learned anything from your parents' mistakes?"

Piper blinked at him, tilting her chin. "Oh, I learned something. And that's why I'm not making any demands at all. As for me walking out of your life, are you offering me a place to stay in it? Or am I destined to become a sob story you can tell future girlfriends, as the reason you believe a woman wouldn't want to stay with you forever?"

He gaped at her, his rampant heartbeat firing so much super-charged blood into his head that any logical thoughts got blasted into oblivion.

"Uncomfortable when the table's turned, isn't it?" She folded her arms and retreated another pace back, the gap between them wider than Foveaux Strait. "If you're not my father, West, then I'm not your *goddamned mother.* I would've come back to you after Police College. I would've loved you, had a family with you, and made a life with you." She flung her arms open and a gull perched on a nearby headstone arrowed into the sky with a flurry of wings. "If a man loved me with all his heart and soul, nothing would make me leave his side for long— ever. But I suspect you're not that man."

She stood there, palms spread wide and tremors ravaging her slender limbs, imploring him to say something, *anything*.

He had nothing. Zero, zip, nada. She may as well have asked him to communicate the contents of his heart to her in Swahili. And so he remained, as impassive as the carved monuments surrounding him.

Piper gave him one last, silent chance to speak, then turned and walked away.

Chapter 20.

Piper waited until she was well out of West's sight before she allowed the tears to come. She swiped at her face as she jogged back along the road, Donny at her heels.

She gave him a cuddle and a belly rub at West's back door and ordered him into his ratty bed of blankets. He whined and shivered. One of life's little ironies—West loved Donny, but he couldn't love her.

Guess the mutt was easier to love.

Piper blew him one last kiss and slipped inside.

It didn't take long to stuff her belongings into her backpack. The whole time she moved around West's bedroom her bruised heart thrashed out a frantic rhythm—wishing, hoping, yearning for him to walk in the door.

She walked over to the bureau, where only a few weeks ago he'd emptied the top two drawers for her without comment. She plucked out the pair of red lace panties she'd bought on that shopping trip with the girls. Remembered him peeling them off her legs, of him teasing her with them the next morning after a night of blissful lovemaking. She winced. Lovemaking, huh? Hot and steamy, mind blowing and world altering, but if she believed he made *love* to her, then *she* was a moron.

Piper grabbed handfuls of panties, bras, and socks, and carried them to her bag. Oh, sure, what West felt for her was more than just sex. He cared about her and probably even loved her, in a way—the way you love someone you've known forever. Someone, perhaps, related to your best mate. He wouldn't cut her out of his life just because she was dumb enough to fall in love with him.

And yep, good folks of Oban, she was just. That. Dumb.

But like hell would she hang around to experience West waving her off from the wharf with a casual, "See ya later." While she tried not to sever her tongue in an effort not to beg him to love her back.

No begging. Begging was bad.

She glanced at one of the framed photos on West's bureau. In it, a much younger West, Ben, and Piper stood in front of Due South, mugging for the camera. It'd been West's sixteenth birthday, a month before Claire Westlake left the island for Los Angeles. Piper stood between the two boys and Claire captured the photo at the same instant Piper and West snuck a glance at each other. The expression on her face was unmistakable: hero worship. Complete and utter devotion, even before she fell in love with him. And on West's face? She shook her head and replaced the photo face down.

West never even noticed.

Piper emptied the drawers and then with still no sign of West, she rang her sister.

"Shaye? You think you can clear your bedroom floor off for one night? I need somewhere to stay until tomorrow."

Three long beats passed before Shaye responded, her voice gentle with unspoken sympathy. "Sure, Piper. My floor is your floor. Just drop your stuff in whenever."

Piper could've kissed her when Shaye left it at that—no sly questions, no demanding explanations, no what-the-heck-happened? "Thanks, sis. I owe you one."

"Yeah, yeah, what else is new."

Piper hung up and hauled on her backpack, the weight of it on her shoulders bowing her spine. Surely it hadn't been this heavy when she first arrived? Well, it weighed a ton now, and every ounce of it killed a little more of her spirit as she trudged down the stairs and out of West's life.

**

"I never thought I'd say this to my own son, but Ryan, you're a fool."

West looked up from his overcrowded desk at Claire, frowning, in his doorway. When he said nothing, his mother folded her arms and huffed down her nose.

"The ferry leaves in twenty minutes and here you are, pretending not to care that Piper will be hugging everyone goodbye right now—everyone but *you*."

He could've switched his laptop off and with a withering tone asked Claire just who was she to judge, but instead he dropped his gaze back to his spreadsheets. He'd blinked at the same one for the last hour, without adding anything. Great improvement to his temperament.

"I'm working. We've already said our goodbyes."

A big, fat lie.

Something shriveled and died in him last night when he returned from work to find her stuff gone. He'd gone straight to Due South after the cemetery. A mountain of paperwork awaited him and why not an end-of-summer stock-take? So he hadn't seen her, hadn't ventured into the restaurant kitchen, and part of him hadn't been surprised walking into a silent house. What he hadn't expected was that the empty dresser drawers and the framed picture turned face down on top would hurt as much as it did.

Piper had left him again. While her barely disguised ultimatum still rankled, he understood the fear driving it. He also understood that by saying nothing, he'd once again pushed her away.

Claire entered his office and turned to shut the door.

As her fingers rattled on the handle he glanced up. "Don't shut it. You're not staying, because you don't get to tell me what to do."

She stopped mid-swing. The door squeaked as she pushed it open again and she stood beside it, cocking her head as she studied him with the same patient look that used to cause him and Del to confess within seconds. "I lost that right when I walked out on you and Bill. Does that about sum up the situation?"

West hissed out the breath he hadn't realized he'd been holding. "Yeah."

"Then I won't tell you what to do," she said softly. "Instead I'll tell you how decisions can change the course of your life. That, at the time, it never occurs to you the repercussions of those decisions could one day come back to haunt you. My decision helped shape who you are today, a man who would let the woman he loves walk out of his life because he's convinced history will repeat. For that alone, I'll never forgive myself."

West leaned back in his chair and tried to maintain a disinterested expression. "Quite a speech, Claire. But Piper made her choice."

"Before or after you told her how you feel about her?"

He swiveled his chair around to face the window.

"I can see why you've made comparisons between the two of us," she said. "However, Piper loves this place as much as you do, and more importantly, I believe she loves you. If you're not in love with her, then tell me to shut up. I won't be offended. But if you're letting her walk away because of fear, then you're about to make the biggest mistake of your life."

"Fuck," West dropped his head into his hands.

"Precisely."

He hated that she was right.

"Make a better decision than I did, son."

The door clicked shut behind her.

He was losing Piper again, this time for good. All because he refused to man up and put his feelings out there. Surely they could work something out about the Nationals, once they talked through it in a rational manner? And if he told her he loved her and she walked away afterward, would it hurt any less?

West stumbled out of his office and was halfway through the kitchen before he answered his own question.

Hell, no—and at least he'd know where he stood.

The wharf, crowded with passengers, was a nightmare to navigate when you were in a hurry. Not a good look if he bowled one of the howling, snot-faced kids into the water in the rush to locate his woman. His head spun from scanning everywhere at once, trying to spot either Piper's distinctive hair or a flash of purple combat boots. He excused himself past yet another dawdling duo right in his path.

"Shaun." He waved at the purser standing by the ferry gangplank and jogged over. "Piper on board yet?"

"The hot punk chick who bought you at the auction?" Shaun scratched his pathetic excuse for a goatee beard.

West gritted his teeth. Also not a good look if he clocked a ferry employee. "That's her."

Shaun shook his head. "Haven't seen her, pal, and she should be on board by now—we're sailing in five."

Hope flickered, died, and then burst into life. Where was she? Maybe she changed her mind? Maybe she was waiting for him back at his place?

He whipped around and nearly collided with Ben, who stood two paces behind him, his hand outstretched, about to tap him on the shoulder.

"Where's Piper?" C'mon, how desperate did he sound? West shoved his fists into his pants pockets and said in a lighter tone. "She'll miss the ferry."

Ben dropped his hand, his face implacable. "She's not catching the ferry."

A silly grin crept onto West's face. Maybe she *was* back at his place, curled up on the sofa with one of those trashy paperback crime novels she loved. Or even better—naked in his bed waiting for make-up sex. Okay, some groveling on both their sides might be in order before that particular fantasy came true but—

"I put her on the first flight out this morning," Ben said. "She left half an hour ago."

His heart stopped. Just stopped dead. Like each artery pinched shut, trapping volcanic amounts of blood inside.

"Back to Wellington?"

"Yep. I watched her kiss Mum and Shaye goodbye and board the plane." Ben tilted his chin, a familiar family gesture, which sucker-punched his heart into beating again.

She'd gone.

Piper had gone.

Then somehow he had to figure out a way to get her back.

***

Nothing like a road trip to put her new unemployment situation into perspective. Piper wound down her Mazda's driver's-side window and sucked in a lungful of cool autumn air. Well, technically, she wasn't unemployed yet—but she'd handed in her notice two weeks ago when she arrived home. After that painful discussion with Tom she'd moved in with a friend for a few days, because left to her own devices in her tiny flat she would've resorted to a pajama-wearing, junk-food eating, ugly-blotched-faced-crying mess.

But today was a new day. Piper coasted down the road to the tourist town of Lake Taupo, the lake a sparkling azure against the snow dusted Mt. Ruapehu rising beyond the far shore. Soon she'd no longer be a cop. It should've made her sad, but it didn't. What a wake-up call. She'd spent years making amends to her father who would've

kicked her butt if he'd known she chose to follow his career path out of
a skewed sense of duty and atonement.

Piper indicated and turned off the road into a bustling lakeside
parking lot. Set up in one corner was a registration desk with a New
Zealand Apnea Association banner staked behind it. She parked and
got out of her car, hoping to catch a glimpse of West's smiling face.
Maybe not smiling after he saw her here.

She left Wellington yesterday on a solo road trip—ostensibly to
take a little me-time to figure out her next course of action. Stowing
her dive gear in the back seat spoke volumes about her intentions.

A late night candy bar session—her go-to vice when life threw
manure-loaded curveballs—had crystallized some stuff in her mind.
Stuff like, regardless of West's stubbornness and sheer male bravado,
he *needed* her for this competition. Ben was a good, dependable diver,
but not in her league. Because she had skills, mad skills. And whether
West loved her or not, she had his back.

She wouldn't let another man she loved drown.

Piper strolled to the registration desk while trying to look
everywhere at once. Where was he? Where was Ben?

She nodded at the elderly man perched on a lawn chair behind the
desk. "Hi. I've come to sign on as a safety diver for one of your
entrants—Ryan Westlake, from Stewart Island."

"Sign on, ay?" The man peered over his half-rimmed specs. "You're
leaving it late, aren't you, lass? Safety diver details were to be
completed with the entry form." He made a sucking noise with his
lower lip. "Let me just check what's on his form." He bent over his
laptop and pecked the keys with his two index fingers.

"Here he is—Ryan Westlake, Oban?"

"That's him."

"Hmm." He scrolled down the screen. "Friend of yours, is he?"

"Uh-huh."

The man sucked his lip again and nodded. "I remember that chap
now. He's a favorite to win, you know—hang on, there's a note added

to his entry." He shoved his specs up his nose and leaned closer. "Oh my. Looks like your friend's pulled out. Rang the organizer last week, it seems."

"Pulled out? You mean he's not here?" Piper pressed her palms on the desk to give her wobbly legs some stability before she collapsed on her ass.

The man looked over his shoulder and then back at her. "Not unless he's here as a spectator."

West spectating instead of competing? Not likely. "Does his file say why he pulled out?"

A brief shake of his head. "Sorry, miss. You'll have to ask him that yourself."

Piper removed her hands from the registration desk and shoved them in her jacket pockets so the old fella wouldn't see them tremble. "Yeah, I'll do that. Thanks."

She walked back to her car, climbed in, and braced her palms on the steering wheel.

West quit the free-diving Nationals. Why?

She thunked her forehead on the steering wheel to knock the answer into her brain. Her mother and Shaye promised to let her know if Bill's health took a downward turn. Not that, then. Maybe West hadn't found another safety diver? Guilt momentarily prickled her skin but she shrugged it off. West had other diving contacts—not a valid reason to prevent him from competing.

Had he changed his mind and quit for her?

Piper thunked her head a second time. Dumb brain inventing a dumb explanation.

She rubbed her forehead and watched the boats ferrying competitors out to the dive site. Even though she denied it, she'd given West an ultimatum. Then, scared he wouldn't pick her, she'd run like a whimpering puppy with its tail tucked between its legs.

Up until this moment she thought West hadn't picked her. That leaving Oban without saying goodbye had been the right thing to do. When West didn't pound on Kezia and Shaye's front door to demand they talk it out, she assumed his silence meant *decision made.*

But maybe he was just a little slow on the uptake, being a guy and all.

Could this be a sign? A hopeful sign?

Piper snatched up her phone and scrolled through her contacts, staring at West's number as if the digits were a code revealing his secret thoughts. She sucked at code-breaking, so she checked her watch: seven thirty-five a.m.

He'd be at the piano, running his fingers over the keys. Did he miss the way she brought him coffee and sat at his side, touching his leg as he wove melodies around them? Did he miss her? She sure as hell missed him. And more than she missed the heart she'd left behind in his hands.

Did West miss her? Did he love her?

One way to find out.

She tossed the phone on the empty passenger seat and started the car. A phone call wasn't going to cut it. Piper preferred to conduct her interrogations in person.

***

Piper was about to throw up. Repeatedly throw up. But instead of dragging her own carcass under a bench to collapse, she had someone else to do it for her.

Footsteps thumped up beside her. She continued to scrutinize the green hills of Stewart Island as the ferry roiled toward it. "Are we there yet?"

"Keep staring at the horizon, you'll be right." Ben leaned his elbows on the railing, glanced toward her and then sidled away a step.

Clever man. She was this close to puking on the new shoes he'd picked up in Invercargill before he met her at the airport.

Piper hadn't expected anyone, but she couldn't stop beaming at the sight of her big brother sprawled on an airport seat.

"I've come to hold your sick bag on the crossing," Ben said with a grin.

"You could hold it, but you *so* won't."

Opting to travel like the locals, since she'd soon be one again? Not one of her smartest ideas. Because even though locals would label this ferry trip glassy smooth, her stomach disagreed, seething with nerves.

Piper shivered as a gust of wind flicked sea spray in her face. No turning back for her now. She was a boots n' all type of gal. She'd debated flying down to have it out with West the moment she returned from Taupo, but the gesture wasn't big enough. She had to show him how serious she was about making their relationship work. So she'd emptied her flat, sold her car to a neighbor's teenage son, and endured a bon voyage party. No one on the island knew her plans except family, and she'd sworn them to secrecy.

She belonged with West—and on Stewart Island she'd either negotiate her happily-ever-after, or—Piper bit her lip, aware of Ben's scrutiny. She didn't want to think about the "or," because she hadn't formulated a plan B.

Plan A consisted of West or bust.

"What if he doesn't...want me?" Even as the sentence slipped out she couldn't bear to jinx it by uttering the "L" word.

Ben draped his arm over her shoulder. Her brother must love her if he risked puke on his new shoes. "Oh, he wants you, all right. He's been a sulky SOB since you left, snipping at everyone."

"West doesn't sulk and he doesn't snip."

"Yeah? He told Mrs. Taylor to butt out of his business when she asked when he was bringing you back home."

Piper forgot her stomach. "Get out! Did she wallop him with one of her sticks?"

"Nope. She whispered something in his ear and patted his ass."

Piper forced a tight smile to her lips. "Incorrigible old woman."

Ben gently shoulder-checked her. "Don't worry, Stubby. He's crazy about you."

"You better hope so," she muttered as the ferry prepared to dock. "Or we'll end up roomies again."

"Not gonna happen." He tossed a wheeling seabird a crust of bread left over from his lunch. "You think anyone can resist a Harland on a mission? West is toast." He chuckled and sauntered away toward the end of the ferry.

Toast, huh? Piper scooped her daypack off the bench seat and followed her brother.

She only hoped it wasn't her that got burned.

***

"If you don't get out of my kitchen—" Shaye said, when West pushed through the swing doors "—so help me God I'll yank something vital off you."

West stared at her flushed face and the pair of kitchen tongs clacking in his direction and moved farther into her domain, risking emasculation. Showing her his palms, he shrugged. "Lunch crowd's getting restless."

"Well, they can wait, I'm busy." Shaye gave him one last baleful glance and returned to whatever sizzled in her pans.

West leaned a hip against a sparkling countertop and tipped his head back to study the ceiling. Up before dawn, he hadn't stopped running. With his dad putting in fewer hours, his best waitress off to greener pastures in Christchurch, and him having to fill three jobs at once, his tank ran on a whiff of fumes.

Worst of all, his chest ached from missing Piper.

He scrubbed a hand down a jaw of the same texture as a baby cactus. When had he last shaved? Buggered if he remembered. Though he did remember letting the woman he loved get away from him—what a dumbass.

Spying the growing pile of pots in the sink, West peered around the kitchen. "So, where's Fraser?"

"Lunch break." Shaye plated the steaks she'd been pan-frying and slid them onto the pass. "Not everyone is trying to work themselves to death, you know." She smacked the bell. "Run to table eight, Lani."

West swore as Lani swooped on the plates and disappeared into the restaurant.

Shaye slapped her hands on her hip and glared. "I'm starting a swear-jar. I figure with your language lately, I'll have a trip to Paris by the end of the month."

"Screw Paris." He strode to the pots spilling out of the sink and jiggled a handle. "Who's going to do all these pots? Me, I suppose."

"No, me."

Piper's voice behind him weakened his legs like someone had knee-capped him with a sledgehammer. Goddammit, had he just hallucinated again? Every morning her whispers tickled his ear and her fingertips ghosted over his back as he stood in the shower, head down and eyes shut, until the water turned freezing. She was everywhere in his house. Every-damn-where except where she should be—with him. So maybe this was another cruel trick.

But when he turned, there she was—silhouetted in the back door with Donny snuffling around her boots, a goofy grin on his doggy face. The same goofy grin he'd have if his muscles hadn't hardened into immobility.

West cleared his heart out of his throat and tried not to pounce on her right then and there. "Piper?"

"Took you long enough," Shaye said. "What'd you do, swim over?"

Piper's lips curved, the smile fading before it touched her eyes. Her gaze skimmed over his unshaven jaw, untucked shirt, and mussed hair. Yeah, he was a right mess, while she looked impossibly lovely in her black jeans and combat boots. God, he could kiss those purple monstrosities, he'd missed seeing them so much.

"Shaye." He kept Piper centered in his crosshairs. "Go and explain to the diners there'll be a delay with their meals."

"That'll go down well."

"I. Don't. Care."

If Piper moved one step he'd go caveman—and to hell with kidnapping being illegal. He'd lock her in his bedroom and pray she came down with Stockholm syndrome.

Shaye moved to his side and jabbed his arm. "I'll tell them their meals are on the house, shall I?"

West shoved a hand into his pants pocket, pulled out a two-dollar coin and slapped it on the counter. "Put this in your jar and tell them whatever you bloody want. Just do it."

Shaye snatched up the coin and hissed under her breath, "Just don't muck things up."

With a toodle-oo wave to her sister, she left them alone.

"I'm hoping you didn't come here just to wash dishes," he said.

Piper shook her head and watched him some more with those big-cat eyes which seemed to peel back the layers of his soul. Well, if she could see into his soul, she wasn't running away screaming.

A good sign.

"You caught me in the middle of chaos." He flicked a hand at the sink. "Things have been crazy around here since I got back from Wellington."

Her brow creased. "You went to Wellington?"

"I flew up to find you, but your flat was empty. The neighbors didn't know where you'd gone, your aunt hadn't a clue, and your boss wasn't helpful."

"Oh. You saw Tom?"

West nodded. What a cheery meeting that'd been, the burly cop refusing to reveal a hint of Piper's hiding place. Doubtful that a fist in the nose would loosen the man's tongue, he'd walked away.

"He refused to discuss you at all, so I had no choice but to return home to try and organize this mess until I could go back and have another go at trying to find you."

Piper scratched Donny's head, studying West from under her lashes. "I stayed with a friend and then drove to Lake Taupo for the weekend. I packed my diving gear."

Donny licked her fingers and she laughed.

Piper. At Lake Taupo. With diving gear. West pinched the bridge of his nose, trying to slow the pulse of blood exploding into his brain. "You went to the Nationals?"

"Yep."

"You were going to be my safety diver?"

"You needed one, and I'm the best."

"Is that the only reason you went*?" Please don't let it be the only reason she went.*

Piper closed the distance and laid a palm on his chest. The simple touch and the warm all-woman scent of her floored him.

"I went because regardless of how you feel about me, I wanted you to be safe."

West gripped the counter with numb fingers, swallowing. Unaware of his feelings for her, she'd pushed past her own nightmare to support him.

"That must've cost you a great deal." His voice came out rough.

She petted his chest and gave him a wonky smile. "Losing you would've cost me much more. I didn't want you down there without me watching your back."

Cupping her face, West brushed a thumb over Piper's lower lip and rested his forehead on hers. Her eyelids fluttered shut and her breathing hitched.

"I shouldn't have let you walk that day—you were right, you know. I didn't realize I'd pushed you away because of how my mother left me." He chuckled bitterly. "I always thought I was a bad prospect for a long-term relationship—disposable, unlovable—feelings that became a shield to stop any woman getting too close. Except you, baby. You smashed that shield to dust. I accused you of being a quitter, of running away—and all the time it was me, scared shitless, and you called me on it. But, like a fool, I let nine-year-old history repeat itself and said nothing."

Her fingers trailed down his chest and stopped at his belly, gripping his shirt. "Why did you quit the Nationals? They were so important to you."

Yeah, so important he'd allowed the stubborn need to prove himself turn him into a complete jerk—when he should've confessed he loved her heart and soul.

"I realized something, someone—" West stroked a hand over her silky hair and left his fingers buried in the soft strands at her nape "—was more important to me than collecting a tag off a two-hundred-foot guideline."

"Is that why you came to Wellington?"

He pulled back, met her gaze. "I came to tell you that, and to look for a job. I can manage a pub anywhere, but I can't manage without you—and I know you need to be there for your dive squad call outs."

Piper's hands came up to cover his. "But Due South needs you. Bill needs you."

"I need you." The words were wrenched from his chest. "*I need you, Piper.*"

She shook her head and his heart shattered, landing in a bloody heap on the floor.

"You'd hate Wellington, West. It's windy and cold—and yes, I know, so is Stewart Island—but it's filled with city people. The kind of people who don't have time to stop and chat, or won't turn up on your doorstep with homemade chicken soup when you've got the flu. And besides—" she rose up on tiptoe, planting a kiss on the corner of his mouth. "—I don't live in Wellington anymore."

"You don't?"

"I handed in my resignation to both the dive squad and the police force."

His brain short-circuited, his head spinning in a dizzying carousel. "You resigned? Why?"

She shrugged a shoulder, but couldn't prevent a small, sly smile. "Something—actually, someone—was more important to me than a job I no longer had the stomach for. Plus, my brother poached me with an un-turn-down-able offer."

"Really. What did he offer you?"

"Partnership. So, as of now, I'm the not-so-silent partner in Ben's dive business." She rolled her eyes. "I'm employed but homeless, so you better come up with something more enticing than *needing* me."

Too much to take in, he just gaped. *Use your words, West, dammit—before you foul this up a third time!*

He swept a hand down to cup her sweet, denim-clad ass in one palm and dragged her flush against him. "How about a home with a man who loves you with all his heart and soul?"

She squirmed closer in his arms and burrowed her face into his neck. "Please say that man is you."

Her lips tickling his skin made him shiver, even as his nerves spiked along his gut. "It's me. I love you, Pipe."

West trapped her against the counter and her hot kisses skimmed up his throat, but he caught her chin before she reached his lips.

"Will staying here make you happy?" He needed her to say to it. "Tell me..." His voice cracked and he waited helplessly for her answer.

Piper drowned in the bluest of blue eyes. The eyes of the man who loved her. He dazzled her so much it took a few seconds to decipher the note of desperation in his voice. The impenetrably cool West wasn't impenetrably cool around her. In fact, West downright vibrated with emotion. She slid her palms up the ridges of his abs she loved so much, and settled them over the wild racing of his heart.

"Staying here won't make me happy, West. You make me happy."
She paused, breathing him in and relishing the security of his arms
around her, the heat of his skin radiating through his shirt. "When I
was little, my mum used to read me a Bible story about Ruth. In the
story, Ruth says, 'Don't ask me to leave or go back and not follow.
Wherever you go, I'll go, and wherever you live, I'll live, and your
people will be my people.' I've forgotten the rest, but not that bit."

His gaze flared hot and a muscle ticked in his jaw. "That's one heck
of a story."

"I've kinda adopted it as my motto." Piper gently pulled his face
down. "I love you, West. Always have, always will. Wherever you go,
I'll be at your side. Whether we live in Oban or Timbuktu, I'll be
happy so long as we're together."

Hoots and catcalls erupted from behind the kitchen's swing doors.
Thuds, bangs, and then a stream of people stumbled into the kitchen—
Shaye, Ben, Glenna, Bill, Ford, and even Mrs. Taylor, who maneuvered
into a better viewing position by wielding her walking sticks like
martial arts staffs.

"Get on with it then, boy," growled Bill, but he chuckled and
rubbed his hands together. "Ask her to marry you, and be done with
it."

Her mother swatted Bill's arm and pointed at West with a mock
glare. "You'll do no such thing. My eldest daughter won't be proposed
to in a pub kitchen—" She flung her hands up. "You haven't even got a
proper ring."

Marriage?

Did Bill and her mother want West to have a coronary before he
turned thirty? She slanted a glance at him, but instead of a bloodless
face and goggling eyes, he grinned. As if he wouldn't reject the idea of
dragging Oban's Presbyterian Minister into the kitchen right now.

In fact, West's face mirrored the same expression she'd seen in the
photograph on his dresser. Love. Pure, and steady. A forever kind of
love. Like her mother had said, she'd been too blind to see it before.

He held up a finger. "Stay right there. Don't move from this spot." West slipped between the growing crowd and through the kitchen doors.

Bill chuckled. "Gone to grab a washer from the toolbox to use instead of a ring, I imagine."

Claire nudged him in the ribs and shushed him.

The murmuring rumble of her family and friends faded into white noise, as she focused on the swinging doors until West shoved through them again. Sucked through time to her first day back on Oban, she could scarcely believe he was the same man. He still sported the same broad shoulders and bite-able butt, but there the similarities ended.

The West walking toward her had mussed hair, overdue for a trim, and about three days of stubble darkened his jaw. His eyes, when they rested on her face, glowed with sensual heat, silently promising she'd never again wake in the night alone. And when she looked at him, she no longer saw through a lens of bitterness and grief. She saw a man Michael would've approved of, and a man she loved enough to finally let her father's memory rest in peace.

West dropped to one knee in front of her combat boots, holding out a small black box. Laughter, tempered with the effort of not bursting into tears, bubbled out of her. She could've sworn Mrs. Taylor squealed in delight from across the room. Raucous applause and whistles erupted, led by her brother.

"Oh, shut up you lot," Shaye said, since Piper could do nothing but gaze at West in mute appeal. "Let the man speak."

Mrs. Taylor's walking sticks poked amongst the crowd until it quieted.

West gave Piper a crooked smile. "I didn't think I'd have an audience when doing this."

"Well, make it memorable, lad," came Old Smitty's voice from the back. "We'll be talking about this for years to come."

West snagged her hand. "Piper."

The way he said her name had every other person in the room fading to oblivion.

"I love you. I've always loved you, but I'm guilty of being a stubborn, proud idiot by trying to deny it for so long."

"Hear, hear," muttered someone.

Piper didn't take her eyes off West to identify the speaker.

"People think I'm never short of a quick comeback or a witty line, but when it comes to you, babe, you leave me speechless—so I'll keep it simple. I want you in my arms and in my life forever. Will you marry me?"

Before she could answer he pried open the ring box, but instead of the flash of diamonds, two rings winked at her. One, a small solitaire and behind it, a gold Claddagh ring, a mirror of the one her parents wore.

"What's with the two rings?" she blurted, looking from the box to West.

West groaned. "Answer the question before I explain the rings, Pipe—I'm dying here."

And so was she—dying to start loving him for the rest of her life. "The answer's yes."

While the ensuing clamoring of celebration exploded around them, West leaped to his feet and hauled her into his arms, spinning her around, and dipping his head to brush his lips across hers. Bubbles fizzed along her nerves—the good kind of ecstatically happy bubbles—leaving her giddy, and not from the spinning.

"Is that the best you can do, West?" Ford hollered.

"Hell, no," West replied. "But I'm not giving you lot any more of a peep show."

"Too right. Everybody except these two out of my kitchen, now!" Bill slapped West's back, winking at Piper over his shoulder. "Since it's not every day my son begs a woman to marry him and she agrees, drinks on the house!"

Once the noisy crowd had dispersed, cheered no doubt by the idea of free booze, West kissed her again. This time his lips weren't quick and gentle. This time they demanded and took, demonstrating just how much pleasure they could give each other over the next fifty-something years.

"The rings," Piper said, when she regained her equilibrium enough to feel the corner of the box digging into her hip. "Why did you buy me two rings?"

West slid his hands to her waist and lifted her onto the countertop, moving to stand between her legs and opening the box again so she could see them. He pointed to the Claddagh ring. "I picked this up in Invercargill before I flew up to find you."

His finger traced over the black velvet to the solitaire. "And this one I bought in Wellington." He hesitated, the intensity of his gaze snatching the breath from her throat. "Nine years ago."

"You bought me an engagement ring?" she squeaked.

"As I said, I've loved you for years—most of my life, come to think of it. I thought I'd done the right thing by driving you away, but God, I missed you so much after you left. I just wanted to take it all back and be with you. Even if it meant moving to the city so you wouldn't get bored and leave me." West shrugged, but the lines around his mouth deepened. "So I sold my Suzuki, flew to Wellington, and bought you this. I went to the Police College, and there you were, training on the field with the other boys in blue."

He removed the diamond solitaire. "You looked so happy. Even being yelled at by the instructor while you did endless push-ups, you looked happy. I decided I had no right to threaten that happiness by forcing my way into your new life, so I chickened out and went home again."

"I never saw you. No one ever told me you'd come up."

"No one knew, except Bill. Dad loaned me a thousand bucks to buy the ring, but he never said a word about repaying it when I returned home without you."

"So which ring do you want me to wear?" She regarded the one in his fingers, which flashed sparks of light on the stainless steel counters.

"Which one do you want, past or present?"

Piper snagged his shirt collar and dragged his face to hers for another steam-coming-out-the-ears kiss. When she pulled back, she wriggled the fingers of her left hand under his nose. "I'm greedy, West. I want it all. Past, present and future."

"That's my girl." He slipped the diamond on her third finger and then the Claddagh ring. "I can't give you back the past, but my present and future are all yours."

West reeled her in for another kiss, running his hands over her back and lifting her into his arms. She fisted her hands in his hair and hooked her legs around him. Cupping her butt in his large, warm hands, West headed inside the pantry.

Piper nuzzled the line of stubble around his jaw, ending at an earlobe, which she sucked between her lips. His speed increased dramatically and the next moment six feet of aroused male had her plastered to the closed pantry door.

Squirming against him as he lowered her to her feet, Piper hooked her fingers over the waistband of his pants. "They say when a couple has been together long enough they can almost read each other's minds."

"So what am I thinking, Pipe?" He let loose a grin that caused her girly-bits to sit up and beg.

His smile widened as his fingers traced the underside of her breasts before hauling her tee shirt off and throwing it to the floor.

Breathing became difficult, she needed mouth to mouth—stat! "You're thinking you love me."

"Yep. And?" Her bra flew through the air and landed on the chest freezer.

"You're thinking you're glad I love you too and that I won't make you wear a tuxedo on our wedding day."

Buttons pinged all over the pantry floor as West ripped his shirt open and shrugged it off. Piper launched herself on him, sealing naked skin to naked skin with a low moan.

He squeezed her bottom. "Beyond glad. And?"

"There's more?"

West backed her to the door again and ground his arousal into her core.

"Okay, you're thinking the twenty bucks you slipped Bill will buy us fifteen minutes before someone comes looking—oh, God—" West's tongue tasted her right nipple, his fingers popping the stud on her jeans.

And ohhh, by the way? She also needed CPR.

"It was a fifty, for thirty minutes." His stare scorched her bare skin as he drew the denim down her legs, stopping briefly to press a hot, wet kiss below her belly button. "But baby, I'll only need ten to have you screaming my name and scandalizing the locals out front."

He slid aside the scrap of her red lace panties and put his mouth on her.

And as it turned out, West only needed five.

ABOUT THE AUTHOR

Tracey Alvarez lives in the Coolest Little Capital in the World (a.k.a Wellington, New Zealand). Married to a wonderfully supportive IT guy, she has two teens who would love to be surgically linked to their electronic devices.

Fuelled by copious amounts of coffee, she's the author of contemporary romantic fiction set predominantly in New Zealand. Small-towns, close communities, and families are a big part of the heart-warming stories she writes. Oh, and hot, down-to-earth heroes--Kiwi men, in other words.

When she's not writing, thinking about writing, or procrastinating about writing, Tracey can be found with her nose in her e-reader, nibbling on smuggled chocolate bars, or bribing her kids to take over the housework.

Follow Tracey on Twitter as @TraceyAlvrezNZ or Facebook as http://www.facebook.com/TraceyAlvarezAuthor
Her website is http://www.traceyalvarez.com and don't forget to sign up to her newsletter here: http://bit.ly/JR3Asu

What Readers & Reviewers are saying about Tracey's books:

"Out of the gate with her début at full throttle, Ms. Alvarez receives a blue ribbon!" ~InD'Tale Magazine.

"In Too Deep (Due South #1) is thrilling, raw and gritty giving the reader a real treat!" ~Amazon review.

"Tracey Alvarez has written an incredible story filled with amazing characters, strong conflict, interesting themes, and an amazing small coastal town setting." ~Amazon review.

"5 stars. Ms. Alvarez has done it again, with incredible, if not one-of-a-kind storytelling!" ~ InD'tale Magazine.

"The story was engaging, funny, heart-warming, sensual, passionate, and brought me back to people and a place I'm growing to love." ~Swept Away By Romance

"Their story is beautifully written, contains sexy and steamy scenes that heat up the bedroom...and the kitchen, and has moments that will break your heart and some that will make you laugh out loud. All this guarantees for an entertaining romance read." ~Amazon review.

OTHER BOOKS IN THE DUE SOUTH SERIES:

The Due South series focuses on family, community, and of course, each book contains a scorching hot romance.

In Too Deep (Book #1) Piper & West
Melting Into You (Book #2) Kezia & Ben
Ready To Burn (Book #3) Shaye & Del
Christmas With You (Book #4) Carly & Kip
My Forever Valentine (Book #5) Short Stories (E-book only)

Far North Series

Imagine an endless stretch of azure blue water and clean, unspoiled beaches.

Imagine a small town surrounded by ancient native forest.

Imagine neighbors who look after their own, who consider them *whānau* - family.

Imagine the secret lives, the hidden passions simmering under New Zealand's sultry, subtropical Far North.

Welcome to Bounty Bay, where the reward of true love is a price only some are willing to pay.

Book #1 *Hide Your Heart*
Book #2 *Know Your Heart*

Made in the USA
Coppell, TX
02 January 2020